HIGHLAND HOPES

Books by

Gary E. Parker

FROM BETHANY HOUSE PUBLISHERS

The Ephesus Fragment

Rumors of Peace

BLUE RIDGE LEGACY

Highland Hopes

Highland Mercies

Highland Grace

A Novel By

GARY E. PARKER

HIGHLAND HOPES

1 | BLUE RIDGE
LEGACY

BETHANYHOUSE
MINNEAPOLIS, MINNESOTA

Highland Hopes
Copyright © 2001
Gary E. Parker

Cover design by Lookout Design Group, Inc.
Smoky Mountain Photo: © 2001 Stone / Marc Muench

Published by Bethany House Publishers
11400 Hampshire Avenue South
Bloomington, Minnesota 55438
www.bethanyhouse.com

Bethany House Publishers is a Division of
Baker Book House Company, Grand Rapids, Michigan.

Printed in the United States of America

Library of Congress Cataloging-in-Publication Data

Parker, Gary E.
    Highland hopes / by Gary E. Parker.
        p.   cm. — (Blue Ridge legacy ; 1)
    ISBN 0-7642-2452-2
      1. Women—North Carolina—Fiction. 2. Blue Ridge Mountains—
Fiction. 3. North Carolina—Fiction. 4. Mountain life—Fiction.
5. Grandmothers—Fiction. 6. Aged women—Fiction. I. Title.
    PS3566.A6784 H54   2001
    813'.54—dc21   2001002515

I dedicate this story
to all the folks I've known,
who liked to sit on a porch and rock
and tell a tale bigger
than the truth could hold.
I don't have to mention any names.
They know who they are.

Acknowledgments

The story of Abigail Faith Porter and her family is fiction. But it is based in the reality of a group of people who were my ancestors. A number of books helped to bring this reality home to me in what I believe and hope are historically correct ways: *Our Southern Highlanders* by Horace Kephart; *The Land of the Saddlebags* by James Watt Raine; *A History of Buncombe County, North Carolina* by F. A. Sondley; *Appalachia Inside Out: Culture and Custom,* edited by Robert Higgs, Ambrose Manning, and Jim Miller; *The Man Who Moved a Mountain* by Richard C. Davids; *Mountain Voices: A Legacy of the Blue Ridge and Great Smokies* by Warren Moore; and *Asheville: A Pictorial History* by Mitzi Tessier. These were the key resources that helped me know the history of the people of western North Carolina. I am grateful for the kinds of study these authors have accomplished. Their work makes my story come alive with truth. Any historical mistakes in this story are mine.

GARY E. PARKER is the author of numerous works of fiction, including *The Ephesus Fragment, Rumors of Peace,* and *The Last Gift.* He also serves as senior pastor at the First Baptist Church of Decatur, Georgia. Gary, his wife, and two daughters make their home near Atlanta.

PROLOGUE

M emories linger a long time up in the coves and hollers of the Blue
Ridge, hang on like early morning mist that won't burn off."

The woman speaking sat across from me in a plain wooden rocker.
From behind her head, the last of the day's sun drifted in through the
double windows and white lace curtains. Although the temperature outside remained near seventy-five degrees, a low fire burned in the stone
fireplace to the woman's right, and the smell of smoky embers filled the
room. I could hear the *ticktock* of the grandfather clock that stood by the
entrance to the hallway.

I smiled at the woman in the rocker. The skin on her hands looked as
thin as wax paper, her hair white and wispy. And her body, though never
heavy, weighed less than a hundred pounds now. She was fully awake yet
bowed her chin to her chest as she spoke, almost as if praying over each
word as it fell from her lips.

"The roads in and out of the highlands weren't much more than a few
ruts and ribbons," she continued. "A path here as wide as a wagon and a
trail there too narrow for anything but a poorly fed horse. With such a
meager means of escape, our memories had nowhere to flee."

The woman talking was my great-grandmother, Abigail Faith Porter Waterbury, or Granny Abby to her family, and she had seen over a hundred years peel off the calendar. The way Granny Abby described things intrigued me. Even though she had more education than most folks born in her time and place, she still sounded like a highland woman—and proud of it. Born on April 23, 1900, she later earned a degree at the teacher's college in Boone, North Carolina. Yet her mountain accent had stayed as pure as springwater.

Granny Abby pointed at the video camera I had set up to make a visual record of our conversation. "We never dreamed of such a thing as that," she said. "We stored up everything in our heads instead. All that we saw and heard, said and did, touched and tasted . . ."

She paused again, her eyes staring into the fire. Standing, I quickly checked the camcorder. Everything was ready, so I sat back down as she went on with her story. The words came softer now.

"Blue Ridge folks keep their tales in their minds," she said, "folded up like a stack of quilts, just waiting for the time when they can pull them out and spread them open."

Granny Abby bent forward in the rocker toward the floor. Her fingers curled around the top of a round wicker basket about two feet tall. Opening the basket, she reached in and pulled out a handful of blue yarn and laid it on her lap.

I smiled again. Granny Abby had knitted and crocheted for as long as any living person had known her. Although I didn't know a crochet hook from a knitting needle, I did know that if somebody handed Granny Abby some cloth and needles of any kind she would make something of them. Every one of her grandchildren and great-grandchildren had a blanket she had made them for their first birthday, their names stitched in bold colors.

Granny looked up. Her eyes, brown as pennies, sparkled. "I got a whole headful of memories, most of them clear as glass," she said.

I nodded. That's why I'd brought along my notebook and camcorder. Within a week over a hundred people would be gathering here in Blue Springs, a two-stoplight hamlet twenty-seven miles northwest of Asheville, North Carolina, to celebrate her next birthday. But before they came, I, her youngest great-grandchild, wanted to put on record the life history of the matriarch of my kin. Taking a deep breath, I told myself to relax. This was just a story: the memories of a mountain woman soon to make what may be her last blanket. But deep inside I sensed something else, something more profound.

Maybe it was because my life was such a mess. At thirty-one years of age, I had recently resigned my position as a reporter for a Washington newspaper. And my love life was in worse shape than my career. Even though I had dated enough men to crowd a classy Georgetown restaurant, none of them had clicked for anything permanent. Plus, I had tried a smorgasbord of religions—a spoonful of this, an ounce of that, a pinch of something else. Suffice it to say, I felt like a cat clinging to a tree limb by one paw. This is what brought me back to Blue Springs. A feeling that I had to come, had to come or . . .

I thought back over the events that had led to my meeting with Granny Abby. A month ago my older brother Todd had phoned me at my D.C. town house to remind me of the family reunion, an annual Blue Springs occasion celebrating Granny's birthday. After hanging up, I immediately decided not to attend. Why should I go? It had been over five years since I'd last seen Granny Abby. Almost two years since I'd seen my mom, three since I'd seen Todd. My dad was dead. Why should I ruin my record of skipping family functions?

But over the next few days, a heavy sadness settled over me. I kept thinking about my great-grandmother, a woman everybody said I favored. Possessor of the same brown eyes, same slender build, and same auburn hair—till hers turned gray, of course.

A week after Todd called, I found myself cleaning out my closet, going through some clothes to give to charity. In a shoe box under a pile of sweaters, I discovered some old pictures. Thumbing through the stack, I ran across a photo my mom had given me years ago: a black-and-white of Granny Abby taken during her days at school in Boone. Goodness, but we did look alike! And I, Lisa Abigail, had her name tacked to me also. I stared at the picture for several minutes, then put it back in the box. I left the closet and tried to think of something else. Yet, in the days that followed, I discovered that the woman in the picture wasn't so easily dismissed.

While it was true I hadn't spent much time with her, Granny Abby had always been a heroine of mine. Growing up in the Blue Ridge Mountains, she'd suffered far more hardships than anything I could imagine. Yet she had a serenity of soul that I envied.

Five days after finding the picture, I woke up and made myself a cup of coffee. Standing by the kitchen window, I watched a heavy rain pouring down. Suddenly the hair on the back of my neck stood up. A new thought ran through my head. Just as I knew that Granny Abby had suffered from the isolation of the remote highlands, so I realized that I'd been living in isolation too. But my isolation came as a single woman in the midst of millions of people—the isolation of rush-hour traffic, high-rise apartments, and acquaintances too busy to truly connect with one another.

In that instant, I made a decision to go to Blue Springs for Granny's birthday. Just like that. While making my travel plans, another idea hit me, a notion I'd tossed around for years but never acted on. I would ask Granny Abby to tell me her life story. Energized, I bought a couple of leather notebooks and an expensive camcorder and plenty of tapes. I even read a book on how to put together a family history. As I prepared, I told myself this visit was just another project to keep my mind occupied, something to prevent me from dwelling on all the explaining I'd have to do at the reunion when people asked me why I didn't have a job, or a husband and family of my own.

But when I was alone, I knew I was trying to fool myself. In my heart I had only one reason for doing this project: I hoped that by hearing about where I came from, I might find a clue as to where I was heading. Maybe by learning the key to Granny Abby's life, I might find the key to my own.

Let me explain it this way. Somebody—I don't know who—once said, "Even if it's true that you can't go home again to stay, it's also true that you have to go *through* home again to survive."

Right now I feel I'm just trying to survive. I'm hoping that going through home again will somehow help me with this.

"You ready to start?" I asked, focusing on Granny Abby once more.

She pulled at the material in her lap and grinned. "Are you?"

Nodding more confidently than I felt, I stood and pushed the Record button.

"Tell me, Granny Abby," I encouraged. "I want to hear."

She licked her lips. "Some of what I got to tell is hearsay," she said. "Things people told me later, memories they shared long after the events happened."

"But you kept their memories and then added your own," I said.

Granny Abby started to rock. I picked up my notebook and pen and sat back down.

Granny Abby started to talk. The camera rolled as I scribbled. What Granny Abby told me is in this story. These are her tales as I wrote them, her memories unfolded for all who want and need to hear.

SECTION I

1900–1908

CHAPTER
ONE

The rain fell fearsome the night she was born. It started right after
dark, sheets of heavy water that came so hard it made folks think
the Almighty had a grudge against the Earth and planned to settle it with
another big flood. Drops of water the size of nickels clattered out of the
sky and knocked the blooms off the dogwoods that had just flowered and
sent every critter in the woods searching for a hole to escape.

Lightning kept company with the rain, as great jags of silver sizzled
from heaven to ground. The thunder that followed sounded like cannons
booming. Wind pushed the rain from side to side, first swirling it to the
north, then to the south. The poplars and oaks and maples and chestnuts
and every other tree on the mountain bent to the wind's will, their spring
leaves bowing as if in homage to sweet Jesus himself. Within a couple of
hours after the storm started, Slick Rock Creek had swollen to nearly four
times its usual width. By midnight the wood footbridge that served as the
only way over the creek had largely disappeared under a rush of muddy
water.

At just past one o'clock a particularly sharp bolt of lightning cut its
way through the black sky. As it did, it showed off a four-room log cabin

sitting on a relatively level parcel of earth no more than a stone's throw up the hill from the creek. The cabin had a narrow front porch and sat a foot or so off the ground on pillars made from oak tree trunks. A stone chimney ran up the left side of the cabin. Barely visible in the rain, three wet dogs lay on the porch, their heads on their paws.

Another streak of lightning flashed. This one lit up an open-sided shed about twenty steps from the cabin. A split-rail fence extended around both buildings. Inside the shed a mule stood with its head down, and a cluster of chickens perched in a variety of poses in and around the mule. In front of the shed rested a black kettle big enough to bathe a body or scald a hog. Rainwater stood about three inches deep in the bottom of the kettle.

The lightning and thunder grew more and more fractious. The chickens fluttered their wings, and the mule kicked against his stall. On any other night that thunder would no doubt have drowned out most every other sound. But this night the thunder took a backseat to another noise, one more shrieky than anything the sky could offer.

Inside the cabin a woman's scream made a powerful racket, its noise cutting through the hand-sawed planks of the cabin's walls. The woman's wailing rose up through the cedar shingles that covered the roof and mingled with the thunderclaps. Another wave of rumbling carried the scream away, and the woman who had made it groaned and momentarily lay back on her sweat-soaked mattress. A tin trunk sat at the foot of her bed, and a kerosene lamp on a handmade table cast heavy shadows over the woman's face. A few drips of water slipped through the roof and splashed onto the wood floor. The woman's eyes were open but glazed. Her lips were dry and chapped.

On his knees by the bed an angular man with dark eyes and a strong chin held the moaning woman by the hand. A single strap over the left shoulder held up the man's worn-out overalls. His brown beard pushed out at all angles from where he had pulled at it during the ordeal of his wife's fifth labor. The long-sleeved cotton undershirt he wore had stains under each arm and down the small of his back. The thickly corded muscles in his shoulders were tense and knotted.

"You got to do something, Francis," the man pleaded, looking up at the plump woman who stood on the other side of the bed. "This birth givin' Rose troubles."

"I know it's goin' hard," said Francis as she dipped a clean white rag into a pot beside the bed and sponged the woman's forehead. "But they is only so much a body can do. It's been many a year since Rose delivered a baby."

The man studied his wife. Her hair had turned dark with sweat. Beads of perspiration covered her cheeks and chin. Her eyes, green as oak leaves in springtime, were focused on the ceiling as if surveying the leaky places that were letting in the rain. She ground a strip of old horse bridle in her teeth.

Breathing heavy, the man bowed his head. Though their lovemaking had stayed regular as ever, eight springs had passed since their youngest boy, Daniel, had come to him and Rose. They thought they had finished with raising babies. Then Rose came up expecting again.

The man felt a hand on his head and raised his eyes. Rose was looking at him. He felt her fingers trembling as she touched his cheek.

"I'm doin' fine, Solomon," she said. "Childbearing is never easy, you know that."

Solomon took her hand, kissed it. The hand was hot but he didn't let it go as he laid it back down. For some reason, an odd sense of fright suddenly rushed over him, made his hands quiver in league with his wife's. He shivered. The face of his ma, dead eleven years now, flashed in his head. A superstitious mountain woman, his ma would tell him that a haint had just passed over the house and given him the cold squeamish touch that rippled throughout his back and shoulders. She'd tell him that the crow that had hopped up onto the porch last night just at sunset had come to say that something bad rode the air, something as black as the crow and just as sharp of beak.

Closing his eyes, Solomon prayed. Jesus didn't take to such superstition, he told himself. Old women's tales that tried to read portents and signs. Silliness that no Jesus man would ever hold to. Yet, he had an awful bad feeling. . . .

He opened his eyes again and patted Rose's hand. The birth pains had started at noon, almost a month earlier than Doc Booth, the medicinal man from down in Blue Springs, had said they ought. Solomon had sent Laban, his eldest boy of fifteen, down to Blue Springs to fetch the doc. But given that the storm had no doubt flooded out the few rocky roads between their holler and the town, he had no real hope he'd see the doctor tonight. When rain fell this hard it made his cabin and property a world apart from everything else, a prison surrounded by a moat of foamy brown water, no way to get in or out.

"Why don't you go sit with Luke and Daniel?" said Francis. "This is women's work here."

Solomon stared back at Rose, then to his sister once more. Although all hadn't turned out just right every time, his wife's earlier deliveries had gone much easier—eight or nine hours of labor at most, then a baby. But something had been different about this child from the outset. Rose had suffered sickness well into the fourth month, and rather than gaining weight, she had actually lost it, at least in her face and arms. Her auburn hair had turned darker, a rusty color. About the only thing that hadn't changed was her disposition. This had stayed fresh as ever, as happy as a young filly throwing up her heels in a meadow.

"This baby gone be special," Rose had said to Solomon about six months into the pregnancy. "Done started to kicking. And she's a girl for sure, I just feel it."

"I done made her a carving," said Solomon, thinking of the ten-inch tall doll figure he'd whittled out of a chestnut branch. "Iffen she is a girl. Shaped it in your likeness, pretty as you please."

"Francis said that horse you cut for a boy looks a lot like you if you gaze at it from the hindquarters."

"Francis always was a kidder."

Rose closed her eyes as Solomon came back to the present and saw how tired she looked. His uneasiness about the delivery sank heavy into his bones. He and Rose had been married for eighteen years. Four boys had come to them in the first nine, the first son two years after their getting married. Three of the boys were still living, two of them waiting by the fireplace in the front room of the cabin.

Solomon pulled at his beard. Francis had helped deliver each of his boys. A mountain midwife—a granny woman as highlanders often called them—she traveled the mountains whenever a baby came due, the only help most mountain mamas ever saw. She knew far more about this than he did.

The storm outside paused for a moment. Rose grunted and bit down on the leather bridle. Her back arched and rose up off the bed as a new wave of contracting came over her. A low moan slipped from her throat.

Francis moved to the foot of the bed, lifted the sheet, and examined Rose's lower body.

"That doctor ought to be here!" Solomon shouted as he stood and stalked to the one window in the room, a single square cut into the wall, covered only with an uneven wood shutter.

"Ain't no use hollerin' about it," said Francis, her voice rising as she lowered the sheets and went to wet her rag once more. "Storms pay no mind to a woman givin' birth. Been happening for thousands of years. We just do our best, then trust in the Almighty and let things be. Now go on out of here."

"But Rose is barely over eight months along!" he said.

"That's far enough," said Francis. "Far enough."

His heart wrought, Solomon stepped back to the bed. The bridle in Rose's mouth had turned black from her tongue and teeth soaking it with spittle. Francis sponged off Rose's face again, then sat down by the bed in a straight-backed chair. Rose suddenly opened her eyes and focused on Solomon's face. He bent low to her.

"This baby mighty slow in the delivery," said Solomon.

"A baby girl's worth the wait," she said. "The boys doing okay?"

"They scared to death," he said. "Men get right mystified by such as this."

Rose smiled briefly and took his hand. "I got more striving to do here. You go and be with the boys. Do your praying. Francis will take care of me and the baby."

Solomon touched her cheek. His calloused hands, strong enough to cut wood from sunup to sundown, were gentle on her skin. He pushed Rose's wet hair from her eyes. "You need me, I'm just in the next room," he said.

"I know. Where else you goin' on a night like tonight?"

He stooped down and kissed her forehead.

Francis stood behind him. "Go on now," she said. "You no help to me here."

Solomon stood, turned to Francis, and whispered so only she could hear, "If this don't go well, you make sure you provide for Rose," he said. "Let the baby go if need be."

"Don't fret yourself," she said. "I will do what ought to get done."

His head down, Solomon moved to the door but then suddenly twisted back. Rose raised a hand and weakly waved it. He faked a smile and stepped through the door to face his sons.

"On your knees, boys," he ordered. "We got prayin' to do."

In the bedroom, Rose motioned Francis to come closer. "I got a bad feelin'," she whispered. "Something ain't setting up right for this baby."

"Don't you worry none," Francis said. "This baby is just taking longer than the others, that's all."

Rose shook her head, her scowl telling Francis to pay attention. "I'm not sure," she said. "I feel . . . feel out of sorts . . . all wrong somehow."

Francis lifted the single sheet again. Her amber eyes widened as she bent closer. A trickle of crimson lay on the sheet.

Moving fast, she grabbed a new rag and dipped it in the pot on the floor. Wiping Rose's face, she leaned low over her. "You got pushin' to do," she whispered. "And you got to do it fast and hard."

Rose gritted her teeth, then said, "If something goes wrong, I want my baby to live. No matter about me."

"Not gone have to make that kind of choice," said Francis.

"But if we do . . . if we do, you got to promise me . . ."

Francis moved back to Rose's feet without comment and lifted the sheet once more. "You ready?" she asked.

Rose bit hard on the bridle and pressed her heels into the mattress. Her screaming once more cut through the storm, and the lightning flashed back as if in unison with her shriek. The baby's head crowned through the birth canal. Rose arched and pushed again. It seemed her insides would surely gush right out of her body and onto the bed, but the baby's head appeared instead. Francis reached for the head and thought for a moment that all would be well. Rose groaned and pushed yet again, and the shoulders of the baby emerged. Rose started sobbing, her body spent from the effort.

"One more hard push," said Francis, trying to keep her voice calm. "One more big one and you all done."

Rose fixed her eyes on a spot on the ceiling. Francis cradled the baby's head in her hands and squared her feet to catch the rest. Biting down on the bridle, Rose gave a final push and the torso of a baby girl slipped into Francis's hands. She pulled the baby from Rose's body and the child's feet appeared in a whoosh of afterbirth. But then Francis caught her breath. The crimson flow from Rose's body became thicker and darker as it followed the baby into the light of the room.

Taking the child from her mama's body, Francis quickly washed away the birth fluids and cleared the child's mouth and nose. The baby sucked in a first breath, then balled up her face and started to cry. Francis cut the umbilical cord with a kitchen knife sharpened especially for this moment, wrapped the baby in a dry cloth, and laid her in her mama's arms.

Her hands shaking, Francis dipped a handful of towels into the water pot and carried them over to the bed. She then shoved them into Rose's lower body in a desperate attempt to stanch the blood that had now become a steady stream. But the blood didn't stop. Francis grabbed a glass jar from her medicine sack by the bed, pulled off the top, and dumped the powdery contents into her hand. Then she dipped a new white cloth into the water pot and wrapped it around the powder from the jar. The wet cloth soaked the powder and it caked into a thick poultice. Francis patted the poultice out flat and moved back to Rose. After removing the towels from Rose's lower body, she pressed the poultice into place. For several seconds she stood and prayed. The poultice—a mixture of creek dirt, spider webs, crushed wasp nests, and ginseng root—had stanched bloody flows more than once. She hoped it would work again. If not . . .

Her heart sank as she saw a trickle of blood escape from the edge of the poultice. Desperate, she picked up the towels again.

"Get . . . get Solomon. . . ." called Rose, her voice shaky. "I need . . ."

After pressing the towels as hard as possible against Rose, Francis dropped the sheet back over her legs and bolted from the room. A few seconds later she returned with Solomon.

A smile came to Solomon's face when he saw the baby nestled against Rose's breast, the child's tiny mouth working for a first meal.

"Got us a girl," Rose said weakly.

"Just like you been wantin'," said Solomon, on his knees by the bed. "Somebody to dress up and show off down to the church."

Rose touched his chin. "Listen," she said. "I got . . . got little time."

Solomon scowled.

"Bring me a . . . a piece of paper," Rose said. "Some in . . . in the middle dresser drawer."

"What you—?"

"Just give me the paper," she whispered.

Solomon watched as Francis stepped quickly to the dresser in the corner of the room. The only piece of furniture in the cabin that Solomon hadn't made with his own hands, the mahogany dresser had an oval mirror in the center and five drawers. The dresser had come from Ireland with Rose's family over fifty years ago; she'd brought it to the marriage as her only dowry.

Francis jerked open the middle drawer and pulled out a stack of gray-lined paper, which Rose had saved from Daniel's schooling this past year. Grabbing a piece of the paper, she took a thick pencil from behind the stack and moved back to the bed. Solomon had pulled up a chair by his wife. Francis gave Rose the paper and pencil and started toward the foot of the bed again. But Rose caught her eye and gave a quick jerk of her head. Francis opened her mouth as if to speak but then said nothing.

Confused, Solomon faced Rose.

"Push me up," Rose said, slowly rising off the bed. "I need to . . ."

"Rest yourself," pleaded Solomon. "You been at this a long time today."

Francis grabbed Rose's pillow and placed it under her back. Her face bunched by the effort of sitting up, Rose shifted the baby so it could suckle easier.

"I need something to write on," Rose said.

"What you doin'?" asked Solomon, his eyes searching Rose's face.

"Shush. Something I got to do now . . ."

Though at a loss, Solomon didn't argue.

Francis brought over the only book in the room—a Bible with a worn black cover—from the dresser and handed it to Rose. She slid it under the paper in her hand. Solomon bent over Rose and kissed her forehead. Touching his cheek, Rose motioned for him to sit. Then she focused on the pencil and paper. He wondered how she had the strength to write after the ordeal of baby labor. But he knew she had a will as strong as the iron in a wash kettle. If she wanted something wrote, she would grit her teeth and scratch it out, no matter what. With the baby cradled under one arm and her fingers trembling, she began to write. Solomon watched her, admiration in his eyes. Unable to read or write himself, he'd said more than once how proud he was that he had married a woman who could. She read to him nightly from the same Bible that now supported her paper.

The storm had completely stopped now, almost as if listening to see what Rose would say. The only sound in the room came from the pencil scratching on the paper. Rose's face bleached out as she wrote, and her eyes fell deeper into her skull. Solomon turned to Francis to ask a question, but she just shook her head. Rose kept on writing, her hand quivering and her breath coming in shorter and shorter gasps. The lamp flickered in the corner. Solomon stood and walked to Francis, who had taken a seat by the foot of the bed.

"She all right?" he asked hopefully.

Francis nodded toward the bed. He saw the bed sheet, noticed for the first time the crimson at the edges. Swallowing a groan, he rushed back to Rose's side.

"Doc Booth's on the way!" he pleaded. "Just stay with me!" He turned to Francis. "Do something!" he shouted. "You've delivered babies . . . lots of babies."

Francis got up and laid a hand on his back. "I done all I know to do," she said. "It's in the Lord's hands now."

Rose set down the Bible, then handed the paper and pencil back to Francis.

"Give this . . . when she's older . . . give it . . . to my . . . my baby," Rose said. "Tell her . . . tell her . . . to remember . . ." Her words faltered and she lay back.

Francis glanced at the paper for an instant and then folded it and laid it on the dresser. Solomon watched but said nothing. He faced Rose again.

"You rest easy," he pleaded. "Doc here soon."

"It's okay," she whispered, her words thin. "I'm not afraid."

"You're gone make it," Solomon insisted. "Rain's let up now. Doc's on the—"

Rose put her fingers to his lips. "Listen to me," she urged, her words easing away even as she spoke. "The baby's name is Abigail Faith, after my mama. Don't blame her for . . . for any of this." She waved her hand over the bed as if pronouncing a benediction. "Promise me you won't blame the baby."

Solomon turned to Francis, his eyes frantic. But she offered him no comfort. He looked back at Rose. He remembered the first time he ever saw her, a sprightly twelve-year-old girl standing by the water trough outside the dry goods store down in Blue Springs. She'd just unhooked a mule from the hitching rail, and he, fifteen at the time, felt tingly all over. Within a year he saw her again, this time when he and his family traveled the nine miles from his folks' place on Settle's Ridge to Blue Springs, to attend the September meeting at the Jesus Holiness Church. She'd sat two rows in front of him. Unable to think of anything else but her, Solomon had heard nothing the preacher said.

The following year he'd started walking her way every Saturday morning, spending the night in her family's barn, returning back home Sunday afternoon. Six months after his first visit to her house, he asked her pa for her hand in marriage. At first her pa hadn't taken much to the idea. Had said he needed time to ponder out a few things. Solomon knew Rose had other suitors, most with lots more to offer than he, but he had no question he loved her more than anybody else. Another half year passed. Rose's pa seemed to hesitate even more. Solomon wondered what kind of offer another beau had made. Back in the mountains, men didn't always give their daughters to marry out of love. A few dollars, a new gun or horse, a parcel of land—any of them made for some mighty good swapping. Not having come into any inheritance yet, Solomon had nothing but his love to offer. Then, just when it seemed he and Rose might have to run off and marry without permission, her pa had given up and granted it.

"You watch over my baby," Robert Toller had warned the day he finally agreed to the match. "You ever hit her and I'll kill you deader than a coon dog chewed up by a bear."

Solomon nodded. He never hit anybody, especially not someone he loved like he did Rose.

"Don't leave me, Rose," he begged, his attention in the present again. "You all I got, all I ever wanted."

Rose closed her eyes, licked her lips. "Bring me the boys," she said.

Solomon started to protest again, but when he looked at Francis and then back at Rose, he knew his protesting would fall on deaf ears. Too shocked to do anything else, he slouched to the next room and motioned Daniel and Luke into the bedroom.

"Your mama's doin' poorly," he told them.

The boys walked past him toward the bed, their heads down. Solomon stayed at the door, his back against the frame, his hands in his pockets. He watched as the boys leaned over their mama to hear her whisper something to each of them. He bent his ear but couldn't hear what Rose was saying. As Daniel straightened, Solomon saw tears in his eyes. But Solomon held back his own tears. When Rose finished with the boys, they stepped away and she beckoned him back to her.

Sitting on the bed, he felt her touch his cheek, felt her lips as he bent down to kiss her one last time.

"You the handsomest man I ever saw," she said.

"I always wondered about your eyesight," he said, trying to cover his hurt by making light of things.

Rose smiled. "You the kindest too."

Solomon opened his mouth to speak again, but his tongue wouldn't move.

"I love you," she said, her voice fading.

"I love you too," Solomon choked.

Rose closed her eyes. Francis came over and took the baby. Solomon felt an emptiness crawl into his stomach, like a turtle shell all hollowed out with a spoon. For almost an hour he sat with Rose and held her hand as her life ebbed away.

Outside the cabin, the sky suddenly brightened as the clouds rolled behind the mountains and the moon and stars blinked on in the dark. But Solomon Porter didn't notice. As Rose took her last breath, he lay down beside her and hugged her as if trying to pass life from his bones to hers. But she didn't breathe again.

A quarter hour later Francis touched him on the shoulder, and he finally eased away from Rose and stood. Daniel and Luke waited in the corner, shifting from foot to foot, their eyes on the floor. Francis handed Solomon the baby. For the first time he looked closely at the little girl Rose had just birthed.

A tuft of auburn hair spiked up from her scalp. Her hands were tiny, her body weighing no more than a medium-sized catfish. He held her close to his face. As if on cue, she opened her eyes. They were green, just like Rose's eyes.

One of the baby's hands grabbed at his beard. Solomon started to smile, but then he thought of Rose who now lay motionless on the bed—the very bed where this child had been conceived and whose life had cost Rose her own. An odd mixture of feelings flooded through him. He knew he needed to love this child, flesh of his flesh, bone of Rose's bone. Yet his love was dulled by the knowledge that had she not come into the world, Rose might still be alive. Rose's eyes would be looking into his instead of this child's; Rose's fingers would be tugging at his beard instead of this baby's.

He knew what Rose would say right now. She would say, "The Lord willed it." She would say, "Blessed be the name of the Lord." But right now he couldn't say such things.

Grinding his teeth, Solomon unhooked Abigail's fingers from his beard, gave her back to Francis, and started to leave. Then he remembered the paper Francis had laid on the dresser. As though afraid of a poisonous spider, he reached for the paper and stared down at the scribbling. He wished he could read what Rose had written, what she'd left behind for her only daughter. He considered asking Francis or Daniel to read it for him, yet he knew that wasn't right. Rose said to give it to the baby. These words were meant for the child, no one else. Maybe someday, when Abigail was old enough and had learned to read, she'd tell him what her mama wrote as she lay dying. But until then he would have to wait.

Handing the paper back to Francis, Solomon roughly wiped at his eyes and slouched out of the bedroom.

CHAPTER
TWO

Everybody knows that when an Appalachian man loses a worthy woman he usually falls prey to one of two temptations: Either he takes to the drink in an attempt at washing away his sorrows with the doublings—that's moonshine for those uneducated in highlander vocabulary—or he throws his shoulders full front into whatever toil he can lay his hands to. Since Solomon Porter was one of those rare mountain men who didn't much fancy the jug, he took to the second pursuit real fast after the death of his sweet Rose.

Almost from the day their circuit-riding preacher, Theodore Bruster, spoke his best words over Rose and the boys hauled her oak coffin to the hill on the cleared-out space about a hundred yards behind the cabin, Solomon had put his hands to laboring. That spring of 1900 he cleared out even more space than he'd already prepared and then planted the biggest patch of corn anyone had ever seen on a poor mountainside. In addition to corn, he planted beans, Irish and sweet taters, squash, tomatoes, cucumbers, and even cantaloupe. From the first chirp of the birds in the morning to the last hint of dusk, he kept himself busy. He furrowed out the stony ground with nothing more than an oak stick he'd cut from a fallen branch, dropped in the seed, and smoothed over the dirt with his toes. He hoed away the weeds when one dared show its head. When not in his cornfield or garden and when daylight allowed it, he hunted for deer or fished for trout in Slick Rock Creek. Always handy with a gun and familiar with every stream running down Blue Springs Mountain, he laid in more venison and caught more fish than ever in his life.

And Solomon didn't stop his toiling with nightfall. Unlike most mountain men, Solomon had a trade and the industry of body to strive at it. So when darkness settled in on the mountain, he pulled out a piece of wood—most often oak, maple, or hickory—and started to shape it. His hands took on a right unusual grace when he cut and carved on the wood. Even though he had no store-bought equipment to aid his production, he sawed and whittled and smoothed in such a way that made his work look almost fancy. Mostly he built rocking chairs, shaping curved legs for easy movement, with firm backs, and arms rounded to fit most anyone. He carved a small *SP* on the bottom of each rocker and then traded them either in Blue Springs or Asheville. The man he traded with in Asheville said Solomon made the best rockers he'd ever seen. Just about every spring Solomon brought the man a few to barter. In the months after Rose died, Solomon sweated even harder over each chair, his eyes squinting in the dim light of the lantern as he finished up three more chairs and cut his initials into the wood.

Only late at night did he seem at a loss about what to do. In the short time between when he quit toiling and fell into bed, he'd often sit on the porch in one of his own rockers, smoke his corncob pipe, and rub Sandy behind the ears. Sandy was the favorite of his three cur dogs. Never a man given to many words, Solomon became even more silent that spring and summer following Rose's death.

He didn't eat much either. Normally a strapping man by highlander standards, his overalls hung on him like rags on a scarecrow, and his deep-set eyes now seemed hollow as a cave. His hair, usually slicked back with a touch of lard, was now left unkempt. He refused to go just about anywhere, even to attend church. And whenever anybody spoke to him on the rare occasions he did venture out, he'd just nod politely and keep moving. Not even his family could draw him out. Francis tried to encourage him otherwise, but he paid scant attention to her or to his sons, unless it was connected with some task he wanted them to do. He paid even less attention to his new daughter.

"You leaving that baby too much to me," Francis said one day after supper while she and Solomon were resting on the porch. "And Laban and Luke stayin' way too late in Blue Springs on most Saturday nights. Last week Laban didn't bother to come home at all till Sunday morning. Missed church all total."

Solomon rocked but said nothing for a while. Like him, the boys had taken their ma's passing real hard. Laban especially seemed lost without her, angry all the time and rebellious against everything and everybody. A couple of times Solomon had smelled liquor on his clothes after a night in Blue Springs, and he figured his oldest had fallen in with some shiftless boys. He had probably taken to gambling too—card playing and the like.

"Abigail's real quick," Francis said, interrupting his musings. "Eyes open all the time, growin' fast. Already made up her weight from coming early."

Solomon remained quiet. He had mixed feelings about the baby. One moment he resented her, the fact that she'd lived while Rose had died. But then he realized that such a view was an unfair way to consider things. The baby had been given no choice. No choice in the conceiving that gave her life and no choice that her mama had bled to death on her birth bed.

"I give her that doll you carved for her," said Francis, her hands busy sewing a repair on an apron. "She already playing with it like she knows what it is."

Solomon shrugged. He had done some fine carving on that wood doll. Shaped it from a piece of chestnut that had washed up on the bank of Slick Rock Creek, where they took their water. He made it look like Rose herself, her chin and cheeks, eyes and forehead. Even the hair, all thick and with some curl. Then he'd stained it with an auburn color to match Rose's hair. But now he didn't care about the doll.

He pulled his pipe from his pocket, tapped it on the arm of the rocker. He knew he ought not blame the child, but he had trouble separating his anger at Rose's dying from the baby girl who had been there when it happened. He felt torn inside, knowing that the girl was the last thing Rose gave him, yet this gift had killed the one he loved most.

Solomon chewed on his unlit pipe for a moment. A wide space lay between him and Abigail. Maybe it was just the matter of her being a girl. Maybe men and girls had a natural distance between them because they were so different from each other. He hoped this to be the case. But deep

31

down he knew he was trying to fool himself. The space between him and Abigail had come because he saw her as the cause of her ma's death, simple as that.

A dog bayed from the woods over the ridge. Francis spoke again. "A man's got a right to grieve," she said, tying off a piece of thread. "Nobody faultin' you for that."

Solomon studied Francis. Her plumpness made her a rarity among the skinny mountain women. Also, she knew some reading and writing. She'd lived with him and Rose for over ten years now.

A barren woman, her husband had died of pneumonia and she seemed unwilling to take on another one. Since she had no one to care for her and Solomon was the eldest of her two living brothers, he took her in. Almost twenty years his senior, she was the firstborn of his siblings, a hefty lady with a head full of gray hair and a heart full of wisdom and quiet love.

"I appreciate your permission for my sorrows," Solomon said with a sincere tone. "Seems like the longer a body lives, the heavier the trouble grows."

Francis nodded as she held up her apron for inspection. Solomon scratched Sandy between the ears.

"Laban's near to sixteen," he said to no particular end. "Almost growed. And Luke's thirteen, Daniel eight." He thought of the one baby who hadn't made it—little Solomon Jr., a stillborn between Luke and Daniel. Buried out by Rose, ten years ago now. He was a perfect baby boy, all his fingers and toes hinged on him just right. After naming the first two after his pa and hers, Rose had told him she wanted to name this third baby after him. But Solomon Jr. never took a full breath. He passed on, like a grain of corn that pushed out of the ground but never yielded any crop.

"Why you think life's so hard?" Solomon asked Francis.

She punched her needle through the hem of the apron. "You askin' the wrong person," she said. "I reckon it don't help much to talk about things such as that."

Solomon struck a match on his boot, sucked on his pipe. The tobacco was strong. Like most men of the Blue Ridge, he grew it himself in a small patch not far from the corn.

"I reckon it's a testing," he said. "A testing to see who is gone stick with the Lord and who is not."

"That's a right deep idea," said Francis.

Solomon rubbed Sandy. "It's got truth of the Book in it," he said as if to convince himself. "Over in the book of . . . I think Hebrews . . ." he paused and tapped his pipe on the chair's arm.

"Let me get the Book," Francis said, rising. "To find what you're saying."

Solomon stared into the sky. The sun was dipping behind the peak of Blue Springs Mountain directly before him. The mountain looked purple and the sky red and orange, about the color of his sweet Rose's hair on the day she died. A whisker of clouds hung near the mountain peak. The dog that had bayed earlier sounded out again. Sandy pricked her ears.

Francis stepped back out, a lantern in her hand. "You thinking Hebrews ten?" she asked.

"That sounds right," Solomon answered.

Francis opened the Bible, pointed her finger at a page, and read aloud, " 'Let us hold fast the profession of our faith without wavering; (for he is faithful that promised.)' "

"That ain't quite it," said Solomon. "Read on over there."

Francis held up the Bible to catch the last of the sun. "Maybe this," she offered. " 'Cast not away therefore your confidence, which hath great recompense of reward. For ye have need of patience, that, after ye have done the will of God, ye might receive the promise.' " Francis closed the Bible and sat back down.

Solomon sucked on his pipe. He recalled Rose holding the Bible, reading from it, using it as a back when she wrote her last words.

"What you do with that paper Rose left?" he asked.

"In my basket," said Francis.

Solomon nodded with understanding. Francis kept a wicker basket by her bed that was filled with her personal belongings. Things like the silver dollar her pa left behind, the hat she wore on her wedding day, a pair of shiny black shoes that Mrs. West from Blue Springs gave her three years ago for helping in the delivery of her twin boys. Now the basket also held the last thoughts of Rose Porter, gone to be with the Lord.

"You think I ought to have you read the letter to me?" he asked.

"Up to you," Francis replied. "She was your wife."

Solomon shrugged. "Might hurt real deep to hear what she said," he mumbled.

"That's a possible truth."

He stood and faced Blue Springs Mountain, his back to Francis. He'd lived here all his life, owning now almost a thousand acres of unsettled land in some of the highest reaches of the Blue Ridge Mountains. His family had pieced together the land over the last hundred years, after his grandma and grandpa had pushed down into the southern highlands from Pennsylvania. Solomon tried to recollect the little that he knew about his people. They were mostly Scotch folks who had come to the New World from Ireland in hopes of gaining both freedom from a meddling government and a chance to make something of themselves. They'd found both land and freedom on the high slopes of the Blue Ridge.

Solomon leaned against a porch post. He loved the land his folks had passed on to him. He loved the laurel, rhododendron, and azalea, the dogwood, maple, oak, chestnut, and pine that covered the mountains. He loved the cool, clear streams that tumbled down in cascades of white water. And he loved the deer and black bear, raccoons and rabbits and squirrels—all the animals that skittered around in the highlands.

He walked back to his rocker.

But the mountains were a hard land for people. Yielded up a living like they had a grudge against those who built on them, as if to sift out anyone who dared test their slopes, to see who had the guts and gumption to survive the worst that might come.

Well, like he always said, some made it and some didn't. He sucked on his pipe. His ma and pa had made it. Had added to the land their folks had staked out and settled, buying up bits and pieces whenever any money came to hand. They'd scraped and scrimped and did without so they could hand something down to their offspring.

Solomon pulled on his pipe again. He'd followed in his pa's footsteps, doing better than most. Working hard and staying away from whiskey, he had learned the carpentry trade, which, as it turned out, was something that came naturally to him. Using this skill, he'd managed to scrape up some cash now and again, a luxury most highland folks never realized unless they made and sold corn liquor.

With the cash that Solomon made from his carpentry, he'd kept the wolf away from the door, sent his kids to as much school as the mountains provided, and built a cabin bigger than many. He wasn't rich, but by highlander standards he had done better than fine.

Solomon scratched Sandy behind the ears. He and Francis had a brother up in Lolley's Branch, whom he hadn't seen in nearly two years.

All the rest of his immediate kin were dead: one brother by a shooting, one by a fall from some rocks while hunting, the third from old age. And a sister had died of mountain measles before she ever married.

Some made it and some didn't. Now he could add Rose to the list, Rose with little Solomon Jr. They did not make it.

He chewed his pipe and wondered once more about the letter Rose had written. Though he would like to know what she'd said, he had no burning to deal with the sadness such a reading might stir up. Men like him didn't deal with the hurts of loss too easily.

"I'll leave that letter be for now," he finally said to Francis. "Not wrote for me no how."

"You'll know when to hear it," Francis said.

"Maybe I never will," he said.

A wisp of a breeze rustled through the big oak that fronted the left side of the cabin. Solomon tapped his pipe on the rocker. Winter would get lonely with no woman to sit with him by the fire at night, no woman to warm his bones when the snow piled up at the door. He thought of Abigail, whom they had taken to calling Abby now. She had no mama, a fate worse than his not having a woman at his side. His arms felt heavy.

"Too much can break a man," Solomon said.

Francis picked up her apron and looked at him, but held her piece.

"Little Junior gone," he said. "Now Rose."

"But Abby and the boys ain't gone nowhere," said Francis. "No matter that the others are passed. It's the way of living. The Lord never promised us we would live without sorrows—you know that. Your boys and Abby are still right here, as alive as anything. And God left you here too, left you here to do for them, to give them every chance." She stopped and wiped her mouth with the apron.

"You think I ought to give Abby up?" he asked.

Francis raised an eyebrow. "Mountain way says she goes to the next of kin with a mama in the house. Daniel too since he's still to home."

Solomon rocked as he stared out at the mountain. He knew that some folks in Blue Springs had started wagging their tongues, wondering why he hadn't followed the code they had all lived by for as long as anyone could remember, why he hadn't parceled Abby and Daniel out to his brother and his wife. But he couldn't find his way to do it, not even with Abby, though he knew she needed a ma.

"I got you to watch over Abby," he said. "Even if you never had no babies. And my kids are fatter than most anybody else's. They doing fine."

"They's better mannered than most others too," Francis added.

"Then I reckon I'll just keep 'em with me," he said. "That suit you well enough?"

"I'm up to what you say," she said, her fingers busy on her sewing again.

Solomon scratched Sandy. "My family been in these mountains since eighteen and forty-three," he said.

"It's a long time."

"The Indians was before them. Preacher says these mountains are thousands of years old."

"At least that," agreed Francis. "Some say a lot more."

"The Book says the good Lord has been here even longer," he said.

"Book says God is always here, never leaving us."

Solomon tapped out his pipe and shoved it in his pocket, then stood and walked into the yard. He took off his hat, held it by his side. "So God is still here?" he asked, his face toward the sky, his voice doubtful.

"I believe it so," said Francis.

Solomon stared at Blue Springs Mountain, its edges barely visible as the dark settled over it. He remembered a time when he was ten, a night he had gone coon hunting with his pa and brothers. In the middle of the hunt, he'd chased a dog on a false scent. The dog split off from the rest of the pack, and Solomon soon found himself cut off from everybody else. Rain started to fall, a rain as hard as the night Rose died. The rain made it such that he couldn't hear if somebody fired a gun so he could follow the sound of the shot out of his lostness.

With his dog at his side he found a small cave in some rocks and hid there until morning, his heart anxious but not yet afraid. When the sun came up, he did what his pa had told him to do if he ever found himself in just this situation, cut off and lost from everyone. He climbed to the top of the highest peak he could find, hauled up into a tree and climbed to the top branch. From there he slowly turned around in every direction.

He saw the bare spot off to the northwest, a spot referred to by mountain folk as a bald. It was a space without trees, an open face of rock on the mountainside that hovered over his family's land.

"Find Blue Springs Mountain," his pa had said. "Find our mountain and it'll take you home."

Climbing down from the tree, Solomon hollered at his dog and set out toward the mountain. It wasn't long before he found his family's cabin. As he stepped into the yard, his pa stood from a rocker on the porch and waved a hand.

"I told 'em not to worry," he said. "Told 'em you would know how to get home."

And so he had.

Staring at the bald again now, Solomon felt more lost than ever before in his life, more so than when he was ten. And this time he wondered if anything, even a mountain, could help him find his way home again.

"I always believed in God," he said.

"I know it," said Francis. "Nothing to change that now."

"But God feels a long way off."

"Death will make it seem so," she said. "Not a surprise in that."

Solomon kept gazing up at the mountain. In the middle of the bald a wide rock face cropped out, almost like a man's chin. The very last ray of the sun hit the bald at a sharp angle, and shadows painted odd shapes above and below the rock. Solomon pulled his beard. The bald took on the form of a human face: the rock a chin, a double shadow for eyes, another one for a nose. Suddenly the mountain seemed to come alive to him, alive and breathing. "Pa always said he could see God's face on the mountain," he said.

"All over it," agreed Francis, "for those who will look close."

Silence came again. The face on the mountain disappeared in the dark.

Solomon turned to Francis and said, "I don't know nothin' about raising no girl. You gone have to see to Abigail."

"Don't you lay all that on me," Francis said. "I'm too old, never know how much longer the Lord gone give me."

The stars blinked on, and Solomon turned away and headed inside the cabin. Francis followed. By the fireplace he stopped and stared at his shoes. "I still miss her," he said. "Sometimes so bad my gut hurts."

"I have no doubt of that," she said. "A man don't get over a woman like Rose any time too soon."

Solomon kicked at the fireplace with the toe of his shoe. Even in the summer he kept a low ember burning for cooking and such. "I'm not good by myself," he said. "Rose helped keep the rough edges wore off."

Francis kept her quiet.

He kept eyeing the fire. Saying what he was thinking made him feel like a traitor, a backstabber to Rose. But he couldn't help himself—it needed saying.

"You reckon Rose would haunt me if I someday took another woman to wife?" he asked.

Francis went to him and placed a hand on his back. "I got no doubt she would recommend it. After a proper mourning time, of course."

Solomon faced her. "Won't mean I don't still love her," he said. "No matter if I marry ten more times, Rose still the best love I ever had."

Smiling, Francis said, "You think they's ten women out there willing to hook up with you?"

He grinned. "Reckon not ten. But one? Maybe? You think so, somebody to help me with Abby?"

Francis lifted his hat up, pushed his hair off his forehead. "You still right decent to look at," she said. "Put on your weight again, comb up your hair. Rose always said you was the handsomest man on the mountain."

"That woman needed spectacles for sure," Solomon said.

Francis laughed.

Solomon set his hat back down, turned, and poked at the fire. As he did, he considered the possibility of a new woman. It wouldn't happen any time soon, he knew that. Still, he suspected he'd get married again someday. In the mountains, men didn't stay widowed long if they could help it.

CHAPTER
THREE

Solomon kept to his toiling all that fall. Mostly he did what all highlander folks do in such seasons. With the help of Francis and the boys, he hauled in and made ready for storage all manner of food, corn—some ground for meal and some stored in jars—and apples, to be dried and made into jelly or apple butter or left uncut in baskets. Kept cold enough, the apples would stay fresh until needed for pies and other things. They made sweet smooth jelly from the grapes that grew along the fence bordering the barn and house. They also put away the taters, Irish and sweet, in a hole dug out behind the barn. After the first frost, Solomon butchered a hog and salted and hung the meat in the smokehouse.

After they'd finished laying up their food, everybody started in with repairing the cabin, re-chinking between the logs and replacing the bad shingles on the roof. Then they cut and gathered fallen trees. The smaller branches would go for kindling, the bigger ones and the trunks for the fireplace. For days Solomon and his sons sawed and axed and hauled the wood close to the cabin so they could get to it when the snows fell.

By the time all this was done, the days had become shorter, and the trees on the mountain had lost most of their leaves. Now the frost blew from their mouths as they worked. Solomon and his family shifted their lives from outside to indoors, their time by the fire increasing in reverse measures to the amount of time the sun hung in the sky each day. By November the shift was complete, and everybody found they were spending far more time in the cabin than they wanted, though somehow they seemed to stay busy. Solomon most of all. Like usual in the winter, he turned his hand every night to his carving and building chairs—rocking chairs for mamas to rock their babies, and straight-backs for men to lean in as they talked and whittled. Building things had always soothed Solomon and never more so than the winter after Rose died.

As the snow built up by the door, he cut and shaved, sanded and stained. Francis sewed, cooked, and cleaned. Daniel left for the schoolhouse—a one-room rectangle about three miles down toward Blue Springs—on the mornings the weather allowed, returning home late afternoon hungry and chilled. Laban and Luke banged in and out like common boarders. The two boys would hunt one day, fish another, and visit the blacksmith's two daughters in Blue Springs on the next.

From time to time Solomon paused long enough to worry about the boys, Laban especially. Laban barely spoke when he came home and only then when asked a direct question. For some reason he seemed to carry a heavy chip on his shoulder, and the natural tendency toward fractiousness every boy his age experiences had become a surly anger. Solomon smelled liquor on his whereabouts about every weekend now. The lazy rascals he'd taken up with kept him out far too late on Saturday nights. Maybe worst of all, Laban pulled Luke right behind him wherever he went.

Solomon knew he ought to deal with Laban straight out. But, given his own melancholy moods and liking for silence, he just kept his hands busy and his mouth shut. Let the boy have his time, he figured. Losing a mama gave a son the right to feel angry, maybe a husband as well.

Solomon watched Abby too, but only at a distance. He saw her in Francis's lap as he and Francis took their meals. Hauling in wood, he stepped by her while she lay on a blanket. He heard her cry when she woke up hungry in the wee hours of the night. As if by magic, she began to take sprout right under his nose. Her red hair growing longer every day, she crawled and pulled and cooed and cried enough to wake the dead. But Solomon gave no sign that he gave heed to any of this. From all outward appearances Abby might just as well have been one of the pups Sandy produced every spring—a cute but separate part of his life. He thought about Abby a lot, of course—far more than anybody knew—yet still felt awkward around her.

Solomon knew that Francis disapproved of his manner around his baby girl. More than once he saw her biting her tongue to keep from having a say at him. But, acting on her Christian ways, she never scolded him. Solomon was glad. It wasn't his sister's place to push him. Better to let him be.

Christmas came but with little cheer. Francis put up a tiny tree that Luke and Daniel had cut and tied red pieces of string on its branches. The tree stood in the corner of the front room and received scant attention. Unlike their mountain neighbors, neither Solomon nor the boys stepped outside on Christmas Eve to fire their guns into the air to celebrate the birth of the baby Jesus. The next morning Solomon skipped the church service down at Jesus Holiness, choosing instead to visit Rose's grave. He stood there for close to an hour, his head bare, the wind and cold turning his ears as red as a summer tomato. He stayed quiet at the grave, as if listening for a voice from somewhere. But none came.

After church Francis gave each of the boys a homemade flannel shirt and then slipped a blue cotton dress on Abby. With little money and no inclination toward gladness, nobody else passed out any presents.

As the January snow bore in, Solomon seemed bent on toiling even harder. From sunup to sundown he worked like a man trying to wear every bone in his body down to dust and gristle. Whether hunting, hauling wood, or making chairs, he threw himself into all of it. The days passed into weeks, the weeks into months. The snows outside eventually slowed up, then stopped falling completely. A couple of weeks after that, a thawing began. The trees dripped like small waterfalls from the melting ice, and Slick Rock Creek swelled with the overflow. By the end of March, Solomon had finished five chairs—three rockers and two straight. He had also built two shelf pieces capable of holding canned goods, books, or any other odds and ends a body might want to load on them.

On the first day of April, three weeks before the anniversary night of Rose's passing, Solomon walked out to his front porch just before dusk, stretched his back, and stared out into the clearing. A circle of budding white dogwoods rimmed the woods past the fence in the front, and the first green leaves had shown up on the hardwoods that shaded his porch.

Laban and Luke both happened to be home, sitting in rockers on either side of Solomon. Luke had a guitar balanced on his knee, his fingers strumming away. Daniel sat on the front stoop with Sandy at his feet. Francis rested beside Daniel. Her hands lay still in her lap for once, and she had a dip of snuff in her left cheek.

"Most of the planting is done," announced Solomon.

Laban muttered, "You about worked us to death."

Solomon grinned and kicked playfully at his eldest. "Hard work never killed nobody," he said.

Sandy laid her head on Daniel's lap. Solomon stretched again. "Maybe we take a trip down to Asheville," he said calmly, as if asking someone to pass the corn bread at supper. "See what we can get in trade for them chairs I been slaving over."

"Yahoo!" yelled Daniel, jumping up and hugging him at the waist. Some people in the Blue Ridge lived their whole lives and never traveled more than ten miles from the cabins where they were born. Sandy waved her tail as though she understood the big news. Luke stopped playing his guitar and looked at Laban.

Solomon turned to his oldest boy. "You think you might like a trip to the city?" he asked.

Laban nodded. "Might be a good time."

"I'll stay with Abby," said Francis. "Asheville is too far for one old as me to go."

"Maybe I can buy some fancy cloth," Solomon said. "Something you can use to make you a new dress."

"Some for a dress for the baby too," Francis said. "That's the true need."

Solomon stretched a third time. "Best that all of us should get a good night's rest. A long way down to Asheville. We'll leave soon as we ready tomorrow."

"It will take a hard day's walk to get there," said Daniel. "That is if we don't get no rain."

Solomon nodded. Weather was unpredictable this time of year, and if a hard rain did come, then one of the streams they had to cross might flood and keep them dead stopped from any traveling they had in mind.

"I know the possibles," Solomon said, not in the least put off. "We will leave tomorrow after chores."

———

They arose the next morning long before first light and started lickety-split to take care of the necessaries. They ate biscuits and jelly for breakfast, then milked the cow, gathered the eggs, and hauled in some wood. Not wanting to wait for water to heat in the kettle in the yard, the three boys and Solomon took baths in Slick Rock Creek just as the sun started to peek up. Shivering in the cold water, they scrubbed off a couple of weeks of dirt and toweled off with some clean rags Francis handed to them. Their bodies pink with chill, they slipped on their best overalls, wiped mud off their brogans, put on their new Christmas shirts and best socks, slid their fingers through their hair and stuck it down with a touch of lard. Solomon trimmed his beard, and Laban shaved off the thin growth he had let gather on his chin.

They then took to loading Bouncer, the mule. Solomon's chairs used up most of the space on the sturdy animal so they stacked the two shelves on a sled—a hand-built conveyance with wooden runners and a rope pulley designed for hauling goods up and down the narrow mountain trails. Finally they stuffed corn bread, coffee, two jars of applesauce, a hunk of ham the size of a shovel blade, and four thin blankets into a burlap bag and stacked it by the door. Before the morning was half gone they were primed and all set to leave.

"Be back day after tomorrow," Solomon said to Francis as she stood by the door with Abby in her arms. "We will do our tradin', then head right back on home."

Francis nodded. "Big towns don't hold much shine for men such as you," she said.

"Air's bad in them closed-up houses," Solomon agreed. "And they got no food worth eating. Take me away from my own house and I get lonesome as a calf without a mama."

"Don't forget my dress cloth," Francis said. "I want to make something pretty for Abby for her birthday."

Solomon tugged down his hat. "Pink if I can find it," he said. "I got my orders."

Turning down the trail, Solomon and the boys set off, with Daniel leading Bouncer, Laban and Luke pulling the sleds, and Solomon carrying the burlap bag on his back. They passed through Blue Springs a little before noon and stopped at the only store there—a faded wood building with a porch where old men sat and played checkers. Solomon bought two cans of beans at the store.

A half hour later he and the boys finished off the beans and a chunk of the corn bread and rolled back onto the trail. The afternoon passed quickly. The boys talked some but mostly stayed quiet, intent on making fast time. They waded through a number of creeks without bothering to take off their shoes, and the water chilled their feet. About nine miles southeast of Blue Springs the dirt trail became a gravel road. They hoofed down the road the rest of the day.

Pulling off the road about an hour before sundown, they built a fire in a meadow close to Wally's Ridge and quickly made coffee. After eating the ham, another chunk of corn bread, and a jar of the applesauce, Solomon pulled out the blankets, and everybody lay up for sleeping, all of them too spent to say much. Within minutes they were snoring and the night passed quickly. When dawn came they washed up in a nearby spring, ate some more corn bread and applesauce, and moved back down the trail. Their path kept up a steady descent.

The boys fell into an easy chatter as they walked. Solomon held his quiet and watched them, his heart proud in spite of his misgivings about Laban's activities over the last few months.

Laban was pretty near a man, the same height as Solomon but with his mama's coloring: auburn hair and greenish eyes. Women loved those eyes and Laban knew it. At church socials the girls kept him busy, their fluttering eyelashes and eager giggles luring him to go walking with first this one and then the next. So far he hadn't singled one out for marrying, but Solomon knew it was bound to happen soon. The boy was close to his manhood. Maybe that was what he needed, Solomon thought, a good woman to gentle him a mite.

Solomon rubbed his beard. He and Laban had clashed at each other a couple of times since Christmas. The boy had a bad tendency to skip out on his chores and disappear off to heaven only knew where. Solomon hoped that such a tendency didn't signal long-term laziness. Bad enough that Laban had already acquired a taste for the doublings. If he turned out lazy too, then he feared for the boy's future. A highlander man wasn't guaranteed to get ahead even when he stayed sober and slaved hard from sunup to sundown, but he was sure not to do well if he didn't. And Solomon didn't take kindly to any signs of either sloth or drunkenness, especially from his own flesh and blood.

Sighing, Solomon told himself Laban was a good boy. Could work most men right to the nubs when he set his mind to it. Could shoot a squirrel between the eyes from so far away he couldn't hardly see it and throw a knife just as accurate. Though he was a touch confused right now, he was still a worthy son.

He turned from Laban to Luke. Luke, the slow one, the one with the tongue that sometimes didn't work too well.

Solomon reset his hat. Luke had lighter hair than anybody else in the family but Francis and skin just as pale. He also had a weak left eye, all white and milky. And he never quite caught on to things like other boys his age. Though no one in the mountains went much past the sixth grade in their schooling, Luke hadn't made it all the way at that. He tried harder than any ten boys, but just didn't take to learning. Never grabbed on to reading, and any kind of numbers muddled him up something awful. Some of the schoolboys teased him about his dull head, yet Luke didn't seem to mind it most times. He just grinned, took up his guitar, and started to picking, his thin fingers flying on the strings quicker than a bumblebee's wings. The music made Luke special, Solomon thought. He had a gift for it.

Smiling under his beard, Solomon glanced over at his youngest. Daniel trailed the older boys, a walking stick in his right hand, Bouncer's lead rope in the other. The boy had dark hair and eyes, hair just like his. But he was going to be taller. The notches on the cabin's doorpost he'd marked on each of the boy's birthdays said Daniel was taller than both Laban and Luke at his age. Thicker too. Daniel had shoulders that would no doubt grow wider than anybody's on either side of the family, including his.

"That boy's thicker than a baby calf," Preacher Bruster had said to Solomon on the Sunday after Daniel's last birthday. "Nobody mess with him, that's for sure."

Solomon knew nobody did. Although young, Daniel had already demonstrated a fierce temper. Strange the way the good Lord had made him up. On the one side he cared more for animals and children than most anybody Solomon had ever met. On the other, he could fly off the handle and work up a flash of anger hot enough to scare a bear right off the mountain. Solomon hoped the boy's temper didn't land him in trouble someday.

Maybe he was smart enough to keep that temper under control.

People said he was the brightest boy in the school, already able to do his ciphers and read the Bible without much stumbling over any words. Though the school down in Blue Springs had only twenty books total for the kids to read, Daniel had already gone through them and more than once. He especially liked the two that told about that King Arthur and his knights, all their noble ways and high adventure.

The road curved to the left and became a packed dirt highway with a lot fewer holes. It was less than two miles to Asheville now. He lowered his head and pushed on. They would reach the city before noon. He reset his hat. Asheville was too much town for him. Almost fifteen thousand people according to the folks at the store where he traded. More than he cared to mix with, that was for sure.

Solomon thought about the city. It had most everything a body could ever want: a barbershop where a man actually paid somebody to cut his hair; a hotel with water that gushed through indoor metal pipes; school-trained doctors with fancy degrees hanging on their walls; schools that went all the way up to the eleventh grade; streets paved with real bricks; and general stores full of enough food to feed a small army. He rubbed his beard. Asheville scared him to death.

A good two hours before noon, he and his boys reached the outskirts of the city. Wagons began to pass them going in both directions. The boys picked up their pace and started talking louder and faster. Solomon felt his own heart beating quicker and he wondered if he might see one of those horseless carriages he'd heard about the last time he came down to Asheville to trade. People said they belched smoke and scared the horses and mules but could roll along on the roads faster than anything anybody had ever seen and could carry loads bigger than five horses. So far none had come to Asheville that he knew of, but it was only a matter of time.

Solomon grunted. He could imagine no reason for a man to go so fast. Whatever speed he couldn't reach by walking or riding a beast of burden he just did not need to reach.

Moving past a sharp curve, he and his boys reached the first row of businesses that fringed the main streets of Asheville—a line of wood and brick buildings that housed all manner of establishments—a doctor's of-fice, a dress shop, a general store, a lawyer's place, a bank. Solomon steered the boys to the general store on the right, a broad white building with a porch as wide as two barns stuck together.

"You reckon old man Stinson still runnin' the place?" asked Laban.

"Hope so," Solomon said. "Stinson always been a fair man to deal with."

"How old is he?" asked Daniel, hitching Bouncer to a post in front of the store.

"Old as dirt," said Laban. "Least that's what he said last time we come by."

"Aunt Francis said to trade for some peppermints," Daniel said.

"And one of them c-c-c-cola drinks," added Luke, his milky eye rolling back in his head like it always did when he became excited.

"A man ain't made out of silver dollars," Solomon said. "We get our necessaries, then see what we got left to trade for splurgibles."

Sighing, the boys followed Solomon up the steps and into the store. They knew their pa wasn't given to much waste when it came to spending.

Inside the store Solomon wrinkled his nose. The place smelled like cinnamon overlaid with freshly cut wood. His boots clomped across the wood flooring. A man and woman studying a metal washtub looked up and nodded his way as he and his boys entered. Solomon tipped his hat, then glanced around the store. A glass counter stretched halfway down the right side of the room and a row of shelves that reached all the way to the ceiling bordered on the left. The shelves held everything from overalls and men's hats to nails and hammers, and cotton and calico and gingham for women to make clothing. Behind the glass counter were such things as men's watches, rows of penny candy, and more cooking spices than Solomon had ever seen.

A bent-backed old man wearing wire-rimmed glasses walked their way, readjusting his spectacles on his nose as he approached. "That you, Solomon Porter?" the man asked, squinting through his glasses.

"I reckon it still is," said Solomon, shaking Bill Stinson's hand. "Back again."

"How long has it been?"

"On to two years almost. August of eighteen and ninety-nine, I think."

"You brought all your sons with you this time," Stinson said, looking over the boys.

"Yep," Solomon said proudly, standing back so Stinson could see his offspring.

Stinson clucked his approval. "They's all bigger," he said. "And more handsome than their pa, that's for sure. So how is Mrs. Rose?"

Solomon studied his brogans for several seconds, pulled off his hat and held it over his chest, his eyes still on the floor. How could he tell the words, say the thing out loud? Truth was he hadn't mentioned it since the day Rose died. Somehow not saying the words made it less real, made it seem like Rose had gone off on a journey somewhere, a long trip past anything he'd ever known. He started to speak but found his tongue uncooperative.

"She's home with the Lord," Daniel said, his eyes on the candy behind the counter. "In April last year."

"I'm much grieved to hear that," said Stinson.

"In childbirth," Solomon added, feeling he ought to explain. "Death meets up with a body in all kinds of places in the highlands."

"Ain't that the truth," agreed Stinson.

"The baby's doing good," said Daniel. "Sister Abby, she is growing fast."

Stinson grunted and pushed his glasses higher on his nose. "Glad the baby is good," he said. "And glad Mrs. Rose got that girl she always wanted. Maybe you bring her in the next time you come down to Asheville."

"Maybe so," said Solomon. "Francis is keeping her now."

Stinson nodded slowly. "Be assured again of my condolences for your loss. Your woman was a fine human being."

"I appreciate your thinking so."

"Abby looks like Mama," Laban said. "Spittin' image."

The door to the store swung open, interrupting the conversation. Two men and a teenage boy walked in, the smell of stale tobacco and several days of sweat announcing their presence. Solomon gritted his teeth as he recognized Hal Clack and two of his sons, Topper and Ben. The Clacks—all of them skinny men with crooked teeth, hair as dark as coal, and noses sharp as hawks' beaks—were rough folks from the other side of the ridge back in Blue Springs. Made their living as blockaders—men who made doublings and then sold the whiskey for the highest price they could find. Clack's oldest boy, Topper, had been tried once for killing a revenuer with a Winchester, but the jury had let him off on self-defense. A friend of Solomon's had told him for a fact that Topper had bushwhacked the man, shot him in the chest as he rounded a curve in the creek bed, which fed into the hideaway where the Clacks kept their biggest still. The government man never had a chance.

Solomon put his hat back on. "We got chairs for trade," he said, dismissing the Clacks as unworthy of his attention. "As good as any I ever done."

"You bring 'em in," Stinson said. "Your chairs are the best anybody brings me, easy as pie to sell."

Solomon turned to his sons. Luke had wandered off to the back of the store. Solomon pointed Laban and Daniel toward the door, then followed them out. At the hitching post he untied the chairs, hauled them down off Bouncer, and sat them on the wood sidewalk. A young woman stepped down the street toward him. Solomon paused and took off his hat. Unlike a lot of highlander men, he tried to treat women with a measure of respect. They worked harder than a lot of the men did and got little or no reward for it.

The woman approaching him had thick hair that flowed onto her shoulders in a cascade of black curls. She wore a straight-lined calico dress that looked almost new. The dress was dark green with yellow flowers on the shoulders and around the neck. The woman reached him, her eyes bold as she stared ahead. Solomon felt his breath catch. The woman had none of the shyness that marked most mountain girls.

Something felt familiar about her but he couldn't place it. Was she a highlander woman? He thought maybe he'd seen her somewhere but then decided if that was so, he wouldn't have forgotten her, not a woman this handsome. Must be a city girl, he decided, living right here in Asheville.

Solomon glanced at his boys, saw that they too had stopped moving, their hats in their hands. The woman raised her right eyebrow for a second as if waiting to see what he would do. But then, when he didn't move or speak, she quickly turned into Stinson's, leaving him and his boys staring at her back.

Several seconds passed. Finally Solomon swallowed, winked at Laban and Daniel, and found his voice. "Stop your gawkin' and finish unloading," he said. "Time is a-wasting."

Picking up two chairs, he stepped back into Stinson's store. At the counter he looked around for the woman, but she'd disappeared somewhere in the back. He saw Luke at the glass counter, his finger pointing at a jar of peppermints. Only three sticks were left.

Bill Stinson stood behind the counter with his head tilted toward Luke.

"Make up your mind, Mr. Luke," Stinson said. "You want the peppermints or not?"

Solomon saw Topper Clack move up behind Luke, and the muscles in his neck tightened up. Men from the Clack clan made all mountain men look bad. They spent most of their time making, defending, and selling their corn liquor. When they weren't at their stills, they were causing all manner of trouble, drinking past all reason, picking fights, stirring up a fracas at every turn. They seldom bathed, ran hard over their women, ruled their kids with an iron hand, and generally served as a pestilence on the land. He had no patience with such fellows and barely managed to hide his disgust.

"Gimme them three peppermints," said Topper Clack, pushing past Luke and pounding on the counter.

"B-b-but I wa-wa-want them," stuttered Luke, his arm on Clack's elbow.

Fearful for his boy, Solomon moved quickly to him. Topper Clack nudged Luke to the side and tossed a couple of coins on the counter. "Them peppermints is mine," Clack shouted. "Bought and paid for."

Luke grabbed for the coins but Clack slapped his hand down on Luke's and pinned it to the counter. Solomon saw Hal and Ben Clack look up from the back of the store. Solomon jerked Topper's hand off Luke's and held the boy's arms at his side.

"We are not lookin' for no trouble," Solomon said, his teeth clenched.

Hal Clack appeared at the counter, Ben beside him. Both men had their hands balled into fists. It struck Solomon that Ben was no more than twelve or thirteen yet he already had the haggard face of a man acquainted with danger.

"Let go my boy," Hal Clack said.

But Solomon held firm. "Your boy started it," he said. "Luke here was mindin' his own business. Your boy butted in a wrong place."

"Don't matter who started nothin'," said Clack. "Just let him be."

Solomon saw Ben move a hand to his boot, knew by instinct that the boy was reaching for a knife. Behind him, he heard the door open, then the sound of boots on the floor. Without looking he knew that Laban and Daniel had stepped inside.

"Back on out of here, boys," Solomon said, never turning his head. "Me and Luke be there in a minute."

"We ain't goin' nowhere," called Laban. "Looks like you got some troubles."

Solomon bit his lip, angry yet in some way proud that his boys wouldn't run from the fracas. A highlander man had to have courage if he wanted the respect of his neighbors. He heard the boots moving again, then felt Laban and Daniel at his elbow. Ben Clack raised his hand, and Solomon saw the knife, a long-bladed shiny thing with a point sharp enough to slay a pig. Ben stepped over to his dad and handed him the knife. Hal Clack held it by his side, his eyes as bright as the blade.

"Now let go my boy," Clack said again. "And give me them peppermints." He glanced at Stinson as he pointed the knife at the glass counter.

Solomon ground his teeth, not wanting to yield, not wanting to show cowardice to his sons. At the same time, though, he wanted to keep them safe. A fight with the Clacks would no doubt turn bloody real fast. Men like them didn't make false threats, and a knife pulled meant a hand ready to use it.

Solomon quickly weighed his odds. His boys were as strong as young bears and all three had knives on their waistbands. Laban especially was mighty good with a knife. But Clack had his weapon already in hand. So by the time Solomon could pull his knife out and take to stabbing with it, one of his boys might take a cutting.

Solomon swallowed hard. No matter about his own pride, he had to do what was necessary to protect his sons. This weren't the time for knife play with the Clacks. Let them win this skirmish, he concluded. He and Hal Clack had clashed at other times before this, and he had no doubt he'd get another chance to even up the score.

A hint of a smile came to Solomon's face as he remembered a previous contest with Clack. He'd won that round, he recalled, and it had meant a heap more than this did. Let Clack have this one.

Solomon started to back away. But before he could move, he heard a commotion behind Hal Clack, heard someone else moving. He saw the woman he'd just seen in the street walk up to Clack and place her hand on his shoulder.

"You causing trouble again, Pa?" she asked with a smile, her language crisper than most mountain women. "Bothering these good people?"

Clack glanced at the woman, then back to Solomon. "Move on, Elsa," he said. "You just gettin' in the way."

Elsa grinned at Solomon and reached for her pa's knife hand. "You know what the sheriff here told you," she cooed. "One more bit of trouble and you're off to his jail. And this jail is different from the one up in Blue Springs. Down here they won't let a man off because they're afraid of him or his kin."

Dropping his eyes like a whipped puppy, Hal Clack took a step back. Elsa grabbed his knife and laid it on the counter. Solomon let go of Topper's wrists.

Clack spit on the floor. "Git your stuff boys," he said. "We're done here for now."

As her pa stalked away, Elsa spoke to Solomon, her eyes as bold as ever. "I hear your wife died last year," she said.

Solomon's brow wrinkled. How did this woman know about Rose? And how come he never heard of her? How could she be Hal Clack's daughter? Yeah, he knew Clack and his wife Amelia had a girl but no one had seen her in many a year. He tried to pull out his memory, remember where and if he'd ever met her before, maybe when she was a youngster. He couldn't place it. But he did find his voice. "My woman passed last April," he said.

"The mountains are hard on women," she said. "Sorry for your hurting."

Hal Clack suddenly reappeared and grasped Elsa by the elbow. She jerked against him, but he just yanked harder as he steered her toward the door. She slapped his hand away and faced Solomon again. "I expect Blue Springs can get mighty lonely for a widow man like you," she said, her voice remaining calm in spite of her pa's rudeness.

"Shut up, Elsa," said Clack, pulling at her arm again. "I won't have you talkin' to mountain trash like this."

Elsa smiled at Solomon, then laid her hand on her pa's arm as if being escorted into a dance and walked primly out of the store.

Stunned, Solomon watched her go. He'd never known a woman who talked in such a forward manner. He turned to Stinson. "How old is she?" he asked.

"Twenty or so, from what I hear."

"Married?"

"Nope, never. Nobody she fancies is brave enough to face her pa and go to courting her, and the men her pa likes don't suit her."

"She is an attractive woman," Solomon said.

"She's trouble from what I hear," said Stinson. "In and out of here every month or so. Her and her ma been living here during school time the last few years, stayed in a boardinghouse not too far up the street."

Solomon remembered that Clack had built his wife a house in Blue Springs, one of the best in town. But he still couldn't remember ever meeting the daughter.

"She is real educated then?" he asked of Elsa.

"Seems so. But she's still a Clack. Got a pretty peeling on her, but I'm guessing the inside is still a bad fruit off that tree. Nice to you, though."

Solomon nodded, mystified again by the ways of women. "She got her reasons for that, I guess," he said.

"You still want to trade them chairs?" Stinson asked, changing the conversation.

"I ain't walked all the way down here just to carry them back," said Solomon. He struggled to settle his mind on his business again. "But they ain't gone come cheap."

Stinson grunted. Solomon turned to the boys for the chairs. He and Stinson started haggling over their value. But even as he bartered Solomon couldn't help but keep thinking of Elsa Clack.

Outside on the street, Hal Clack steered Elsa to a wagon and pushed her into it. "You stuck your nose in where it don't belong," he said. "Messin' with a man's business."

"You were about to get yourself thrown into jail," she said. "I'm just using some brains, unlike the rest of this family."

"Just shut up and stay here. Me and your brothers goin' to the stable, check a horse."

Elsa propped her chin in her hands, her face flushed and angry.

"I mean it," said Clack. "Keep yourself put."

Elsa bit her tongue.

"I'll be back in a few minutes and I better find you right here in this wagon," he said as he walked off, his sons following.

Elsa shifted and watched them go. As they disappeared around a corner she faced Stinson's store again and thought of Solomon Porter. Though she could tell he didn't remember her, she had actually met him six years ago on a cloudy October day in Blue Springs. A politician of one kind or another had come there to make a speech. In town to purchase winter supplies, she and her mama had stopped to listen as the politician hopped up on the back of a wagon to woo the voters. Not knowing his name at the time, she saw Solomon Porter standing near the politician's wagon, his hat off, his hair neater than most mountain men, his clothes better kept. He had a dark look about him, though not an unkind one. And he was strong as an ox. She could see this in his forearms as they hung from the rolled-up sleeves of his shirt.

Elsa felt her face flush. Although she was just fourteen at the time, she'd already blossomed into her full womanhood, and more boys than she bothered to count had called on her. But the boys her age seemed like babies when they made their advances. They stammered when they tried to talk to her and kicked at rocks and kept their eyes down, studying their bare feet. Elsa dismissed such boys as far too backward for her liking. She needed a man who would know what to do with someone like her, a man she couldn't maneuver so easily as she did all the others. She needed a man who had a sense of what he wanted and could teach her the things about loving that she didn't know already. There were still a few things left for her to discover.

Blushing, Elsa had asked her mama about the handsome man near the front of the crowd.

"He's a married man," Amelia Clack said.

"What's his name?" insisted Elsa.

"Solomon Porter and he's at least thirty years old, in addition to his married condition."

Elsa crossed her arms. "He's a handsome man," she said.

Amelia chortled. "That he is."

"What you know about him?"

"Not much. People speak of him as real quiet. And he's trustable too, most say."

Elsa sighed, feeling instantly drawn to a man like that. Not many people trusted her pa. That made her sad.

The politician finished his speaking. Rain started to fall. Elsa and her mama moved to do their purchasing. An hour or so later they came by chance out of the store just as Solomon Porter walked by. With her eyes on Solomon, Elsa slipped on the wet steps of the wood porch. Solomon grabbed her, pulled her up straight, tipped his hat, and kept on walking. She'd watched him as he walked off, her skin still tingling from the strength she felt in his hands, the warmth in his fingers.

A door opened at Stinson's, and Elsa's attention focused again on the present moment. A man and woman walked out carrying a washtub.

Elsa thought of her pa. She knew what people said about him. He was a moneygrubber. Made corn liquor for sale to all that had the dollars to pay. True, not too many folks other than a few in Jesus Holiness Church begrudged him his liquor making. In the mountains almost everybody made some doublings, at least for their own personal use. But people did resent the strong-armed ways that Hal Clack and his kin ruled everybody else. If somebody crossed him, he visited a quick beating on that person. When faced with competition from other stillers, he'd been known to collect a gang and go riding into the coves, pistols and rifles drawn to shut down the offender. That way he closed down the competition and kept his prices up. Worst of all, some said that more than once he had told government revenuers where another man kept his still so they could go tear it up. And that's one thing a body best not do in the mountains—tell revenuers where to find another man's makings.

Elsa sighed. Some of the time she liked the power her pa wielded. And she certainly enjoyed the dollars his business brought to them, liked the clothes the money bought, the extra fine house it allowed her to sleep in every night. But she wished he'd come by his fortune in a more respectable way. She wished that all of his blessings had made him a more refined man, less prone to drink and gamble, chase women and cuss, go without shaving and bathing.

Elsa bit her lip and pouted. Her mama was powerless when it came to Hal Clack. She just cowered in his presence. When Hal got all liquored up and came home angry and found something to his dislike and took to hitting Amelia, as he did about once or twice a year, Amelia just wailed and took the beating. Having watched it for years, Elsa nursed a deep but mostly unspoken fury at her pa. No way would she take this kind of treatment from any man, husband or no.

Getting warm in the sun, Elsa shaded her eyes and shifted in the wagon. Her brothers weren't much better than her pa. All four of them were bullies. Following their pa's example, they had little or no respect for women or anybody else for that matter.

Elsa hugged her arms around her waist. With no sisters, she had nobody to talk to. Life sure got lonely sometimes, she decided.

She thought of Solomon Porter again. Was he any different than the boys her age? Did he have the stomach to stand up to her pa? He seemed mighty brave just now inside Stinson's store. Calm and steady. Was he like that all the time?

She heard a door open again and saw Solomon and his sons walk out of the general store. With her heart thumping heavy, she watched Solomon coming down the street. Her face flushed. Her body warmed up, and this time it wasn't from the sun.

As if pushed by a force she'd never experienced and couldn't control, Elsa decided right then and there that she wanted Solomon Porter, wanted him more than anything she'd ever wanted in her life. Not that she wanted to be as poor as he was. But she wanted him, the kind of man he was, the . . . For a second she tried to figure out the feeling. Why did he draw her like he did? She didn't even know the man.

Her mind reasoned through it. Maybe she wanted Solomon because she knew it would make her pa furious. Or maybe she wanted Solomon because she instinctively wanted something better than what she had in her own family, something more noble, something gentler and kinder.

She told herself to let it go. It didn't matter that she didn't know exactly why she felt so attracted to Solomon Porter. She didn't need to puzzle it all out. It was enough that she knew that Solomon was a strong, handsome, honest man and that such a combination was rare in the mountains, and she wasn't getting any younger, and things in her family weren't getting any better. So if she wanted him, she better do something now or the moment would pass and Solomon would marry someone else. Then she would end up stuck with some rough highlander boy that her pa would approve and she would hate.

As Solomon approached her wagon, Elsa weighed the matter one last time. Her pa would no doubt roar like a wounded bear. He would threaten to cut her off from all his money. That notion scared her. But she knew she could woo him back like she always did. After a while she would sidle up to him and call him "Papa" and smile real big and he would get over his anger and once again provide her with the financial provision she deserved.

Assured by her reasoning, Elsa hopped down to the street and placed herself in the path of Solomon Porter.

Watching Elsa Clack jump from her wagon, Solomon came to a stop and eyed her suspiciously. "Where's your pa?" he asked.

"Does it matter?" she asked in return, her eyes sparkly.

Solomon looked around as if he was eager to cross the street but didn't want to get hit by a wagon. Something was bothersome here, though he didn't know for sure just what it was. Laban stepped up behind him and pulled on his shirtsleeve. He faced his eldest son. Laban's jaw was firm.

"She's trouble, Pa," he said, loud enough for Elsa to hear. "Let's go home."

Solomon nodded. What Laban said made sense. But a woman like Elsa Clack made a man lose most of the good sense God had given him. He was a thirty-six-year-old man who had need of a woman, and he wasn't afraid of anybody, much less a bully like Hal Clack.

He pulled his pipe from his pocket, chewed it for a minute. He'd known Clack since he was a boy, hadn't liked him then and didn't like him now. Owed him for more than one slight. Might be pleasurable to make him mad by courting his daughter, whether he ever took after Elsa serious or not.

Laban pulled on his sleeve again. Solomon took a heavy breath and realized that courting Elsa Clack to get back at her pa wasn't exactly a kindly thing to do. Truth was, the idea was beneath a man who claimed any connection to sweet Jesus. No matter how much he owed Hal Clack, he couldn't do that. He started to walk away.

But then he thought of Abigail. The girl did need a mama. Yes, she had Francis but for how much longer? Women died young in the highlands, and most of the bloom had long since fallen from Francis's flower. Solomon considered the notion of spending another winter without a woman. It would be bleak like the one just past, full of long cold nights with nobody but him in the bed. Nobody to hold, to talk to before he fell asleep. Though he knew he could never find anybody as precious as Rose, he still didn't want to stay alone forever. No two ways about it, he needed a wife. But Elsa Clack? With all the calamities her family might cause? It would be complicatious, that's for sure.

His head all jumbled, Solomon faced Elsa again. "You just climb on back up in your wagon," he said. "Maybe I come see you later."

Elsa stared hard at him for several seconds, then hitched her dress and eased back into the wagon. Sitting up straight, she nodded and said, "Make sure you come soon now. A girl like me won't stay free forever."

Tipping his hat, Solomon turned and walked away, his sons trailing. His heart pounded heavy in his chest as he moved up the street, and he couldn't tell for sure whether this was because he was worried or excited.

CHAPTER
FOUR

Elsa and her ma moved back to their house just outside of Blue Springs in early May, and Elsa spent the next four weeks waiting on Solomon Porter to come calling. But he failed to show up. In response to his tardiness, Elsa grumbled to herself, made life as miserable as possible for those around her, and wondered at night before she fell asleep what had happened to him. Had he gotten so busy working that he had no time to think of her? Or was he just like all the other men she knew—too scared of her pa to make the advances he needed to make?

As June rolled by, Elsa took to thinking bad about herself. Maybe Solomon hadn't thought her pretty enough. She looked in the mirror over her dresser one morning. Average height, dark curly hair, blue eyes, more buxom than most mountain women, good teeth, straight and strong. A clear complexion too, creamy and soft. A whole lot more like her pa than her ma, a fact for which she was most grateful.

She patted her hair, felt pleased with her appearance. It couldn't be her looks. Everybody swore she was beautiful. Then what? Why hadn't Solomon Porter come to spark her?

She thought of his dead wife, a woman she knew only by reputation.

Rose Porter had been a decent looking woman according to those who spoke of her, but nothing out of the ordinary. A lady given to soft words and a gentle heart, everybody said. A beloved figure in her mountain community, somebody always ready with a bowl of soup for the sick, a smile and good word for the disheartened. No doubt Solomon still carried some bleakness in his heart about her passing. But how long did a man need to grieve before he could acceptably go courting again? It had been over a year now, a respectful enough time for anybody, even the most loyal. So what was wrong with him? Why had he not made any advances toward her?

Still pouting at Solomon, Elsa moved away from the mirror and considered another possibility, one she didn't rightly want to face. Solomon Porter had scruples. Everybody said so. But her kin weren't known for their high moral code. Truth was, her family wasn't known for any moral code at all, high or low. What if Solomon hadn't made any advances because of the ill reputation of her pa and brothers? What if Solomon Porter saw himself as too good for someone of Clack blood?

Elsa rolled the notion around in her head. A cousin had been hanged three years ago for shooting a man in the back during a brawl down at the general store in Blue Springs. And seldom did a month go by without one of the Clacks ending up in a jail somewhere for at least a few days. No doubt her kin and Solomon's would mix like hound dogs and coons. Had he figured that out and rejected her because of it?

Sitting on the edge of the bed, yet another possibility came to Elsa. Had her forward ways come on too strong for Solomon? Perhaps he thought she had too much of her pa in her, all brash and loud. Was that it? Did he want a quiet little mountain woman? Somebody to cook his meals and tend his kids and keep his cabin swept clean? Well, she could do that as capably as any woman could. But she was more than that too. She had education, all the way through the eleventh grade from a school right there in Asheville. Her mama, for all her faults, had seen to it that Hal Clack paid for her boarding so she could attend school.

Her jaw set, Elsa sprang up from the bed and told herself to forget Solomon Porter. If he didn't want her because she was a smart woman with some sense of her own mind, then he wasn't good enough for her! Simple as that.

June became July and Elsa gradually turned angry at the whole situation. Her daydreams about Solomon Porter's strong arms and dark eyes became episodes of genuine dislike. How dare he ignore her this way? If he thought she was just going to sit around forever and wait on a coward like him, he had another think coming! Plenty of mountain boys with their tongues hanging out were just dying for a chance to take up with her. She would show Solomon Porter a thing or two, she decided, surely she would!

As the first light dawned on the morning of the Fourth of July, Elsa dressed in her prettiest outfit: an ankle-length green dress with yellow rosebuds around the collar, a wide-brimmed hat with a yellow chin strap, and a pair of black shoes so shiny she could see her face in them. Checking herself in the mirror, she had no doubt she would have on better clothes than any woman in Blue Springs.

Her pa and brothers rode up just as she and her ma climbed into the wagon for the ride into town. From their flushed faces she could tell the men had taken early to their jugs. Though it was only midmorning, she knew they'd soon reach a state of total drunkenness.

Elsa and her ma led the procession in their wagon, her pa and brothers following on their horses. She and her ma stayed quiet through most of the short trip, while her pa and brothers gabbed like town gossips. Elsa listened with embarrassment to their slurred words. No wonder Solomon Porter wanted nothing to do with her.

In town she found a spot under a big oak and stopped the wagon. Climbing down, she quickly nodded to her ma and turned to leave, to separate herself from her loutish kin.

"You check in with me before the firecrackers," said her ma. "I'll stay near the general store."

Elsa waved and walked away. Afraid of her husband's jealousy, her ma always stayed in one place on days like this, stood around with a group of old women, their tongues wagging as they caught up on gossip and bragged about their children.

Wiping her face with a cotton handkerchief, Elsa eased down the street, her eyes wide with excitement. More people came to Blue Springs for the Independence Day celebration than for just about anything else. Beat-up old wagons were parked everywhere, some empty, some filled with folks sitting and talking, resting, or eating. Every hitching post had a horse or mule tied to it, the smell of the animals heavy and moist in the July sun. Wherever a tree made any shade, somebody sat under it, their picnic baskets open, with a cloth on the ground and food spread out over it. Elsa sniffed the air—fried chicken, potato salad, apple pie—the town was filled with the aroma of a summer's plenty.

She reached the Jesus Holiness Church, a plain white structure with peeling paint that seated maybe fifty people if most were fairly thin. Preacher Bruster, a stalky man with a raspy voice, who preached at Jesus Holiness about once a month when his travels brought him that way, stood out on the front steps, his floppy black hat down on his forehead, his long black coat hanging almost to his knees. His long arms moved wildly as he shouted, as if he were fighting off a swarm of angry bees.

Bruster's face was wet with sweat, and his voice already scratchy from his preaching. "JESUS IS RIGHT HERE IN BLUE SPRINGS!" he bellowed. "COME TO THE MASTER, COME TO JESUS TODAY!"

Ignoring the preacher, Elsa kept walking. She saw scattered groups of men here and there, loitering under trees, by the livery stable, behind the general store. Many held round white jugs in their hands. They pressed the jugs to their lips, their throats working hard to suck down the sharp-tasting liquid inside. In spite of the fact that making and drinking moonshine was against the law, none of the men seemed worried about their open consumption of spirits. In Blue Springs the only lawman was kin to half the folks in the county. No way he would do any arresting on a day like today.

Elsa licked her lips. She'd tasted the doublings more than once, even drunk to excess a couple of times. But the drink had never established any true hold on her like it had her pa and brothers. Unlike a lot of folks around her, men and women, she didn't like that it made her feel all loose and light-headed. A woman who wanted to keep her wits about her at all times, Elsa had determined that the doublings weren't much for her partaking.

She reached the town square. Drapes of red, white, and blue bunting hung down from the ceiling of the building that served as both the sheriff's office and the postal service. Four men standing on a wood platform in front of the building banged away on their musical instruments. One man held a mandolin, another a fiddle, a third a banjo, and the fourth a guitar. They wore plain overalls and floppy black hats low on their eyes.

Liking the music, Elsa stopped and found a shady spot under an awning across from the platform. She recognized three of the players, Luke Porter among them. His fingers flew over the guitar strings, sharp and fast. She knew from what she'd heard that he was slow in the head. But goodness, he sure did have a gift for the musical. Leaning against the building, Elsa felt someone moving to her from the side. She turned and saw Laban Porter at her elbow, a red apple in his hand. A lump rose in her throat. Except for his reddish hair and green eyes, the boy looked just like his pa. She glanced past Laban, wondering if Solomon was about, but she didn't see him. She took a breath and hoped that Laban hadn't noticed her quick search for Solomon.

"Your brother is mighty good with that guitar," she said, trying to distract Laban. "Where did he learn?"

"A man at the church got him started," said Laban. "Traded Pa that old guitar for one of his rockers. Luke took it from there. Plays all the time, sunup to sundown."

They listened to the music for a couple of minutes. Laban munched his apple. Elsa said, "Your pa does all right with trading his chairs I guess."

Laban shrugged. "Not many ways to make any money in the mountains if you don't do doublings."

"Your pa is a hard worker it seems."

"All of us are. Pa always says, 'Laziness don't become a man.' " Laban bit from the fruit.

Elsa leaned against a post, tried to appear nonchalant. "Your pa here today?"

Laban tossed the apple core to the ground. "He's about here somewhere, I reckon."

"He over his grieving for your mama?" The words came out before Elsa had time to think about them.

Laban grunted and studied his bare feet. "You have to ask him about that I guess."

"He loved her powerful, didn't he?"

Laban looked up, his eyes straight into hers. Though Elsa couldn't tell for certain, she thought she saw confusion in his face, a mixture of anger and attraction, almost as if he wanted to like her but feared to do so, as if he knew she was dangerous somehow—dangerous yet tempting.

"We all loved Mama," he said softly. "She was a good-hearted woman."

"I hear so," said Elsa. "Everybody says it."

Laban watched his feet again.

"Your features like your pa," she said. "But your coloring is all different, hair and eyes."

Laban stared at her for several seconds. Then he spoke, an edge in his tone. "Why you so talkative about my pa?"

Elsa shrugged. "No special cause. You bring the baby down with you?"

"You quick to change the subject," Laban said.

"You didn't seem to like the other one," she said, hoping he would drop his suspicions.

"Aunt Francis got Abby," he answered, his voice relaxing a bit, his eyes becoming gentler. "Down at Jesus Holiness with the other babies. Abby's napping, I reckon. Maybe Aunt Francis too."

The band stopped playing, laid down their instruments to take a break. For a few seconds, silence fell on the crowd. Elsa heard a chorus of birds chirping in the trees. A group of children came running by, their bare feet kicking up dust, their shouting wiping out the quiet.

Elsa wiped her face and nodded at Laban. "Guess I better be going," she said. "Hope you enjoy the day. Tell your pa I said hello."

Laban stepped to her, grabbed her elbow, and stopped her in her tracks. His eyes had lost all their gentleness and seemed to have turned darker now, like the sky before a thunderstorm. "You stay away from my pa," he said with his teeth clenched and his grip tight on her arm.

Momentarily stunned, Elsa stood dead still, feeling his fingers digging into her flesh. Her heart pounded. Laban hated her, she could see it in his face, hated her and feared her too. For a second she felt panic. How could she ever woo Solomon if his eldest son stood so fiercely in her way? But then her jaw set itself. No way would she let a mere boy keep her from what she wanted.

"Don't be ugly at me," she said calmly. "Didn't your mama teach you any manners?"

"I don't think a Clack has got any room to talk much about manners."

She started to reply but then thought better of it. The best way to handle a threat was to face it with action, not words. Her pa had at least taught her that much. Better to do than to talk, he always said. Somebody threaten you, you don't wait around to see if you can argue them out of it. Shoot first and clean up the mess afterward, that's the Clack way of thinking.

Placing her hand on Laban's, Elsa pried his fingers from her elbow, pushed them off, and stepped away. Then, without another word, she headed toward Jesus Holiness. She would show Laban Porter a thing or two about what she thought of his threats. She would go straight to Francis and see if she could steer her toward Solomon. After that, who cared what Laban thought?

Still seething, she reached the church a few minutes later. Her anger calmed some by the walk, she decided she should try to appear disinterested. Slowing, she eased past the church building. A number of mules shuffled their feet at the hitching post. A table of pies and cakes waited for someone to eat them in the shade on the side of the church. A circle of women stood by the table, their hands busy with fans shooing away an army of buzzing flies.

To the left of the church, Elsa spotted a pack of men sitting under a mammoth oak, the tree's branches acting as a leafy curtain against the heat. A couple of the men had their pipes out, using them as pointers as they talked. Others spat streams of brown juice out past their feet, the spray spreading out in the dust. Several squatted on their haunches. Others talked with a leg propped on a nearby stump. A couple leaned back in wooden chairs.

Searching the group for Solomon, Elsa saw him leaning against the thick oak. He had his hat off and his hair glistened with oil. He'd trimmed his beard back real short since she saw him last.

He spoke as she watched, and the other men in the group stopped and listened, some nodding their heads in agreement. Elsa's heart rose in her chest, and all her anger disappeared as she saw again what she liked about him, what made him so attractive. Solomon Porter held the respect of all that knew him. A woman like her met so few men like that. He carried himself with a handsome dignity, and everyone bragged on his wisdom.

Without thinking about consequences, Elsa determined that she wanted to talk to him right then, wanted to tell him she forgave him for not calling on her, that she didn't care about any of that now. What mattered now was that he should know how she felt. She took a step toward the oak tree, but then suddenly stopped and dropped her eyes in dismay. Not even a woman as bold as her could interrupt a group of men in a situation like this. To do so would not only destroy any reputation she had but it would also embarrass a man like Solomon, would embarrass him to the point he might never forgive her.

Her shoulders slumped, she walked away. Spotting a well by the church, she went to it, picked up the long-handled dipper that hung on the side of the water bucket, and pulled up a long drink. The cool liquid felt good on her throat. It was so hot, at least ninety or so. Several drops fell from the dipper onto her chin and down the front of her dress. She licked her lips and took another drink. More water sloshed down her chin. She liked the way it felt, cold and moist. She rubbed the water down her neck, wiped it over her hands and face.

As if waking from a long sleep, Elsa suddenly felt the men under the oak staring at her. Without looking at them, she took another drink, liking the sensation of power that came as they admired her beauty. Like a queen reminded of her high station, she remembered she could move men to do her bidding, that her looks and smarts had always made that true. From early in life, she had recognized this reality. When she talked to a man, he always listened and was ready to do what she asked. When she fluttered her eyelashes, men licked their lips as if preparing for a kiss.

Pleased with the strength she felt, Elsa sipped from the water once more and wondered if Solomon was watching. She wiped her brow, then threw the remainder of the water in the dipper to the ground. She heard someone walking her way, the scratch of boots on dirt.

Holding her breath, she looked up and saw Solomon Porter standing in front of her.

"Got any of that water left?" he asked, as calmly as if asking a man for a light for his pipe.

"If you ask me nice," said Elsa, trying to appear equally as relaxed.

"You like teasin' a man, don't you?" he said as he took the dipper from her hand.

She shrugged, pouted her lips. "Seems to me that most men like some teasin'."

"I ain't one of your boys," Solomon said. He pulled some water from the bucket and drank it. "I'm a growed man. Got no time for silly games." He sipped more water.

"I expected you to call on me," Elsa said, deciding to talk directly in hopes of keeping Solomon off stride.

"I been too busy to call on anybody. Thought the timin' might be better when fall come, after I got my corn in, cleared my garden, cut wood for winter."

Elsa flushed just slightly. Her words came a bit quicker now. "So you were planning to call on me?"

"I gave it a thought or two, yes I did." Solomon dipped back into the water bucket.

"Taking your sweet time about it," she said, pouting again.

"I ain't seen the rush," said Solomon.

"I'm twenty-one come September. Not waiting on a man forever."

"Practically an old maid," he said with a sly grin.

"Now who's teasing who?" Elsa said, glad to see that his initial gruffness wasn't a permanent condition.

Solomon hung the dipper on the bucket and faced her. His eyes turned serious. "Why you doing this?" he asked.

"What do you mean?"

"Playing so straight after me. You could have any man in the county, single or married. But you seem set on coming my way. Don't make sense. Other than some land, I own little or nothing. And I got kids close to your age, plus a baby. We would make a right peculiar match."

Elsa weighed his question. Did she really know how to answer? Did anyone know how to answer such a thing? She thought of all her reasons for feeling attracted to Solomon Porter, and a swirl of emotions ran through her. She wanted a mature man, not a boy. She would run right over a boy, would have no respect for him. She needed somebody strong enough to handle her, somebody who wouldn't feel frightened by her power.

She turned away from Solomon and studied the grass at her feet. Her motives weren't all pure. She also wanted him to spite her pa, to show him that she had a mind of her own, that he couldn't control her forever, that she would make up her own mind on some things. No question about it, she wanted away from her pa and his brutish ways.

Solomon touched her shoulder. She twisted back to him and gazed into his eyes. Intuitively she realized that she wanted something else too. She wanted Solomon Porter's integrity, the fact that others trusted him. Repelled by what her pa represented, she knew that Solomon probably gave her the one and only chance she would have to make something valuable of herself, something special. Maybe with a man like Solomon she could find a way to fill up some of the emptiness in her soul, an emptiness as deep as the well from which they'd just drawn water.

Why did she want Solomon Porter? Well, she wanted him because he was a good man. True, she feared she didn't deserve such a man and that she might corrupt him if she ever got him. In spite of this, she wanted him anyway.

Solomon touched her cheek, and she felt her stomach warm. She wanted a pretty man too, she decided, a man with good teeth and wavy hair, a man with a square chin and a powerful back and shoulders. Solomon delivered all that and more.

Elsa sighed. Could she reveal all this to Solomon? Could she voice the truth of these mixed motivations? Or should she make up something? She stared at Solomon, saw the honesty in his eyes, the strength that most men didn't have. But she didn't know how he felt about her, if he felt anything at all. She decided to hold her thoughts to herself.

"Let's just say I got my reasons for speaking so straight with you," she said, stepping a stride away from him. "What about you? What made you consider calling on me?"

Solomon grinned again. It made his eyes bright. "I'm a widowed man," he said. "And my daughter needs a mama."

Elsa poked him in the ribs. "That the only reason? You expect me to nursemaid your girl?"

"You thinking there is something else?" he asked, his grin widening. "You think you so pretty I just can't help myself?"

"You're not funny, Solomon Porter." She felt herself getting lost in his eyes.

"I'm a regular clown," he said.

They stood still for a moment. A light breeze played through the tree overhead. Elsa felt like she and Solomon were all alone, like everyone else in the world had suddenly disappeared. Without warning, Solomon touched her chin again. His hand was cool to the touch.

"I don't know that I'm ready for this," he said softly. "Gone cause troubles for sure."

Elsa covered his hand with hers, felt the strength in his fingers. Her heart pounded, and her cheeks reddened. "I know it won't be easy," she said. "My pa will not take kindly to you courting me."

"Then it is really gone upset him when I petition him for your hand in marriage, ain't it?"

"You plan on doing any sparking of me before that marriage?"

"I thought I might. You think we ought to go right now and ask your pa if that would be okay?"

She laughed at him now, her laughter pouring out like water over a cliff. "You're a bold man, Solomon Porter," she said, "a brave and bold man."

"No bolder than you," he said.

"The two of us together might be a dangerous thing."

"I have no doubt it will."

The two of them walked away from the oak tree then and down the path out past the church. As she left the church, Elsa saw her brother Topper standing by the hitching post, his face a scowl, his hands clenched at his sides. For a second she almost pulled away from Solomon, her fears threatening to make her stop and think all this over one more time. But then she remembered her pa's rough treatment of her mama, and she pushed away all thoughts of him and gave her full attention to Solomon Porter. The fact that her brother watched with such hatred on his face just made it all the more exciting.

CHAPTER
FIVE

Pulling her blue shawl tight over her shoulders, Aunt Francis took a last look around the church house and wished she could have a dip of snuff. Times like today made her stomach feel scratchy with nerves, kind of like a baby cat had got inside her belly and started dancing around, claws out. Though the sun had warmed up real good for the first Sunday in March, she still felt chilled. Maybe her nerves made it so, she didn't know for sure. When she felt unsettled, she always had a tendency toward the shivers.

Blowing on her fingers, she watched as Solomon and Elsa walked toward Preacher Bruster. Solomon was glancing down all shy and all, but Elsa was staring at him bold as you please. Elsa wore a white dress that reached to her ankles, a thin lace veil over her face, and patent leather shoes—all bought by her mama from Asheville. Solomon had put on the best clothes he owned: a secondhand black suit with a white shirt and string tie. All together the clothes cost him two chairs in trade at the general store in Blue Springs.

Francis felt a twinge under her rib cage. She put a hand on her stomach and pushed in on the hurt. More indigestion, she figured. Been bothering her off and on a lot over the last few months. Telling herself she needed to cut down on what she ate, she swallowed and focused on the matter at hand—her brother's marriage to Elsa Clack.

Francis glanced over the crowd and counted thirty-two people—Hal Clack and his no-account sons not among them—who had gathered to watch the vow exchanging.

"Do you take this man as your lawfully wedded husband?" the preacher asked, his tone indicating he had suspicions about the possibility.

"I do," said Elsa, eyes on Solomon.

"Do you promise to honor and obey him?"

"I do."

"Do you promise to keep him in sickness and health. . . ?"

Her side grabbing on her again, Francis sat in the front row of the hard-backed pews and worked hard to stay attentive to the ceremony. Not that she felt real steady about this marriage. Never much pleased with the prospects of her kin hooking up with the Clack crowd, she'd watched Solomon's eight-month-old courtship of Elsa with an ever-increasing sense of unease. At first she had hoped it was only a passing thing—a healthy man taking up with the first handsome woman that run his way. After all, the girl was a looker. No one of any sound mind questioned that. And Solomon was still close to his prime. He needed the attentions of a woman. But then, as summer had passed and winter had come on, she saw that Solomon seemed intent on something more than a casual acquaintance with the woman. And apparently Elsa Clack had the same notions about him.

Never one to come to church, Amelia Clack had started showing up at Jesus Holiness about halfway through the autumn time, her daughter in tow. After a couple of weeks, Elsa moved to Solomon's side in the pew, her mama sitting behind her. Not too long after that, Solomon started staying in Blue Springs with Elsa and her ma when the services had ended. He came home only when darkness forced him back up the mountain. For a while, Francis wondered why Hal Clack didn't stop all the nonsense. After all, he wouldn't take to such a match any more than she would. But when she had asked Solomon about it, he just shrugged.

"Don't even know that he is aware that I'm courting Elsa," he had said. "He don't come down to Blue Springs too often. And her ma ain't saying nothing."

Surprised, Francis had pressed him. "You not aiming to hide this thing from him are you?"

"Clack don't scare me. But I ain't going looking for him either. He will find out soon enough. Things like this don't stay quiet for long."

Francis had nodded. "True words there," she'd said.

"Is there a ring to show the tie between this man and this woman?" asked Preacher Bruster, pulling Francis back to the present moment.

Solomon produced a ring, handed it to the preacher. He held it up, turned it around for everyone to see. In the mountains, not many people could afford such a fancy thing. Solomon had promised Bill Stinson his next ten rockers for it. Francis had just shaken her head when she found out that he planned to trade for a ring. Rose never did have one.

Preacher Bruster said, "This ring says to everybody here that this man and woman are bound to each other, bound by Jesus Christ hisself, bound . . ."

Francis lost concentration again as Bruster took off for some more preaching, his voice picking up the pace as he warmed to the task. She recalled the past months as time had moved through Christmas and into the new year. Her unease about Solomon and Elsa had become downright disgust. She had tried to warn Solomon against the prospects of a marriage to a Clack.

"I got nothing against Elsa herself," she had said one night in February while she and Solomon sat by the fire, his dog Sandy at his feet. "But there is no way Hal Clack is gone let you go through with any marrying of his daughter. He just won't cotton to a man who won't do the doublings with him."

Rocking easy, Solomon puffed on his pipe. "Don't rightly matter what he cottons to," he said. "It is what Elsa and me wants, no more, no less."

Francis stared into the fire. She knew Solomon wouldn't back down from Hal Clack. She tried another way at it. "I don't know Elsa Clack too good," she said, "but I wonder why she's so set on this. Maybe she's up to something, maybe something no good."

Solomon placed his hands on the arms of the rocker. "Now what could she be up to?"

"Don't know. But it just feels—"

"You ever think she might just find me worth her while?" he interrupted, a slight hint of upset in his voice. "That maybe I am the kind of man she wants?"

Francis nodded, recognizing the possibility. Lots of women wanted a man like Solomon, a steady man who didn't take of drink, a man who wouldn't cuss a wife or beat on her. A man who would keep his hands busy at some passable trade, keep food on the table. A man trustable with other women. Easy on the eyes too, everybody said that.

"I got no doubt of that," Francis said. "But I still don't trust a Clack, you got to give me the truth that I got good reasons for that."

Solomon rocked harder. It was silent for several minutes. Sandy raised her head, licked her lips, then lay down again.

Maybe Elsa did love Solomon, thought Francis. But that possibility did nothing to make her feel any better. Something about Elsa, or maybe it was her family, gave her the sweats. Francis tried one more notion. "You sure she's the right kind of woman to raise your children?" she asked.

Solomon's rocker stopped moving. He squared his feet, leaned forward at the waist, his hands on his knees. He pointed his pipe at Francis, and his eyes told her she'd treaded on a path not to his liking. "You already know what I'm gone say," he said firmly. "I plan on marrying up with this woman. Laban and Luke are most grown anyway. She won't have much to do with them."

Francis sighed. Laban had let his dislike for the woman known from the beginning. He'd almost come to parting with his pa over it.

"She is barely older than me, Pa!" Laban had shouted the night Solomon made his intentions clear to all of them. "And she's a Clack to boot. You always told me to have no dealings with such as them. Now you say you plan to marry one?"

Solomon set his jaw. "Not fair to hold her kin against her," he said. "She has taken to me and me to her. That is the way of things, like it or not."

Laban stared at his pa, the vein over his eyes bulging hard, his face flushed. "It will be a real pleasure to call her *Ma*," he said, the sarcasm dripping.

Solomon had taken off his hat, lowered his eyes. "She ain't your ma," he said. "Nobody expects you to treat her as such. But . . . I . . . well, I'm in need of a woman. Abigail is too. And it has been right near two years." He looked up at Laban, walked over to him, and put his hand on his shoulder. "Look," he said, "I will always love your ma best. Nothin' is gone change that. But Elsa is a good woman, I believe it true. You'll see it too. Just give her a chance, take the time to know her, see—"

But Laban didn't want to hear it. Storming out, he had disappeared for three days, then returned with the sour smell of liquor on his clothes, his mood sullen. Since then, he and Solomon had barely spoken.

"Now repeat after me," said Preacher Bruster. "With this ring, I wed thee. . . ."

Francis came back to the moment.

Solomon repeated the preacher's words.

Francis took a deep breath and remembered her last try at changing Solomon's mind. Though knowing she'd already pushed farther than most highlander men would have allowed, she'd decided she had nothing left to lose. Might as well ride the mule as far as it would carry her.

"You still got Abby," she had said to Solomon only about six weeks ago, again as they rested by the fireplace. "She needs a good mama. You sure Elsa Clack is the kind of woman you want for her?"

Solomon bit his pipe. Francis saw his eyes narrow. "I ain't gone do nothin' deliberate to hurt my daughter," he said. "You know me better than that." He leaned back in the chair. "Besides, Abby's got you to raise her, look out for her."

Francis started to speak, to tell Solomon about the pains in her side and about her worries over her health, but then she changed her mind and held her piece. If her suspicions proved true, Solomon would find out soon enough without her saying anything. She spit snuff juice into her cup. She had done what she could. Whatever the future held, she would just have to face it.

Preacher Bruster's voice drew her back to the church house again, to the wedding taking place right before her eyes.

"This marrying is serious business, huh!" Bruster shouted, staring out over the crowd as he began the serious part of his sermonizing. "It's what the Lord intends for man and woman, huh." His voice took on the singsong rhythm he used when moving from talking to preaching. Francis liked the way it sounded. He picked up the pace as he spoke.

"The Lord commands us to hold marriage up high and honorable!" called Bruster. "The good apostle Paul called it a mystery."

His tones became breathless as he reached the end of a phrase.

"Today our brother Solomon Porter and Miss Elsa Clack are betrothin' to each other, huh. Right here in front of us and God. Betrothin' to love, huh, and stay faithful, huh . . . and stick together, huh, in thickness and thinness, huh, in times when they is sick, huh . . ."

Another prod of pain rolled up under Francis's rib, and she grabbed at the spot and pushed in on her side. A clammy dampness broke out on her forehead. Trying to ignore the pain, she glanced over at Amelia Clack, wondered how the woman could stay with a man like her husband. Amelia had a black bruise on her right cheek. Though no one asked, everybody knew full well how the bruise had come to be there. Clack must have doled out some of his anger about this wedding on her.

Francis gritted her teeth. Hal Clack had made his way to Solomon's place not more than a month ago, his boys at his side, all of them on horses. The morning air around them had been thick with the smell of liquor. Hopping down from his saddle, Clack had staggered to the cabin door, pounded on it, and shouted for Solomon to come out and to face him like a man.

After drying her hands on her apron, Francis met him on the porch. "Solomon ain't here," she said, nodding to the boys who had stayed mounted. "Back by dark I guess. You boys want to wait? I got some corn bread bakin'."

Clack looked around, his eyes confused. "Ain't here?" he asked as if the possibility had never come to him. "Where's he gone?"

Francis lifted her head toward the woods. "Out there," she said, "doing whatever men do." She hoped Solomon hadn't heard the commotion up at the spring where he was digging a trench to draw down some water.

Without warning, Clack grabbed her by the shoulders, shoved her out of the way, and rushed into the house. Francis heard him stomping through the rooms one at a time, his heavy boots on the plank flooring.

A few seconds later he stumbled back to the porch, his face all flushed. "Tell me where that coward is!" he shouted at Francis. "He ain't gone marry my Elsa, he knows that, don't he?"

Francis stood her ground. "You better take up with him what he knows or don't know," she said.

Clack drew back his hand. "You got a smart mouth, woman! I ought to—"

"You ought to hold it right where you stand."

The voice came from the woods to the left of the cabin. Everybody turned to face it but they saw no one.

"Come out where I can see you!" shouted Clack.

"Tell your boys to drop their guns on the ground," Solomon said. "Then I will come out, easy as that."

"How do I know you really got the draw on me?" asked Clack.

"You know only a crazy man goes into the woods without packing his piece," Solomon said. "And you know I ain't no crazy man."

Clack stared at his sons. Francis could see his mind working. His lips were drawn back like a bear about to attack. His teeth were spotty, several missing in the front and several dark with decay. His beard was untidy, badly in need of a trim.

"I ain't got all day," shouted Solomon. "You need to do somethin', even if it is wrong."

Clack wrinkled his nose, nodded to his sons. They eased their rifles from the sheaths on their saddles and dropped them to the ground.

"Waist pieces too," Solomon said.

The boys pulled pistols from their pants, tossed them out.

Solomon stepped out of the woods, his rifle at the ready. He moved quickly to the porch and stood there with his weapon pointed at Clack. "Now say what you got to say," he said calmly.

"You know what I come to say," said Clack. "I been watching this since last summer. But now I have waited long enough. My patience has no more stretch in it. This nonsense has to end, right here today. My Elsa ain't for the likes of you."

"She's got her own mind and she has set it on me. I'm gone marry her. Planned on doing it the right way and askin' you proper, but I guess that won't take place now."

"I won't let it last," Clack said.

Solomon lowered the rifle but only a bit. "Time will tell," he said. "But for now I want you off my place. Off, and don't come back." With his rifle still ready, Solomon moved off the porch and picked up the weapons the boys had dropped. "I will deliver these down to the sheriff in Blue Springs," he said. "You can pick them up there."

Scowling heavily, Clack climbed onto his horse. "You ain't heard the last of this," he said, jerking his horse around.

"I expect not," said Solomon.

Clack kicked his horse and galloped off, his sons following close behind.

Solomon faced Francis. "You okay?" he asked, stepping onto the porch again.

She had shrugged and led him into the house. They hadn't spoken of the episode since.

Now watching Solomon as he held Elsa's hand, Francis hoped this marriage didn't get him or somebody else killed.

"By the power of the Lord Jesus!" Preacher Bruster announced, his voice still raucous, "and the authority of this here state, I do now say that the two of you are joined as husband and wife. What God has put together, let no man tear . . ."

The pain in Francis's side eased some. Maybe it was just a sour stomach, she figured. Maybe she would live long enough to see Abby all grown and married up with a man as good as her pa. Blinking back a flow of tears, Francis closed her eyes and said a silent prayer for Abigail Faith, the last child and only daughter of Rose and Solomon Porter.

CHAPTER
SIX

When she got older Abigail realized that her aunt Francis's funeral was the earliest thing she could remember. It took place just over three years after Pa and Elsa's wedding, on a May morning so bright the sun blinded her eyes when she stepped out of the cabin to say her hellos to the folks gathered to pay their last respects. Aunt Francis's body remained inside the cabin in a wood box in the front room. It had been there for two days, never alone for a second, as her neighbors came by for the Sitting Up—the time between the moment somebody died to when the family laid the dead into the ground. In the highlands, a body didn't face the grave alone. In the Sitting Up Time somebody always stayed by the deceased. It was a matter of courtesy.

Two of her pa's straight chairs had been placed on either side of the burying box, one chair supporting the end of the box at Francis's feet, the other the end at her head. Unlike the custom of many of his fellow highlanders who buried their dead but held the funeral service sometime after the harvest, Solomon wanted Preacher Bruster to have his say over Francis as soon as possible.

"Let a body go on to its reward," he had said, explaining his reasoning for not waiting. "Francis deserves it, that is for certain."

Nobody argued with him, and all those in Blue Springs who could manage to take the day off traveled in for the burial. They came all morning long, one after another, to stand over the wood box and look down at Aunt Francis as she lay out plain as day.

Right before noontime Solomon stepped to the porch and called everybody to attention. The hum of conversation that covered the yard suddenly stopped. "It is time for Preacher Bruster to do the necessaries," said Solomon, his hat in his hands. "Time for us to hear a word from the Lord."

With his Bible in hand, Preacher Bruster moved to the edge of the porch. A couple of the dogs barked. Bruster raised his hand. The dogs shut up. The preacher lit into his preaching for almost forty-five minutes. The crowd stood in the sun and listened.

Dressed in a yellow dress that her aunt had made for her only a few months before she passed on, Abigail stood on the porch beside her pa but she didn't understand much of what the preacher said. When he'd finished, he wiped his face with a white handkerchief, then turned and went into the front room where Francis lay. Standing over the coffin, he raised his right hand into the air and thanked the Lord Jesus for saving the immortal soul of Aunt Francis Rachel Wilson. After that he read a few Scriptures, mostly from the Psalms, and then said a prayer.

What he did next made Abigail want to cry. As calmly as if closing a barn door, he shut the coffin's lid, snapping down the two leather hinges on the sides. Then he nodded to Laban.

Stepping over to the coffin, Laban took hold of the metal handle on the right of the box. Luke took hold of the handle on the left. Four other men grasped the coffin too, two on each side. Lifting all at once, they moved the box outside.

Abigail led the procession up the hill behind the cabin, all the while holding her pa's hand. They reached a spot under a pair of old oak trees. Abigail knew her ma was buried under the same trees. Her legs suddenly felt like somebody had tied a pumpkin to each ankle.

She felt heavy in her chest too, mostly because she wanted to talk to Aunt Francis about all this but could not. Plus, she didn't quite know what to do in such a time. Aunt Francis was gone, her pa had told her. But he hadn't said *where* Aunt Francis had gone to, at least not in a way Abigail could understand.

"Aunt Francis is in heaven," he'd said when she asked where Aunt Francis had gone.

"Where is heaven?" she asked, truly curious.

Solomon pointed to the ceiling of the porch where they sat at the time.

"On top of the porch?" she asked.

Solomon breathed heavily, obviously at a loss. "With God," he said. "Aunt Francis is in heaven with God."

"Preacher Bruster says God is everywhere."

"That is the truth," said Solomon.

"So Aunt Francis is everywhere?"

"Not quite."

"But you said she was with God and God is everywhere."

Solomon stared off into the woods, scratched Sandy behind the ears. Abby had the feeling she had upset him.

"Is Aunt Francis with my mama?" she asked.

Solomon faced her, his eyes sad. "That is right," he said. "Aunt Francis is with your mama."

Abby had nodded and looked out toward the woods like her pa. Nothing there seemed any different than usual. Trees still swayed in the wind. The sun still warmed her hair when she stood under it. Sandy still liked it when she scratched her behind the ears. Bees still buzzed around her head when she stood close to flowers. Though not quite sure what it all meant, it came to Abby that a person's death didn't seem to change much of anything. The world just kept on going, moving on past a body's death like a river flowing by a piece of driftwood that a flood had thrown out of the foam.

Somehow pleased with the thought, Abby felt satisfied for the moment. Death was natural, she decided. Life moved on after it happened. Hopping up, she had run into the yard, Sandy trailing after her. . . .

Now Abby walked in front of the coffin that held her aunt Francis. Her pa stopped as they reached the oaks. Abby rubbed her eyes while staring at the grave, a hole in the ground somebody had already dug. They were going to put Aunt Francis in the hole. Her pa had said so.

Abby stepped as close as she could and looked down into the hole. Was heaven in the hole? Pa said Aunt Francis had gone to heaven. But now they were putting her into a hole.

Her pa pulled Abby back from the grave. Laban edged forward. Then, looping ropes around the front and back ends of the coffin, the men who had carried the box now lowered it into the hole, slid out the ropes, and tossed them to the ground. Preacher Bruster nodded to Solomon. Solomon picked up a fistful of dirt from the pile at the foot of the coffin. He tossed in the dirt. It was mostly black but had some rust in it too. Everybody else grabbed a handful of dirt and tossed it onto the pine box. The dirt sounded like heavy raindrops landing on a roof as it fell on the coffin.

Abigail took a handful of dirt and threw it onto the box, then stooped to pick up another one. But then Mrs. Elsa—that was what Pa had told Abby to call his new wife—grabbed Abby's hand and shook her head at her. Abby felt confused but didn't whimper. Preacher Bruster nodded to Laban, who then picked up a shovel. Luke and Daniel did the same, and the three of them began to shovel dirt into the hole around the coffin.

Watching her brothers, Abigail pulled away from Mrs. Elsa and ran to Daniel, her little hands grabbing for his shovel. He gently pushed her away.

"No, Abby," he said, raising the shovel so she couldn't reach it. "We will do this."

Abby stared at her pa to see if he'd tell Daniel to let her help shovel the dirt, but Pa had his eyes on the coffin and didn't look at her. Abby felt like crying. Pa had seemed so sad in the last few months, his normal calm breaking down at least once that she'd seen, into a red-eyed bout with real tears. But he had pushed them back, and she had realized she'd never seen him cry. Her thoughts about death coming so natural didn't make any sense now. Anything that made her pa almost cry wasn't natural at all. And nobody lived in a hole in the ground. She wondered what it meant to die.

Abby knew of course that her ma had died. Aunt Francis had told her one day when she asked why she didn't have a ma like most everyone else. Taking her up to the oak trees, Aunt Francis had pointed to the wood marker, to the words written on it.

"That says *Rose Sharon Porter*," she said. "She died giving you birth. She loved you that much."

Though she did not know all that such a thing meant, Abby did know that what Aunt Francis told her about her ma both comforted and scared her all at the same time.

"What did my ma look like?" she asked Aunt Francis.

"Like you."

"Like my doll?" asked Abby, thinking of the carving her pa had made for her before she was born.

"Yes, just like your doll . . . only taller of course, and softer too. Soft as a feather pillow."

Abby smiled at the memory. She had always loved her doll, stared at it for hours at a time. Talked to it too sometimes. After Aunt Francis took her to her ma's grave and told her that the wood doll looked like her ma, she started laying it beside her when she went to bed every night, looking at it the last thing before she closed her eyes. Sometimes she dreamed about the doll, dreamed that it came to life as she slept, came to life and got taller and softer, that it became her ma in the flesh, that it held her safe in its arms as it sang sweet lullabies to her. But then she would wake up and see the carving, and though it was pretty and she loved it, it was hard too and not able to talk to her, to hold her in its arms. Feeling sad because she'd awakened from her dream, Abby would start the day again without a ma.

Now she wouldn't have Aunt Francis either. Aunt Francis had been sick a long time. She'd suffered from a hurting in her sides and heart for at least a few years. The doctor said she had got the tumors, that they'd filled up her insides like a jar full of pig's feet.

At first Aunt Francis didn't seem no different than she had ever been. She kept doing her work, cooking and cleaning, sewing and canning. Yes, she grabbed at her sides every now and again, and her face drew up in a ball of hurt, but she kept going anyway. Pa said Aunt Francis was a "tough old gal, stubborn as a tree stump that didn't want to come out of the ground."

"She has been sickly for a spell," he said. "But she won't slow down none."

But then the hurting started coming more often. Aunt Francis slowed a lot, her pace not half of what it had been. Then March came and she took to her bed. Lost weight faster than a dog with no food. Her skin sagged on her face, and her eyes fell back into her skull till it seemed they almost disappeared. She stopped talking too. Waved off anybody who wanted to come see her.

"Leave me my peace," Abby had heard Francis say to Pa. "Don't want a bunch of folks coming by so they can say how bad I looked in my last days."

Pa respected her wishes, and Aunt Francis suffered in silence. Her only companions were her immediate family and a black Bible she kept by her side at all times. Mystified by her aunt's illness, Abby sometimes peeked through the crack in the door to her room to see what lay inside. She wondered if she could see the sickness that had taken such a hold of her aunt, if the tumors in her belly might show up like a band of strangers come to do bad things. From time to time she heard her aunt take to coughing, the racking so hard Abby wondered if her insides might come up in one giant heave. Sometimes she saw her pa sitting by her aunt's bed, his hands wiping Francis's face with a cloth wet with springwater. Often he held the Bible open for her, the Book in one hand, a lamp in the other so she could read the verses even as she lay there with her head propped up on a pillow.

Sometimes when her strength allowed, Aunt Francis read the words aloud. " 'In my Father's house are many mansions,' " she would read. Or " 'I am the way, the truth, and the life. . . .' " Or " 'He that believeth in me, though he were dead, yet shall he live.' "

Though her aunt had read these words to her at other times and she'd loved hearing them, they thrilled Abby even more now. She loved hearing her aunt reading from the Book. The sound of it drew her like a salt lick drawing deer. And it wasn't just what the words said either, as much as she liked that. It was also the sheer fact that someone could take the mysterious markings from a page and actually make sense of them.

Abby knew her ma had been able to read. Aunt Francis had told her so. Rose Sharon Porter could read and write. Aunt Francis said her ma used to read every day from a Bible just like the one that she had.

Sometimes, when it got too cold to play outside, Abby sat on her pa's bed and held her ma's Bible in her lap, trying to imagine what it would be like to hear her ma's voice speak out the words from the Book. The notion made her shiver with a feeling she didn't yet know what to call. At the same time, it made her set her jaw too, made her tell herself that someday she also would know the words her ma and her aunt had read. She too would have the ability to arrange the words in her head and make sense of them. If words from the Book meant so much that her ma read from them every day, and her aunt spoke of them even as she faced the death stranger, then the ability to handle such words was a prize Abby wanted to possess. For some reason she couldn't yet understand, the desire to read and write became a hunger deep inside, a hunger that gnawed at her. Her ma and Aunt Francis had known how to decipher words. And one day so would she.

Bound to Francis and her ma by this decision, Abby watched as Laban worked on with the shovel, as the dirt piled up on the box that held her aunt. The sides were already covered. The top was disappearing fast.

Aunt Francis was gone, dead and almost covered with mountain soil. Who would read to her from the Book now? Pa? No, he didn't know how. And he didn't pay enough attention to her to do it on any regular basis. What about Daniel? No. Even though he knew how to read, he was a lot like Pa, never slowed down enough to do much reading. Luke? No, he didn't read too good. Even if he could, his speaking came out too hard and slow. Laban? No, he had built himself a small cabin almost a mile away and wasn't home much anymore. When he did come home, he seemed mad at everybody. Laban and Pa didn't talk much to each other, and Abby had the sense that something was not right between them.

Abby stared back at the coffin. She'd have to do it herself. If she wanted to know more of the mysteries of the Book, she'd have to become the reader of it.

Laban tossed another shovelful of dirt onto the coffin. The coffin was covered, the last spot of wood now buried. The pallbearers kept heaving their shovels till soon it was all finished. Then Solomon stepped to the graveside, smoothed out the dirt with his hands, and laid a handful of wild flowers at the head of the grave. Laban moved to the oak tree to his right and pulled a wood cross from behind it. He handed the cross to Solomon. Solomon jammed the cross into the soft ground near where he'd placed the flowers, pressing down on it with both hands. It slid into the dirt. Solomon stepped back and took Mrs. Elsa by the hand. Preacher Bruster raised his right hand over his head again. Everyone closed their eyes. Abby kept her eyes open. She watched the dirt on top of the grave to see if it might heave up at any moment, as Aunt Francis came busting out with the new resurrection.

Wasn't that what the Book said? That those who believed in Jesus would break out into a newness of life? That they would live forever with Jesus in heaven? She knew it was so. She had heard Aunt Francis read it. So why wasn't Aunt Francis rising up into the air above the oak trees to go to heaven? To be with God and Mama?

Abby squinted to see if it was happening. But Aunt Francis did not come out of the dirt. Nothing moved except the wild flowers as a soft breeze blew across them. Preacher Bruster stopped praying and everyone lifted their heads. Several people stepped to Solomon and shook his hand. Abby felt a hand on her shoulder. She looked up to Mrs. Elsa.

"Time to go, Abigail," said Mrs. Elsa. "Aunt Francis is with Jesus now."

Abby rubbed her eyes. Her auburn hair hung to her shoulders, her curls touched by the breeze. She looked back to the grave, knew that something vital had changed in her life but wasn't sure what it was or how to describe it. Walking back down the hill toward the cabin, she held Elsa's hand and thought of what she knew so far.

Her real mama had died during her birth. Although she didn't know enough to feel guilty about this just yet, she did know she felt funny about it sometimes without understanding why.

Her pa, while a hardworking man, didn't spend much time with her. He said little, and what little he said, he mostly said to other people. On those few times when she sat close to him, mostly down at the Jesus Holiness Church on Sunday mornings, he smelled like tobacco and fresh wood all mingled together.

Mrs. Elsa had come into the family a couple of years after her mama's death. Mrs. Elsa had a pa that never spoke to her and some brothers who people whispered about but never mentioned out loud. Sometimes Elsa saw her mama down in Blue Springs, but her mama had never come to the cabin where her daughter now lived. Abby had never seen any of Elsa's family, and when she asked about them, her brothers told her she wasn't missing nothing.

Abby didn't quite know what to feel about Mrs. Elsa. She was a smart-looking woman, everybody knew that. And she was younger than Pa too. But she spent most of her time with the baby boy she had birthed last November. That boy looked a lot like Elsa, all black-headed and fair-skinned. Elsa doted on him like he had royalty in his blood. At least that is what Aunt Francis had said when she explained to Abby that the word *royalty* meant like being a queen or king or something.

Abby didn't mind the baby too much. But Pa seemed to pay more attention to him than to her, and that bothered her every now and again. Aunt Francis said that was natural with babies.

"Don't worry," Aunt Francis had said. "When the next baby comes, little Solomon Jr. will get bumped out too."

Abby watched and waited. So far no new baby had come, so she didn't know if Aunt Francis was right or not.

Mrs. Elsa had helped Aunt Francis do some of the work around the cabin, taking her place in the corn patch, hoeing and picking and shucking. Hauling water from the creek. Stitching the boys' shirts and overalls. But she did not do much with Abby. Around Abby she seemed hesitant, almost scared, as if she might break something if she rushed in too strong and all. She left most of Abby's raising to Aunt Francis.

Her brothers were lively and lovable but mostly absent. Only Daniel paid her any attention at all, and most of that came in the form of teasing. Aunt Francis had done most of Abby's raising to this point. She had cooked her meals, made her dresses, sat by her in church. In good weather she had taken walks with her in the woods and told her about Asheville and other big cities that lay at the foot of the mountain trail where Abby had never traveled. Often at night, she read the Book to her, told her that the keys to life were all tied up in two things—getting right with Jesus and acquiring knowledge. Said the Book was the way to do both.

Abby loved Aunt Francis. And, in a way she couldn't really understand, Abby suddenly realized that Aunt Francis had been her mama, had done all the things a mama did for a baby girl. She had fixed her hair for her, tied it up with a green ribbon every Sunday. She had kissed her on the neck in the softest spot she could find, laughing hard as Abby squirmed all ticklish. She had let her stand by her on a chair while she pounded out biscuits. She had whispered that she loved her as she kissed her and tucked her into her bed in the loft each night.

Abby felt tears in her eyes. Now Aunt Francis was gone.

Twisting back for a last look at the grave, it occurred to Abby that for the second time in her life, she had lost a mama. Not many other girls could claim that. Brushing away her tears, Abby's tiny feet walked heavy down the trail.

Back at the cabin, Mrs. Elsa took her to the porch, then let go her hand and moved through the door. Abby took a spot in a rocker on the porch and stared out into the woods. Though many of the folks lingered for the meal that was to follow, a score of others who had come to the funeral were already on their mules, headed away from the cabin. Watching them go, Abby rubbed her eyes once again. Aunt Francis was dead. Now Mrs. Elsa would raise her. For some reason, she didn't quite know what to feel about that.

CHAPTER
SEVEN

Almost two weeks passed. It was late afternoon. Solomon had gone down to Blue Springs with the boys to settle up with the undertaker who had made the box for Aunt Francis. Elsa found herself alone in the house except for her boy, Solomon Jr., who was napping. Abby was in the yard tossing sticks with Sandy. Taking a deep breath, Elsa moved to the room where Aunt Francis had slept, a ten by ten square with a single mattress bed, a couple of handmade tables with a coal lamp on each, a rocking chair in one corner and a spinning wheel in the other. A single square window was cut in the left wall of the room, and the wood shutter that covered it during the winter was pulled back to let in the air. A bee buzzed through the open space, then back out again.

Elsa wiped her hands on her apron. For some reason, she felt lonely. Not that she and Francis had ever been real close. They hadn't. She knew that Francis, just like her own pa, had opposed the marriage from the beginning. That knowledge had made it difficult for her to move into Francis's house, to become the lead woman of the place. For the most part she had tried to stay out of the way, to do what she could to help but not to challenge Francis head on. But, given the stout personalities of both women, that arrangement hadn't always worked.

Elsa went over to Francis's bed, sat down on the edge. Francis wasn't the only one who had suffered in the last few years. True, Elsa's suffering wasn't from a physical illness, but other kinds of suffering cut almost just as deep. To Elsa's surprise, her pa had not forgiven her for her rebellion against his wishes. The finances from him she'd counted on had never come through, and though Solomon labored hard at his trade, she never had as much money as she wanted. Her mama helped by bringing a few dollars to the church now and then and sneaking them to her in a white handkerchief, but those meager dollars never stretched far enough to do much good.

Elsa placed her head in her hands. Solomon had found some of the money once, a few days before last Christmas. She had mistakenly left three dollars wrapped in the handkerchief on the dresser after they returned from church. He picked up the handkerchief to put it away as he laid his only collared shirt down on the dresser. The handkerchief fell open, the dollars showing. Without touching the money, he called Elsa into the room. She saw right off that something had stirred him up.

"Where did you get this?" he asked calmly, pointing to the money.

She shrugged, trying to appear unconcerned. But dollars were rare in her neck of the woods. Mountain people mostly dealt with barter, not real cash. Only a blockader like her pa ever handled much paper money.

"Mama gave me it," she said. "Said I should use it to buy the baby some new clothes for Christmas."

Solomon stayed still for several seconds, and she had a thought that he might let it go. But then he grabbed the money, wadded it up in a clenched fist, and stuck it in his pocket. "I will give this back to your mama next week," he said, his tone remaining even. "And don't bring no more liquor money into this house. If we cannot make do on what I can provide, then we just won't make do. You understand me on this?"

He stared at her, and she felt the strength in his look and she both loved and hated him for it. She had married him because of this kind of strength, a strength that refused to back down from her pa, a strength that said he could make it on his own, no matter what. But at the same time that strength also showed sometimes as pride, a pride that kept her from living in the manner she deserved.

Elsa balled her hands into fists. A woman like her deserved more than Solomon could provide. She deserved finer clothes, a few pieces of store-bought furniture in her house, and a horse with a saddle for riding. Why should she live with so little when her mama could pass on a few dollars from time to time and make her life and that of her new baby more at ease?

She felt her face turning red. It wasn't fair what Solomon was telling her to do, not fair at all! How dare he return that money, money meant for his own baby boy? How dare he let his silly pride stand in the way of doing what was right for his family? Didn't he see that she just wanted the best for them all, her and Solomon and the baby? That's all she wanted, the best for them all. . . .

Sitting on the bed, Elsa remembered that she hadn't challenged Solomon the day he found the money, but she hadn't forgotten the matter either. In fact, the next time she traveled down to Blue Springs, she'd asked her mama if she had the dollars, and when she said yes, Elsa got them right back from her. She loved her husband and respected him, but if he thought he could just boss her around with no response, he had another think coming.

Elsa heard a bee buzz through the window and she focused back on the job Solomon had given her just before he left.

"Go through Aunt Francis's personables," he had said that morning. "Keep what you want, give away what you don't. Might as well clean out the room and move Abby to it. Give her some space from that little loft where she sleeps."

Standing, Elsa tried to shake off the weariness that had settled over her shoulders since Francis's death. She had to care for the whole family now, and that made her real tired. She had too many chores and too little help. Luke was slow. Except for his music, he had little ability to do anything else. And Daniel, though bright and full of gumption, challenged her at almost every turn, defying everybody's authority except his pa's. While still too young for anybody to know for sure, Abby seemed more like Daniel than anybody else. If so, that meant even more trouble down the road.

Feeling resentful of all the responsibility, Elsa moved to the window and stared out toward the woods. This was more than she had bargained for when she married Solomon, she decided, more by a long ways. For a moment, she wondered if she'd made a mistake, if her spite for her pa had taken her down a wrong path.

Yet she knew she loved Solomon. She had married him not simply because she wanted to escape her pa but also because of all his good traits, and he had a bunch. But could those good traits make up for the mess that now surrounded her? Too little money and a house full of kids to handle?

She touched her stomach, ran her fingers over the gradually rounding surface. Another child was on the way. Though she had not told anybody else just yet, she knew it was so.

Elsa turned back to the room, ground her teeth, and made a quick decision. If her mama wanted to give her money, then she would keep on taking it. She would take it and spend it on her babies and dare Solomon Porter to do anything about it.

Anxious now to do the distasteful task ahead of her, she moved to the table by Aunt Francis's bed. A wood cup sat there, the snuff cup that Aunt Francis kept close by most of the time. Other than a coal lamp and a Bible, nothing else lay on the table.

Elsa placed the cup in the pocket of her apron to throw away later and walked over to the other side of the bed. She noticed a round metal can. Inside the can was a variety of sewing materials—needle, thread, cloth, and yarn. Under all of this she came to a bunch of crochet hooks and a mixture of small cloth pieces. Deciding to keep the can and its contents, Elsa placed it on the mattress. She then turned to the wood trunk sitting at the foot of the bed. Opening it, she saw what few items of clothes Francis had owned. Two pair of old shoes, three dresses, all of them worn and faded from washings in the kettle in the yard. They had buried her in her Sunday dress—a collared navy one with white lace at the neck and wrists.

Under the dresses Elsa found a blue shawl, a floppy hat like men wore, and the blanket Francis had used in winter to cover her legs while she warmed by the fire. Lifting the blanket, Elsa saw a basket in the bottom of the trunk. The basket, sitting upright in the corner, was almost as tall as the trunk and as round as a small water bucket. It had a top with a hook to keep it closed. The hook was snapped shut. Elsa had never seen the basket before.

Her breath came quicker now. She knew instinctively that Aunt Francis had kept her personal things in the basket, those possessions that made her distinct from all other women. Bits and pieces of life that no one else owned in quite the same way she owned them. Staring at the basket, Elsa eased down onto the bed. Her fingers trembled. In this basket she knew she would find Francis's most cherished possessions.

She breathed deeply. Though she and Francis had clashed every now and again, the woman had generally treated her kindly, tried to help her adjust to her place in the Porter household. Was the key to Francis's kindness in here? Even more, could she learn how to live in a like fashion by studying what made Francis who she was? Was such a thing possible? Would she want it if it were? Did she truly want to take on some of the traits that made Francis so beloved?

Elsa wiped her hands on her apron and realized she didn't know what she wanted. Did she have the desire and courage to change if she could? Who knew? For now, all she knew was that she was what she was, what her family history had made her—a combination of the best and worst of the kinfolk of Hal and Amelia Clack.

Deciding to leave such questions to a future time, Elsa snapped open Francis's basket and looked inside. She saw a white hat with a piece of lace down the front. She lifted out the hat, placed it on her head, spread the lace out over her face. She wondered for a minute what Francis had been like the day she got married. Thinner for sure, less wrinkles too. Full of dreams, maybe? Too ignorant to know that life came along and knocked most of those dreams right out of you? That life reached up and stole those dreams when you were not watching? Or even when you were?

Elsa pulled off the hat, laid it on the bed, and continued picking through the basket. A pair of shiny black shoes lay under the hat. Under the shoes she found a silver dollar, minted in 1897, in a brown box. She wondered why Francis kept the silver dollar, what it meant to her? Shrugging, she saw a couple of books: *The Pilgrim's Progress* and *David Copperfield*. She fingered through the books, remembering that Francis had liked to read, especially the Bible. Near the end of *The Pilgrim's Progress* she found a piece of paper, folded square and neat. Without thinking, she unfolded the paper and started reading the words on it.

My dearest Abigail, I will not be with you when you read this. . . .

Elsa's breath caught and she stopped reading for a moment as she understood what she had found. She stared over her shoulder to make sure no one was watching. Satisfied she was alone, she started reading again. It didn't take long to finish the letter. Her fingers clutched the paper tighter and tighter as her eyes soaked up the words. She read the letter a second time, then a third. Her face flushed. For several seconds she sat there motionless, the letter now in her lap. What should she do with this, the last words of Rose Porter, a letter to her only daughter?

Should she give it to Solomon? But he couldn't read. But she could read it to him. Did he even know about the letter? If so, he'd never said anything about it.

Had Rose Porter written the letter, then handed it to Francis to keep until Abigail could read it? But now Francis was dead, and the letter had fallen to her. What should she do?

Why not tell Solomon? What did she have to gain from keeping it a secret? Nothing, that's what. No reason to stay quiet.

Standing, she knew she had to tell him about the letter. If he already knew of it, fine. But either way, she had to make sure.

That night, after everyone had bedded down, she slipped into bed and kissed Solomon lightly on the cheek. "You sleepy?" she asked.

He faced her, his eyes bright. "What you got in mind?"

She laughed. "You a loving man, Solomon Porter, but you got the wrong idea this time. I need to talk about something."

His look turned serious. "Everything all right?"

"I found a letter in Francis's things," she said, deciding to say it straight out. "Words from Rose to Abigail."

Solomon turned onto his back, stared at the ceiling. "I know about it," he said. "She wrote it the night she died. Francis been keeping it."

Thinking of the letter's contents, she asked, "Francis read it to you?"

"Nope, not Francis or Rose. Meant for Abby, not me."

"You might ought to hear it."

Solomon propped his hands on his chest, steepled his fingers. "I feel tempted," he said. "But I don't think I got the strength."

Elsa laid her hand on his shoulder. "What you mean?"

His jaw worked tight. "It is her final saying," he said. "I figure it will hurt something fierce to hear it."

Elsa felt her heart skip. A scary notion came to her. Solomon still loved Rose! Five years had passed but he still had not put away his grief. Maybe he never would.

She pulled away her hand, rolled onto her back, and joined Solomon in staring at the ceiling. "You ought to read the letter," she said. "Like a man running from a bear. Sometime the best thing is to turn and face it down. Maybe the only way to scare it off."

"Maybe so," said Solomon. "But right now all I can see is that it is a mighty big bear."

Out of nowhere a sharp jealousy sliced through Elsa. She tried to ignore it but couldn't. It hit her hard, a jolt of resentment against a dead woman, a woman who had all of a sudden reached out from the grave to crawl into her life, into her bed. In that second, she suddenly hated Rose Porter, hated that she still held such power, such influence over her husband, such a hold on his heart. Without thinking, she spoke harshly. "Time for grieving her is past," she said. "Reading that letter ought not be such a fearsome thing."

Solomon faced her, his eyes sad. "You don't know nothing about it."

"I know Rose is dead," she said. "Buried up there with Francis and not coming back."

Solomon ground his teeth. Elsa could see she had angered him. Well, so be it. He had angered her too.

"You just keep that letter," said Solomon. "When Abby grows up and learns her letters, we will let her read it then."

Elsa started to tell him to take the letter, to take it and keep it wherever he kept all the rest of his memories of Rose. But then she remembered the contents of the letter and decided to leave it alone. Maybe the letter would help her later, she figured. Help her in ways she could not today even imagine. She closed her eyes and tried to fall asleep, but found it difficult. Though she knew it shouldn't matter, she couldn't push away the idea that her husband still loved his dead wife far more than he ever had or ever would love her. And that idea hurt her in her insides.

She tried to calm herself, to remember that Solomon had been kind to her in every way, loving and attentive. But then she saw the hurt in his eyes again when she mentioned the letter to him, the letter that brought back memories of Rose. That look made her anger boil up all over again. By the time she did finally go to sleep, her anger had become a smoldering fire—a fire that grew as she dreamed, grew and grew till it burned through her dreams like a wildfire consuming a mountainside.

CHAPTER
EIGHT

The wind cut at his face, and Laban wiped his nose with the sleeve of his denim shirt. The autumn after Francis's death had come with an early frost. A cascade of leaves whipped off the trees overhead, orange and yellow and red and brown. Laban rested on his hunkers, a jug of doublings in one hand and an apple in the other. A stack of playing cards lay on a rock at his side. He and a man named Respert—a distant cousin three years his elder on his mama's side—had been flipping the cards, gambling a penny for the highest card on each flip. Now the cards lay quiet. Luke sat beside Laban, his guitar slung over his back, his bad eye roaming as he watched the leaves blowing. A squall of ravens perched on a tree limb directly overhead, their black wings shining in the late afternoon light. The sun dipped low in the sky.

Laban sat for several minutes just watching his brother. A touch of guilt swept over him, and he felt chilly. He knew he shouldn't have brought Luke up here, shouldn't have led him to this hidden cove more than seven miles from the one-room cabin he'd built after his mama died. In the back of the cove sat a liquor still. A thicket of laurel and rhododendron hid it from anybody who might be hunting nearby or out looking for their pigs. Several bags of corn lay by the still. The air held the smell of mash and a low fire burning. Three main parts made up the still: the cooker where the corn mash was kept warm enough to ferment; the worm that carried the fermented liquid from the cooker; and the condenser where the collected steam turned into liquid.

A fire burned under the condenser. A copper wire ran out of it. The steam vapors from the liquid in the condenser were cooling in the wire and running as newly made liquor into the container sitting next to it. A stack of jugs sat by the still to collect the doublings for hauling to the buyer.

Respert and another man sat across from the still, both as liquored up as Laban, and both anxious to stay that way. Laban didn't know Respert's sidekick too well, but his name was Bluey and his left ear was bigger than his right and he had blond hair way down on his forehead. A fifth man lay on the ground between Laban and his companions. This man had ropes around his ankles and wrists and a dirty rag stuffed in his mouth. Bruises covered his face, and a scab of dried blood caked up on the back of his head.

Laban took a swig from his jug and considered how it was that he'd ended up in such a spot. Mostly it came from the fact that he had pretty much rejected everything his pa had tried to teach him. Even though he had a Bible name, he seemed bound and determined to do most anything and everything he could to act just the opposite of a Bible man.

Not that he thought about the Good Book that much. Truth to tell, he tried to avoid any and all talk about all that Jesus stuff. For his money, a man didn't earn no extra credit with God or anybody else by studying the sky every day hoping to see some sign of the Lord. The notion of God came up in his head about as often as the question of how many ashes it took to fill up a fireplace. In other words, not too often.

Tossing away his apple, Laban shook his head, his heart heavy. He and Luke had come up to the still less than an hour ago and found Respert and Bluey with the government man. The revenuer had made the mistake of stumbling onto their still, and they had beat him up real bad, pretty near to death. If he did not see a doctor soon, he might just die on the spot.

At first, Laban tried to act like it didn't matter to him. Hunkering by the fire, he started sipping on the jug and tossing the cards with Respert. But despite the fact that he'd fallen a far way down from what his pa wanted for him, he still did not take well to the notion that a man might die while he sat by and played cards. He had to help the revenuer if he could. So, while flipping cards and swigging doublings, he tried to figure what to do. But nothing came to him. After a while, as the drink took its effect, he gave up his hopes of helping. But he felt bad about it all.

Luke started playing his guitar. A few seconds later, he lifted his voice—a smooth tenor—into a song. Laban listened to the mournful tune and ruminated some more about the state he'd reached. Dispensing with the notion of a God who dwelt somewhere way out there just waiting to pounce down on a man and give him *what for* if he happened to break one of the commandments, Laban trusted nobody but himself. A man with a strong body and a sharp wit didn't need much of anything else. If he had a good brother or two, that was a good thing, but not necessary in most cases.

The way he saw it, a man did just fine if he did a few simple things. One, take care of life's necessaries. Lay up food and wood for the winter that always comes; keep your clothes sewed and washed whenever the opportunity allows; keep the roof of your cabin as leak-proof as possible by chinking up the wind cracks in the summer.

Two, treat other folks with respect as long as they live in ways that are respectable. A body does this because if you don't, then the other person will one day treat you poorly too and no man, no matter how able, can fend forever all by his lonesome.

Three, never let down your guard 'cause if you do, something will punch you in the gut right then and there. As Laban saw it, a highlander man faced danger most every day. He had seen that danger play itself out on more than one occasion. Like the time in Blue Springs that Tommy Talley, all liquored up, took a knife and jabbed old Billy Kinder three times in the stomach for the simple transgression of saying that Tommy's horse had a bad case of the swayback. Or the day a mountain rattler bit one of the Roper twins, and the baby bloated up till his face looked like a fat balloon and then died a day and a half later. And none of that even counted what had happened to his mama just over five years ago. That still galled him something awful.

Laban had loved his mama more than he dared to admit—what with him almost a man and all. But the dying of his mama proved to him once and for all just how close at hand danger really was. One minute a woman lives and breathes and pushes out a new baby girl from her body. The next minute that woman bleeds out on the bed, and her life passes onto the sheets with her blood. Then somebody pulls the sheets off from where she'd died and washes them in the pot in the yard and that seems the end of it.

But it wasn't the end, at least not for Laban. He remembered. He remembered and swore to himself that he wouldn't place too much trust in life again. Or God either, for that matter.

"What you gone do about him?" he asked Respert, pointing his jug at the government man.

Respert shrugged, his round shoulders slumped. "Nothin' I can do," he said. "Man finds my makings, I got to make sure he don't mess 'em up." He kicked a foot at the revenuer. "He come to the wrong place. Bluey cracked him with a rock; he didn't even see it coming. Right out of the trees, Bluey jumped on him."

Laban touched the jug to his lips. Mountain men had learned to fight from the Indians. They were sneaky smart, most likely to spring at you from ambush, even from behind the back. No one saw any shame in it. A man comes for what is yours, you got to protect it with the most handy means available. That included knife and gun, bushwhack, or fair fight.

"We got the right to defend what is ours," continued Respert.

Laban nodded. Everybody in the mountains felt this way. The government had no right to tax a man's makings. Just as logical to tax a man for making corn bread to eat or a shirt to wear. Moonshine was just as necessary. Folks used it for medicine, for warmth when the snow fell, for cleaning out a cut, for making meat tender. And liquor came from natural things—corn, springwater, fire, sugar. God made the makings for moonshine. Why should the government tax such a natural thing?

If the government wanted to send a revenuer into the hills to cause trouble, then they deserved whatever fate came their way, good or ill. Nobody in the highlands saw no wrong in that. Then why did he still feel so blue?

Laban stared at the revenuer, saw that his breathing had fallen shallow. His head wound looked right nasty. The man might die any minute.

Laban glanced at Luke, who continued to strum his guitar, his eyes on the sky as if listening to some distant music only he could hear. Laban wondered how much Luke understood of what was happening. Did he know the trouble that Respert had caused? If this man died, would Luke realize the danger they were in and keep his mouth shut? Or would he go back home and tell what had happened?

"You reckon we ought to take him to a doctor?" Laban asked, hoping Respert would see some wisdom in the idea.

Respert grinned. His teeth showed gaps in the upper middle of his gums. "You too drunk to know what you saying," he said. "We haul him to a doctor, he gets better, he spies us out and hauls us up to trial for both the still and molestin' him. Not much smart in that."

"But what if he dies?"

"Comes with his trade," Respert said. "He knowed the risk when he signed on to do the work he does."

Laban set his jug on the ground as he studied what to do. He knew that if he tried to move the man, Respert and his pal Bluey would stop him. And even if they didn't, what could he do? If he carried the man to a doctor and he recovered, what would stop the man from blaming him and Luke for his injuries? After all, the revenuer hadn't seen his attacker. For all he knew, it was Laban who did it.

Laban figured another possibility. If he carried the revenuer to a doctor but he died anyway, then the sheriff would surely arrest him and Luke on the spot as the prime suspects.

Torn with confusion, Laban stood and leaned over the revenuer. What if he just took Luke and left, he wondered, walked down to the sheriff in Blue Springs and reported what he'd found? But then he knew that wouldn't work either. Respert and Bluey would just lie about their part in the matter and blame him and Luke. It would be his word against theirs. In a highlander court, the truth didn't always matter a whole lot. In a highlander court, the man who could put the most members of his kin on the jury always won.

Still weighing the matter, Laban saw another truth too. A reputable highlander man did not speak ill of a kinsman to a legal authority, no matter how bad the deed the kinsman had done. If a kinsman brought dishonor on the name of the clan, then the clan took care of the matter in its own way. To go tattling on Respert to the government broke every taboo known to the Blue Ridge. To do that meant to put himself and Luke outside the family circle, and though he might do that to himself, he couldn't do it to Luke. To do so would make them both marked men, men that others would either shun or seek vengeance against. Laban knew he couldn't bring such a fate to his brother.

"So what you gone do with him?" he again asked Respert.

Respert spat on the ground. "Reckon I'll just carry him off a few miles from here and leave him to his own possibles. Let the natural ways take care of him."

Laban looked into the trees. A man all hurt and tied up wouldn't make it more than two or three days, and that was only if some critter didn't have at him before then. He felt a bite of regret at his stomach. A man put himself in some bad spots, he decided. Bad spots that showed no way out, bad spots that made a man hate himself for what he'd done to bring him to that bad spot and for what he would have to do to escape the consequences.

For several minutes he thought back over the last few years, knew he had squandered them in ways that displeased his pa, put a stain on his family's name. A sense of shame came over him, and his head dropped.

Laban knew that his heathenish life made his pa fearful for him. Solomon wanted his sons to stay right with the Almighty. As Solomon saw it, God gave life, God took life away. Everything that takes place does so because the good Lord wanted it that way. A baby gets born normal, everybody celebrates and praises sweet Jesus. A baby gets born with a clubfoot . . . well, the Lord had good reasons. A corn crop stands as tall as a man's head. Thank you, Jesus. A summer passes without rain, and the corn dries up till it flakes away in the palm of your hands. Somebody done broke the law of the Lord, and a punishment had to come.

Such simplicity made Laban mad as a hornet. As he saw it, such a notion took a man's gumption away from him, his need for striving. Taken to its logical end, this notion led to a weakness he couldn't abide by—a weakness that just bowed its head and shut its mouth as if struck mute with puny fatalism. Whatever happens, just accept it. Don't complain, don't rail out at it, don't kick against the will of the Almighty.

Well, he wanted none of that. Pa's ways were too simple, too weak for a man full of his own strength. Fact was, right after his mama's death, Laban decided he would kick against the Lord's will if he chose. But that kicking had brought him to such things as this, things he knew would end in no good.

He felt movement at his side, turned, and saw Luke beside him, his guitar on his back.

"We g-g-go home now?" asked Luke.

Laban wished he could do exactly what Luke suggested. Go home and put all this behind him, all this and everything else he'd done in the last few years. But he knew he could not, knew that if he left this revenuer on this mountain to die, that he would be cutting himself off forever from the good name and family of Solomon Porter. But he saw no way to escape the sad fact that he had to do exactly that. He faced Respert again.

"Where you gone leave him?"

"Don't rightly know. Somewhere lonely like, don't want nobody stumblin' by and finding him too soon, know what I mean?"

Laban nodded. The revenuer would die within a couple of days. He sighed. But then an idea came to him. "Maybe take him up to Edgar's Knob," he said. "Nobody up there much."

Respert stuck a jug to his lips, kicked the revenuer again. "Edgar's Knob sounds good. Nobody find him there."

"I reckon me and Luke will head on home," Laban said. "Seems you boys got this covered."

Respert sucked from his jug, then stood and motioned to Bluey. "Night coming soon," he said. "Let's move this man along."

Laban waved at Respert and walked away, Luke at his side. Going over the mountain, he knew what he had to do. Three hours later, he left Luke at his pa's house and headed out toward his own cabin, his shoulders slumped and his heart weighing as heavy as a sack of coal.

The moon that came up over Edgar's Knob that night had a face that turned down at the edges as if in an infinite frown. A steady stream of feathery clouds floated over the moon, making it visible one moment, invisible the next. On the ground beneath the moon, behind a cluster of chunky rocks, a man with bound wrists and ankles and a rag in his mouth slowly came to consciousness. Struggling to breathe, he tried to sit up but found he couldn't. His head hurt real bad, and his eyes were swollen almost shut. He fell back to the ground, stomach and face first. For several seconds, he just lay there, considering his circumstance. Then he rolled over and tried again. Pulling at his bindings, he sensed that if he didn't free his hands soon and find some help he might not survive. Fear threatened to panic him, but he pushed away the fear and kept at his work. But his attackers had done their job well. His hands were tight in the ropes.

Taking a breath, he paused and stared at the moon. To his left, he heard something move. "Hey!" he said with a muffled shout, his hopes rising. "Anybody there?"

No answer came. He supposed he had imagined it. He raised up, leaned against a rock. He closed his eyes. Something to his left moved again. He turned that way but saw nothing. For a second, he wondered if his attackers had come back to finish the job. But no one stepped out. He breathed a little easier, then drew his legs to his chest in an attempt to hide against the rock. What if a critter was out there—a bear maybe, or a wolf? Even a panther? A few still roamed these mountains at the higher elevations.

He heard movement again and felt something touch his back. He jerked against the rock, banging his head. A hand pressed over his eyes.

"Don't move," said a voice from the dark.

He felt the hand against his head now, a wrap going around his eyes, a blindfold covering his face. He struggled against the blindfold, but the hands held him still, and he found himself losing consciousness again. His head throbbed painfully, his eyes unable to stay open. He fought against passing out and managed to remain conscious.

The man eased the revenuer over to his side. Then, his hands gentle, the man lifted a knife from his belt. Squatting over the revenuer now, the man took the knife and raised it into the air. The steel edge glinted in the moonlight. The man lowered the knife and cut loose the ropes at the revenuer's wrists and ankles. Slipping the knife back into his belt, the man pulled the rag from the revenuer's mouth and tossed it behind the rocks.

Still squatting, the man pulled a jug of water from behind the rocks and set it down by the revenuer. A piece of corn bread wrapped in a white cloth joined the water jug. As he stood up, the man took a deep breath and looked around. Then he wiped his hands and walked away. Above his head, the moon peeked from behind a row of clouds and stared down at what he had left.

The revenuer quickly pulled off his blindfold, spun around, and watched the man walking away. He'd seen the man earlier in the day, him and his brother Luke. The revenuer rubbed the back of his head where the rock had banged his skull and thanked his lucky stars that at least one of the men who had earlier held him prisoner had enough conscience left not to let him die.

CHAPTER
NINE

When the day finally came for school to start in the fall of 1907, Abby Porter rose before sunup, washed her face and hands, and threw on an old brown shirt and overalls. After that she ran out of the house and started in on her chores. Hurrying as fast as she could, she gathered eggs, milked the cow, and fed Bouncer. Then she rushed back to the cabin to eat her breakfast—a biscuit and some buttermilk. Though her whole family joined her at the table, she hardly spoke a word. After she'd finished eating, she ran to her room, yanked off her work clothes, and slipped into the best outfit she owned: a simple blue dress, a tan sweater with four buttons, a pair of thin white socks, and a pair of black shoes with a buckle that Pa had traded a chair for down in Asheville. Next she pulled her hair, still auburn and curly, into two matching pigtails, splashed water onto her face one more time, and headed outside. Somebody had already brought Bouncer from the shed.

Climbing onto the mule's back, Abby hooked her lunch pail over the crook of her elbow and yelled as loud as she could, "Come on, Laban! First day of school gone be half over before I make my arrival."

A few seconds later Laban stepped to the porch, his floppy hat in his hand, his beard all scraggly. Pa trailed after him with his hands shoved in the pockets of his overalls. Daniel and Luke came soon after Pa, each of them smiling.

"You got over an hour before starting time," Solomon called to Abby, stepping to the mule. "And it's only three miles or so down there."

"Won't hurt to go early," said Abby. "Find me a good seat by the front."

"You an eager girl," Solomon said.

"You would think she was going to see a circus," Daniel said.

Solomon faced Laban. "You deliver her the first day," he said. "After that, I suspect she and Bouncer can make it on their own."

"I don't even need him today," Abby said. "I been down to Blue Springs by myself more than a few times."

Solomon grinned. "Mighty true, girl, but you best let your brother take you at least this once. Don't want folks thinking we not taking proper care of you."

Abby nodded. No reason to argue with her pa, just so she got there. Laban took Bouncer's lead rope, tipped his hat to the family, and headed toward the path that led down to Blue Springs.

"I appreciate your company to school," Abby said to him. "Even if I could go by my lonesome."

Laban grunted. "Pa says I ain't much good for working anyway," he said. "Might as well take the carrot head to school."

Abby didn't mind him calling her carrot head. Lots of folks did. It didn't bother her much, so long as she knew they weren't funning on her.

She sat up straight on Bouncer's back, her body almost twitching with excitement. Today she started school. She had waited for this day for as long as she could remember. Pestered Pa last year to let her start, but he had said no, said she was too young and small to travel out and back by herself, and he couldn't spare one of the boys to escort her every day. In addition to that, Elsa had birthed her second baby—another boy, this one named Walter—in August of last year and she needed Abby to help her around the house until she found her strength again.

The whole year had just dragged by with Pa and Daniel and Luke working from sunup to sundown and her having to spend most of her time serving as nursemaid to her two half brothers. It wasn't that she did not love them. But she did get mad at them sometimes, because they howled a lot and pulled at her pant legs and kept her from starting school when she wanted. When this happened, Abby remembered that Mrs. Elsa had been pretty nice to her since she'd come to live with them and real appreciative of her help. Which made the time go smoother.

But all that was past now. The day had finally come, the day to sit in a room with a real teacher and open a book and learn to read and cipher. The best day of her life, Abby figured it, no question to ask about that.

Birds chirped in the trees as she passed. She wondered what made them sound so spry and happy. Would she learn that in school? And why did the rain fall in some years and stay away in others? Or what made apples taste so good when you cooked them up and spread sugar and cinnamon on them and put them in a crust for a pie?

Abby leaned back on Bouncer. She had so many questions she wanted somebody to answer. Like, why do leaves turn green in the spring, then all kinds of colors in the fall? And why do they drop off the trees when the frost comes? Or, why do dogs and cats hate each other so much?

Laban steered Bouncer sideways to miss a mudhole. Abby stared at her big brother's back. A sense of sorrow settled in between her shoulders as she thought of more questions she needed somebody to answer. Like, why did men like Laban find life so hard? Why did he and Pa not get along better? Why did men drink so much liquor?

She shifted the lunch pail to her other arm. Maybe a teacher could guide her toward the answering of such things. Or show her a book that could.

Abby took a deep breath. The morning air smelled so fresh, like water bubbling up from a spring, all foamy and white and clean. She imagined a book in her hand, the feel of the cover, the smooth pages, the sound of it as she turned from one page to the next. She couldn't wait to read one all by herself.

Since Aunt Francis's death, no one had read a book to her. Not even Mrs. Elsa, and she read real good. Mrs. Elsa sometimes pulled one of her two boys up on her lap and read poems to them from a book she'd brought from her ma's house. But she had never invited Abby to listen. From time to time, though, Abby had hidden behind a door with her ears to the wall, her body tight with fear that Elsa might see her hiding there.

One part of Abby wanted Elsa to discover her. That way she could admit she liked to hear books read out loud. Maybe then Mrs. Elsa would ask her to listen too. But Mrs. Elsa never saw her. Or at least she never said anything if she did.

Abby felt hungry for books, for the sound of the words that Aunt Francis used to read to her. The hunger grabbed at her throat sometimes when she heard Mrs. Elsa reading to her boys, and she felt sad and lonesome like she did on the day of Aunt Francis's funeral. Strange about that, how the feelings were so alike. Maybe her studies at school would teach her why this was so. Maybe they would also teach her why people died before anybody wanted them to. That was a good question for somebody to answer.

"You mighty quiet," said Laban, breaking her thought.

"Just pondering some," she said.

"All ready for this school, ain't you?"

"Sure am."

They made a few more yards, rounded a curve in the trail. Bouncer stepped past a big rock.

"You ever read many books?" she asked.

Laban kept walking. "Nope," he said. "Nothing much worth reading."

"Oh, I think everything is worth reading."

"You are like Ma," Laban said. "She read whenever she got a moment to sit down. Bible mostly."

Abby's eyes sparkled. She loved hearing about her ma. "Ma read to you?"

"Ma read to everybody—me, Luke, and Daniel. Pa too, most every night. All of us sitting on the porch when the season allowed it, by the fire when it didn't."

"I wish I had knowed Ma," said Abby.

Laban kept walking.

"Aunt Francis read to me," she said. "Like Ma did to you."

"Aunt Francis was a good woman," Laban said.

Bouncer eased around a switch lying on the road.

"She as good as Ma?"

"Nobody as good as Ma. But Francis was mighty fine, just the same."

Now Bouncer stepped over a log that had fallen in the way.

"You miss her still?"

"Ma or Aunt Francis?"

"Ma."

Laban pulled Bouncer to a halt, then turned and faced Abby. His eyes looked red. "I miss her every day I live," he said. "Every day I live." He turned and moved Bouncer forward. Abby knew enough to say no more about Ma.

They arrived at the school in less than an hour. The building sat in a clearing about half a mile out of Blue Springs, a single room rectangle of faded white wood and a peaked roof with a stone chimney on the right side. An outhouse sat on the left, and a well with a covered top fronted it. The yard was mostly dirt except for a big maple tree that gave shade to the front steps of the building.

Abby's eyes danced as they entered the clearing. Before they reached the school's front door, she hopped off Bouncer and ran on ahead, Laban trailing. At the door she pushed right through the clump of children standing around the entrance. Without saying hello to anybody, she ran to the front of the room, took the seat closest to the teacher's desk, and glanced around to look for the teacher. She saw her to her left, a woman no more than Laban's age, standing holding an apple with a short boy Abby knew as Jubal waiting at her knees. The teacher had brown hair that she had tied in a bun behind her head. Her face was round—like the top of a butter churn. She wore a plain brown dress with black boots that came up past her ankles. Her eyes were as black as the boots.

Abby decided she was a rather stern looking woman but still attractive in a rather curious way. The teacher leaned down to Jubal and patted him on the head. Abby felt someone beside her, looked away from the teacher, and saw Laban at her elbow.

"I will leave Bouncer hitched outside," he said. "You come right home when school is out."

Abby nodded, and Laban turned to leave. The schoolteacher stepped over to them. Abby noticed a scar under the teacher's chin where her cheek ran into her neck.

"You joining us for school today?" she asked Laban, her voice just a touch surprised.

"No, ma'am," said Laban, his hat in his hand. "I'm done with my schooling many a year ago. I'm bringing my sister." He pointed the hat at Abby.

The teacher's face flushed. "I'm sorry," she said. "But we take all ages here."

"I know," he said. "Don't fret about it."

The teacher looked at Abby. "And what's your name, young lady?"

"I'm Abigail Porter," she said proudly. "Most folks call me Abby."

The teacher stuck out her hand. "Pleased to meet you, Abby. I'm Miss Eugenia Brennan. Glad to have you in my school." Miss Brennan turned back to Laban. "You be picking her up later?"

"No, ma'am. She will ride Bouncer, that's the mule, back up to home when school is out."

Miss Brennan looked slightly disappointed, and Abby couldn't figure out why. Laban put on his hat, tipped it, then turned and left. Miss Brennan watched him go before facing Abby again.

"Nice of your brother to bring you," she said.

"I don't see him much," said Abby. "Just now and again. He happened to come home for a spell this week. Pa sent him down with me."

Miss Brennan nodded and said, "I see you got the seat closest to the front."

"Yes, ma'am. I come to learn."

"It pleases me to hear it."

"I want to read," continued Abby. "Read books."

Miss Brennan smiled big. "Any particular book?"

"All of them," Abby said. "But start maybe with the Good Book. My ma read it every night."

"You've set your sights right high," said Miss Brennan. "But I expect we can start you on your way, let you work up from there."

Abby felt so happy she wanted to shout. But she held it to herself.

Miss Brennan clapped her hands together and went to the door to call all the children in to start the day. As the boys and girls ran to their seats, Abby studied them. She knew most of the children, many of them from Jesus Holiness. But a few of them were strangers to her, boys and girls from nooks and crannies of Blue Springs Mountain she had never traipsed. Several grades of students were in the classroom together, with the oldest boys in the back, the oldest girls in front of them. The rest of the kids arranged themselves pretty much in order of age from back to front. A black iron stove sat in the center of the room. A single chalkboard ran across the front behind Miss Brennan's brown desk. A stack of paper tablets lay on top of the desk, thick pencils by the tablets. A shelf about four feet across with two sections to it stood to the left of the desk. Abby quickly counted about thirty books resting on the shelves.

Seeing the books, Abby could barely contain herself. She would finally learn to read. Like her ma before her, like Aunt Francis after her ma died.

Abby stared at Miss Brennan. This woman could show her how to open the books, decipher the words on the page, find the key to so much she didn't yet know. She would do anything to gain such knowledge, anything to please Miss Brennan.

Miss Brennan clapped her hands again. "I'm Miss Eugenia Brennan," she said. "I moved here two weeks ago from Charlotte."

Abby had a sense of dizziness in her head. She would study so hard Miss Brennan would think she was wonderful. Miss Brennan would love her as if she belonged to her, love her more than anybody else.

"I studied at State Teacher's College," continued Miss Brennan. "I have wanted to teach all my life. This is my first year."

Abby suddenly wondered if Miss Brennan had a husband, maybe children too. But then she remembered how she had introduced herself as "Miss," and how she'd let her eyes follow Laban when he left the school. She was single, sure as anything. Abby wondered why. Women in the mountains married real young, thirteen or fourteen sometimes.

"It will take me a while to learn all your names," Miss Brennan said.

Abby wanted her teacher to know her name in a hurry, to know her name and smile at her, to smile at her like a woman smiled at her child, to . . .

With a start, Abby suddenly realized with the insight that occasionally comes to children that she had never really experienced the fullness of love that she craved. No one at home gave it to her—certainly not Mrs. Elsa, even though she was nice to her most of the time. Junior and Walter took almost all of Mrs. Elsa's time and attention.

Pa didn't give Abby much favor either. He worked most of the time and rarely spoke directly to her, so she never knew for sure what he felt about her. For the most part, she stayed by herself a lot. Daniel talked to her now and again, but not nearly as much as she wanted. And Luke played his guitar for her when she asked, but he stayed out with Laban all the time.

Miss Brennan continued to talk, and Abby tried to listen, but in her head the word *lonely* suddenly rose up and she rolled it around several times and knew that it belonged to her. Though she had more by way of house, food, and clothing than the majority of highlander children, she knew with a flash of recognition that she had a pa that had kept his distance since the day she was born. As she realized the truth of this painful thing, it came to her that her pa probably knew exactly how she felt. In spite of his getting married again, his having a new wife and two boys to keep him company, he still had an air of sadness about him. This sadness showed up at odd moments, but it still hung around, much like a stray dog looking to grab a bone when nobody was watching.

Abby sighed. She knew about that sadness. She knew it and sensed that she shared it with her pa, and she felt drawn to him because they held that sadness in common. Her head drooped and she started to lay it on her folded arms on her desk. But then she glanced to her left and saw Jubal beside her. He grinned real big, and she saw he'd lost two teeth in the front. She smiled back at him, then faced the front again.

Miss Brennan took the writing tablets from her desk and started passing them out. Abby's heart pumped faster as her tablet came her way, and the sadness fled her as fast as it had come. How could she feel sad today? She had started her schooling. Soon she would be able to write her name and read a book, and the whole world would open to her. Then all her sadness would disappear forever.

CHAPTER
TEN

From September until the end of April, Abby traveled down to school every morning that the weather didn't stop her. Studying harder than the other students, she picked up her ABC's in a hurry, then moved to learning some words. She wrote the words down on pieces of the gray tablet paper that Miss Brennan gave them and carried them home when the day ended. At night she looked at the words over and over again by the light of the lamp that sat on a table by the fireplace. Whenever somebody came within earshot she pointed to the words on the paper and called them out loud.

At the same time that Abby studied the words from her books, Laban took a more than passing interest in Miss Brennan. All through that fall and winter he kept showing up at the school, at first with the excuse that he wanted to make sure Abby made it okay, but then later with no excuse at all. After a bit of early standoffishness, Miss Brennan gradually began to reward his attentions with a shy smile and flirty eyes. By the time Christmas came and went, Laban and Miss Brennan had taken to holding hands and showing up at just about every social function held in Blue Springs.

The fact that her brother had taken to courting her teacher made Abby happier than a cat with a new ball of string. *Maybe Laban will marry Miss Brennan,* she thought. Then she could spend a lot more time with her teacher, pull out of her head everything she knew, all the words that had ever been written. Miss Brennan would read thick books to her, books filled with stories of kings and queens, romance and wars, treasure and journeys.

Abby figured the match between Laban and Miss Brennan pleased her pa too. Solomon liked it because Laban's wildness had settled down a lot as a result of Miss Brennan's womanly influence. Abby had heard her pa tell Mrs. Elsa his thoughts about the pair.

"Laban is not so fractious these days," he had said. "That school-teacher got him tied up in so many knots he can't get loose to go do his carousin'."

Elsa laughed. "A woman can do that to a man, that's the truth."

"It is a good thing," said Solomon. "That boy was headed for a meeting with a bad end the way he was going . . . a bullet or knife blade, no doubt."

Abby knew her pa was right. Laban had settled more than a measure or so since he started courting Miss Brennan. Not that he had stopped all his drinking. Abby still smelled liquor on him sometimes after he'd spent a night out with his buddies. But he'd cut down on the doublings something considerable. And, far as she knew, his gambling had pretty much ceased altogether. A man considering the possibility of marrying didn't have much money to lose on a shiftless card game.

By the time the dogwoods had started to bloom again and the first year of Abby's schooling had almost reached its close, most everybody in Blue Springs had concluded that the schoolteacher from Charlotte and their own Laban Porter would no doubt marry up sometime during the summer. Abby surely expected as much. And why not? Laban and Miss Brennan sat real close down at Jesus Holiness on Sundays and they held hands when Laban walked her home. And once, right after the school day had ended, Abby had gone out to climb on Bouncer, then she remembered she'd left her writing pad on her desk. Hurrying back inside, she caught Laban and Miss Brennan in a kiss, his hat in his hands, his lips touching Miss Brennan's.

Her heart beating fast, Abby had run back outside before they saw her. After that day, though, she often pretended she had gone out to the schoolyard to play while Laban visited with Miss Brennan. Then, after she'd given them a few minutes alone, she would tiptoe back to the door, quietly crack it just a little, and look in to see if she could catch them kissing again. Sometimes they rewarded her spying with a kiss or two, sometimes they didn't.

On the Friday that would change all their lives, Abby didn't see any kissing going on when she eased back in and hid herself behind the door. She'd remember that day forever. A last blast of spring wind blew at the schoolhouse, making it shake and creak. Dust blew up behind her as Abby peeked silently at her brother and his woman.

Laban sat on the edge of Miss Brennan's desk with his hat on his knee. Miss Brennan stood beside him, arms folded across her chest. Her eyes were red, and she touched the back of her hand to her face to wipe away tears. Suddenly scared for reasons she didn't understand, Abby leaned in closer.

"He wrote me a letter," said Miss Brennan.

Abby's breath caught, and her heart started thumping harder.

"Don't care about no letter," Laban said. "He is back in Charlotte."

"But I've known him all my life," she said. "I thought we were going to get married last year. But he broke it off. Wasn't sure he was ready, he said. That's . . . well, to tell the truth . . . that's when I decided to come up here and teach. Get out of Charlotte, away from where I had to see him every day."

"But that is behind you," he said, standing from the desk and taking Miss Brennan's hands in his. "You got me now, you and me . . . we got plans."

Abby could see her brother loved Miss Brennan, and, figuring what was happening, she felt sorry for him.

"But he has asked me to come home," said Miss Brennan. "He wants to come back to me, marry me like we have said we would do ever since we were little kids."

"But I have asked you to betroth with me. And you been thinking about that. Now you say you want to throw that all away, run back to a fella that already left you once, walked away and made you so upset you come all the way here to Blue Springs? Don't make no sense for you to go back to him."

Miss Brennan pulled away, turned her back to Laban, and wiped her eyes again.

"But you and I are so different," she said. "You know that, we talked about it from the beginning. I don't fit here, not really. I'm not a high-lander woman, not like those up here anyway, all cut off from everything. I'm not cut out for these rugged places. I just came to get away, to escape. . . ."

Laban stepped over and hugged her from behind. "Maybe I can come to Charlotte," he said. "If you're not a mountain woman, maybe I become a city man. Find a job at the livery stable, do some blacksmithing maybe."

Miss Brennan faced him again and smiled but only briefly. Her hands clasped Laban's. "You say that now," she said. "But you would die living anywhere but in these mountains. I can't ask you to move to Charlotte, and you know you couldn't anyway . . . not for any span of time, not for me, not for anybody. It just wouldn't work."

"You ashamed of me," Laban said, letting go her hands. "I'm good enough for you while you're here in Blue Springs, all cut off from your folks and friends. But you don't want nobody from home to know you tied up with the likes of me."

Miss Brennan started sobbing, then covered her face with her hands. But she didn't argue with Laban, and Abby knew he had hit on a truth that Miss Brennan didn't want to admit. Mountain folk were like a different breed of people who didn't often mix well with those beyond the coves and hollers they called home. Miss Brennan had come to see this in her year in Blue Springs, had come to understand that, though she'd spent a year in the mountains, she remained an outsider to a true high-lander, a stranger to the ways of Laban and his kin. In a like fashion, those born and reared within the mist-shrouded circle of the Blue Ridge Mountains didn't ever truly fit below it.

Listening to her cry, Abby decided that maybe Miss Brennan was doing what was good for everybody. Break it off with Laban and stop any foolishness before it spread too far. But, even though she recognized the rightness of Miss Brennan's decision to leave her brother, Abby didn't like the way it made her feel. More than anything she wanted to run to Miss Brennan in that second and hug her at the waist, tell her she needed to stay and marry Laban, make him happy, make her pa happy, make *her* happy. Lots of people depended on her marrying Laban. How could she leave him and everybody else and go back to some man in Charlotte?

"My folks want me to come home too," Miss Brennan said. "They think I'm crazy for ever coming up here in the first place. And if they knew that you and I—" She stopped and put a hand on Laban's hip.

"Look," she continued, "I've come to . . . well, I don't know that it's love . . . but I'm fond of you . . . and you've been so kind to me . . . you and your family . . . and Abby is so smart . . . so eager to learn. But—" She stopped again and walked to a window and looked out. Laban followed, touched her elbows from behind.

Watching him cross the room, Abby saw that his face had changed, had taken on a sullen frown. Abby knew from his look that anger was boiling in him. His shoulders looked bunched, his neck stiff and tight.

"You done made up your mind, ain't you?" he said. "Nothing I can say to change it."

Miss Brennan nodded slowly, her eyes looking downward. "It's the right thing," she said. "I know it, right for both you and me." She faced him again. "You'll get over this. You're still young, all these mountain girls are just dying for you to come calling on them. I see it everywhere I go."

Laban took her in his arms then, hugged her close, and she didn't resist. Abby felt tears rising up in her as she watched her brother say good-bye to the only woman he'd ever loved. For several seconds he held Miss Brennan in his arms, his face buried in her hair. Abby figured his heart was breaking, and it felt like a death to her. She decided maybe to Laban it was. If he never saw Miss Brennan again, what was the difference between that and death?

Rubbing her eyes, she saw Laban raise his head. He kissed Miss Brennan one more time on the back of the neck. Then, quickly dropping his arms from her, he grabbed his hat and stalked out, never looking back. He passed Abby without a word, and she, too scared to move, didn't try to stop him.

As Laban stomped down the schoolhouse steps, Miss Brennan ran to the front door and watched him go, her tears flowing and her hands at her mouth. Abby watched him go too, and her heart broke—not only for Laban but also for herself and her pa. Without thinking about it, she knew without a doubt that Laban's life had just taken an awful turn, a turn back toward the life he'd led before Miss Brennan came to Blue Springs. The anger Abby had seen on his face scared her more than anything she'd ever seen, and she had a feeling that this anger wouldn't go away anytime soon. And, maybe worst of all, she realized that if Laban wasn't happy, then Pa wouldn't be happy either. He would start worrying again that Laban might come to a bad end, and his worry for Laban would touch everybody in the family.

Her heart heavy, Abby stayed still for another minute or so and then turned and walked out of the schoolhouse. At home that night she kept quiet about what she'd seen. Let Laban tell what had happened, she decided. Let him tell Pa and everybody else that Miss Brennan had left him. Maybe then he could start over with his life.

While dark fell, she waited on the porch for Laban to come but he never did. A couple of hours later, as she dressed for bed, she said a prayer that Laban would keep his anger under control and not come into the path of a bullet or a knife blade as the result of it.

When Laban left the schoolhouse he walked immediately to a liquor man he knew about a mile out of Blue Springs and used most of the coins in his pocket to buy a jug. Within an hour of the purchase he found himself pretty near to drunk already, his eyes glassy with the doublings, his gait unsteady. The afternoon shadows started to lengthen on the ground, and the late spring air still had a touch of chill in it. But, filled with liquor as he was, Laban didn't much feel the cool. Sitting on the porch of the general store in Blue Springs, he saw Luke come out of the blacksmith's stable, his guitar on a rope around his back.

Feeling lonesome, Laban stood and stumbled toward his brother, called out to him. Luke turned and smiled big, threw up his hand. Laban fell in step with him.

"Time to g-g-go home," Luke said, obviously pleased with the idea.

"Nope," said Laban. "Got no home."

Luke's brow squinted. "What you mean?"

Laban shook his head.

"Where you headed?" asked Luke.

"Don't rightly know. Wherever . . ."

"C-c-can I come?"

Laban thought for a second. He had an idea that he ought to send Luke home, but his mind was so fuzzy with the drink, the notion passed through before he could grasp it firm. "Sure, come on, you bet," he said.

By sundown the two of them had walked almost five miles, their trail bending off the main path over two miles ago, becoming little more than a deer track now. Their steps took them through a leafy canopy of hardwoods and pines on a steady move upward toward a spot no stranger could've ever followed. Breathing heavy from the climbing, Laban pushed through a thicket of mountain laurel and stepped behind a rock more than twice his height into a clearing. The sound of running water muttered through the quiet. The air had a sour smell—the smell of warm, fermented corn mash. Glancing around the clearing, Laban saw four men sitting by a small fire next to the rock. Each had a jug at his elbow and a rifle within arm's length. Laban recognized his cousin Respert. Respert jerked up his rifle as Laban emerged from the dusk.

"Relax yourself," called Laban. "Just me and Luke."

Respert lowered his weapon when he saw it was Laban. "Hey, boys," he said. "Come and sit." He motioned to the fire.

Laban and Luke joined the circle. Bluey and the other two men—brothers named Conduff and Mikey who Laban knew from over at Slatesville—gave them a nod. Luke and Laban returned the gesture. Respert swigged from his jug, and Bluey followed suit. Bluey and Mikey had their knives out, Bluey cutting at a thumbnail, Mikey jabbing his into a stump and pulling it out, jabbing it into the stump and pulling it out.

"You boys just knockin' about?" asked Respert, poking at the fire with a stick.

"Reckon so," Laban said. "Not much else . . . else to do in this . . . godforsaken place."

Bluey laughed as he concentrated on his thumbnail cutting. "You sound like you about drunk," he said. "Been working long on that jug?" He pointed his knife at Laban's whiskey.

Laban lifted the liquor and took a snort. "Not long enough," he said.

The men settled into silence. Luke took out his guitar, started to strum on it. Respert pulled a deck of cards from his pocket, and he and Conduff started flipping cards, making penny wagers on which one would draw the highest. Laban leaned back and took another shot of his jug. He thought of Miss Brennan and then pulled again from the liquor. Luke's guitar sounded mournful. A breeze clicked up in the trees overhead. Laban felt his anger rising again, even worse than down in Blue Springs. What was he to do now? Stick around in the go-nowhere, do-nothing world of Blue Springs? He sucked from the jug.

Before Miss Brennan came along, he never asked such questions in his head. But she had awakened him to the world beyond his tiny mountain hamlet, had led him to see that a man didn't necessarily have to live and die within ten miles of the cabin where he was born. A man who wanted to work hard and keep his nose clean could leave such a place and make something of his life.

Laban sighed. That idea had no running space now, no chance to come true. Miss Brennan had as much as told him so. He wasn't good enough for her, wasn't good enough to go out with her into the world past what he had always known.

Bluey stopped his nail cutting, stood and tossed his knife at a tree about thirty feet away. The knife point bit into the tree, straight and true.

Respert and Conduff glanced up. "You can sure throw that knife," said Respert. "Better'n anybody I ever seen."

Laban kept nursing his jug. Luke's fingers stopped moving on his guitar for a second but then picked up the playing again. Bluey pulled the knife from the tree, wiped the blade on his pant leg.

"Throw it again," Respert said. Bluey stepped back another five steps, cocked and threw the knife. It cut through the air, stuck dead into the tree again.

"Whooee!" shouted Respert. "Best I ever seen!"

Mikey stood with his knife. "Let me have a try at that," he said, holding his knife by the blade.

"Hold on there," Respert shouted as he jumped up and ran over to the tree. "Let's make a target to hit." He took Bluey's knife and quickly cut a crude circle into the tree bark. "Now have a go at that," he said to Mikey. "A quarter says Bluey can hit it, and you can't."

"I will take that bet," said Mikey. "Might as well just hand over that money."

Respert grinned and handed the coin to Conduff to hold. Mikey did the same, then squared his feet, reared back, and flung his knife.

"Too low!" shouted Respert, checking the tree. "Couple inches outta the circle." He pulled the knife from the tree and handed it to Mikey.

Laban watched closely as Bluey took his place, set himself, and threw his blade.

"In the target," hollered Respert. "Right in the top line."

"Try her again," Conduff said.

"Another quarter on Bluey," said Respert.

Shaking his head, Laban stood and gathered his balance. "I will whip you both," he said. "Fifty cents says so."

"You ain't got two quarters to your sorry name," Bluey said, grinning.

Laban searched through his pockets, took out his last two quarters, and set them on a stump by the fire. "Show me your coins," he said.

Bluey quickly laid the money on the stump.

Mikey shook his head. "Just lost my last quarter. Broke as a beggar."

"Me and you then," said Bluey, looking at Laban as he grabbed his knife. "Let's do her."

Laban stepped back and pulled his knife from its sheath.

Bluey drew a line with his foot about thirty feet from the tree. "Behind the line," he said. "And no cheating."

"I'm the judge," Respert shouted. "I say the winner."

Bluey and Laban nodded their agreement.

"It suit you if I go first?" Bluey asked.

"No matter to me."

Bluey nodded and stepped behind the line. Laban glanced at Luke, gave him a wink. But he didn't feel near so confident as the wink indicated. Truth was, his vision was a touch blurred, his hands unsteady from the liquor. And it was getting darker by the second. When it came his turn to throw he hoped the light from the fire would be enough for him to see the target.

Bluey squared his feet, then reared back and threw his knife. It spun through the air, over and over, then stuck into the tree about three inches left of the circle.

"Missed it!" shouted Mikey, pulling out the knife and running back to Bluey. "Two quarters up to Laban!"

Laban sat his jug on the ground, then walked to the line and closed his right eye. The target looked small but at least he could see it. He set his feet and whipped the knife at the tree. *Zzztt.* Its point cleaved the tree, dead in the center of the circle.

"That's a winner!" shouted Respert.

Laban grabbed at the money, but Bluey pulled his hand away. "Why don't we liven up the throwin'?" Bluey said. "I got two dollars against your one I can best you on the next throw."

Laban glanced at Luke. He had his guitar in his lap but he wasn't strumming it. A big grin creased his face. "You the best with the knife," he said. "Always win at throwin'. Win the dollars," he said. "Give me one."

Laban chuckled and left the quarters on the stump. Emboldened by the whiskey in his blood and the thought of the money in his pocket, he decided that if Bluey wanted to lose some more of his money, then let him have at it. He knew he was good at this. Maybe Miss Brennan didn't think much of him, but he could do some things right well.

Bluey placed two bills by the coins, took his knife and readied himself.

But Laban stopped him before he could throw. "How much money you got on you?" he asked suddenly.

Bluey looked at him, confusion on his face. "I ain't tellin' the likes of you," he said. "But I can cover whatever you are thinking."

Laban stepped to Luke, pointed at his guitar. Luke handed it to him. The guitar in hand, Laban faced Bluey. "This here guitar," he said, "against ten dollars."

Bluey cackled his pleasure. "You a sporting man," he said. "Let's do her." He pulled a five-dollar bill, four ones, and four quarters from his pocket and piled it all on the stump.

Laban set the guitar by the money. Luke's eyes grew big. Laban knew the dollars were more than he'd ever seen. Yet he felt confident, maybe foolishly so. He faced Bluey. "Do your best," he said. "You throw first again."

Bluey nodded, took a breath, and set his feet on the line.

"Closest one to the bull's-eye," Respert said. "I judge the throws."

Mikey and Conduff rubbed their hands together. Luke kept his eyes on Laban. Bluey threw the knife. It jammed into the tree inside the circle, bottom left corner. Laban tugged at the bill of his hat. He would have to throw good to win. Respert pulled the knife out, marked the spot where it hit, then stepped back.

Laban took the line, looked at Luke but didn't wink this time. His hand shook as he raised the knife. But then he steadied himself and let it go. *Zzztt.* It zinged at the tree, straight to the center of the circle.

"That's the winner!" shouted Respert. "A bull's-eye. Anybody a-doubting it?"

Mikey and Conduff ran to the tree. "That's the truest," said Mikey. "Dead center. Ten dollars to Laban Porter."

Laban stepped to the stump, handed Luke back his guitar, then picked up the money. A surge of pride came over him and he laughed out loud. "Not smart to make wagers against your betters," he said to Bluey, pocketing the money. "Make a man poor in a hurry doing such as that." He straightened and nodded at Luke. "Reckon we ought to head on home now," he said. "Got to worry about what to do with all my winnings."

"You a real kidder, ain't you?" Bluey said, his tone cold.

"I make a joke from time to time."

"Ten dollars ain't no joke," Bluey said. "Not where I come from. Give me a chance to win it back."

Laban paused, stared back at his opponent. "I didn't start the wager," he said. "But I got all rights to end it."

Bluey glanced at Mikey. Laban saw Mikey make a step toward his rifle sitting by the rock. Laban blinked his eyes hard and suddenly felt a lot more sober. His mind cleared up real quick.

"I want one more chance," said Bluey. "That is the sportin' thing to do. Let me try to square it all up."

Laban looked over at Mikey again. He was another notch closer to his weapon. Laban weighed the odds. Mikey and Conduff had come with Bluey, would no doubt stand by him if it came to shooting or knifing. Respert would run for the nearest cover. That made it him against three. He thought of Luke. If it came to fighting, Luke would try to help him, maybe catch a bullet or the point of a knife.

Laban ground his teeth. Bluey had him in a bad way. If it was just him, it wouldn't matter. Caring little about his own miserable life, he would jump into them like a panther pouncing on a fawn. Better to have it out here with Bluey than to go on with his miserable future. But that meant placing Luke in the line of danger, and he didn't want that. He couldn't bear to think of what it would do to Pa if something bad happened to Luke. Deciding he didn't want to make any trouble even if it meant losing the dollars he'd just won, he relaxed his fists.

"I'm a sportin' man," Laban said. "Ain't that right, Cousin Respert?"

Respert grinned.

"What is the wager this time?" Laban asked.

Bluey stared at his feet for a second. Then he turned, walked past the still and disappeared behind the rock that hid it. Soon he came back with a saddlebag slung over his shoulder, his hands busy with the leather straps. Standing by the stump, he pulled out a leather pouch and opened it, its contents laying out for all to see. Laban's mouth dropped open, and the last of the liquor seemed to flush out of his veins.

"How much is there?" asked Respert.

"Right near two hundred and forty dollars," Bluey replied.

Everybody stood around the stump now, their eyes wide as saucers, their mouths almost watering. Laban looked up at Luke, then back at the money, more dollars than probably anybody in Blue Springs had ever seen, more money than any of his kin had ever owned.

"Where did you come by all this money?" asked Respert.

Bluey laughed. "Not from selling eggs," he said. "I can tell you that for sure."

Liquor money, thought Laban. They all knew it. Only way to earn such money in the mountains was to make and sell illegal whiskey. But Laban knew Bluey didn't have a still big enough to provide enough liquor to make this many dollars. Where did he. . . ?

It came to him then. Bluey was a nephew of Hal Clack. He must've just sold a good-sized load of his uncle's whiskey.

"I got nothin' to match up to a wager like this," Laban said. "Need to whittle the bet down a long way for me to meet it."

Bluey shook his head. "You done beat me twice," he said. "You gone scared on me now?"

Laban shrugged. "I just ain't got nothin' to match it," he repeated. "Can't bet what I don't have."

"That's a fact," Respert said. "He's my cousin, and I'm a witness to the fact that Laban Porter is as poor as a bad preacher."

Mikey and Conduff laughed. Ignoring them, Laban said, "Make it ten dollars even; that will give you a chance to square up with me. But then we quit. That is the fair thing, and you know it."

Bluey paused, obviously considering the matter at hand. But then he shook his head again. "I hear you got land," he said. "I will wager my money against your land."

"The land belongs to my pa," Laban said quickly. "Not mine to wager."

"You the oldest boy," said Bluey. "The land will be yours someday, most of it anyway. If I win, I won't claim it until your pa passes on."

Laban's heart rumbled in his chest, and he shook his head hard. He had no reason to make a crazy wager like this. "Make it for the ten," he said. "I ain't goin' no higher."

"I didn't think you was no womanish man," challenged Bluey. "But maybe what they say about the Porter clan is true. No gumption in their spines when things get down to the nubs."

Laban ground his teeth. He had already suffered a big humiliation today. Another one seemed more than a body could stand.

"You done beat him twice," said Mikey, egging Laban on. "You going coward on us now?" He placed his hands under his armpits and flapped his arms and clucked like a chicken. "Laban Porter is a chicken man," he called. "Chick . . . chick . . . ch-ick-en."

Respert leaned close to Laban. "Man can do a lot with that much money," he said. "Buy a fancy horse, a new rifle, spanking new suit of clothes."

Laban stared at the dollars and knew that Respert had it right. A man with that much money could do most anything he wanted. A likeable notion came to him. A man could leave the mountain with that much money, go down to a town, and start up in a school to gain a real education. A man could better his life, rise up out of ignorance and poorness, find himself a wife—somebody like Miss Brennan.

A feverish feeling took hold of Laban as he ruminated on the idea. He couldn't hold it back. With this money he could go down to Charlotte, prove to Miss Brennan and her folks that he deserved her, could take care of her. He could go back to school and make something of his future.

In an instant he knew he had no choice but to take the chance. It was as if fate had thrown this opportunity at his feet, had thrown it there to see if he had the bravery to claim it. His whole life lay right there on the stump of an old oak tree, and all he had to do was grab it up. Bluey was right. The land, at least a major part of it, would fall to him someday. It was his to wager, his to do with what he wanted. And he had already won two tosses. No reason he couldn't win a third.

Another notion came to him. What happened if he did win? Would Bluey let him just take the money and leave? Maybe not. Maybe Bluey would have Mikey shoot him and Luke. Then they would swear to the sheriff that the killings were in self-defense.

Laban faced Bluey, his jaw tight. "My brother leaves now," he said. "Mikey and Conduff go with him. And they take our firearms when they go."

Bluey grinned. "You are not a trustin' man," he said.

"Just making the odds fair."

"But Respert's your cousin," Bluey said. "What is to keep you and him from jumping me if I win, taking the money and claiming I lost the wager?"

"We both know Respert is without spine," Laban said. "No danger to nobody."

Bluey considered the matter for a second, then nodded. He turned and dismissed Mikey and Conduff. "Meet me at Barrow Point," he said. "I'll come along directly."

The two men picked up their rifles, took Bluey's pistol and shotgun, then stopped to wait on Luke.

Laban went over to Luke and handed him his pistol. "Don't say nothin' to nobody about any of this," he said. "I'll come home before morning."

"You gone be okay?" Luke asked.

"Sure, just keep your tongue in your head."

Luke nodded and trailed out with Mikey and Conduff, his guitar on his back.

Now Laban and Bluey were alone with Respert.

"Draw a circle on that tree," said Bluey, pointing to a big hickory at least thirty feet away. "Make sure to make new marks."

"You can see that okay?" asked Respert.

Bluey nodded. "There is a little light left. And the fire is bright enough."

Respert ran to draw the circle.

Laban wiped his hands on his pants. His mouth turned dry. He wondered if Bluey felt the nerves as bad as he did. He thought about his pa, then remembered Miss Brennan. He rubbed his forehead. Best not to think of nobody right now.

Respert yelled, "It's done," and then ran back and made a line in the ground with his toe. "Behind this here line," he said. "Flip a coin to see who goes first. Bluey calls it."

Laban and Bluey nodded, and Respert tossed a quarter into the air.

"Tails," Bluey said.

"Tails it is!" yelled Respert. "Let's do her."

Bluey turned to Laban. "You bring me the deed the day your pa dies."

"I'm gone enjoy buying a new set of clothes with your money," said Laban. "Good clothes too, from Asheville, maybe."

His knife in hand, Bluey walked toward the line.

Less than a hundred yards down the trail, Mikey and Conduff glanced knowingly at each other and slowed down their walk.

"That's a looker of a guitar you got there," Mikey said to Luke.

"I . . . I . . . like to p-p-play it," Luke said.

From behind Luke, Conduff raised his pistol and cracked Luke on the head. He fell in a heap. Mikey caught him before he hit the path, dragged him behind a thicket of laurel, and dropped him to the ground. Then he rushed back up the trail toward the campfire. Twenty seconds later he and Conduff took up positions behind the rocks that hid Bluey's still. Mikey held his breath as he peeked out.

Not more than seventy-five feet away, he saw Bluey, knife in hand, his feet square. Bluey slowly took aim and then whipped the knife through the air. It split a dead center cut into the carved circle on the tree.

"I don't believe it!" shouted Respert. "He stuck it in the heart!"

Bluey and Laban ran to the tree to check. Bluey laughed when he saw his knife in the middle of the circle.

Respert jerked out the knife and faced Laban. "You got your work cut out for you, cousin," he said. "All you can do is match him and make him throw her again."

Knife in hand, Laban moved to the line and toed it. He balanced his knife in his fingers. "Bluey got lucky," he said. "The both of you just steady your eye on this."

Watching him, it was all Mikey could do not to cackle with glee. He had no doubt that Laban's hands were all clammy. The man's voice sounded thin, in spite of his bold talk. Mikey knew that since Bluey's earlier throws had hit more than a touch off center, this third one had surprised Laban quite a bit.

He glanced at Conduff, his grin wide. Bluey was pulling the oldest gambling trick in the book. Draw Laban in by making two decent but losing throws. Up the wager on each throw yet not so much as to scare him off. Since Laban had won twice already, he just knew he could win again. But then, when the stakes have been raised to the breaking point, Bluey ups and throws his knife like nobody's business.

Mikey licked his lips as Laban tensed for his throw. He knew that Laban had to finish the wager no matter how low-down Bluey's methods. No way could he back out now and still keep any kind of respectable name on the mountain.

Laban raised the knife to a position behind his right ear, closed his right eye, and took a deep breath. Mikey slipped his pistol out of his waistband, finger on the trigger.

Laban reared back, then whipped his hand forward. The knife was almost out of his hand when Mikey fired his pistol. Laban's hand twitched just a mite at the sound.

When Laban heard the pistol shot he thought instantly of Luke. Then the knife left his hand. He ducked and rolled to the ground away from the sound of the gun. Had Mikey and Conduff shot Luke and left him dead in the woods? Were they coming back now to kill him too?"

"Bluey wins her!" Respert shouted. "Laban's throw a inch too high!" Mikey and Conduff rushed out from behind the rocks.

"Where is Luke?" demanded Laban as he scrambled to his feet and ran over to them, his mind forgetting the wager to worry over his brother.

"He's fine," laughed Mikey. "A lump on his head, I suspect. But nothin' to harm him too long."

Laban didn't know whether to believe him or not. "Luke!" he shouted. "You all right?" No answer came. Laban stood by the fire, unsure what to do.

Mikey and Conduff slapped Bluey on the back. All of them laughed at their exploits. Bluey took a large swig from a jug that Mikey handed him and made his way to Laban.

Laban's hands started shaking as he realized what he had done.

"You keep a close eye on that land deed," Bluey said with a smirk. "Maybe your pa is not long for this world."

Laban threw a punch at his face. It landed hard and something cracked. Bluey's nose started bleeding as he stumbled back and fell down.

Mikey pointed his pistol at Laban's chest. "Back yourself away," he said. "I don't prefer to shoot you, but if you turn fractious on me, then it's a true case of self-defense. Maybe we will finish off your half-wit brother too."

"You cheated!" Laban snarled at Bluey, who was still on the ground holding his nose. "Respert knows it."

"I stumbled," said Mikey, grinning. "The gun went off by accident. You missed your throw. Must be the Lord's will."

Picking himself up, Bluey went to Respert and slapped him on the back. "You see this fair and square here?" he asked.

Respert shrugged. "Two men throw a knife," he said. "One man hits a bull's-eye, the other man misses a inch off. That is all I can judge."

Bluey patted him again. "Respert is a fair man," he said to Laban.

"Gutless but fair, everybody will tell you that Respert is both."

His desire to fight struggling with his concern for Luke, Laban knew that Bluey had him. In the highlands, people didn't cotton to excuses when it came to a wager. A man made a bet and lost, nobody asked how it happened. The man covered his loss or he got shot. No questions, no excuses.

"Okay," Laban said, his shoulders slumped. "You bested me. But you cheated and you know it."

Bluey took another shot of liquor. "You take care of my property," he said. "I'll stop by from time to time to make sure you do."

Although furious, Laban picked up his jug, took a snort of liquor to calm his nerves, and walked out of the camp. A few minutes later he found Luke in the laurel. After checking his head for damage, he sat down and laid his brother's head in his lap and stared up at the sky. He felt lower than a skunk's belly and knew he'd come to his end. Letting his pride and greed take the upper hand, he had gambled away his family's only valuable. For several long minutes he mulled over the notion of just taking his pistol from Luke and ending it all right there, putting himself out of his misery, stop shaming his family with his wayward deeds. But then he knew he didn't deserve such an easy end. To take his own life meant that his family would have to bear his shame. They would have to lower their heads in embarrassment when they passed people on the street. Truth was that was what *he* deserved, not them.

Laban hung his head. So long as he lived, he could keep that shame off his kin. So long as he lived, everybody would point to him, not his family. They'd whisper behind his back and laugh at his foolishness. Nobody but him deserved such a fate.

As the night pushed on, Laban stayed by the trail, holding Luke's head. Tears pushed up in his head but he refused to let them free to do their cleansing. He knew what he had to do. He had to live and wear the shame. That was the punishment he deserved. To take his own life would make it too easy.

CHAPTER
ELEVEN

Three days later, just before supper, Abby picked a stick off the ground and tossed it in the direction of the smokehouse. Sandy, her teeth showing as if in a smile, darted after the stick, grabbed it up with her tongue, and scooted back to Abby with her feet tossing up dust. Taking the stick from Sandy, Abby threw it again. Sandy fetched it again. Then hearing horses coming, Abby lifted her head toward the trail that led to the creek. Sandy rushed back and stood at Abby's side, her head even with Abby's waist. Sandy's lips curled back as she dropped the stick. But this time she wasn't smiling. Sandy growled.

A man wearing a slouchy black hat and mounted on a stout brown horse suddenly broke out of the overgrowth that covered the trail just past where Abby's pa had cleared it. Sandy snarled, then started barking. The man on the horse thundered closer. Four others followed him, each in floppy hats, each stirring up dust as they prodded their animals ahead. Sandy stood in front of Abby, the dog's ears laid flat, her barking loud enough to wake the dead.

The men looked mean. Abby yelled and started running toward the cabin. The horses drew closer. Abby reached the porch and hollered, "Pa!

Horses coming!" She ran inside and saw her pa peering out the window.

"Grab the shotguns, boys!" he shouted. "Trouble approaching!"

Everything moved in a whirl. Laban and Luke grabbed the shotguns that always stood by the door. Elsa appeared, wiping her hands on her apron. Solomon ran out to the porch, his gun ready. Behind him hurried his sons, each one equally armed. Solomon twisted to Abby and Elsa and ordered, "Stay inside!"

Abby rushed into Elsa's apron, buried her face in it. Elsa had Solomon Jr. on her hip. Abby twisted about and edged to the door, Elsa beside her. Abby peeked around the corner. The horsemen had come to a halt and arranged themselves, still mounted, in a line in front of the porch. Sandy stood by Solomon, and Abby's brothers were on either side of him. They held their shotguns at shoulder level, pointed at the horsemen.

"State your business, Hal Clack!" called Solomon. "Then take your leave from my land."

Clack grinned and tipped his hat, as happy as a man eating ham on a hot biscuit.

Abby held her breath. Hal Clack was Elsa's pa. What did he want? She looked at the other men, hoping they could give her a clue. Three of them looked like Hal Clack. The fourth one did not. She recognized him as the sheriff from down in Blue Springs. She had met him at Jesus Holiness once. Sheriff Rucker was his name.

"Ain't got all the night for waiting," Solomon said.

"Ain't you gone ask me to climb down?" said Clack, spitting tobacco juice to a spot near Solomon's feet. "Invite me to come in to set a spell?"

Abby thought that Mr. Clack had made a reasonable request even if on such short notice. Mountain people like her pa usually acted real hospitable to visitors.

"You and I got nothin' to say to each other," said Solomon. "So I reckon I won't be inviting you in this time."

Abby could tell her pa didn't like Hal Clack. She wondered why. But then she looked at Clack real close. He had a scrubby beard, and his clothes looked all slept in. And he kept spitting tobacco juice near her pa's boots. She wrinkled her nose. Though too far from him to tell for positive, she had a sure suspicion that Hal Clack did not smell good.

Clack shifted in his saddle, looked at the four men who had rode in with him, then shook his head and spat once more. When he spoke again, his voice had turned even meaner. Abby decided she didn't like him any more than her pa did.

"I come to claim what's mine," Clack said. "Brought the sheriff with me."

Solomon lowered his shotgun but only a touch. "What you meaning?" he asked.

Clack indicated Laban. "Ask your eldest," he said. "Reckon he knows what I mean."

Solomon faced Laban. Abby saw the question in his face. She eased away from Elsa, squatted at the side of the door so she could see Laban better. He looked awful, even worse than in the last few days. And that was bad enough. She'd figured that he had turned so grievous because Miss Brennan had put away his proposal in favor of the man in Charlotte. But what did that have to do with Hal Clack?

"What you got to do with what Clack is saying?" Solomon asked Laban.

Laban studied the ground near his bare feet, not saying anything.

"Tell it out, boy," Solomon demanded.

Laban took a heavy breath. "Guess he is talking about a wager I lost," he said.

"You owe this man money?" asked Solomon. "What have I told you—"

"Ain't money he owes me!" interrupted Clack. "More than that."

"Tell me straight out!" Solomon said, his eyes flashing anger now. "Laban, what is he saying?"

Laban sagged down onto the porch and laid his shotgun on his knees. He stared into the dirt, and Abby saw his shoulders start shaking. She heard him crying. Her pa knelt over him, his hand on his shoulders. Laban shook his head but said nothing.

Abby heard Sheriff Rucker speak. She looked up at him.

"He wagered your land," said Rucker. "Lost it in a knife toss."

Solomon's spine went stiff. He stood up, faced the sheriff. "Say that again?" he said.

Rucker climbed off his horse, stepped over to Solomon, and squared his shoulders and feet. "Three days ago," he said. "Your boy and Bluey Willers, Hal Clack's nephew by his wife's sister. They were up near Edgar's Knob. Started tossing a knife around . . ."

Rucker told the story. As he talked, Abby eased out the door to the edge of the porch. From there she watched her pa. As Rucker talked, Solomon seemed to shrivel, like bacon frying in hot grease, getting smaller and smaller as the heat burned it up.

"Laban put up your land," Rucker said. "Against two hundred and forty dollars. Bluey outthrew him. Respert saw it. So did a couple of other boys. I got no reason to believe it didn't happen like they said."

Solomon faced Laban. He didn't sound angry when he spoke, just bewildered and sad. "He speaking the truth?" he asked.

"I didn't know Bluey would tell this to Clack," Laban said.

"That don't matter," said Solomon. "Is he telling it true?"

"He said he wouldn't claim it till you died," he said, his eyes still studying the dirt. "Swore it to me."

"But you did make the wager?" Solomon's voice sounded impatient, louder too.

Laban looked up at his pa. Though she'd never seen it until now and didn't know how to label it, Abby saw something empty in Laban, something broken—a jar smashed, all the water spilled out.

"I had done outthrew him twice," he said. "And could do it again, no question . . . But Mikey and Conduff, they shot a pistol. I thought they had hurt Luke . . . thought—"

"You had Luke with you?" interrupted Solomon.

Laban shrugged. "Yeah, I had him with me. He—"

Solomon slapped him then, hand across cheek, flesh against flesh. The shock of it stunned Abby so much it took a few seconds for her tears to come. But then they flooded her eyes, running instantly down her face and onto the front of her dress. She stuck out her tongue and licked up the salty liquid and knew in her heart that things in her family had changed forever.

Solomon hollered at Laban now, his voice hurt and angry and scared all at the same time. "You throw away your own life!" he yelled. "But you want to wreck your brother's too! I won't abide that. He depends on you, trusts you, and you go off and mix him up in your carousin'." He drew back his hand as if to strike again and Laban cringed, but Solomon suddenly caught himself and clenched his fist and slowly lowered it to his side.

Abby could see the strength of will it took for him to pull back the second blow. She both feared him for what he'd done to Laban, yet loved him for not hitting him again.

Laban buried his head in his hands, while Solomon faced Sheriff Rucker. Abby held her hand over her mouth, pushing back her tears so she could hear. Her pa's voice sounded tired, unable to resist whatever it was he knew was coming.

"What you wanting me to do?" he asked.

Rucker sighed, then shook his head. "I don't usually get involved in the settling of wagers," he said. "Not my line of work. But Clack, well you know he—"

Solomon held up a hand, halting Rucker. "I know his family has got Blue Springs all tied up. Nothin' a man in your spot can do."

"I want you off this property," said Hal Clack before the sheriff could answer. "Cleared out with all your cheap belongings. Want you gone by this time tomorrow. Give this place the rest of the summer to air out from the smell of the likes of you."

Abby felt movement from behind, glanced back and saw that Daniel had raised his shotgun. His face was tight, the skin stretched over his cheekbones. His eyes had become narrow slits, and his skin was all red.

"Ain't none of us goin' nowhere!" called Daniel. "But you are leaving right now!" He pulled back the hammer on the shotgun. Clack and his sons tensed. Abby's body shrunk inward.

"Put it down!" Pa yelled, stepping over to Daniel. "I ain't gone have nobody getting kilt over this." He pulled at the gun, but Daniel resisted.

"Give me the gun!" insisted Solomon, his teeth clenched. "I got enough trouble without you making more."

Hanging his head, Daniel relented.

Daniel's shotgun in hand, Solomon faced Rucker again. "If Laban made the wager and lost it, we got no choice but to abide the loss," he said. "No honorable man can do anything other."

The sheriff twisted toward Clack. "Give them a week to get gone," he said. "Fair is fair."

Solomon shook his head. "We will go tomorrow. No use putting it off."

Solomon faced Clack. "You been wanting at me for a long time," he said. "Reckon you are enjoying ever minute of this."

Abby saw movement at the door of the house. Elsa stepped onto the porch, her face a mask of determination. She walked to Solomon and stood at his side. She looked up at her pa with her hand over her eyes, shading against the last of the sun. "You don't have to do this, Pa," she said.

"It ain't because of you," Clack said. "This goes back before you were born."

Elsa tilted her head, obviously not understanding.

"Me and your pa got a long history," Solomon said, his eyes still on Clack. "This is just the most recent outcropping of it."

Elsa nodded, though Abby could see she didn't understand. "What's to become of me and my boys?" Elsa asked.

Clack grunted. "Don't matter to me. I wrote you off when you married up with the likes of this." He indicated Solomon.

For several moments no one spoke. One of the horses snuffled. It suddenly dawned on Abby that this meant her family had to leave her cabin. But where would they go? Where would they live? Her head ached at the problem, and for the first time in her life, real fear came on her—the kind of fear that gnaws at the stomach, like a hunger that can't be satisfied. She wanted to run to her pa and have him assure her that he would take care of her. But she couldn't do that, because he'd never taken the time to assure her of much of anything, so why should she expect him to start now? Abby's tears fell again, harder this time, and she couldn't stop them from coming. She shoved her hand into her mouth and bit down on the meat of it.

"I will hand you the deed tomorrow," Solomon said. "Tomorrow by noon. I will give it to Sheriff Rucker here."

Clack nodded, a crooked smile cutting across his face. "I'll be here to see that you do," he said, turning his horse. "Right here." Clucking to his horse, he kicked his heels and took off his hat and whirled it in the air, then galloped out of the yard, yelling like a banshee on the loose. His boys followed him, their cackling joining in with their pa's.

Abby watched them leave through her tears. Luke and Daniel stood on the porch like statues. Laban remained seated, head down. Elsa and Solomon stayed still in the yard, her arm around his waist. All by herself, Abby felt a loneliness in her chest, a desire to stand by somebody and have them take her in their arms and tell her it would be okay, things would turn out just fine. But she had no one to hold on to, no one to dry her tears and hug her neck. From out of nowhere, a sharp feeling of anger came. Even if they were kin to Mrs. Elsa, she hated Hal Clack and his dirty sons, she decided. They had made her pa hit her brother and were running her off from her house. They had made her feel afraid and alone. They were awful men, and she knew right then and there that she would hate them for the rest of her life.

CHAPTER
TWELVE

The sadness that settled on her family the night after Hal Clack came felt to Abby a lot like the sadness that came after Aunt Francis died. No one talked much, and when they did, they mostly whispered. Everybody's skin seemed to have turned gray, like all the blood had drained out of their bodies. Their faces looked as colorless as a metal washtub.

As she watched her pa sit by himself on the porch long past the time that dark had come, Abby wondered if he had felt any sadder when her ma died. If so, she did not know how he could have stood it.

Laban left after the Clacks rode away. Without taking any provisions or speaking a word to anybody, he just walked down the path in front of the cabin and disappeared in the woods. Abby listened for the splashing of his feet as he crossed Slick Rock Creek, but she heard nothing. Like a puff of smoke from the chimney, he just disappeared into thin air.

Elsa busied herself around the stove, but when she put out the bacon and collards she had cooked for supper nobody paid it much attention. Daniel and Luke walked out to the porch and sat with Pa for a while but then the two of them left him and went out to the barn. A few minutes later, Abby heard the sound of Luke's singing and playing rising up toward the cabin. He chose lonesome sounding tunes.

Not long afterward, Mrs. Elsa put her boys down to bed and then walked out to the porch. She said something to Solomon that Abby couldn't hear, then moved back inside and made herself ready for sleep. Abby followed her example, slipping into a nightgown and crawling into her bed for the night. But sleep didn't come for a long time. Holding the carving of her ma, she kept thinking about what had happened and what it meant for her and her family.

Life sure did play some tricks on a body, she decided. One minute you are skipping around in your yard throwing sticks with your dog with not a care in the world, and the next somebody tells you they own your land and you are as good as gone. Gone where, she did not know, just gone.

Rolling over, she held up the carving so it caught the light from the fireplace. For a moment she studied its smooth lines, ran her fingers over its face. Living and dying was tricky too. One minute a mama is planning what to name the baby about to come, and the next the man who sired that baby and loved that mama is saying his good-bye to her and looking for a place to dig a hole where he can plant a pine box.

Shifting about on her tick mattress, Abby fell to considering the place of the Almighty in such matters. Was all the suffering that came to a body simply the coming to pass of what the good Lord wanted? That is what the Primitives said, the Baptists who shouted and sang out to all that would listen that whatever happened took place because sweet Jesus willed it so. What will be, will be. Nothing to be done but accept whatever comes your way and move on.

Abby sighed. Moving on was hard. Bad things took your breath away, and who can move when you can hardly breathe? Who can just wake up the next day after a great sadness and square their shoulders and head out to the field to plow?

She wondered if her pa had moved on from her ma's death. He had married again. But all mountain men who could find a wife did that. But what did he feel? Did he still miss her ma? Did he ever think of her? Did he accept her dying as the result of God's desire?

Unsettled by the notion, Abby decided to lay her questions aside for the time being. Deal with such things after she growed up some, she told herself. After she got more of a grip on matters pertaining to sweet Jesus.

Yawning, Abby set her carving on the table beside her bed and concluded that about the only good thing that had come from pondering such weighty thoughts was that it had made her sleepy. Glad for the weary feeling, she closed her eyes. But then she heard her pa come through the front door and make his way to his bedroom. Wide awake again, Abby sat up and eased over to the ladder that led down from the loft. For several seconds she just sat there, wondering what to do. She heard her pa close the door to his room. Without thinking, she did something she would never have considered on any normal night. Maybe it was because she wanted to feel close to somebody on the last night she lived in her family's cabin. Or maybe she wanted to see if she could hear her pa tell Elsa where they would go the next day. She didn't know for sure why she did it. But she climbed down the ladder and tiptoed to the door of the room where her pa and Mrs. Elsa slept.

Sitting down by the door, she leaned her ear as close as possible to it. For a couple of minutes she heard no sound. Waiting, she suddenly realized where she was. What would her pa do if he found her listening in on him and Mrs. Elsa? Ashamed, she almost stood up to go back to bed. But then she heard a voice, and she forgot all her misgivings. She leaned close to the door again. She heard Elsa talking.

"What are we going to do?" she asked.

Abby heard fear in her words. Solomon didn't answer right away. Abby wondered if he would. Finally he spoke.

"I'm studyin' on it," he said.

Silence came again to the room. Then Elsa said, "I can go talk to Pa. He'll let us stay here, he'll listen to me, I know he will. No matter how hard against me he sounded today."

"I won't abide you begging your pa for nothin'," said Solomon. "I am a poor and ignorant man, but I still got my pride."

"Then what's your notion?" Elsa asked. "Easy enough to say I can't talk to Pa but not so easy figure out anything better."

Abby heard the challenge in her words.

"I got it figured this way," said Solomon. "I got a brother—"

"I am not going to live with your brother!" interrupted Elsa. "That place of his has dirt floors, and his wife hates me. And they have no room for us, you know that."

Abby thought of her uncle Pierce. He had a bad hip from the time he broke it falling out of an apple tree when he was a boy. That bad hip kept him from doing much hard labor. His corn was poorly kept, and he didn't have the handiness with a trade like her pa. He and his wife Erline had four kids, two of them already moved out, one about Daniel's age and one a year younger than her. Compared to Pierce and Erline Porter, her family was right wealthy. No way could Uncle Pierce provide shelter and keep for all of them. For once, Abby found herself siding with Elsa.

Abby heard feet touch the floor, and she jumped away from the door and was about to run back to her bed. But when the feet didn't move, she paused and listened again. Maybe Pa had just sat up. Maybe he had his head in his hands like he sometimes did when he had hard thinking to do. She could see him that way now and she wanted to run through the door and hug his shoulders and tell him she trusted him to take care of things. He had always provided for them; no reason to think he would do anything less now. Yeah, life had hit him with some hard blows, but he had always stood up to them, always reset his hat, said his prayers, steadied himself, and put his hand back to the task of living. Though he didn't say much to her or hold her close like she wanted, she still knew she could count on her pa.

Closing her eyes, Abby held her palms together under her chin and tried to pray like she figured Pa would. As she prayed, she set her mind on the framed picture of Jesus that hung behind the pulpit down at Jesus Holiness, the only decoration in the place. She liked that picture—the long brown hair, the hazel eyes, the sunlight breaking in on Jesus' face.

"Jesus," she started, her voice a whisper. "I pray that you will lift off some of the burden that weighs down on my pa's shoulders. Tell him what he needs to do to care for his kin. Hang on with him now, and don't leave him on his lonesome in such a tight spot."

Abby thought of Laban. "And another thing, Jesus," she said. "About Laban. Wherever he is and whatever he is doing, don't let him go off and do anything any more foolish than what he has already done. Keep him—"

Hearing her pa talking again, Abby opened her eyes and forgot her praying.

"You ain't going with me to Pierce's place," Solomon said. "You nor our baby boys neither."

Abby caught her breath. What did Pa mean?

"You're going to your ma's place."

Abby breathed again but a frown came to her face. She knew that Elsa's ma lived by herself down in Blue Springs. Hal Clack didn't go there very often. But what did Pa mean when he said Mrs. Elsa and her boys would go there?

"I thought you didn't want me talking to Pa," said Elsa.

"You don't talk to him. You just go to your ma's. He ain't there most of the time anyway."

"And you go to your brother's? Split up the family?" Abby heard sadness creeping into Elsa's words. Maybe a touch of a challenge too.

"Won't be forever. Give me until fall and I will get us some kind of cabin built. Then everybody will come under one roof again."

"But why don't you just come to Ma's with me? Pa won't care. He just wants to best you, we both know that. You having to live there would please him."

"You know I can't do that," said Solomon. "Can't live that close to a town. In a house all boarded up like that, with glass winders and all. I would go plumb loco in a week. Besides, I won't live in no house owned by Hal Clack."

Silence fell in the room again. Abby wondered if they had stopped talking for the night. She curled her toes under her nightgown, rubbed her eyes.

"Your pride is a powerful thing," said Elsa.

"Sometimes it is all a man has got left," he said.

Abby felt like crying. But Elsa's next question cut off her tears.

"What about your kids? Where are they staying?"

For a long time, Solomon didn't answer. Abby again held her breath. She thought surely she must be turning blue in the face. Then Solomon said, "I'll take Daniel and Luke with me. You gone have to keep Abby."

The words hit Abby like somebody had clubbed her with the limb off a hickory tree. Her pa didn't want her! He was casting her out of the family, sending her to live somewhere she had never seen with a woman not her ma, a woman so busy with her own children she had no time nor love for anyone else. Now the tears did come, a flood of salty wet down her cheeks and over her chin. She knew her pa had always kept his space from her, but she still thought he loved her, still thought he claimed her as one of his own, even if she wasn't a boy, even if she was the baby who had come the night her ma had died. After all, he had made the carving for her, the doll that looked like her and her ma. But now this latest thing showed that she was wrong, he did not love her, did not want her in the family with him.

Solomon kept talking, but Abby barely heard him.

"Piney Gap is no kind of place for her. What if things happen to drag on longer than I planned? There ain't no school up there and it's too far for her to come down to Blue Springs every day. And she loves her schooling, you know that."

No longer listening, Abby pulled herself off the floor and ran back to her bed. Pulling her blanket over her head, she shivered in the dark. She wanted to cry but refused to do it, and her body shook even as she fell asleep. As the night moved on, she finally stopped quivering. But her sleep was troubled and filled with dreams that made her sadder than she ever imagined a person could be.

The sun had not come up when Daniel awoke. For several minutes he just lay in place on his mattress and wondered if he had dreamed the bad things swirling around in his head. He looked over and saw Luke beside him, his body peaceful. Beside Luke was an empty mattress, and Daniel knew then that he hadn't dreamed the awful things from yesterday.

Standing, he pulled on a shirt and overalls over his long johns and quietly made his way to the porch to watch the sun come up on the last day he would have in this cabin. In the rocker he hugged his arms to his chest and looked at the sky. The stars twinkled down on him as if nothing had happened. His body quivered as he thought of Clack's visit and the news he had brought. He could still feel the hard stock of his shotgun on his shoulder, the cool of the steel barrel, the roundness of the trigger that he had touched with his index finger. He wondered what he would have done had his pa not stopped him from his intentions. Would he have shot one of the Clacks? He had no doubt of it. But how many could he have killed afore one of them put a shot into his chest or head? The answer to that he did not know. And what would it feel like to shoot at a man? To point a gun at human flesh and squeeze off the trigger?

Standing from the rocker and moving to the edge of the porch, he concluded that he had no answer to such things. All he knew was that Hal Clack had come to take something that belonged to his family and that such a transgression had made him so fierce he would've shot at every one of them until they shot back and killed him dead.

Mystified by his feelings, he walked into the yard. Without thinking about it, his feet took him out behind the house, headed him up the incline toward the ridge beyond the pasture. His bare feet toed the earth as he walked, and he decided that a man ought always to hold a solid acquaintance with the dirt. A man ought to know how it smelled as rain wet it down at the end of a summer day; how it felt as it rolled between the fingers when you broke up a clod; how you could plant corn seed in it and make a crop at summer's end.

Daniel stuck his hands into the pockets of his overalls. Laban had lost their land for them, Pa's land and his. Daniel's hands balled into fists. Laban had no virtue, he decided. None at all to do such a thing, to hurt his pa in such a way, to take from him the only thing next to Jesus and family that meant anything at all.

As if drawn by a magnet, Daniel moved farther up the incline, his steps faster as he let his anger at Laban take greater hold. *How could a body make such a mistake?* he wondered. *What got into the man? Was it the drink?*

Daniel had tried the doublings a few times—all boys his age had done it. But the stuff burned his throat like a hot coal going down and he hadn't taken to it. Why did Laban like it so well?

He decided it was just another thing he did not know and could not fathom. But right then and there he vowed he wouldn't do the doublings and bring ruination to his life as Laban had brought to his.

Breathing harder as he reached the top of the ridge, Daniel saw that he'd moved to the twin oaks that sheltered the graves of his ma, his aunt, and the brother he never knew. His head down, he walked toward the wood crosses that marked their spots. When he stepped past the biggest of the oaks, he saw his pa standing between the two graves, his hat off and held at his waist.

Not wanting to bother his pa, Daniel turned to walk away. But Solomon had already heard him.

"Hey," said Solomon. "Just making a last visit."

"I'll leave you be," Daniel said.

"No . . . stay on. I been here a spell already." He put on his hat, hunkered down by the graves. "I am gone miss this place," he said, a hand patting the ground that covered his wife's body.

Daniel held his breath. The moment felt scary. For some reason it brought to mind the times down at Jesus Holiness when Luke sang one of the old songs, his sweet tenor reaching out so pure that it seemed to reach heaven itself, a tone that not only reached heaven but extended an invitation once it got there—an invitation to move on back down to earth with the music and wash down on everybody blessed enough to hear it.

Solomon patted Rose's grave again. "Elsa is a good woman," he said. "Fine looking too." He glanced up at Daniel as if expecting a response.

"That she is," said Daniel.

Solomon nodded. "I got no complaints with her."

Silence came again. Daniel knew it wasn't his place to add anything.

Solomon patted the grave once more, then stood up and repeated, "I am sure gone miss this place. I come up here from time to time, you know. It is a peaceful spot."

Daniel heard the shaking in his pa's voice, and he knew that his pa wasn't just talking about the land. More than anything else he would miss coming up to the ridge, sitting down on the ground and talking to his dead wife when things took on a dark turn. He moved to Solomon's side, put a hand on his shoulder. But then his pa turned away, and his shoulders firmed up. Daniel knew that Solomon felt ashamed of his needing to cry. Daniel didn't know what to say. Solomon had said more than once that "Crying never did nobody any good," and such a saying could trap a man at a time like this. He stayed quiet as his pa fought off what his heart wanted to do, as he pushed back the pain of leaving the land.

After a couple of minutes, Solomon faced Daniel. "We got to stay strong today," he said. "Strong for everybody."

Daniel nodded his agreement. Inside his head, though, he wanted to let his pa know that it wasn't a sin to show emotion, not a sin to show that a matter like this hurt deep, hurt like a knife wound stuck full in the back. But he had no words for such a thought and so he did not say them.

Solomon started walking back toward the cabin. Daniel hurried after him, his heart pounding. He had to say something, couldn't let Pa just walk away from Ma's grave and never hope to see it again. Before he knew what he wanted to say, he grabbed Solomon by the shoulder and spun him around. Solomon looked at him with wide eyes.

"I . . . I . . ." Daniel sputtered.

"What you want to say?" asked Solomon.

Unable to hold it back any longer, Daniel blurted out what he'd been thinking ever since Clack and his boys had rode off their property. "I will get our land back," he whispered.

Solomon nodded his head, but Daniel could see he had no conviction in it.

"I mean it!" he said, his teeth clenched in the effort to give his pa some hope. "I will find a way to claim back what belongs to us, to you . . . to you and . . ." he pointed back at the grave. "To you and Ma and all of us."

Solomon laid a hand on his shoulder. "We will do okay," he said. "The Lord will not leave us."

"I will get back the land," Daniel said again, his body now shaking with the pressure of tears as he realized what he'd just said. "As Jesus is my witness . . . I make you that promise."

Solomon pulled him close. For several long minutes the two of them stood that way, Daniel's head resting on his pa's shoulder. "We will . . . will come back to . . . to Ma's grave. . . ." sobbed Daniel. "As God is my witness . . ."

When Abby woke up that morning, she made her way down the ladder with heavy steps. At breakfast she ate a cold biscuit covered with molasses and drank her buttermilk without speaking. Everyone else did the same. When they had finished, her pa stood at the head of the table and rapped his knuckles on the wood. Everybody came to attention.

"Here is the way it is," Solomon said. "We have come to a bad patch of the trail, no two ways to look at it. Life is gone be hard for a while. But we got to move on, do the best we can." He stopped and stared around the table. Everybody hung their heads.

Solomon started up again. "I have made a hard decision," he said. "But there ain't no easy ones to be had."

He took a heavy breath. "Daniel and Luke will come with me to my brother Pierce's place. I am sure he will take us in. We will start us up a cabin." He turned to Abby. She gripped the table with both hands. Solomon said, "Elsa will take Abigail and the two babies to Blue Springs to stay with her ma. In a few months, God willing, we will get enough of a cabin built for us all to come together as one family again."

Abby studied the crumbs that had fallen from her biscuit onto the table. For a long time no one said anything. Abby waited for Daniel or Luke to stand up to Pa, to tell him he could not send her away like this, couldn't send her to live in a town with Hal Clack's wife. She was a highlander girl, born wild and free. The thought of living all stuffed up in a house with a tin roof and glass windows scared her to death. But no one said anything, nobody stood up for her.

"We will do okay," said Daniel, his tone determined. "Build us a cabin, then collect everybody together again."

Abby glanced up. Solomon shrugged. "With enough hard labor a man can overcome most anything," he said. "We got a bad deal but it won't do no good to moan over it. Crying never did nobody no good. All we can do is put our shoulder back to the wheel and trust in the Lord to see us through the low places."

"W-w-we will m-make do," said Luke. "Yes, sir, w-we will make d-d-do."

"We will come back here someday," Daniel said, his eyes wet. "Find a way to reclaim what is ours. Get rid of Clack and his kin and move right back in this old place."

Solomon breathed big again, then nodded. "Okay, let's get loaded. And remember to keep your dignity. Don't give Clack no cause to think he has beat us down."

As they stood from the table, Daniel tried to put his arm around Abby, but she pushed him away and ran up to the loft and sat down on her mattress. But she didn't cry this time. Pa had it right, she decided. Crying never did nobody no good. Her heart turned bitter, as cold as the ice that gathered at the edges of the spring in January. Since last night she had come to the conclusion that she was truly all alone in the world, and that realization had driven her to the decision that if her pa didn't want her, then she didn't want him either—him or her brothers or anybody else. From now on, she would take care of herself. She felt like she'd been doing that pretty much since the day she was born anyway.

Moving slowly but steadily, Abby left her mattress and started to pack her few belongings. Her nightshirt, two pairs of overalls, two dresses, three cotton blouses, and two pairs of shoes—one brown brogans, one black for church. And a few odds and ends to comb and brush her hair. When she picked up the carving of her ma, she stood and held it for several seconds. One part of her wanted to break it in half and leave it behind. Leave it behind like her pa was leaving her behind, she figured. Leave it and never see it again. But another part knew she could not do such a thing no matter how mad she got at her pa, no matter how hurt she was. Without really knowing how she came to it, Abby sensed that to leave the doll behind meant to cut herself off from her pa forever, to break the last chance she had for ever knowing him up close.

She threw the carving into a burlap bag with the rest of her belongings and carried the bag out to the porch. She saw three or four other bags already there and knew that the others had brought their stuff out too. Finished with her clothes, she drifted in and out of the house, first in this spot, next in another, helping for a few minutes, then stopping, helping for a few minutes, then stopping. The work didn't take long. Some cooking pots, an iron skillet, a few wood spoons and forks came from the kitchen. Plus a large knife for cutting up hog meat and such and two smaller ones they used for chickens, rabbits, and squirrels. Helping Elsa, she folded up a few blankets and bedclothes and packed the curtains that Aunt Francis had made for the front room.

Outside again, she saw Daniel bring Bouncer toward the porch. The mule was already sagging in the middle from the tools from the shed: a hoe, some blacksmithing tools, the saws Solomon used to cut wood, the ax, the post-hole digger, along with the small plow that made the hillside ready for corn and tobacco.

Before Abby knew it, almost half the day had passed. She found herself sitting on the front porch, Sandy at her side, her fingers scratching her ears. Elsa walked to the steps, holding a large basket.

"That belonged to Aunt Francis," said Abby, recognizing the wicker basket.

Elsa nodded. "I been keeping it," she said. "You want to see what's in it?"

Momentarily tempted, Abby started to stand. But then she shook her head. What difference did it make? Just a dead woman's old raggedy stuff. Here today, gone tomorrow. Like everything else. "Guess not," she said.

Elsa hesitated for a second, and Abby thought she might say something else, but instead she shrugged and moved on.

At just past noon, Sheriff Rucker returned with Hal Clack and his sons right behind him, the same high and mighty posture in their shoulders that they wore the day previous, the same look of open pleasure on their unshaven faces. To Abby it seemed that even their horses pranced, all puffed up with their triumph.

While she and her family finished loading, Clack and his sons waited under the trees by the shed. From time to time they took a swig off a jug that they passed around, and every now and again they laughed like somebody had told the world's funniest story.

Daniel and Luke led the cow from the barn. Pa placed a box full of chickens on a sled sitting by Bouncer. They would have to come back for the hogs. Sandy and the other dogs gathered in a group on the porch, their tails wagging at all the commotion.

"That is about all of it," said Daniel to Solomon. "Loaded and ready to go."

Everybody moved to the porch. Hal Clack and his boys made their way over, the jug in Clack's hand now, his steps unsteady. Abby figured he must be almost drunk. Sheriff Rucker waited by the porch, his head down.

"I will see that deed now," hollered Clack. "In the palm of my hand."

Solomon stepped inside the cabin, returned a few moments later with a worn leather pouch. Opening it, he brought out the deed to his land, a piece of parchment paper he had kept under his mattress. For just a second he held the paper in his fingers. Abby thought he trembled just a little but, looking around, she realized that no one else had seen it. Pa handed the deed to Rucker, who then gave it to Clack.

Clack turned to Elsa and said, "You and your boys can come home with me if you want. Just walk away from this man and come back where you belong."

At first Abby thought she saw Elsa hesitate, but then she took Solomon's hand. "I am staying with my husband," she said.

Abby liked the way she spoke out so strong. Maybe living with her would not turn out so bad.

Clack took a swig from his jug. "Suit yourself." He faced Solomon again. "You get all your trash out?" he asked.

"We got our personables," Solomon replied.

A grin crossed Clack's face. "I been hating you a long time, Solomon Porter," he said.

"I know that," said Solomon.

"Ever since you took Rose from me."

Abby grabbed a porch post at the mention of her ma's name.

"I did not take her from nobody," Solomon said, his tone indicating he had heard all this already.

"My pa and hers had already made the arrangements," said Clack. "Fair and square. She was set to marry me. My pa would give her old man four new horses and all the gear to match."

Abby gulped. Had her ma and Hal Clack ever courted? Was it true that Rose had been promised to him? Was that why he hated her family so much?

"I reckon Rose had other ideas," said Solomon. "Me too."

Clack swallowed from the jug, took a step closer to Solomon. The two men stood nose to nose. Abby thought they might come to blows.

"You sayin' she married you for love?" asked Clack.

"No other cause. I had little else to offer."

Clack suddenly looked at Abby. She dropped her eyes, then slowly raised them again. Clack stepped toward her, now stood only inches away. She smelled his breath. It smelled sour and sharp, whiskey mixed with foul food. She wanted to throw up.

"Your ma is dead," he said as if she did not know it. "You mighty near just like her."

Abby dropped her eyes as Clack's hand touched her chin. With his fists clenched, Pa stepped toward her. But Sheriff Rucker moved between the two men, and Clack dropped his hands to his side. Her pa stopped moving.

Clack's voice was soft when he spoke. "You got the same hair as her," he said. "The same mouth and cheekbones, same . . . same everything."

Abby felt everyone staring at her and Hal Clack. She felt like she ought to say something but didn't know anything to say.

Clack stepped closer still, his mouth now only an inch from Abby's ear. "I . . . I loved your ma too," he whispered, his voice so low no one but Abby could hear. "But your pa took her from me, cheated me. I swore then I would repay him someday . . . make him sorry he—"

As if suddenly coming to consciousness, Clack stopped talking. His eyes blinked, and he looked around as if he didn't know where he was.

He rubbed his chin and then faced Solomon again, pointed at him. "You killed Rose!" Clack shouted. "Making her live out here, dirt poor, delivering her babies without no doctor. If she had married me, she would still be living, still be . . ." He started walking toward Solomon, and Abby could see that something had tipped over in him, something had become meaner than she thought a man could be. Close to Solomon's face, Clack stopped and screamed, "You took her and married her and now she is dead, and I have come today to wreak my payment from you!"

Solomon stood his ground, his face a mask. But Abby couldn't help but wonder if maybe he half agreed with Clack, if somewhere deep down he was nodding his acceptance of the awful truth of his worst enemy's words. Maybe her ma would be living today if she and Pa hadn't married, if she had chosen Clack over him, if . . .

Abby shook her head against the thought. She would not exist if that had happened. Yet Rose would still be living, and which was the better of the two? She tried to figure out the thing, but found it past her mind to do so. She gave her attention to Clack again as he stepped back from her pa, his face black as night, his eyes vacant with anger. Abby knew without him saying anything else that Clack had decided to do something awful, something no man ought to do to another.

Clack turned to his boy Topper. A wicked grin lit up the boy's face. Abby could see that they had already planned their next deed. The rest of Clack's boys stepped to their pa like a pack of wolves about to close in on a helpless calf. Clack faced Solomon again. The two men locked stares, neither of them blinking.

"Burn it down," said Clack, waving his hand over the house and property. "Burn it all down."

Topper took a match from his pocket and looked over at his brother Ben. From a pouch on his saddle Ben pulled out a rag. Topper struck the match and touched it to the rag. The rag lit up fast, and Abby could see that they had put kerosene on it before they came. Riding his horse up to the porch, Ben tossed the rag through the front door.

SECTION II

Summer 1908–Fall 1918

CHAPTER
THIRTEEN

All through that summer Abby had nightmares about the day the Clacks rode in on horses to burn down her family's cabin. She saw the flames licking at the heels of the house, barn, fences, everything that would hold heat. She tried to twist her head and not watch but didn't have the strength to turn away. Only when the flames had burned everything to ashes did she wake up.

The days in Blue Springs were not much happier for her than her nightmares. The hours passed slowly. She kept expecting her pa to come fetch her. When she wasn't helping Mrs. Elsa with Solomon Jr. or Walter, she sat on the steps on the front of Amelia Clack's white house and stared down the one-lane dirt road that fronted it. She expected to see Daniel leading Bouncer around the curve at any second, her pa right behind them. But nobody ever came.

So Abby waited on the steps some more and hugged her knees to her chest and cast mournful eyes to the sky. But she did not cry. Having taken her pa's words about tears to heart, she had kept her eyes dry and her mind as firm as cherrywood.

Pa and the boys didn't even come down to Jesus Holiness that summer. Too much work up at Uncle Pierce's place, Abby figured. Cutting trees, hacking off the branches, hauling them to a clearing, stacking them on top of each other to form the walls to a new cabin, chinking the walls with moss and mud. Though she had never built a house, she spent a good smart of time through July and August thinking how a body might do it. First they would find a spot level enough to put a house. That spot would sit as near to a spring as possible. Then they would cut down all the trees on the spot, chop off all the underbrush, and clear the ground of stumps and loose dirt. Finished with that, they would next put four stone pillars where the corners of the house would go. A floor of smoothed logs would sit on the pillars, and the walls would go up from the floor. When they had finished the walls, they would place the roof on, a peaked top probably made of cedar shingles. All of it chinked solid to keep out the worst of the wind and rain. Her pa would build a solid house, she knew that, even though it might not look real fancy.

The Clack house was totally different from this. Made of planks smoother than any she had seen before, probably from down in Asheville, she figured. The walls in the rooms didn't even have cracks in them, the floors neither. The wood on the floors was as even as those on the walls and had been painted with dark varnish. The house had six big rooms, three of them for beds, a separate kitchen, and a parlor room with store-bought furniture. The inside and outside of the house were painted a shiny white, and the windows—made of real glass—had curtains of different colors in each room. The curtains in the room they gave her were as blue as the sky and matched the covering on her bed.

Abby knew she ought to feel grateful that she got to live in the nice house. She had her own room with a bed, dresser, night table and kerosene lamp. Although she still had to go to an outdoor privy, she had a metal chamber pot for night use, and a water basin for washing her hands and face sat on her dresser. Most folks would feel like a queen staying where she lived. But it wasn't home and never would be. She missed the sound of the wind as it whistled through the walls right before a storm, the *drip, drip, drip* of the water falling through the roof where the chinking sometimes wore out, and the dogs barking as they chased some critter in the night.

As August rolled through, Abby let her mind imagine the new place her pa was building. It would no doubt look a lot like the old cabin, only fresher, the smell of the new wood still hanging in the air, not yet covered with the aromas of a family living within its walls. With that picture firm in her head she awoke every morning, thinking that day her pa would show up. Then she would hug Mrs. Elsa tight and tell her to pack up, the time to go had come. But August passed, and Solomon never showed. Abby tried to convince herself it did not matter. She had pretty much made it on her own so far, so she could keep right on doing that.

For the most part, she stayed out of the way of Mrs. Elsa and Mrs. Clack. Neither of them seemed to mind her being around. So long as she didn't say much, did the chores they gave her, and didn't break anything, they left her to her own doings.

From time to time Abby caught Mrs. Clack watching her from the corner of her eye, almost as if she had some curiosity about what kind of child she might be. But Abby could never tell if Mrs. Clack was watching in hopes of catching her in some mischief or because she felt some liking for her.

Of course, Mrs. Clack and Mrs. Elsa both had their hands full. With Solomon Jr. four now and Walter two, the women had plenty of chores to do to keep up with the boys and the house. Washing diapers, scrubbing walls and floors, cooking meals, making beds, and whatnot made for more than enough toil for any two people. To make it worse, especially on Mrs. Elsa, Solomon Jr. had taken sick since the day Clack had burned down their cabin. The day they moved into Mrs. Clack's house, Junior took a cough to his chest and started sniffling at the nose something awful. Leaving most of his food on his plate at meals and running a fever off and on all summer, he soon became a puny boy without much warning to anybody.

Abby could see that Junior's illness was taking a toll on Mrs. Elsa. She had brought in Doc Booth only a few days after Junior came up sick.

"Must be the heat," Mrs. Elsa said as the doctor checked Junior over. "Everybody knows it's hotter down here than up in the hollers."

"Or the water," said the doctor, closing his black bag. "Some babies born in the high parts of the mountain don't take to the water here in town."

"It's been raining a lot too," Mrs. Clack added. "Sometimes when things get all moldy, a body takes to coughing."

"Give him this morning and night," Booth said as he handed Elsa a bottle of dark liquid. "See how he takes to it."

Elsa nodded, lifted Junior to her hip.

"Maybe he will just grow right out of it," said Mrs. Clack. "Whatever it is."

Abby studied Mrs. Clack. A thin woman, she seemed almost weightless, her body like an ear of corn that somebody had shucked, leaving only the husk behind. Her face was white as flour, and her dresses hung on her like empty sacks. When she spoke she tended to cover her mouth with her hands, as though hiding the fact that it was she doing the talking. She started a lot of her sentences with *maybe*, giving the person listening the idea she didn't want to say anything just flat out as true. For some reason she could not put her finger on, Abby found herself feeling sorry for Mrs. Clack.

Contrary to Mrs. Clack's hopes, Junior didn't grow out of anything, and the medicine seemed to make no difference at all. As the humid summer days went by, he kept on coughing and sniffling. Doc Booth came back a second time and tried out some new medicine on the boy, but the new remedy did no good either, and Junior dropped even more weight. His clothes hung on him real loose, and his hair, usually a shiny black, turned a dull color and lay flat on his head.

Abby tried to play with him from time to time, but he whined a lot and that made it hard for her. After a while she pretty much gave up on the effort. Without Junior to play with, Abby spent even more hours alone.

This didn't mean that she had no friends. Jubal, the short boy from school, had started following Abby around some, and she saw one or two others she knew from the school or from Jesus Holiness. But much to her sadness, most of the kids were too busy in the fields to have much time for playing.

Abby did some chores too. She made her own bed and kept her room neat. Plus, Mrs. Clack kept a small garden behind her house, and Abby hoed and weeded in it without being asked. But the truth of it was the size of the vegetable patch was pretty small and so didn't keep her too busy. Abby ended up with more spare time than she had ever known.

Bored in her idleness, she took to taking long walks around Blue Springs, stepping up and down the few streets all by herself, dropping into the storehouse, the post office, the sheriff's building, the two churches—Jesus Holiness on the north end and One Way Baptist on the south. The churches held services on different Sundays of the month: Jesus Holiness on the first and third, and the Baptists, proud folks of the

Primitive branch, on the second and fourth. Both took the fifth Sunday off. Neither of the churches kept their doors locked, and Abby often walked inside them, her bare feet liking the cool feel of the plank floors. The churches looked a lot alike. The soft light streaming through plain square windows, the hard-backed wood pews, the pulpit in the center at the front. The only difference seemed to be the fact that Jesus Holiness had a picture of Jesus hanging behind the pulpit. Maybe that was why they put the picture there, because the church was named after the man in the picture.

Abby liked the quiet she found in the empty churches, the way her breath slowed down, the way her hands unclenched and her mind drifted upward. Sitting on the hard pews, she often stared up at the top of the buildings and wondered how she had come to such a spot—no ma, no pa, no real home.

Not liking the way such thinking made her feel, she always hopped up fast and ran outside the churches, her jaw gritted against such bad notions. She would not feel sorry for herself, she concluded over and over again, would not allow what Hal Clack had done to get her down.

Somewhere in those summer days running out of the churches, she caught up to the idea of leaving Blue Springs. It came to her all of a sudden, like Sandy, her old dog, darting out from behind the shed. But once she ran onto it, the notion hung close, became a stubborn companion that stuck with her no matter what. She would not stay all alone in Blue Springs forever, she whispered to the sky every time she left Jesus Holiness or One Way Baptist. She would find a way to escape this awful place, to leave the mountains that caused the kinds of heartaches that had come on her.

The days passed slowly. But they did pass. By the end of the summer, Abby had learned about most of the people in Blue Springs, about two hundred folks total, she counted, scattered out within a four- to five-mile area from one end of her snug little valley to the next. Almost all of the houses in the area were made of hand-hewn logs; only the Clack's place and Doc Booth's were made of any kind of shaved wood. On the south end next to the One Way Baptist Church sat the corn mill, the place where Blue Springs Creek cut its widest channel. A blacksmith's shop bordered the mill on the right.

For the most part, Abby avoided going by the schoolhouse that summer. It brought up too many bad memories—images of Laban and Miss

Brennan and all that followed their sad parting.

Abby often wondered about Laban. Was he okay? Had he gone home to Pa yet? Did he even know that Pa and the others had gone to live up to Uncle Pierce's? And what ever happened to Miss Brennan? Did she marry that boy from Charlotte?

Before Abby knew it the days started to grow shorter. Birds flocked up and pointed their beaks southward, their wings flapping overhead as they headed to warmer spots to nest for the winter. As she, Mrs. Elsa, and Mrs. Clack finished up with supper one night at the end of August, Elsa told her that school would be starting in a few weeks.

"I hear you got a new teacher," Elsa said, her hands busy in a bucket of water. "A man this time."

Abby tried to appear like she didn't care. Took a bite from a piece of corn left over from the meal.

"He has two kids," said Elsa. "Twins."

Abby fingered her corn. "Boys or girls?"

"One of each. And they say they are the same age as you."

Abby glanced up in spite of herself. "My age?"

"That's right. From way off near Knoxville, Tennessee."

Abby drank some milk. "Why would anybody come here from Knox-ville?" she asked.

Elsa dipped a plate in the bucket, washed it in soapy water. "The teacher has a ma here," she said. "Came back so his ma could help with his kids."

"What's wrong with his wife?"

Elsa faced her, wiped her hands on her apron. "I hear he is a wid-ower."

Abby spoke without thinking. "Like Pa?"

Elsa raised her eyebrows. "Like your pa used to be," she corrected.

"Sorry," said Abby.

"No offense. I know all this has been hard on you."

Abby shrugged. Mrs. Elsa didn't usually seem to care whether any-thing was hard on her or not. With so much to do with her own boys, she pretty much left Abby to her own self.

"I like school," Abby said.

"The teacher's name is Mr. Holston," said Elsa. "Kids are Lindy and Thaddeus."

A dog barked outside. Abby thought it sounded like Sandy. But Sandy was with Pa. The dog barked again. Though scared to let her hopes loose, Abby jumped up and ran to the window. Her heart pounded at what she saw.

"It's Pa!" she shouted, running to the back door. "Pa and Luke! Sandy too!"

Leaving Elsa, she jumped down the steps and into the yard. Solomon opened his arms and she ran into them. He lifted her up and twirled her around and around. Unaccustomed to such a show of pleasure from her pa, Abby closed her eyes and held to him so hard she thought her fingers might crack. He twirled her some more. Sandy barked and barked. Solomon's hands felt so strong Abby wanted them to hold her forever. She grew dizzy from the spinning. But still she held on. Pa's calluses pressed into the flesh of her wrists, calluses so solid they seemed like rocks. She opened her eyes, and the ground spun around and around. She thought she would sail right off the edge of the earth.

"Glory be, child," panted Solomon. "I am gone fall from the dizzies."

Abby squeezed him harder. But gradually he began to slow. The ground settled some. Abby took a breath, and Solomon let go of her arms. Sandy stopped barking and ran over and licked her hand.

Catching her balance, Abby saw Solomon move to Mrs. Elsa, open his arms, and hug her. For the first time, Abby had the thought that the two really did love each other. A look of confusion crossed her face. Did Pa love Elsa more than he did her ma?

Even if unsure what to call it, Abby felt jealous at the notion, then angry at both her pa and Mrs. Elsa. If Pa loved Mrs. Elsa more than her ma, maybe he loved Solomon Jr. and Walter better than he did her. She twisted a strand of hair in her fingers and wished she had not run to him so eager and all. Abby looked over to Luke. He bowed at the waist and grabbed her up off the ground.

"H-h-how you doing, sister?" he asked. "Y-y-you miss me?"

Abby hugged his neck. "Where's your guitar?" she said, noting he didn't have it slung over his back.

"L-l-left it. Too f-far to carry." He placed her back down.

"And what about Daniel?" asked Mrs. Clack.

Surprised that she spoke, everybody looked at her.

"Left him to watch home," said Solomon. "Somebody needed to stay and feed the livestock, milk the cow."

Abby nodded. Farm work took no days off.

"Let's go in the house," Mrs. Elsa said. "You boys must be dying of thirst."

"Could use a swallow of something cold," said Solomon. "Long way we have come today. Where are the boys?"

"Inside," Elsa said. "You won't believe how much they have grown, Walter especially."

They all poured into the kitchen. Mrs. Clack brought in Junior and Walter. Solomon hugged them each and took a seat at the table. He held Walter on one knee, Junior on the other. Luke and Abby pulled out chairs and also sat down.

"Here is some water," said Mrs. Elsa, handing Solomon a dipper. He handed it to Luke, who drank it dry. Mrs. Elsa filled it again, and Solomon followed Luke's example. Finished, he passed it back to Mrs. Elsa, pushed back his hat, and wiped his lips. Night had come outside. The sound of katydids filled the air. Elsa placed a plate of cut tomatoes and biscuits on the table and took a seat.

"We got us a place finished," Solomon said through a bite of tomato. "Not the fanciest lodging you ever saw but passable till we can build better."

Abby glanced at Mrs. Elsa. She looked pretty, her hair all pinned back, her clothes neat and washed clean like always. Her ma sat beside her, hands over her mouth like she wanted to keep something from escaping from between her gums.

"We know you been working hard," said Mrs. Elsa.

"Ever morning from sunup to sundown," Solomon said. "That is, when the weather let us."

"A l-l-lot of rain," said Luke.

"Seemed like every other day," Solomon added.

"Been some wet here too," said Mrs. Elsa. "Junior took sick from it, been real poorly. Doc Booth has seen him twice, but it seems he's not much better. Might be hard for him to make the trip up the mountain."

Solomon looked at Junior, patted his head. "I thought he looked some peaked. But he will do fine. We can ride him on Bouncer. Luke can carry Walter. Take us most of a day, but then we will be home, all one family again." His eyes lit up as he talked, and Abby could see that the notion of getting everybody under one roof again pleased her pa something fierce. Abby glanced at Mrs. Elsa and saw her looking at her ma.

Watching the two women, Abby felt something passing between them, something maybe they had already discussed. Abby looked back at her pa, a hundred questions in her head. What did the cabin look like? Did it have a loft where she would sleep like the last one? Did her pa plant a garden this year? How far from the creek was the cabin? Did Sandy still like to fetch sticks? Had Laban come home? Had he and Pa made up, or did Pa want to hit him some more?

Solomon handed Luke a slice of tomato. Abby figured it was not the right time to ask her questions. Junior hopped down from Solomon's knee and crawled up in a chair beside him. Solomon handed Walter to Mrs. Elsa and returned to his eating. For several minutes everyone stayed quiet as Luke and Solomon ate.

Then, licking his fingers, Solomon pushed back from the table and patted his stomach. "I'm thanking you for the food," he said to Mrs. Clack. "Me and Luke walked hard today."

Mrs. Clack nodded her acceptance of the thanks.

Mrs. Elsa said, "I guess we ought to make ready to leave in the morning."

Abby didn't think she sounded too pleased with the idea. *Why not?* she wondered.

"Early as we can," said Solomon. "Get home midafternoon maybe."

Abby's stomach turned quivery. Home before dark! She had never heard such happy words. She wanted to jump up and down to show her joy but nobody else moved, so she stayed quiet. Pa and Luke talked on a while longer, filled everybody in on the news from their summer of toil. But Abby barely heard it. The biggest thing she wanted to hear had already been said. All the rest was just a lot of gab.

A little over an hour later Solomon stretched his back and stood, and everybody took that as the signal to leave the table and prepare themselves for the next day. Within another hour Abby had packed everything she owned into a tow sack and had it ready to go. Soon everyone else was ready too, and they all turned in for bed—Luke with Walter and Junior, Abby on the floor in the parlor, and Mrs. Clack in her room.

The night went quickly, and the whole household woke up with first light. Nobody talked much as they ate gravy and biscuits and started making ready to leave. Her eyes on Mrs. Elsa, Abby saw her shoulders were slumped, her hands slow at the packing. She wondered again why Mrs. Elsa wasn't acting happy. Her husband had come to gather the family under one roof again, yet she seemed almost grumbly about it.

Deciding not to worry, Abby quickly packed her sack on Bouncer, then helped Mrs. Elsa load hers. The chore took no more than a half hour. Abby watched as Mrs. Elsa hugged her ma and whispered in her ear. Then the two women pulled away from each other, and Mrs. Elsa turned to face Solomon.

"Gone be hot today," Elsa said.

"Cooler up the mountain a ways," he replied. "Sooner we get up there, the better it will be."

Mrs. Elsa nodded, and they all took to the path that led out of Blue Springs. Abby trailed along with Luke, her heart skipping now. The morning went quickly, the group stopping only for water now and again and for a bite of food at midmorning. Everybody remained pretty quiet. Abby liked it. After living all summer in the noisy town, she enjoyed the peacefulness of the mountain trail. To her right the waters of the Blue Springs Creek bounced over the rocks, twisting and turning between its banks. The air smelled like the earth under a boulder that somebody had just moved. Sandy padded beside her, her pink tongue hanging out longer and longer as the trail became steeper.

The sun burned hot on Abby's neck. About noontime the group came to the fork they would normally have taken to reach their old homestead. But Solomon kept his nose straight ahead, and they walked past the fork without a glance. The trail switched off to the right and headed up even higher on the mountain. Abby had never come up this far.

Her breath straining a little, she wondered about the new house. Then she thought of the school down in Blue Springs, knew she would have a harder time getting to it from up here. For the first time she wondered if she might have to stop her schooling for a while.

Not liking the notion, she pushed it off and told herself to leave well enough alone. She would live with her pa and brothers again. If that meant giving up schooling for now, she would do so.

The day got even hotter. The sun moved past the sky's center point as Solomon led them higher and higher up Blue Springs Mountain. They reached another fork. Solomon steered them to the left this time. A mile or so beyond the turn Abby saw a clearing and a small cabin snuggled down in the middle of it. A curl of gray smoke drifted up from the cabin's stone chimney. She stopped and faced her pa. Everyone halted.

"I know it ain't much," Solomon said, indicating the cabin. "But we are fortunate that Pierce and Erline don't need this spot. It will do us until spring when we can build on bigger."

Abby stared back at the cabin. Like her pa said, it wasn't much. Didn't have a smooth log anywhere on it. Just one window that she could see and it was covered with a wood shutter, not glass like Mrs. Clack's windows down in Blue Springs. No barn yet, just a lean-to out to the right of the cabin. The cow stood under the lean-to, its tail swishing flies. An outdoor privy waited out behind the lean-to, the wood of the outhouse freshly cut.

The group slowly approached the cabin as if careful not to step off the edge of a cliff. The cabin had no porch. As they reached the front, Daniel stepped outside, his hands waving. Abby ran to him and hugged him, and he toed the ground in his bare feet. Soon the rest of the group arrived, so Abby stepped back. Elsa looked over at Solomon.

"Go on in," he said. "Give her a good going over."

Elsa climbed up the two steps that fronted the cabin, turned back to look at Solomon for another second, then walked on inside. Abby followed close behind, while Luke brought Junior. Holding Walter, Solomon trailed in last.

Abby saw that the cabin had only two rooms, the one she was in— about the width of three grown men lying end to end—and a second room, which was past an opening in the wall to her left. She strained to see through the opening to examine the second room, but couldn't manage it from where she was. Abby glanced at Mrs. Elsa and saw her jaw working. She could tell that what Mrs. Elsa saw in the cabin did not please her.

"It's right rough," Mrs. Elsa told Solomon. "More so than I figured."

"The rain slowed us," said Solomon, placing Walter down. "We did the best we could."

Daniel nodded his agreement. "Laban didn't help us none either," he said. "Never showed up. You hear any from him?"

Mrs. Elsa rubbed her face but didn't answer Daniel. Abby watched her as she examined the cabin again. The place had no loft or cellar. The floors were but rough planks, so bare feet would pick up splinters real easy if they didn't walk careful. A black pot hung from the side of the fireplace. Long nails poked out from the wall by the door. A couple of hats hung from the nails.

Abby studied Mrs. Elsa again. She had her fists clenched at her sides. A hint of bother came to Abby. Though the cabin was rough, her pa and brothers had done a lot of work in the weeks since she'd last seen them. The logs had good chinking in the cracks, and the fireplace was big, covering most of a whole wall. Although small, the cabin would stay warm in the winter. And they had a shed for the mule and cow and a privy with a top on it. The way she figured it, her pa and brothers had done about as much as three men could do in the short spell they had to work. Abby felt proud of the three of them.

"Junior has been real sickly," Mrs. Elsa said, her tone indicating she wanted to explain something to everybody. "A place like this might go hard on him."

Solomon put an arm around her waist. "We will make it through the winter," he said, "then add on and fix up everything next spring. We will do fine, you just wait and see."

Mrs. Elsa took his hands, squared up her body with his. For several seconds they just stood there, neither of them moving. Abby sensed that Mrs. Elsa had made up her mind about something and now planned to say it. Her neck tightened.

Elsa said, "Maybe me and the boys ought to stay down in Blue Springs until you can do some more on the cabin." Her words were spoken fast but firm. "To make sure that Junior is strong enough for this."

Abby knew that Mrs. Elsa had thought about the words before she said them.

Solomon looked confused. For a while he didn't say anything. Everyone else froze in place. Finally, Solomon said, "You want to go back down to town?"

Mrs. Elsa nodded slowly.

Solomon dropped her hands, rubbed his beard. "I reckon I don't understand," he said. "It is not right to keep a family split up. Not when they got a place worthy of living in."

"I'm worried about Junior," said Mrs. Elsa. "If he gets the pneumonia, as sickly as he is he might not make it through the winter."

"He didn't get sickly until he lived in a town," Solomon said. "Maybe some mountain air is all he needs."

Elsa's voice matched Solomon's stubborn tone as she replied, "I think I know what's best for my children," she said, her hands on her hips, her posture like a post dug deep into the ground.

Solomon moved to the fireplace, stared into the flames. "Now, don't go getting riled," he said. "No reason for hard words. Let's just think a spell on this, that's all."

Abby wanted to leave the room, to let her pa and Elsa do their arguing in private. But nobody else made a move to go, and she didn't know how to leave on her own.

Solomon rubbed his beard again. "You say you want to stay in Blue Springs. That what you are telling me?"

"I believe it is," said Elsa. "I think it better for the boys for now."

"But I believe you ought to stay here," he said. "Not right for a man and wife to stay apart if they can help it."

Elsa moved to him. Her voice became softer, wooing him to her view. "We don't have to split up. You and the boys can come to Blue Springs, live there with me and Ma until you finish the cabin next spring."

Solomon chewed his lip. "You know that ain't doable for me," he said. "We done talked about it more than once."

"And this won't work for me and my boys," said Elsa, stepping back and indicating the cabin.

"You said you took me for better or worse."

Elsa sighed. "Come to Blue Springs. You can stand it for one winter."

But Solomon shook his head. Abby knew that just like Mrs. Elsa had made up her mind, so Pa had made up his and nobody could change it, not even his wife. A scary quiet fell on the cabin for a long moment. Abby studied the flooring, noticed the smell of the fresh wood.

Solomon cleared his throat. "I am your husband," he said. "A woman ought to follow what her husband says."

Abby stared at Mrs. Elsa to see how she would respond.

"I am not wanting to make this hard," Mrs. Elsa said, "but a mama knows what is best for her children."

Solomon shrugged, rubbed his beard again. "I ain't a man that forces his woman to something she don't want," he said. "Even if I think she is wrongheaded in her wanting."

Mrs. Elsa sighed, then stepped over to him and took his hands. "And I am not a woman that wants to make her husband a henpecked man. But I am worried about Junior. He is not a strong boy."

Solomon looked at Junior, and Abby could see that Mrs. Elsa had won her point. Then, without warning, Solomon glanced over to her. "What about Abby?" he asked Elsa.

Mrs. Elsa shrugged. "She can stay in Blue Springs too," she said. "Or here, whichever she wants. She is old enough to say which."

Everyone looked at Abby. Not expecting the sudden attention, she didn't know what to do.

Solomon went to her, bent down, and put a hand on her shoulder. "Me and your ma don't see eye to eye on this," he said. "So we gone have to part our ways for a mite longer. But she is right about one thing. You are old enough to have some say in what happens to you." Solomon looked around the cabin. "It will be rough here. Cold this winter, and without much food of a passable nature. And no school either—too far to go every day."

Abby felt tears creeping up, but she quickly brushed them away. She refused to let them see her cry. She thought about her choices and knew that neither made her happy. She didn't want to leave her pa and brothers. But she didn't want to stop going to school either. Who knew if she would ever get to go back if she quit this year.

She stared into her pa's eyes. A note of hurt came to her then, a sense of grief that he hadn't just told her that she needed to stay with him, that no matter how hard it came that winter, she needed to live where he lived. She wanted him to take her in his arms and assure her that he wanted her by his side no matter what, that he would care for her in spite of the cold, in spite of the scarce food. But she knew he would not say that. He never had, so why should he start now?

"Here is your chance to speak," said Solomon. "Tell me what you want to do."

In that second Abby knew the choice she had to make. If she ever wanted out of the mountains, she had to learn enough so she could leave and make a living beyond these hills, which she both loved and hated at the same time.

She pulled away from her pa. "I will go with Mrs. Elsa," she said, her voice flat. "I will stay with her and go to school."

Solomon patted her hand, then stood and faced Elsa. "It is still my druthers that you would all stay here," he said.

"I know that," Elsa said. "But I fear for Junior."

"Then do what you got to do," he said.

"We will leave in the morning."

"Luke will see you safe back to town," Solomon said.

Elsa nodded, and Solomon hugged her. With her feelings all mixed, Abby stood and watched them. She would spend a whole year down in

Blue Springs going to school. But she would not see much of her pa and brothers. Was this the way life was? she wondered. A combination of the good and bad, of what made her feel low and what made her so happy she almost busted? Not yet knowing the answer to her question, Abby decided she would need some more time to ponder it.

CHAPTER
FOURTEEN

The cloudy skies that had covered so much of the top of the mountain that summer moved lower and lower through the fall and winter. The water from one rain after another poured off the roof of the Clack house, the sound of it a constant *drip, drip, drip* as the days grew shorter and shorter. The house took on the smell of a wet dog, and the flames in the fireplace turned smoky as water dribbled down the chimney onto the embers.

The weather made Junior even more sickly, so Doc Booth visited about once each week but didn't know much more to do than to give Junior another bottle of the same medicine that had failed every other time he had prescribed it. Junior cried a lot more now and at all hours of the day and night. Mrs. Elsa held him and sang to him and poured honey mixed with spoonfuls of liquor down his throat. But none of it seemed to make any difference.

Abby began to wonder if Junior might die. *Is this the way children die?* she thought. They cry and cry and cry until they just cry away the life that is in them, like a creek bed that runs dry in the summer after the spring rains have washed through it? She couldn't recall Aunt Francis doing much crying, and she knew her pa didn't take to it, so maybe this was just the way it was with young'uns.

Abby felt sad when she heard Junior wailing, and she prayed for him every night when she lay down to sleep. She didn't know much else to do to make him better. So she stood by and watched and waited for his body to run dry and then to die. But Christmas came and went and Junior stayed alive, and she thought maybe her prayers had done some good.

She saw her pa, Daniel, and Luke at Christmas when they traveled down from the cabin to attend services at Jesus Holiness. Yet, to her sadness, Hal Clack and his boys also chose that time to come to town, and since they stayed at Mrs. Clack's, that meant her pa and brothers had to sleep in the blacksmith's shop under heavy blankets. The cold of the night put frost on Pa's beard, but neither he nor the boys seemed to mind. On Christmas Day everybody but the Clack men dressed up in their best clothes and met at Jesus Holiness for a sermon and some singing. Luke played his guitar, and afterward everyone told him how good he was.

"You ought to go down to Asheville and play for some big churches down there," Preacher Bruster said after the service ended. "They will take up a love offering of money for you. You play too good to keep your light under a bushel basket up here."

Luke kicked at the ground and thanked him for his kind words. Abby didn't understand what the preacher meant. Would people really pay cash money to hear her brother play his guitar?

Though Abby wanted everybody to go back to the Clack house to eat, she knew her pa and brothers couldn't do this so long as Hal Clack and his sons stayed there. With the holiday and all, Clack and her pa seemed to have agreed to some unsaid bargain to make no trouble, but that didn't mean the two of them would sit down at a table with each other.

As for her part, Abby tried to stay quiet and out of the way with the Clacks in the house. They talked loud and swigged from their liquor jugs, and Topper knocked over the kitchen table once by accident. Other than that, Christmas Day passed with no troubles. And as drunk as he was, Hal Clack hardly seemed to know that Abby was even there.

That night, after the men fired their guns into the air and everybody ate a big piece of fruitcake, the Clack men took to drinking even heavier. Before long they were sloppy drunk and sleepy by the fire. Mrs. Elsa and Mrs. Clack cleaned up the floor from where the men had spilled ashes from their pipes and dribbled tobacco juice when they missed their cups.

Throwing a shawl over her shoulders, Abby told Mrs. Clack she wanted to go for a walk. Mrs. Clack nodded, and Abby eased out the back door and on toward the street. Ten minutes later she slipped through the door at the blacksmith's shop and glanced quickly around. A kerosene lamp hanging on a post by the door gave her enough light to see her pa and brothers asleep on the straw to her right, resting for their trip back up the mountain in the morning. For several seconds she stood and listened to their breathing. Solomon snored, and Abby remembered how that sound had brought her comfort when she used to lay in the loft in their old cabin, back before Laban lost the land.

She felt bad for Laban. Daniel had told her he didn't come around anymore. He'd taken up with the same boys who had swindled him out of their land, spent most of his time carousing around with them, drinking, gambling, and going after women who never went to Jesus Holiness or the One Way Baptist either.

Sighing, Abby tiptoed across the shop, stepped over Daniel and Luke, and stood motionless over her pa. His beard had turned a mite gray since she had last seen him and he had lost weight. A whole row of wrinkles pulled at his eyes, even while he slept. His hat lay beside him on the straw. Abby saw gray in his hair too.

Quietly, so as not to wake him, Abby lay down by her pa and stretched out. She rested her head in the straw by his hat. The smell of horses filled the air. The straw pricked at her arms. But Abby found no complaint with any of it.

She took a deep breath and closed her eyes, imagined her pa's arms around her, her head resting on his shoulder. Why couldn't she have that? Like she saw Lindy from down at the school do with her pa from time to time, go right up and hold his hand and walk down the street by his side. Why did God let some girls have a ma and pa with both of them as easy to touch as a month-old puppy? Why did some girls find so much good fortune everywhere they walked and not others? She pulled her knees up to her chin and decided she had no answers to such deep questions. Maybe nobody did.

For the rest of the night Abby lay there and listened to her pa's snoring, the sound of it more settling than anything she had heard in a long time. Every now and again she thought she might reach out and touch his face, play her fingers through his beard. But she worried about waking him and so kept her hands to herself. As the kerosene lamp burned lower and flickered and then went out, she inched closer and closer to her pa, yet never allowed herself to nudge against him. She wanted to touch him so bad it hurt her in her stomach. But he had never been one to touch too much, and she didn't know what he might do if he woke up and found her so close. So she stayed at her distance.

Sometime in the wee hours of the morning she dozed off. Her head moved with the dreams that bothered it. She saw her ma and pa together and her in between them, the two of them holding her so tight it made her feel like she couldn't breathe. The dream made her smile in her sleep. She wanted the dream to last forever. But then she heard a rooster crow, and the sound awakened her. She opened her eyes and saw her pa at her side and knew she better go before he woke up and found her there. Brushing sleep from her face, she stood, slipped out of the blacksmith's shop, and ran back to the Clack house. Still, the memory of the dream stayed with her all the rest of the day and into the weeks and months that followed.

The day after Christmas, the Clacks and her pa and brothers all left, and Abby and everybody else settled once more into the routine that had marked them since the fall. In early February she returned to school, her seat still in the front row by the stove, and her joy in learning not one bit lessened by any of the calamity that had come her way. If anything, the hardships she had faced made her more determined than ever to learn about everything that passed her way. From what Abby could see, only educated people got to make choices about how they lived. They got to move from place to place, live in Charlotte or Asheville or Knoxville. They got to talk about things like fashion and politics and science and medicine. They got to decide what they wanted to do and where they wanted to take up residence. That was what she wanted too—the chance to leave this mountain and all its troubles, to make a decision about where and how she wanted to spend her days.

Determined as she was, Abby studied harder than anybody and made better grades too. This kind of effort made her a teacher's favorite in no time. Abby liked that just fine, though it did mean a few of the other boys and girls in the class decided they didn't much care for her. From time to time they called her "teacher's pet, teacher's pet" and stuck out their tongues and threw dirt at her. Yet she didn't mind it much.

"Let them poke fun," said Lindy, the teacher's daughter and Abby's best friend. "When they are all grown and still dumber than a fence post, they won't make fun then."

Abby laughed and stuck her tongue out to match her tormentors, then walked away with Lindy.

The winter moved on, still rainy and cold and without much snow. Abby spent a lot of time studying the assignments Mr. Holston gave out each day for homework. She read by the fireplace, did her adding and subtracting on the kitchen table, and practiced her writing on her gray-colored tablets by the lamp in her room.

"You have excellent penmanship," Mr. Holston told her one day as he checked her homework. "Fine lines, and easy on the eyes to read."

Abby blushed and then worked even harder on everything Mr. Holston gave her to do. She liked him a lot. He had a head as round and bald as a cantaloupe, wore glasses with thick black rims, and constantly wiped his nose with a handkerchief. Some of the kids laughed at him behind his back. But Abby told the kids who talked bad about him to shut up, and when they didn't, she threatened to put her brother Daniel on them and that generally made them turn real quiet.

The way Abby saw it, Mr. Holston took it personally when a student didn't do very well on something. He would bow up his thick neck and strain even harder to make sure the boy or girl with the bothersome subject figured it out. That counted for something in her book, and so even if Lindy had not become her best friend, she would've liked Mr. Holston anyway.

"I'm glad your pa moved to Blue Springs," Abby said one afternoon near the end of March as she and Lindy headed home from school.

Lindy looped her arm around Abby's. Overhead, the sun warmed Abby's back. The air smelled like a flower about to bloom.

"Pa takes his teaching real serious," Lindy said.

"He always been a teacher?"

They passed the sheriff's office. A stray dog ran past them, tongue hanging out.

"Long as I can remember," said Lindy. They turned down the street and walked toward the house where Lindy and Thaddeus lived with their pa and grandma.

"What about your ma?" Abby asked. "Was she an educated woman too?"

Lindy nodded. "She met Pa at the college. Both of them taught when they first married. Same school in Knoxville. Then me and Thaddeus came along, so Ma stayed home with us."

Abby thought about that a few steps—the idea of a man and woman working side by side, both able to read. She wanted to know more about Lindy's ma, yet didn't know whether to ask. Though she and Lindy had spent a lot of time together in the last few months, neither of them had spoken of the thing they had most in common.

Lindy suddenly stopped, pulled away from Abby, and swung up to the top of a fence and sat on it. "My ma died New Year's Day a year ago," she said, her voice as calm as if announcing the weather. "Took a fever on a Friday, never stood back out of bed. Nine days later she passed on. Doctor said he did all there was to do for it. Just one of those things, her time to go, he said, nothing else he could do."

Lindy jumped down, started walking again. Abby followed. "Least you got to see your ma," she said. "Mine died the day I was born."

Lindy sighed. "I saw the carving in your room. That your ma?"

"Yeah, Pa did that. He carves good."

"You look like the carving too," said Lindy.

"Most folks say so," Abby said. "You favor your ma?"

Lindy laughed. "Most say no, more like my grandma. I'm gone be taller than my ma was, skinnier too. And my hair is straight and black, hers was a dirty blondish color."

They reached Lindy's house and stopped in the middle of the street. The stray dog ran up to Abby, stuck his nose into her hand. She rubbed him behind the ears.

"Knowing your ma don't make you miss her any less," Lindy said.

The dog licked Abby's hand. "I wish I could have talked to her just once," she said. "Heard her voice, you know, just been able to touch her face, see what she smelled like."

"I'm glad I got to know my ma," said Lindy. "But maybe that makes it sadder. You know, if you never had nothing, you can't miss it. But once you got something, you don't want to let it go."

Abby pondered the idea for a second. It made some sense. But that didn't help her any when she thought of her ma. "I never spoke to my pa about her," Abby said. "He's not the talkative kind about such things. My brothers, Daniel mostly, he told me some things. How she baked the best sweet-tater pies anybody ever tasted. Sang pretty too. Daniel said that's where Luke got his musicals. And everyone swears she loved everybody, a saint kind of woman. But that's about all I know. Except that we look some alike."

Lindy nodded, then crouched down by the dog. "My pa ought to remarry," she said. "Like your pa did." She stood again.

Abby shrugged. "A new wife can bring some troubles."

"You seem to do all right with your new ma."

Abby patted the dog. "I reckon," she said. "But she ain't my ma, let's just keep that straight no matter what."

Lindy walked to the steps of her house and onto the porch. "You want to come in?" she asked. "Do some reading together?"

Abby paused. "You reckon Thaddeus is home yet?"

Lindy smiled at her. "Which way you hoping?" she teased.

Abby blushed. She and Thaddeus aggravated each other. Picked and pulled like a puppy and a kitten. She did not like him a bit. The fool boy said he loved Blue Springs better than anywhere he had ever lived. Loved owning his own rifle, shooting it out in the woods whenever he wanted, the creeks where he could swim naked in the summer, and the lack of noise of a night when he sat on the porch.

She had blushed when he told her about swimming naked, and she told him he must surely be lying to her. But he said come and see next summer if you like, and so she shut up about it. Still, she had no doubt he was telling her the truth about how he loved Blue Springs. He swore on his mama's grave that he wanted to grow up and stay here forever, become a lumberman who cut timber off the hills and made a fortune from it.

"I'm gone fish these streams and shoot deer for food and mount the antlers on the wall of a cabin I will build," Thaddeus bragged. "The biggest cabin anybody in Blue Springs has ever seen."

"You plumb crazy," Abby had said to him when he told her his big plans. "Nobody in their right mind wants to come up here to stay. Nothing here but hard living and grave holes ready to swallow you up early."

But Thaddeus only laughed at her and swore even harder that he would never leave the place.

"I'm hoping he never comes home while I'm here," said Abby, bringing herself back to her talk with Lindy. "You know he pesters me bad."

Lindy smiled again, then opened the door and called for Thaddeus.

"He ain't here," yelled her grandma from the kitchen. "Ain't seen him."

"It's safe," Lindy said, holding open the door. "Thaddeus is out running around somewhere."

"Maybe he's with Jubal."

"Probably so. He and that boy do about everything together."

Leaving the stray dog and stepping into the house, Abby couldn't help but feel a little disappointed. Though she found Thaddeus Holston more than a mite pesky and would never admit to anybody that she liked him even a little bit, he did make her laugh. And in her present situation the ability to do that made him right valuable to have around.

CHAPTER
FIFTEEN

E aster came late that year, the third Sunday in April. All the dog-woods had bloomed, the azaleas too. The trees had greened out a couple of weeks earlier. The steady rains of winter and spring had given way to gentle breezes and soft sunshine, and a whole army of bees, butterflies, and birds had taken up their work of repopulating the earth.

Walking home from Jesus Holiness on Easter Sunday in her best dress—a bright yellow one with white lace at the neck that Mrs. Clack had bought for her—Abby sucked in the sweet spring air and found herself feeling almost peaceful. Her tenth birthday had come and gone only a few days ago, and though nobody had paid any mind to it, she didn't really care. With Lindy and the stray dog that she'd kept and named Patch at her side and Thaddeus and Jubal trailing behind throwing rocks at trees, she knew she had friends. In addition, she had learned more during the school year than she could ever have imagined. She could now read at least some from just about any book she picked up, and Mr. Holston had somehow managed to keep a new one in her hands most of the time. He kept saying to her, "You got a brain too big to fit in your head." And although she didn't exactly know what all he meant by that, she could tell by his smile that he meant it as a compliment.

Except for the fact that she hadn't seen her pa and brothers but one other time since Christmas, Abby didn't see a whole lot that gave her much cause for griping. Given her situation, she had decided that though life sometimes dealt a body a few poor hands, whining did not help much, and so she might as well play the cards she was given as best she could. Keep her chin up and her heart strong and move on.

"You want to come home with us?" asked Lindy as they reached the fork leading to her house. "We can probably set you a place for Sunday dinner."

Abby thought about it but knew she better not accept the invitation. "Mrs. Elsa and Mrs. Clack are expecting me," she said. "They do a fancy table for special days."

"Then I'll come by later after I eat," Lindy said. "We'll go up to the creek and do some wading."

Abby and Patch left her at the fork and walked home and into the kitchen. Ten minutes later, after setting the table, she joined Mrs. Clack and Mrs. Elsa for dinner. Though he was six years old now, Elsa held Junior on her lap. He held a biscuit in his hands. He wore overalls and a brown shirt and looked a lot like Solomon in his angular frame yet had a thicker jaw and lower eyes, like the Clack side of the family. His hair fell down in his eyes and every now and then he coughed, a lingering sign of his ongoing puny health.

Fried chicken, mashed potatoes, biscuits, and spring greens had been spread out on the white tablecloth. Mrs. Elsa had gathered some early white daisies, arranged them in a clear jar, and placed them in the middle of all the food. Abby felt almost royal in the presence of such fine things. Patch lay at her feet.

"Let's say grace," said Mrs. Elsa.

Surprised, Abby bowed her head. While Elsa attended Jesus Holiness on most days when it met, she didn't do much praying on regular days. Abby thought for a second of her pa, wondered when she would see him again. He prayed aloud before every meal, his head down, his voice slow.

"Bless this our food," Mrs. Elsa prayed. "And each of us as we try to live right. And bless those of our family not here today as they—"

The sound of feet clomping on the porch interrupted her prayer. Immediately thinking of her pa, Abby almost jumped up and ran from the table. But she fought off the urge and stayed put as Mrs. Elsa finished.

"As they strive to do your will. Amen."

When Abby opened her eyes, she saw Mrs. Elsa remove Junior from her lap, push back her chair, and head toward the door. Abby, Junior, and Mrs. Clack followed, Patch behind them. The door swung open before they reached it, and Hal Clack pushed his way into the house. As always, the smell of stale liquor came with him, and Abby could see he hadn't shaved nor bathed in quite a while. Mrs. Clack stepped to him, Junior at her side. Without warning, Clack grabbed for the boy, held him up over his head and examined him as if inspecting a prize pig. Junior puckered up his face and started bawling. Clack put Junior on the floor, but that didn't stop his crying. Clack slammed the door behind him and motioned them all into the kitchen.

"You got some food out?" he asked, his words slurred from the drink.

"Plenty," said Mrs. Clack with her hands at her throat. "Chicken, greens, all the things you like."

They returned to the table and arranged themselves in their chairs. Junior's crying had turned into a low whine.

"I come by this morning," said Clack, the accusation plain.

"We went to church," Elsa said. She handed Junior a biscuit.

"You going to church a lot," Clack said, obviously not happy with the idea.

Mrs. Clack and Elsa didn't answer. Abby wondered why Hal Clack didn't like his wife and daughter going to church. Wasn't church a good thing?

"Church ain't nothin'," said Clack as if reading her mind and wishing to answer the question. "God never did nothin' for nobody."

Mrs. Clack dropped her eyes. Elsa dipped greens onto her pa's plate. As if sensing the bad feeling in the room, Junior notched up his whine a mite. Elsa hefted him up to her lap again. He wiggled to get down but she held him tight.

"Shut that boy up," Clack ordered as he grabbed a chicken leg and started gnawing on it.

Elsa shushed Junior, but this only seemed to make it worse. He cried louder, his wailing filling the room.

"Let me have him," said Mrs. Clack, standing to take him from Elsa. "See if maybe he wants a nap." With Junior in hand, she turned to leave the room. But then Clack grabbed her arm and twisted her back around.

"Worthless Porter baby," said Clack. "Just a whiny brat not worth nothin'. Gimme that boy. I'll give him cause for such a screeching." He reached for Junior, but Mrs. Clack turned away, her body shielding the boy from Clack.

Abby's eyes widened. She had never seen Mrs. Clack act in such a contrary way toward her husband. Clack seemed shocked too. His mouth fell open.

"I said hand me that boy!" he demanded. "Time he started taking on some manliness."

"Let him go rest, Pa," Elsa interjected. "You just sit here and finish your eating."

Clack scowled at her. "You stay out of this," he said. "This between your ma and me." He faced Mrs. Clack again. "I said hand me that boy."

If she hadn't been there to see it, Abby would not have believed what followed next. For the first time she caught a glimpse of what a woman pushed to her limits could do. For whatever reason—maybe because she loved her grandson or maybe because she'd just finally had enough of her husband's bullying—Mrs. Clack disobeyed him.

"Let me take Junior to bed," she said. "Give us all some peace and quiet."

As quick as a mad bear, Hal Clack rose from the table, kicked his chair across the room, and smacked Mrs. Clack across the shoulder. She fell down hard but never let go of Junior.

Elsa jumped up and grabbed her ma. "Take him," yelled Elsa. "Take him out!"

Clack moved to hit his wife again, but she dodged by him and ran from the room, Junior still crying.

The veins in his neck bulging, Hal Clack stepped to his daughter. Abby sat frozen at the table, too scared to move. Elsa glared at her pa, her eyes wide. Abby could see that she knew something bad was coming. Clack drew back a fist.

From the corner, Abby saw Patch run toward Clack, his teeth bared, a deep growl rumbling in his throat. Clack spun around to face the dog and grabbed a pistol from his pants' waist. Patch snapped at Clack's leg, but Clack kicked him away and raised his pistol, pointing it at the dog's head.

Without thinking, Abby rushed at Clack. He fired his pistol but Patch dodged away and the shot missed. Patch snapped at him again, this time snagging Clack by the ankle of his pants. Clack raised the gun again.

Too mad to feel afraid, Abby grabbed at Clack's leg, her arms clutching him at the knee. He shook his leg to throw her off but she held on. He drew back his pistol again, knocked her on the neck with it. She bit him on the knee, and he screamed and whacked her on the head again. The pain cut through her skull and she fell off of Clack.

Lying on the floor, Abby saw Mrs. Elsa jump on her pa from behind, her arms and legs wrapped around him. Patch growled and snapped again, but Clack kicked him full in the jaw. Patch yelped and rolled away.

Abby noticed the door to the cellar by her head and started to pull open the latch to climb down the ladder and drop into the black hole where they kept the taters and jarred jellies. But then she looked back up and saw Mrs. Elsa clawing at her pa and knew she couldn't leave her alone to fight her mean daddy.

"Leave us alone!" sobbed Mrs. Elsa, her hands reaching for her pa's eyes. "Just go on out of here before you hurt somebody bad!"

Clack shook his shoulders like a bull throwing off a rag doll, causing Mrs. Elsa to fall and roll to the floor. He then stepped to her and raised a booted foot. Abby quickly got up and ran at him once more. But he grasped the back of her dress with one hand and held her still. His other hand squeezed her neck. Abby squirmed against him. He jerked her off the floor and pushed her against the wall and held her there for what seemed like an hour, his eyes boring into hers, his sour breath pouring from his lips.

Abby tried to kick him, but he held her at arm's length. Mrs. Clack suddenly came back into the room, a shotgun in her hands. Abby looked at her eyes, saw the determination in them. Elsa pulled up from the floor and eased to her ma's side.

"You have . . . have done enough meanness for . . . for one day," Mrs. Clack panted. "Just let that girl down and leave us alone."

Clack drew back a fist, and Abby thought he was about to hit her for sure.

"Let her down, Pa!" Mrs. Elsa shouted.

Clack spat on the floor.

"I will shoot you in the knee," said Mrs. Clack, calmer now.

Clack opened his mouth as if to speak but instead released his grip and said nothing. Abby dropped to the floor. Looking suddenly tired of all the commotion, Clack blinked twice and swallowed hard. Abby had the feeling she was watching a man who had just awakened and found himself in a place he didn't recognize. His shoulders sagging, he slid his pistol back into his pants and headed for the door. Patch eyed him, a low growl still coming from his throat.

At the door, Clack stopped for a moment and looked back at Abby. "Stupid Porter kids," he said. "Not worth shootin'." With that he stomped out and down the front steps.

Watching him leave, Abby felt Mrs. Elsa at her side, her hand touching the bump that had already come up behind her ear.

"You okay, honey?" asked Mrs. Elsa. "Got some bleeding here where he pistol-whipped you."

Abby nodded. "It hurts some but not too bad."

Mrs. Elsa pulled her close, wiping her head with the hem of her apron. "Let's get some water on that," she said. "Maybe it won't swell up too much."

"I'll get a towel," Mrs. Clack said as she leaned the shotgun in the corner.

Standing by the table while Mrs. Elsa used a wet rag to clean the wound on her head, Abby wondered if this was what it felt like to have a mama. If so, she decided she liked it, liked it a lot. Mrs. Elsa's hands were gentle as she wiped around the cut and washed off the light blood.

"You are a mighty brave girl," said Mrs. Elsa.

Abby stayed quiet. Patch moved to her side, and she scratched his ears.

"My pa is a bad man when he drinks," Elsa said. "Sometimes I don't know what pushed Mama to want to marry such a person."

"You ain't the only one who wonders about that," said Mrs. Clack, patting Abby on the back. "I must have been crazy as a loon."

The three of them laughed.

Abby looked up at Mrs. Clack, sympathy in her eyes. "Most every time I see him, he is drinking," she said.

Mrs. Clack chuckled just slightly and gave her a hug. "You got that right, child," she said. "You got that right as rain."

Hearing their laughter, Abby closed her eyes and enjoyed the hug in spite of the meanness that had caused her to end up on the receiving end of it. Facing down Hal Clack had scared her a lot but it had made her stronger too, made her feel that if it came to it, she could take care of herself. And, even better than that, the battle with Hal Clack had made her see that Mrs. Elsa and Mrs. Clack did have some feeling for her, even if they didn't often take the opportunity to display it in any real noticeable way.

CHAPTER
SIXTEEN

After the day Mrs. Clack and Elsa had stood up to Hal Clack, Abby's feelings about her situation in Blue Springs took a noticeable turn. Whereas before she had prayed every morning for the day her pa would come down to take her back to the new cabin, now she pretty much lost her fancy for such a thought. In fact, by fall she had altogether stopped praying about it. So, when he did finally show up in early September and make the pronouncement that he had added a third room and a porch to the cabin and shaved down the floors to a smoother finish, Abby found herself touched with dread. Truth was, she did not want to go. She had friends in Blue Springs now and she loved her schooling. And, though Mrs. Clack didn't exactly pour the loving on her, the fact that the three of them had faced down her husband seemed to have changed Abby's feelings toward her, at least a little. Once or twice they had even laughed about how Abby had bit him on the leg and Elsa had gouged at his eyes and Mrs. Clack told him she would shoot him in the knee. And Mrs. Clack had asked Abby to call her "Amelia," and Mrs. Elsa said to refer to her as just "Elsa." So the laughter and name changing had to mean something, Abby figured.

Sitting at the table as everybody ate their supper the night her pa came to fetch her, Abby was quiet, her insides feeling tore up. What kind of daughter wanted to stay separate from her pa and brothers? And how could she tell Pa her feelings?

After supper Abby watched as Elsa gathered together her belongings to leave in the morning. She wondered if Elsa had mixed feelings too, if maybe she also wanted to stay put in Blue Springs, to keep her boys, Junior especially, near town where Doc Booth could see to him in a rush. To Abby's eyes it seemed that Elsa drug her feet some as she packed, that she didn't have any particular relish for the job.

Her own few possessions piled on the floor by her bed, Abby did not sleep well through the night. She kept thinking that it wasn't fair she had to leave the one place where she'd started to make real friends, the one place where people thought she was smart, the one place that gave her a chance to rise up and become somebody. But none of this thinking stopped time from passing, and before she knew it the sun had started to come up and she had to prepare herself for leaving Blue Springs. Waking up early, she took the carving of her ma off the night table and stared at it as the sun broke through the window. She ran her fingers over the finely cut features of the face, features everybody said looked just like her ma, just like her too. She held the carving up in the light, tried to imagine her ma in the flesh. But no feeling came to her, no sense that her ma had ever truly lived.

She heard feet on the floor and knew that everybody else was now waking up too. It wouldn't be long before Pa would want to head back up the mountain. Abby laid the carving on her stomach and gazed up at the ceiling. Truth was, her pa felt about as distant to her as her ma did. Even though he was a flesh-and-blood person, he'd never given her much more love than her dead ma had. At least her ma had given her a life, had in fact died in the effort to do so. No greater love than that, the Good Book said, than to lay down your life for another person. But what had her pa ever done to show his love? Put food on the table? Clothes on her back? Roof over her head? He had done all that, she had to admit it. And she appreciated him for it. But even that provision had ended when Laban lost the land.

Sighing, Abby sat up and fingered the carving once more. From what she could see, she and her pa had come to a fork in their living, him going one way, her going another. She wanted to stay here with her friends, keep on with her schooling. No way could she do that from up in the holler.

So decided, she climbed out of bed and quickly dressed. In the kitchen five minutes later, she saw her pa sipping a cup of coffee. No one else was there. Solomon nodded at her. She dropped her eyes, studied the floor for a second, her heart thumping heavy. Then she looked up.

"I want to stay here," she said, her eyes locked on his.

Solomon set his cup down on the table, cleared his throat. "I wondered maybe you would," he said. "Nice house and all."

"Nothing to do with the house," said Abby, her voice surprising her with its mature sound. "I got friends here. Lindy and Thaddeus and little Jubal, they are my friends."

Solomon swigged his coffee, then said, "Friends ain't family."

Before Abby could stop herself, the words poured out, words she hadn't put into any order in her mind, words she knew would hurt her pa even as she said them. But in spite of this, the words had to be spoken. "My friends feel closer to me than my family," she said.

Solomon's hands shook some as he put down his coffee cup again. "I expect that's possible true," he said slowly. "Your family ain't been all it should be to a young girl, myself included. And we have had our troubles . . . things to keep us apart, but . . ."

His voice trailed off, and Abby could see that he wanted to say more but didn't quite know how. She felt sorrow in her throat, a wad of sadness welling up like a lump of bread dough she couldn't swallow. Yet the sorrow didn't change the truth of what she'd said, what she felt.

She stepped closer to her pa, placed a hand on his shoulder. "I got my schooling here, Pa," she said.

He nodded, studied his coffee. "Nothin' more vital than family. Not even schooling."

Abby heard determination in his voice, which meant he was going to dig in his heels. On instinct she knew what she had to say, the one thing that would make him let her stay. But to say it sounded so grown up, so much older than her years. But there it was, the right thing to put before him. "You want me to do good with my life, don't you, Pa?"

He faced her, his hands on the table, palms down. "You know I do."

"Then I need to stay here," she said, "where I can keep learning, where Mr. Holston can teach me. He says I got a brain too big for my head. He thinks I am smart and he tells me I can do anything I want. But

I can't do that if I go back to the holler, I just know it."

Solomon's eyes watered, and Abby thought he might cry. But he always fought such signs of weakness. Her heart sank. She didn't want to hurt her pa, to make him do something he hated the thought of doing. But she'd spent so little time with him she felt as though she scarcely knew him. This made her even sadder and she wished she could change it, but she couldn't. That was the way the world had made things for her and him, and she just had to live with it—live with it and make the best of things for her and everybody else.

Solomon said, "You mighty growed up for such a young thing. But I guess maybe your way of living pushed you up quick, made you wise beyond your days on earth." He took her hands then, ran his rough fingers over her skin. "You got your own mind. Like your ma did. Smartest woman I ever knew . . ." He laid her hands down and stood and moved to the window, stared out at the morning sun.

Abby wanted to ask him more about her ma, ask him to tell her everything he knew. But before she could, he faced her again, his hands in his pockets.

"You take after your ma in a lot of ways," he said, a light of remembrance in his eyes. "Sometimes when I see you it makes my breath want to stop, makes me think Rose is standing right before my eyes. . . ."

Abby's throat felt as if someone had pushed a rock down it. She couldn't remember her pa ever saying anything so personal to her. She wanted to press him for more, to beg him to tell her all that he remembered about Rose Porter, how she sounded when she talked, how she smelled on Sunday when she dressed up for church, how she looked when she got mad. She wanted to make him . . . but she knew she couldn't. Pa didn't work that way. He talked when he wanted to talk, and asking him to go beyond that only caused him to shut down as tight as a turtle in his shell.

"You loved Ma powerful, didn't you, Pa?" Abby asked, her voice barely a whisper.

Solomon grinned sheepishly. "More than I could ever speak out plain," he said.

Silence came to the room for a while. Abby didn't know what else to say. Her pa would either let her stay or not. It was in his hands.

He rubbed his beard, sighed. "I reckon I got no right to take your schooling away from you. Your ma would not want me to do that. Neither do I. So you just stay on here for now."

Abby's emotions mixed all up in her. She wanted to run to her pa and throw her arms open and hug him for his kindness. At the same time, though, she felt sad she had hurt him earlier with her words. She wanted to tell him she loved him in spite of feeling cut off from him. He was her pa and that was reason enough for love. But since neither he nor she had ever said such a thing before, she didn't know how he would respond, and so she just smiled real big and thanked him and let it go at that. He nodded his head, picked up his coffee cup again, and took a sip from it. Then he turned and left the kitchen.

Not sure what else to do, Abby went back to her room. She took the carving of her ma from the table, held it up to the morning light and fingered its fine features. Without understanding why, she got the sudden feeling she was not a child anymore. She had fought Hal Clack. She had spoken out plain to her pa. While it was true the two were hardly the same things, they did give evidence that she wasn't just a piece of driftwood at the mercy of the creek water. She was a person with the wherewithal to stand up for herself, a person with the gumption to steer her own course, at least a little bit. Pa was right. Things that had happened had pushed her up quick, given her smarts beyond her days.

The carving in hand, she moved to the closet by her dresser. Then, standing on her tiptoes, she slid the carving onto the top shelf of the closet. Since she was so growed up now, it was time to put away childish things.

———————

After her pa left with Elsa and the boys, Abby's life settled into an easy routine. She studied at school every day with Lindy, Thaddeus, and Jubal, played outdoors when the weather allowed, then came home to do chores, eat a bite of supper, do some reading and go to bed. Though she and Amelia never talked to each other with the closeness of real relatives, the fight with Hal Clack and the fact that they lived under the same roof had brought them into a friendly and agreeable relationship.

Amelia liked to work in her garden on warm days and was always tinkering around the house, sewing new drapes, painting a room, or refinishing a floor or piece of furniture. Abby helped her some when she wasn't studying, and Amelia always thanked her for the assistance.

Abby got the feeling that Amelia was glad for the company since she never saw Elsa much anymore and her husband and sons didn't come around too often. Of course, when they did come around, they mostly caused trouble. For her part, whenever she got put out with Amelia, Abby just remembered back to the day Amelia had pointed a shotgun at her husband for her protection and that settled her down. Truth was, she liked Amelia and she knew Mrs. Clack liked her.

About the only time any problems arose was when Hal Clack or one of his sons dropped by. Then Amelia turned real tense and didn't speak hardly at all to Abby. Abby wondered what it felt like to live in such fear. She wanted to tell Amelia to stand up to them again, but then she decided such courage as Amelia had shown that one time didn't just show up on any regular day. So Abby figured she should just leave well enough alone. So long as she stayed quiet and out of the way, Hal Clack and his sons usually ignored her. And she knew that was the best thing for them all.

From time to time Pa or Daniel or Luke would drop by. For the most part Abby saw little of them over the next couple of years, except for the times they came down to Jesus Holiness for meetings. But ever since a rattler had spooked Preacher Bruster's horse and the horse bucked him off, causing Bruster to break his knee, the services at Jesus Holiness had become unpredictable. One Sunday a preacher showed up, the next he didn't.

She didn't see Laban at all during this time. Daniel told her he had taken up with a woman on the other side of Epsom's Ridge, but that hadn't slowed down his carousing any.

"Pray for him," Daniel had said to her, "because he is bound for trouble for sure if he don't get his life straight."

Abby did pray—for Laban and everybody else. One of the good things about learning to read meant she could read the Good Book for herself. And she had taken to doing that every night before she shut out the light. She had dusted off the Bible from Amelia's front room table and brought it to her bedroom and started working her way through it. Even without regular services at Jesus Holiness to keep her spirit up, she felt drawn to the words in the Book. Every now and then, though she didn't know what many of the words meant, the Book seemed to take on some kind of mystical power, and the writing would rise up right off the page and walk out and speak to her. When this happened, Abby got a shivery feeling up and down her spine and she thought someone else must have entered the room and was standing behind her. Another presence was near; she just knew it.

The shivery feeling didn't come every night of course, but she kept reading regular all the same. Some days she closed the Book all confused, wondering what in the world she had just read, why God had seen fit to put this passage or that one in there at all. Lots of mysteries in the Book, she concluded, more than she could settle in her lifetime.

On other days, though, she closed the Book with the sense that sweet Jesus himself had talked to her through it. That made her feel like the words had danced into her head on lively feet and settled in places that gave her all the knowledge she would ever need.

Sometimes Amelia asked her about the words in the Book, and Abby did her best to explain. But she didn't always know what to say, and Amelia didn't ask very often, so their discussions about the Book weren't all that regular. Abby wondered if she ought to talk with Amelia about Jesus, about the need to live right with the Lord as her Savior. Yet, since she'd never exactly come to this experience herself, she didn't rightly feel she should tell Amelia she ought to do anything. Besides, she and Amelia were still not so close as a mama and daughter, and talking about Jesus as Savior wasn't something a body did with just any old stranger who happened to be walking down the road.

And so the next three years passed. Preacher Bruster's knee finally got better, and services at Jesus Holiness took up their twice-a-month timetable again. Abby grew taller. Her body, while still slender, began to fill out some, taking on the first signs of womanhood. Her monthly flow started the summer after her twelfth year, and Amelia told her what to do, and Abby went through that change of life without too much being upset.

Horseless carriages came to some of the big cities of North Carolina, and Abby got to see one when Amelia took her to Asheville in the fall to purchase some new clothes. Amelia started talking about the day she would get the electrical run to her house for lights and some pipes put in for an indoor privy. Lots of folks in Asheville had them now, Amelia said, and although the electrical hadn't reached up to Blue Springs yet, she told Abby they would get it first thing when it did come.

Mr. Holston told everybody in school about moving pictures and brought them a newspaper from Charlotte or Asheville every now and again and made them read it to keep up with the events happening in the world.

The post office put in a telephone, and about thirty more people moved to Blue Springs to work with a timber company that had come in to cut down trees in the area. And the newspapers all said some trouble had started up in Europe. Mr. Holston told them he hoped the trouble in Europe didn't lead to a war but it might.

Abby's life took on a gentle sameness, like a quiet river moving from one place to another, one year to the next—no foam, no white water— just a calm drift toward whatever was ahead. Pa and Elsa and everybody but Laban came down more regular now that church had started up again, about a dozen times a year, usually for just one or two days at a time. During the summer and at Christmastime they stayed longer, the men putting up in the yard of Amelia's house, while Elsa, Junior, and Walter slept inside.

Many of the times they came, at Christmas especially, Luke pulled out his guitar and played and sang. His voice had caught up with his guitar playing now, and he sounded real smooth, a rich baritone that warmed up the room with its crooning. Churches in a bunch of valleys began asking him to come to sing and play for them. The churches often took up a love offering after he had finished to show their appreciation for his time and testimony.

"Luke is getting famous on us," Daniel said one August night the summer after Abby turned thirteen. "Everybody in these parts is just dying to hear him pick and sing."

"A-A-Asheville too," said Luke, a big smile on his face. "I d-d-done played there a couple of t-t-t-times."

Abby grinned with her brothers. Both of them had grown bigger than her pa, and Luke had taken on a good-sized belly. "From all the church f-f-food," he'd said when they teased him about it. "And you're movin' on toward thirty years now," said Daniel. "An old man, for sure."

Abby laughed with Daniel. Luke was only twenty-six, five years older than Daniel. "Sing me 'When the Roll Is Called Up Yonder,' " she said to her brother.

Luke grinned big and played it for her. Abby tapped her foot and sang along with him, her heart as happy as she had ever known it to be. She could read as well as most anybody in town, had three of the best friends a body could ever want, and though she didn't live with them, she got to see her family at least once a month. How much better could life get?

The night passed, and she loved every minute of it. Abby felt sad the next morning when everybody was loading up to leave, but she felt content too, satisfied in her soul that things had turned out as well as possible given the circumstances that had come her way.

CHAPTER
SEVENTEEN

Winter struck early in the year of 1913. A bitter wind blew down from the high corners of Blue Springs Mountain, its cold fingers cutting through even the heaviest shawl that Abby owned. The wind blew the leaves off the trees earlier than usual, and the mountain took on a barren look. Everybody said that if it was this bad in October and November, no telling what the good Lord had in store come January. The sun disappeared with the leaves, and the days turned as gray as a washtub and as cold as a block of ice.

On her way to school every morning, Abby ducked her head as low as she could, covered her nose and mouth with her hands, and ran hard. Always the first to arrive, she helped Mr. Holston start the fire in the black stove that stood in the center of the classroom, then held her hands close to the stove as it heated up. The kids that followed her huddled as close to the heat as possible while they did their schoolwork, but it was so cold outside even that didn't help much. Mr. Holston let them out early almost every day, so they could rush home before what warmth the day produced had disappeared on them.

Like the other pupils, Abby hurried home on the days the teacher let school out early, Lindy at her side most of the time. Thaddeus and Jubal came with them less often now, what with them being young men and all and too shy and afraid to spend time playing with girls, no matter how pretty and womanlike Abby and Lindy had become.

Tired of the gray days, Abby kept her eye on the sky all through November, hoping for a break in the cold. But none came. The month ended, and December rolled in just as bad. Mr. Holston called school off completely until the weather broke, and Abby found herself sitting in the front room at home one morning the first week of the month, with a book in her lap, her eyes still sleepy from not having woke up good just yet. Amelia was in the kitchen, knocking around with some dishes.

Abby heard heavy feet stomping on the porch. She got up and walked toward the door, but it flew open before she reached it, and there stood Topper Clack big as day. He pushed past her in a rush, his big face red with cold. The smell of liquor came with him, and again Abby wondered if the Clack men ever had a waking moment where they weren't drinking.

"Git out here, Ma!" Topper yelled. "Pa's been hurt!"

Ben Clack banged through the door next, his pa hanging on his shoulder. Abby saw a trail of blood streak out on the floor from Hal Clack's left leg. She looked at his pants. His left leg was torn up at the ankle. Hal Clack's face had turned white, and Abby knew by the color that he'd lost a lot of blood. His eyes were closed.

Amelia ran into the room, her hands over her mouth and her eyes wide as saucers.

"A rusty bear trap got him!" said Ben. "Set up on the ridge behind Solomon Porter's old place."

"Bring him into the bedroom," Amelia said, instantly taking charge. "Get him stretched out."

"I'll go fetch the doctor," Topper said.

Amelia and Ben hauled Hal to the bedroom and laid him out on the covers.

"I'll get some water boiling," said Abby.

Ben Clack glared at her. Abby dropped her eyes and ran to the kitchen. Pulling a pot from a wall shelf, she filled it with water from a bucket by the sink, carried it over to the stove and set the pot on top of it. She then threw in a couple more pieces of coal. As she waited on it to boil, she had the thought that maybe Hal Clack had finally come to his just rewards. A man as mean as him had to pay a price sometime. Maybe the good Lord would use this bear trap to give Hal Clack the gangrene and move him on past this earth to the fiery hereafter he deserved. A shiver of gladness ran down Abby's spine. Hal Clack had taken her pa's land, cast her family out on the trail. He deserved every bad thing that happened to him.

She checked the water. It was beginning to boil. She suddenly felt a pang of guilt. Would a true Christian person think such vengeful thoughts about Hal Clack? She heard footsteps and turned to see Amelia running into the kitchen.

"Need some rags," Amelia said, grabbing some white cloths from a drawer. "His ankle is all cut up, broke maybe. Got some infection in it already. He was by himself when the trap caught him. Boys didn't find him till a day later. Brought him right here."

Abby nodded. She knew that men had set traps out years ago when bears were more plentiful. Trapping was about the only way to keep a bear away from a cabin. Maybe her pa or his before him had put out the trap that got Hal Clack.

"Water is about hot," Abby said as she watched the steam rising from the pot.

"We will clean that ankle up good," said Amelia. "He will be good as new in no time."

Within five minutes Amelia had hauled the water and rags to the bed, pulled off Clack's shoes, and shoved up his pant leg to clean the ankle. He moaned and pulled away as she pressed in to wash out the wound. Ben had to hold him down so Amelia could swab the torn flesh.

Watching her work, Abby pondered the frailty of the human body. All hurt like this, Hal Clack didn't seem fearsome at all. His ankles were skinny, his face was white, and he seemed to have aged a lot since he had burned down her home a few years ago. The skin on his neck hung loose like a hound dog's, and his chest looked awful shrunk in for a man she'd once thought so strong. Years will do that to a body, she realized. Wear it down as surely as the wind and rain will wear down a mountain given enough time to have at it. She felt bad again about her earlier thoughts of revenge on Clack.

A door rattled open. She glanced up to see Topper step into the bedroom with Doc Booth at his side.

"Found him at the general store," Topper said to Ben. "Brought him straight."

Doc Booth pushed by everybody and put his medical bag on the bed. He leaned over Clack and checked his ankle, gently twisted it in different directions. Clack moaned and jerked again, but Booth held the ankle steady for a couple more seconds before laying it down. He pulled a bottle from his bag, opened it, took one of Amelia's white rags and poured some of the bottle's contents onto the rag. Then he dabbed at the cut with the rag.

"You say this is from a bear trap?" he asked without glancing up.

"Yeah, a rusty thing up on Porter's old place," growled Ben. "Way up high near the bald. Before he passed out, Pa said he had been there a day, no more. You think—"

Doc Booth held up a hand, poured more liquid onto the rag, washed the wound with it. Putting the top on the bottle, he reached back into the bag and took out another bottle. He opened it and held it to Hal Clack's lips. Clack mumbled but didn't wake up. Booth poured the liquid into his mouth anyway. About half of it dribbled down Clack's chin, but then he swallowed and the other half disappeared.

Booth wiped away the spilled medicine and turned to Amelia. "He has a broke ankle," he said, "and some infection too. Don't know how far gone it is. I will need to set the ankle." He turned to Topper and Ben. "You boys need to pitch in here. I expect he will object right smart to what we gone have to do."

"It gone hurt him?" asked Ben.

Doc Booth chuckled. "That is a sure enough bet. Now, one of you take him by the shoulders, the other by the waist. And when I lift up his ankle, hold on like you got a bull by the horns."

Topper and Ben looked at each other but did what the doctor said. Doc Booth picked up the ankle as Clack's sons grabbed their pa. Booth set his feet square and gave a heave on the ankle. Abby heard a snap, and Hal Clack rose up off the bed. All the weakness Abby had seen earlier seemed to have suddenly disappeared. Clack thrashed about like a caught trout, throwing his sons off him as he bellowed out. Booth jerked the ankle once more, and Abby thought Clack would kill him on the spot. But the boys grasped their pa again and pushed him back onto the bed. Then Booth let go of the ankle and stepped back. Pulling yet another bottle from his bag, the doctor opened the top and took a swig of drink. Clack thrashed a couple more times and then lay still, big beads of sweat all broke out on his forehead.

"He gone get better, ain't he, Doc?" asked Ben, easing away from his pa.

"It will take a couple of days before we know for sure," Booth said. "He has got a fever but maybe the infection hasn't reached into the bone yet."

Ben licked his lips and glanced at Topper. Amelia moved to her husband, wiped his forehead with a rag.

"I have to go," said Booth. "I'll check back again tomorrow." He handed Amelia the two bottles he'd opened. "Keep the wound clean and give him a drink of this every four hours or so." She took the bottles. "And if you believe in it, say a prayer or two for him."

His bag in hand, Booth left the bedroom. Amelia followed the doctor out. Abby started to go with her, but Topper stepped over and grabbed her arm. Abby was about to call Amelia back yet didn't feel right about asking a mama to face conflict with her son, so she stayed quiet. Ben looked out the door, then back to Topper.

"They on the porch," Ben said.

Topper nodded, frowned at Abby. "Your pa set that trap," he said.

Ben moved to a spot behind her, like a wolf sneaking up behind a rabbit.

Abby's breath shortened, but she swallowed it down and spoke braver than she felt. "You don't know that," she said.

"Who else?" asked Ben from behind.

Abby jumped at the sound. It sounded so close, so sinister. But inside something told her that she better stand up to Topper and Ben, that she better not let them see her fear. Bullies sometimes back down when a body stands up to them.

Though flushed and trembly, Abby pulled her arm away from Topper. "I don't know who else might have set it," she said. "But men sometimes put traps out to protect their stills. You sure you or your pa didn't set it yourself, then forgot where it was?"

"That is a smart-aleck answer," Topper said, stepping closer. "What makes you think my pa has a still up there?"

She felt Ben edge closer too. His breath touched hot on the back of her neck. Abby thought quickly. "Why else is your pa going up so high on the bald? I don't expect he was hunting in this weather."

Topper looked at Ben, and Abby knew she had hit on the truth. Hal Clack did have a still up there somewhere, probably near the spring at the head of Slick Rock Creek. But whether or not Clack had set the trap himself, she had no way of knowing. Maybe he did, maybe her pa did.

She stared at Topper. While she couldn't tell for sure, he had to be almost to the middle of his thirties—a grown man with no more education than a creek rock. He had a wild streak and a taste for liquor that no amount of the doublings seemed able to quench. Like his pa, he smelled bad too.

"You better hope he don't die," said Ben from behind in a voice that chilled her blood. "You and your sorry excuse for a pa too."

"I don't want anybody to die," Abby said, not turning around. "Not even your pa."

Topper raised a fist. She ducked, but he didn't swing at her. Abby waited another second, the touch of Ben Clack's breath on her neck making her want to throw up. Ben touched her neck where it joined at her shoulders. She jerked but didn't turn.

"Get on out of here," mumbled Topper, dropping his hands to his side. "Afore I do something I might regret."

Not waiting to argue, Abby pulled away from Ben's touch and scurried from the room, her heart beating fast. For it wasn't what Topper might do that scared her the most. Without knowing why, she felt that he wasn't the Clack she had to worry about. Something about Ben, maybe Topper's junior by ten years or so, made her more anxious than Topper ever did.

––––––––

Clack hung on between life and death for over a month. Christmas arrived and passed while he still lay in bed. Elsa brought Junior and Walter down from the holler for a couple of days but Solomon and the boys stayed away because Clack's sons had set up in an abandoned cabin only a mile from Blue Springs. Placing the blame for their pa's broken ankle on Solomon, Topper and Ben made it known to everybody that would listen that they wanted a face-to-face meeting with Solomon Porter. Elsa told Abby and Amelia that Solomon didn't think it the right time to deal with the Clacks. After their pa's situation cleared up—whether he lived or died—then he would give the Clack boys the meeting they wanted.

At least one of the Clack sons dropped by almost every day to see their pa, each of them seemingly drunker every time they came. They traipsed in mud with their heavy boots, demanded hot food whenever they snapped their fingers, and sometimes fell asleep on the floor of the front room without any kind of attention to the mess they made.

Abby did what she could to help Amelia, but, remembering her last encounter with Topper and Ben, she stayed out of sight as much as possible, often spending the night with Lindy whenever the opportunity presented itself. No use throwing a mouse in front of a rattlesnake, Abby figured. Stay quiet, out of the house, and out of trouble.

About mid-January the weather turned warmer all of a sudden. The sun seemed to take on new life, its heat betraying the fact that it was still dead winter. All of the snow melted, and the streets soon became muddy from the runoff. Almost overnight a whole bunch of different kinds of birds appeared and began singing their sweet songs. If Abby hadn't known better, she would have sworn it was April.

Walking back from the general store late one Saturday afternoon near the end of the month, Abby rounded a corner and headed up the hill toward Amelia's place. She passed through a pasture and through a shoot of cedar trees, their branches shady green as the light dimmed behind the mountain. Abby had some canned goods and a sack of flour in a burlap bag over her shoulder. She ducked under a cedar. Someone moved up from behind, wrapped a hand over her mouth, another hand to her throat.

"Keep your quiet," said a voice she recognized immediately. "No reason to rile yourself."

Abby held her breath. What did Ben Clack want with her? She hadn't hurt his pa. Another thought rolled in her head but she didn't think it possible so shoved it away.

Ben dropped the hand from her neck down to her waist, placing the hand firmly around her body. "You a mighty pretty thing," he whispered, his other hand still covering her mouth, his hot breath on the back of her neck. "Growed up to womanhood this past year."

A wave of nausea rolled through Abby's stomach as she realized her instinct had been right. In the last year or so she had noticed boys looking at her in a different way than when she was a child, a way that made her both pleased and somewhat scared. The notion that Ben Clack had noticed her in this way created pure disgust in her.

"This can go easy," said Ben. "Up to you." He moved the hand on her waist up to her shoulders, ran his fingers over her neck. Abby's skin crawled. His fingers felt like a spider's legs. She tensed herself to fight him but found herself unable to move, her body frozen in place by his chilling touch.

Then she wanted to faint, to close her eyes and black out, to fall into a sleep so deep she could disappear forever. She closed her eyes and sunk into herself. What Ben Clack was doing no longer affected her or made any difference in who she was, what she would be. Her body relaxed. She knew Ben was moving but she no longer seemed a part of the present moment. It was all happening somewhere outside of her, beyond the boundaries of her body and mind.

As if in a dream, she sensed Ben grabbing the back of her blouse. Air touched her skin and she knew he had pulled the blouse from her ankle-length skirt. His fingers edged under the blouse and touched her back. Feeling as though struck with a bolt of lightning, Abby suddenly returned to consciousness. No way could she stand by and allow this to happen without a fight! The bad things that had happened to her so far had come from forces beyond her control. She could do nothing to stop her mama and Aunt Francis from dying, nothing to keep Laban from gambling away their land and forcing them to move. But she was almost grown now; she had choices in the way she handled things, what she did or did not do. No longer would she just let things act on her. Now she would act on them!

On instinct, Abby willed herself to stay still.

Ben's hand ran up her spine toward her neck. "You doin' fine," he said, his voice low. "Real fine." He touched her shoulder and eased her slowly around to face him. One hand stayed over her mouth, the other now stroked her neck near her collarbone.

Gritting her teeth, Abby forced herself to wait. He turned her further around. She saw his eyes, bloodshot and narrow. She hated him. From some unknown place, a strange calm washed through her, a sense of detached precision. She knew exactly what she had to do.

She moved quicker than she knew she could. Her teeth bit into the flesh of the index finger of the hand on her mouth. She tasted blood. Her right leg kicked upward, and her foot struck home. Ben Clack cursed. Abby jerked away as he doubled over and grabbed his groin area. She started to run, but Ben cursed again and threw himself in her direction. A hand latched on to her ankle, and she tripped and fell. Ben jumped on her then, his heavy body pressing her into the ground. She fought hard, yet when she opened her mouth and tried to scream, no sound erupted. Her vocal cords seemed to have dried up. Her fingers poked at Ben's eyes. Her teeth found the flesh of his shoulder, and he screamed.

Abby heard the sound and liked the pain it voiced. She had caused that pain, and that knowledge gave her even more courage. She pushed her fingers into the sockets of his eyes. He pushed her to the ground again, grabbed her hands, and pinned them at her sides. She tried to continue the fight, but his weight pressed harder and harder, and she knew she couldn't go on forever. He weighed too much. He slapped her then, and tears welled up in her eyes, but still she didn't cry out.

Abby heard a dog bark, and she recognized the sound. Patch! She opened her mouth to call the dog. Ben tried to cover her face, but she bit his hand once more and yelled to Patch. This time her voice worked, and she heard Patch bark again.

"Abby!"

The sound rose from the hill below the line of cedars, and Abby instantly knew it was Thaddeus's voice that called for her. Her strength doubled. She rolled sideways and yelled again. "Thaddeus!"

She heard movement in the trees, footsteps coming closer.

Ben Clack let her go and jumped up. "I ain't done with you," he growled, moving away toward the trees. "Don't you forget it." Then he was gone.

Abby pulled herself up. Thaddeus was on the way! She shoved her blouse back into her skirt. She didn't want Thaddeus to see her like this. How could she explain it? What would he think? Maybe that she encouraged Ben in some way? Embarrassed by the idea of talking about what had just happened, she forced herself to stand.

"Abby!" Thaddeus yelled out again, not far away now.

Abby smoothed down her hair but didn't answer. Taking a deep breath, she wiped her eyes and hurried off through the trees. No reason to tell anybody about any of this. She had stopped Ben Clack. She could take care of herself.

———

Three days later, Mr. Holston called school back into session for all the kids who could get there. So Abby joined Lindy, Thaddeus, Jubal, and about ten others back in school on Monday just as January reached its conclusion. It was so warm they didn't even need the stove.

In the first row as usual, Abby, having taken off her shawl, sat with a gray tablet in front of her on her desk and a thick pencil in her hand. Mr. Holston had given her an old math book from his college days, and she was busy copying down some problems from it. She stuck the end of the pencil into her mouth and chewed on it. Though she'd come to the point where she could read just about any book anybody gave her, math did not always sit as well, took more labor than all her other subjects put together. And Mr. Holston had told her she had to do every problem in the book, beginning to end.

"You will need this math for college," he had told her the day he handed the book to her. "So set your head to it."

Abby thumped the pencil against her jaw as she took a breath. If she didn't do better on her math, maybe she couldn't go to college. No matter how smart Mr. Holston said she was.

The door to the schoolhouse opened. Abby heard it but had math on her mind so didn't turn around. Mr. Holston left the blackboard and walked toward the door. Abby kept her eyes on her math problems. She heard muttering behind her head. A few seconds later she felt a touch on her shoulder. Glancing up, she saw Mr. Holston at her side.

He whispered into her ear, "Mrs. Clack is here."

Abby quickly switched around, waved to Amelia, who stood by the door.

"She says you need to come," said Mr. Holston.

Abby's brow wrinkled. "She say what for?"

"No, just asked for you."

Though confused, Abby nodded, put down her pencil, and left her tablet and math book on the desk. She got up and followed Mr. Holston to Amelia.

"You need to come with me," Amelia said without explanation.

Abby could see from her eyes that Amelia had been crying and guessed it had something to do with her husband. Had he died? But was that a reason to cry? A sense of shame came over her at the bad thought, and she asked Jesus to forgive her for her meanness. No matter how rough Hal Clack and his sons were, Amelia no doubt loved them, and Abby didn't want Amelia to suffer any more grief than had already come her way.

Following Amelia, Abby left the schoolhouse. She wanted to ask about Mr. Clack, but since Amelia didn't seem ready to say anything about him, she let it pass. They stayed silent all the way home. At the front door Amelia reached down and took Abby's hand. Amelia's hand was warm, and Abby wondered how it would feel to a wife for her husband to die. Would it feel like losing an arm or a leg? Something you had grown accustomed to and then suddenly were without? Yet Hal Clack didn't stay much with Amelia, so why would she miss what she didn't have around that often? And even when he did come home, he treated her without respect. Better not to have a husband than to have one who acted so coarsely.

Amelia opened the door, and they entered the front room. "Things are rough," said Amelia, shaking her head.

Abby wanted to give her a hug and tell her that she could make it through this, no matter how sad she felt today. She had experience in such things and could say the words in a way that would offer comfort to Amelia.

Still clutching Abby's hand, Amelia led her to the door of the bedroom where Mr. Clack had stayed all these weeks. "Stay here," Amelia said.

Abby nodded, then Amelia stepped into the room. Abby wondered if she was covering up her husband's body, making him presentable for the folks in Blue Springs to come see him. She heard muttering inside the room. Were Clack's boys in there too? Her body tensed. She hadn't seen Ben Clack since the episode in the cedars, which had made it easier to shut it out of her mind. Though Thaddeus had asked her once about why she had called out to him, she had told him she didn't know what he meant. He had shrugged and let the subject drop.

The door opened. Amelia stepped back to let Abby enter. Abby walked into the bedroom and saw Hal Clack sitting up in the bed, his back propped on a pillow. His eyes were dull but open. They bored in on her as she drew to a quick stop. A stab of disappointment ran through her stomach when she realized he was alive, and she again told herself she ought not think such awful things. Clack licked his lips, which were cracked and gray-colored. Abby glanced at Amelia, who stood in the corner with her hands over her mouth, her body shrinking in on itself.

Topper and Ben stood by their ma. Both were slouched against the wall and as relaxed as a couple of wolves with full bellies, lying in the sun. Abby's face flushed. Ben and Topper looked at each other, then grinned at her. They appeared too happy for her liking. The pleasure on their faces told Abby something bad was about to happen to her. She wondered if Ben had told Topper about the episode in the cedars. She hoped not.

Topper stepped to his pa's side. Ben moved over to Abby, slipped behind her back where she could barely see him from the corner of her eye. Abby cringed, her senses now sure that Ben and Topper planned to throw something evil her way.

A crooked grin broke out on Topper's face. "Pa's gone make it," he said.

"No thanks to your sorry pa," whispered Ben.

"He has started to eat," said Topper.

"And he took to the jug again today," Ben announced. "Man gone make it so long as he can lift his own jug to his lips. A sure sign, no escapin' it."

Abby looked to Amelia. What did any of this have to do with her? Yes, she had given fleeting thought, even hope, to the idea that Clack might die. Make a lot of lives easier if he did. But the Clack boys didn't know that. So why call her in this way? Why put so much focus on her on the very afternoon their pa started regaining his strength?

Amelia held her eyes for just a second before lowering her head. Abby suddenly knew that something had already been decided, something that affected her. And Amelia could do nothing about it this time, not even take a shotgun to her husband and make him back away.

"Ain't no Porter gone stay here any longer," said Topper, making plain the tidings Abby had already sensed.

"We already let it go on too long," Ben said. "I been trying to tell Pa that from the beginning. You can't mix a skunk pup in with a litter of good coon dogs."

"We let you stay for Ma's sake," said Topper. "She ain't had nobody since Elsa took up with your trashy pa. We been kind to you for Ma's cause, more than you deserve."

Ben added, "But all that's gone end now. No matter what Ma says. She don't need the likes of you around. Pa has finally seen it my way. You leave here tomorrow."

Abby heard a sob from the corner. Amelia was taking this hard. She wanted to go to her and put an arm around her and tell her not to fret, that she had done all she could, more than Abby ever expected. But she knew it wasn't the time or place for such a thing.

"Where will I go?" Abby said, suddenly dealing with the reality of the situation.

Topper shrugged. "Don't matter to us," he said.

"I will go back to my pa," she said, quickly sizing up her options and knowing it was the only one that made sense.

"Like Topper says, it don't matter to us where you go," said Ben. "Just so you take your leave of this place."

The sobs from the corner grew louder, but Abby avoided looking at Amelia. No reason to make her feel any more ashamed than she already was, she figured. No reason to make her any more grieved.

Abby squared her shoulders. The Clacks had made their choice, and she couldn't change that. But she would not let them see any fear in her. Solomon had at least taught her that. "I will go at daybreak," she said, her jaw firm.

"That you will," said Ben. "That you will."

CHAPTER
EIGHTEEN

Abby's feet moved heavy the next morning as she packed up her belongings, said good-bye to Amelia, and hurriedly left the house. The good-byes to Lindy, Thaddeus, Jubal, and Mr. Holston broke her heart.

"I have already taught you about all I know anyway," said Mr. Holston when she told him she had to leave Blue Springs. "But I'll still be giving you assignments every time you or one of your kin come to town. You can do the work at home and then get it back to me the next time someone makes it down to Blue Springs. That way you can keep on studying. It won't be long before you'll be ready to try your hand at college."

Abby wanted to believe the teacher's plan would work but suspected it would not. Though she'd never walked it straight out, she figured at least six miles separated the school from her pa's new place. True, such a distance was not impossible to walk in good weather at her age, but it would prove real troublesome in cold or rainy weather. Even if she tried it, her attendance would surely fall to almost nothing, and she might as well not go to all the bother for so little as that. Also, if she lived with Pa and Elsa, she would feel guilty if she didn't spend her time helping with the chores. But she didn't say this to anybody.

Lindy started crying when Abby told her she had to go. "I will not let you leave," she moaned. "You can come live with me."

Abby shook her head. "You got no room for me, you know that. Your house is already filled more than needed."

Lindy nodded her understanding. Her grandma had taken in two of the timber workers who needed board. No more space for somebody new. She walked with Abby as they reached the border of Blue Springs. Thaddeus and Jubal hung back, too shy and unsure to say much.

"This will break Thaddeus's heart," said Lindy, glancing over her shoulder to make sure he wasn't close enough to hear.

Abby looked surprised.

"You know he has set his hat for you," Lindy said.

"I don't know any such thing."

"Then you are blind," Lindy said as she glanced at him again. "Thaddeus is so smitten with you that he can barely talk when you come around."

Abby shrugged. "I just thought he was shy."

"Oh, he is shy all right. Tongue-tied if you get within fifty feet of him."

Abby didn't know what to say so she said nothing. She liked Thaddeus fine, but what had happened with Ben Clack had scared her so much she didn't think she wanted anything to do with any boy for a long time. And now that she was moving back up the mountain, she would not see much of Thaddeus anymore.

They reached the fork where the road started its upward trail. Lindy hugged her. Thaddeus and Jubal kicked at the ground, told her they would maybe come see her in the spring. Then Abby left them, not looking back.

The trip up the mountain passed slowly. She had left Patch behind to keep Amelia company, so she felt lonely. It had rained overnight, and the trail had turned slick. Abby picked her way up the path with her chin set firm. One more trial, she thought, one more rock she had to climb to see what would become of her life. Her most pressing question was the matter of her schooling. How would she manage until she could find a way to continue her learning? Though she already had more education than most of the folks on the mountain, she knew that what she'd learned was not even a scratch on the surface. Mr. Holston had told her as much. "A whole world of learning out there," he had said to her more than once. "You study hard enough and learn some of those things and you can do something with yourself, something you never even imagined."

Mr. Holston's words had filled Abby with a desire she had never dreamed possible. Not only did she still want to leave the mountain, but Mr. Holston had convinced her she might actually have a chance to do it. But now that her schooling had come to an end she figured she was stuck on the mountain forever.

Her shoulders feeling like lead weights, Abby forced herself on home. When she arrived at her pa's place in early afternoon and explained to everybody that the Clack boys had thrown her out, they just nodded as if expecting such a thing all along, then stepped back to let her in the cabin. Elsa gave her a glass of buttermilk, and Walter and Junior stared at her like she'd come from a circus or something. But nobody asked her too many questions. Abby smiled to herself. Mountain folks figured a body would talk when she wanted to talk. No purpose served by jabbing her with questions about anything.

When it was near suppertime, she helped Elsa fix it and put it on the table. They all sat down to eat, and Elsa commented on how much help Abby had been on her first day home. Junior and Walter—both of them big boys with white faces and dark hair—wanted to sit beside her. Abby noticed how healthy Junior looked. Apparently the hard mountain life agreed with him. Daniel teased her about how much like a woman she had become, and later, Luke played her a new song he had written. Abby asked them if they had a place of their own yet. Daniel said no, but they planned on building something in the spring. Pa chewed on his pipe and listened as everyone talked.

Watching him, Abby recognized for the first time that she and her pa had more than a few mannerisms in common. In a crowd they both stayed pretty closemouthed. Neither of them was given to any big or sudden motions. They both could sit for a long period of time and reflect on the matter at hand. And both kept their emotions in tight rein, all dammed up like a river wanting to bust out over the banks.

Everybody finished supper yet no one pushed away from the table. Solomon lit his pipe and started puffing. The conversation slowed to a low ebb. Elsa filled a bowl off the table, stepped to the door, and threw out the scraps to the dogs. Luke held his guitar but didn't play it. They all stared at Abby, and she knew they wanted to hear her talk, hear her tell what had happened to her in the last few years. But she didn't know if she felt ready to say much, to say out plain how she'd come to a place where she wanted to leave the mountain, how she'd come home but only long enough to figure out what she wanted to do next and how to go about the accomplishing of it.

"Y-y-you more like M-m-ma than last time we s-s-saw you," said Luke, taking her off the hook to speak. "All g-g-growed up and all."

Abby dropped her eyes. She hadn't talked about Ma in a long time. Her arms felt heavy, and the grief she had felt when she left Blue Springs deepened. For the first time the reality of leaving her friends and school hit her hard.

"Your ma would be proud of you," Solomon said. "All the learning you have taken."

Abby's eyes filled with tears. Her pa seldom said such personal things. She liked hearing it, but the day had hurt enough already without dealing with such a matter as this.

"Y-y-you look like that carvin' Pa g-g-gave you," said Luke. "S-s-spittin' image, I always said."

"That was maybe my best work," said Solomon.

Abby froze as she realized she had left the carving in the closet at the Clack house where she'd put it years ago. She held her breath and hoped Pa didn't ask her about it. If he did and she had to admit she had left it behind, he would think she didn't care about the one thing he had given her. Here he had finally said something about her ma to her, and she had forgotten to bring home the carving he had made in her likeness. If he found out he would never forgive her, and she couldn't blame him.

To her relief Elsa moved back to the table right at that moment, and nobody else mentioned the carving. Abby promised herself that she would get it the next time she visited Blue Springs. Everybody kept looking at her, but she was so worried about the carving that she said little. Apparently giving up on getting her to talk, Solomon stood up a few minutes later, shook out his pipe in the fireplace, said his good-night and took off to bed. Everybody else soon followed.

The night passed and the next day. Everybody accepted Abby as if she had never left. She joined the family in their daily labor. A week followed and then a month. Another followed right after, and before Abby knew it, spring had blossomed. The trees budded out fresh and green as they always did, and the birds landed back from their nesting spots to the south. With no way to go back to school, Abby gave up hope and settled down to the routine of taking care of life's necessities. She filled her days by making herself handy around the cabin. Junior and Walter trailed along behind her like two puppies following a gravy bowl. When she got a spare moment, she took out the few books she owned and read to them. They seemed to like it, their round faces staring up at her with steady attention. Since they lived so far up the mountain, neither of the boys had attended any school. Elsa had taught them some letters and numbers, but now Abby became the one they turned to with their many questions. Without planning it, they started a morning routine of study after the early chores, the two boys sitting at the kitchen table as she gave them the benefit of her studies.

Daniel and Luke stayed gone a lot, though Abby was sure they weren't off drinking and making trouble like Laban. Luke played his guitar all over the region, in churches mostly and some county fairs in the fall. Daniel traveled with him when he could but he had other matters to tend to as well, matters that kept him plenty busy. Even though he didn't talk much about this, Abby saw quickly that Daniel had a knack for picking up odd jobs: timber cutting in the warm dry months, helping build a bridge down near Asheville, or filling in when anybody took sick at the general store, post office, or livery stable. Without anyone showing him much, Daniel took to bricking as well. Once or twice in Abby's first year back home, somebody asked him to go to Asheville to do some brickwork there. He accepted their invitation and stayed gone for a couple of weeks both times. He often gave Abby a quarter from his wages, and she knew he handed Pa a couple of dollars every now and again too. But other than that she didn't know what he did with his earnings. Remembering Laban, she hoped Daniel wasn't gambling or drinking it away.

Abby traveled down to Blue Springs every month or so, mostly to go to Jesus Holiness on the Sundays when Preacher Bruster showed up. She would sit by Lindy at the church, with Thaddeus and Jubal silent as fence posts in the pew behind them. Mr. Holston gave her a new book to read on some of the Sundays she showed up. Abby gratefully accepted them as the treasures they were. Every time she traveled to Blue Springs she wanted to go by the Clack house, not only to see Amelia, who she discovered she missed a lot, but also to keep her pledge to retrieve the carving her pa had made. But every time she came down, the Clack boys were at home to see their pa, who was still laid up there. So she could not bring herself to stop by, not even for a minute. As long as Ben Clack was anywhere within five miles, she wanted nothing to do with that house.

Her fourteenth birthday arrived, and Elsa gave her a new piece of yellow ribbon for her hair. Nobody else said much of anything. Spring passed and summer started off hot. Abby toiled in the fields and taught the lessons to Junior and Walter. All the while she tried not to think about another school year soon to begin without her. But she couldn't help herself. Her mind wandered and she thought of all the learning she would no longer receive, and she felt as though her life had ended. She would live and die on Blue Springs Mountain and never travel more than twenty miles from the cabin where she was born.

———

June and July moved along with each day seeming to grow more heated than the last. By the time August pressed in, the sun scorched down so hard that the dogs Hal Clack had brought with him to his house in Blue Springs hardly moved off the porch. Now with his ankle pretty much healed up, Clack was beginning to stir some in spite of the heat. All the infection in the bone had disappeared, the scar had turned from a bright red to a dull brown color, and Clack could walk again. Though Clack figured he owed some appreciation to a lot of people for the fact that he could still draw breath, he was also convinced that only a man of his particular stoutness would have survived the ordeal. Therefore, he offered no one any thanks.

On the last day of August he crawled out of bed around midafternoon, quickly ate the ham and collards Amelia had prepared for him, and leaned back in his chair, his jug handy on the table. He had been drinking off and on since waking up, and his mood was now generous. Amelia sat beside him, her hands cupped on either side of her throat, her eyes staring at the table. Having seen the look more than once, Clack knew his wife had something she wanted to say but was afraid to say it. A sympathy he didn't feel very often passed through him then, and he decided that since she'd taken such good care of him, maybe he ought to speak nicely to her for once.

"You make good collards," he said, nodding toward his plate. "Best I ever ate."

Amelia kept her eyes down. "Pleased you partial to them," she said.

Clack took a drink from his liquor jug, and his head felt dizzy. But his good feelings stayed steady for the time being. "You doctored me good. I ain't forgettin' that."

Amelia looked up, her eyebrows bumping together in a confused look. Even though drunk, Clack could see she didn't trust him. He almost chuckled with pleasure at the thought. A man who didn't surprise a woman every now and again lost his control over her. If a man was too easy to figure out, a woman had him under her thumb.

"Maybe I will buy you something down in Asheville after awhile," he said, taking another drink. "A new dress maybe."

Amelia laid her hands on the table, one on top of the other. "I want to go see Elsa," she said quickly.

"I don't know about that," Clack said. "She is still with Solomon Porter." His words slurred.

"I know that," said Amelia. "But I want to see my grandbabies. Abby too. She left some things when she took off from here so fast back in the winter. I want to put those things back in her hands."

"What kind of things?" Clack's head cleared. He took another drink.

Amelia's hands covered her mouth. Clack noted the reaction and knew his wife had said more than she wanted. A surge of thrill rolled through his bones. What had Abby Porter left at his house that his wife needed to deliver?

"You gone let me go?" asked Amelia, ignoring his question.

Clack's thoughts jumbled some. The liquor was clouding his head. But he still had enough sense to know something was fishy. Was his wife trying to move him off the subject? Or were the things Abby Porter had left behind not worth mentioning? An old coat? A hairbrush? A few books that the teacher down at school gave her?

He licked his lips. Faced his wife again. "I want to see what that Porter girl left," he said. "See it right now."

Amelia shrugged. Clack thought it looked forced.

"Nothing to see," she said.

Clack reached over and put a hand on her neck. She tensed. "I'll make judgment on that," he said.

Amelia stayed still.

He squeezed her neck. His mind cleared momentarily. "I ain't . . . ain't forgot how you come at me with a shotgun to protect that girl a few years back," he said. "You done took to her, no question. And I ain't faultin' you for it, what with you all alone here and all. But I got to make sure she ain't got twenty dollars put away that you tryin' to take back to her."

"That child never saw no twenty dollars in her whole life," Amelia said. "You know that."

Clack moved swiftly, his hands grabbing both of his wife's shoulders and pulling her up before she could react. He held her before him now, his hands tight on her elbows. "Show me what she left!" he growled. "No more smart talk from you!"

He pushed her out of the kitchen and into the hallway. She stopped and pressed up against the wall as she struggled to fight back. But Clack yanked her off the wall and threw her to the floor.

Amelia buried her head in her hands. "I won't do it!" she cried.

He jerked her back to her feet. "Where you got her things?" he yelled. "Show me or I will throw you out of this house and sell it and you will have to live with me and the boys up on the mountain. And you'll never see those mongrel grandkids again, or Elsa either. Not when they come down to church, not when they come down to buy goods. Not ever, you got that? You will never see them again!"

Amelia sobbed into her hands and shook her head. Clack could see that he had broken her. Even if she could stand the notion of leaving her house, she could not face the possibility of never seeing her daughter and grandbabies again.

Although continuing to cry, Amelia led him into the bedroom where Abby had slept. She walked to the closet, opened it, and pulled out a large wicker basket. Hauling the basket over to the bed, she set it down and flipped it open. A wood carving lay on the top of a stack of things that filled the basket.

"Where did you get this basket?" he asked.

"Elsa brought it when she lived here with her boys," said Amelia. "Left it when she took off back with Solomon."

Clack picked up the carving and studied it closely. "Well, I'll be . . ." he whispered. "Looks just like Rose Porter! Solomon did it; nobody else with the skill with wood that he has. Have to give him that."

He tossed the carving on the bed and then dumped out the rest of the basket. He saw a fancy hat, a pair of black shoes, some crocheting materials, a piece of cloth, all wrapped up together. He held up the cloth and shook it. A piece of tablet paper fell out. The paper looked old, brittle at the edges.

Picking up the paper and unfolding it, he asked, "What we got here?"

"Nothing," Amelia said. "Just an old letter."

"Who from?" he said, squinting at the letter as if doing so would help him read it.

Amelia sat heavily down on the bed, her hands over her mouth. Clack almost laughed. She was so easy to figure. Her posture said she didn't want him to know the letter's contents.

He took a step toward her, shoved the letter in her face. "Read it to me," he demanded.

She shook her head.

He threw the letter on her lap. "Either read it or start packin'!"

She picked up the letter, looked up at him, her eyes begging.

Clack pointed to the letter. "Read it."

"I wish that bear trap had done you in," she said quietly.

He chuckled and took no offense. "You ain't the only one," he said. "But it did not and so you still got to deal with me. So read me that letter now or make ready to suffer the consequences."

She read him the letter, every word wracked by her tears. Clack drank from his jug and listened, his eyes widening as he realized what he was hearing. When Amelia had finished, she laid the letter on her lap. For several minutes neither of them spoke. Then Clack pulled his wife from the bed and pushed her out the door. She did not resist.

Closing the door behind her, Clack moved back to the bed and picked up the letter in one hand and the carving in the other. He lifted the letter to his nose and sniffed it. Though he knew it was fourteen years old, he had the hope that he might catch a whiff of Rose Porter on the paper, some touch of aroma that would help him remember a woman he'd truly thought he loved. But no such smell rewarded him.

He held up the carving next and studied it from every angle. Solomon had made it in the likeness of his wife. But it also bore a powerful resemblance to his girl, Abby, a girl who had rounded out into womanhood now. Still holding the two treasures, Clack eased down onto the bed, his jug in hand. As the sun disappeared outside, he drank swig after swig of liquor. Just after dark he fell into a drunken sleep, the carving and letter beside him on the bed.

———————

Amelia Clack waited for almost an hour after her husband fell asleep. But then, as quiet as a cat, she slipped into the room and made her way over to the bed. Her husband's snoring filled the room, and the air smelled awful. For a few seconds Amelia stood over him and watched in disgust. Then, her hands shaky but determined, she rolled him over and pulled the carving and letter from his side. Quickly escaping the room, she wrapped the two items in a piece of gray cloth and headed to the back of the house. If she was lucky and hid the things well enough, he wouldn't even remember the pieces, she figured. A man as drunk as he was forgot a lot of things. He had done it in the past. She hoped he would do it again.

CHAPTER
NINETEEN

September bore in as hot as August, the days so warm that none of the birds seemed willing to fly south, and the squirrels paid no attention to the task of gathering nuts for winter. A few wispy clouds drifted through the broad canopy of blue sky that gazed down day after day on the mountains in and around Blue Springs, but not even the foliage responded to the change in the calendar. The leaves on the trees remained green, and barely a one of them dropped off when the wind, light as a soft breath, fingered its way through the air. About the only thing that seemed active on the mountain that fall was the Solomon Porter family. As always, Solomon had them all toiling hard—gathering corn, canning fruit, preparing the cabin, cutting and hauling wood. From sunup to sundown everybody kept their hands busy and their heads down.

Abby joined in with everybody else. Her body, now unmistakably that of a fully developed woman, firmed up strong under the strain of the rough work. Her hands took on calluses, and her face turned brown with the sun. Her shoulders and arms had developed a muscular tone. She liked the way this felt. She could handle herself, she decided one day as she hauled in an armful of wood she had helped cut. Just let Ben Clack make a play on her now. She would pick up a stick and knock him down, yes she would.

For a moment she enjoyed the rush of anger that surged through her stomach. Ben Clack deserved to hurt, he and all his mean-hearted kin too. But then she knew she ought not desire such a fate on anybody, not even on a Clack. A good Christian wouldn't think such an awful thing. She was no better than the Clacks herself, an attitude she needed to work on if she wanted to make sweet Jesus happy with her.

After supper one evening about halfway through the month, Daniel walked in from Asheville and surprised everyone with the announcement that he had a break in his labor due to a lack of the right brick color. They all welcomed him home, and he sat down at the table. Elsa brought him a dipper of water.

"You come through Blue Springs on the way up?" Solomon asked.

Daniel nodded.

"So what is the news?" asked Elsa.

Daniel shrugged, swigged his water. "Preacher Bruster is planning on conducting a fall meeting beginning on Sunday," he said. "You heard that yet?"

Solomon shook his head. "We had to skip the last couple of preachings, with work and all. And I had to go see your uncle Pierce one weekend. He broke a toe."

"He doing all right now?"

"Yeah, just don't get around much."

Daniel nodded. Everybody knew that Pierce and Erline Porter hardly ever set foot off their property. "Preacher Bruster said everybody needs to come," said Daniel, back to the revival. "We got trouble brewing in Europe and these new folks are moving into Blue Springs; nobody knows anybody much anymore. Preacher Bruster said the whole town could use some revival."

"Y-y-you reckon w-w-we can go, Pa?" Luke asked.

Solomon made a couple of cuts on a piece of wood in his hands, blew the shavings off and held up the wood for inspection. "We made good progress on the corn," he said. "And most of the canning is done already. Reckon we can go to meeting for a few days."

Abby wanted to jump for joy. She hadn't spent more than half a day in Blue Springs since she left last winter. Going to meeting meant she and her family would stay down there for at least a whole week, maybe more if the Holy Ghost took hold strong enough. Elsa and her two boys would stay with her ma; Daniel, Luke, and Pa would no doubt bed down in the woods, and she would stay with Lindy.

"We will head on down there on Saturday," said Solomon. "So everybody needs to make their preparatories before then."

The rest of the week passed in a blur. Abby packed up her only Sunday dress, a bright blue one that Amelia had given her the last time she'd traveled to Blue Springs. Like most everybody else who didn't have the money for much variety in clothing, she would wear the dress every night of the meeting. In addition to the dress, she folded up her two pairs of overalls and her three best blouses and placed them in the burlap sack she used for travel. Her black shoes and undergarments joined the other clothes in the sack. She pretty much had packed all the clothing she owned of any passable nature.

The trip down to Blue Springs went without incident. When they reached the outskirts of town, Abby left everybody and headed straight to Lindy's house. Lindy's mouth fell open when she opened the door and saw her. She hugged Abby hard and took her right on in. Mr. Holston hugged her too and asked if she had kept up with her reading, and she told him she did the best she could with the time she had. Though she sagged a little at the thought of how much school she had missed, she quickly told herself this wasn't the time for self-pity and so pushed the feeling away.

Thaddeus greeted her that night when he came in from his job with the timber company. Abby noted that he had filled out some and taken on the appearance of a young man. He had some fuzz coming in on his chin, and his voice sounded deep as a barrel. His head seemed to reach almost to the ceiling, his blond hair falling into his eyes except when he brushed it back with his large, slender hands. As always, Thaddeus said little around her. Abby kept her quiet too.

Lindy watched them both with a silly grin on her face. Abby wanted to poke her and tell her to keep her thoughts away from such matters, but knew it would do no good. Lindy often saw things that simply weren't there. Like the notion that Thaddeus cared a whit about Abby or her for him. A silly idea.

As she lay down to sleep that night, Lindy on the other side of the bed, Abby offered a word of thanks to God that the church meeting had given her the chance to come to Blue Springs and spend some time with her friends. While she prayed, she suddenly had a revelation, an insight as plain as a voice speaking to her. Here she had come to town for a meeting, yet she hadn't given any attention to the purpose of the meeting itself. All she had done was see it as a chance to visit with her friends. Of course, this wasn't a bad thing in itself, but surely not the most God-honoring way to consider the matter.

Disturbed by her callous disregard of what was most important, Abby rolled over and stared at the wall. What a sinner she was! She had given no thought to God.

She remembered her bad feelings about Ben Clack just a few days previous. She hated him, no way to deny it. Hated all his kin too, except for his ma. Abby wondered how a true Christian could wish harm on another person like she wished on all the Clack men. Had she broken some commandment with those mean hopes, a commandment that maybe even the Lord could not forgive?

She considered another of her transgressions: her resentment about moving back in with her pa. Her skin warmed with shame. Nobody right with Jesus could feel so sad about living with her own flesh and blood! How selfish of her to want to leave her family just so she could attend school, advance her own self with little care for anyone else.

The moon outside moved to the one window in the room and peeked in at Abby. Another insight stood up and looked at her. She had never made any public testimony of her belief, had never given any witness to the church that she had trusted Jesus as the Master.

Abby drew her knees to her chest and pondered the matter. She'd seen people do this all her life—stand up before all the church folks and tell how God had come to them in a vision, how God had spoken to them, called them to the arms of Jesus. How Jesus had cleansed them in the blood of the Lamb and made them as clean as water from the spring, how He had washed them of their sins and handed them a new way of life.

Elsa had given such a testimony a year or so ago, Daniel the summer after he turned twelve. Luke too, only somebody had told Abby about that since she was too young to remember. And Solomon, of course, who served as an elder down at the church. What about Laban? Though she expected not, Abby had never come right out and asked.

But maybe he had. Maybe she was the only one in her family—other than Walter and Junior who were still too young—who hadn't seen a vision, hadn't heard any word. Did this mean she didn't really know Jesus as her Savior?

The question stayed with Abby as she fell asleep. And it was still with her when she woke up the next morning and moved through the day. As she dressed and headed for church, the question cut through her brain like an ax through a piece of wood. Yet she didn't know what to do about it. Yes, she knew she had to do some squaring up with the Lord, but wasn't sure what all that meant. She could not fake an encounter with Jesus. If one came, she welcomed it. But if not, she wouldn't stand up and give testimony to something she knew wasn't completely true. Better to not meet Jesus than to pretend she did for the sake of somebody else.

The week moved with the speed of a trout darting by in a shallow creek. Abby sat through every service, her spirit almost aching for Jesus to talk to her, to whisper in her ear or shout in her face. Preacher Bruster shouted up a sweat every evening, his voice raspy by Wednesday night, his slender body becoming even skinnier as he wore himself out with his sermonizing.

"Jesus is the way, huh," he would say every night when he drew near the close of his message. "You gotta get right with Jesus, huh, if you want a pillow reserved for your head, huh, up in heaven's golden mansions, huh, on the day that you lay down your weary bones from this earth and pass into the black night of eternity."

Abby had heard such words before. She just about knew them by heart. She believed every one of them.

"We're all sinners, huh!" shouted Bruster. "Sinners most foul, huh! The stains of our sin are worser than tobacco juice on a new shirt, huh! And we can't clean that shirt, oh no, we can't clean it ourselves, huh. You need the blood of Jesus to cleanse your heart, huh! The blood of the Lamb, slain for you on the high Cross of Calvary, slain for the forgiveness of your foul sins."

Abby agreed that she needed forgiveness. Forgiveness for her hatred of all things Clack, forgiveness for her resentment about leaving school, forgiveness for her bad feelings about her pa—the way he never talked to her, never paid attention to her. But she had felt no touch of the Spirit's breath on her heart, no rush of the wind on her body and mind, no cleaning water washing over her awful ways. No vision had come to her; no word that she could stand up and share with the church had sounded in her ears.

Bruster brought his sermon to an end, his scratchy voice pleading with the folks there to make their lives right with Jesus. "You need to put your hand in the hand of the Master, huh, the Master Jesus whose hands were pierced by the nails, huh. Put your hand in His and He will save you . . . save . . ."

Abby looked down at her hands. Thick calluses covered her palms. She had lost all tenderness in her hands. They were not a lady's hands any longer. She ran a finger over the palm of one hand, touched the spot where the spike had cut into the flesh of the Lord.

Later, when she described it to the church, she said she didn't know how to explain what happened next. She could only tell it and they had to determine whether they believed her or not. Sometimes she didn't believe it herself, that maybe she'd just imagined it because she wanted to come to Jesus so bad she could taste it.

Her hands felt warm. The heat started in her fingers, a feeling like when she came in from the cold and held her hands, palms out, toward the fireplace.

The warmth in her fingers moved from the tips to where they joined the hand. It intensified too. The fingertips were now burning hot, like she had actually touched her fingers to the flames of the fire. The fingers seemed to quiver with the heat.

Abby put her hands in her lap, palms up toward her face. Her heart thumped in her ears. Now the heat in her fingers ran into her palms, and sweat dripped off her face. She wanted to cool her hands, to run outside and take a dipper of water from the well and pour the chilled water over her hands so they wouldn't burn anymore. She glanced toward Lindy, who sat right beside her, to see if her hands were burning too. But Lindy appeared normal as ever, looking up at Bruster as he preached on. Abby could hear him shouting in the background.

"Jesus died for your sins, huh! Took the penalty for your black heart into His own heart, huh!"

Her palms burned, as if someone had dropped a hot coal right into the center of them. Abby wanted to scream, to tell somebody that her hands were on fire, that she could feel the embers sizzling into her flesh and could smell the charring of her skin.

"Take the hand of Jesus!" shouted Bruster. "He alone can wash away your sins!"

Abby lifted her hands from her lap, studied the palms as if by staring at them she might cool them down. But they remained hot, and she knew now that she had to leave the church before the heat in her hands burned through her skin and made sizzling holes in the center of her palms.

"Give Jesus your hands!" shouted Bruster. "Jesus can . . ."

Without thinking, Abby raised her hands further, almost to her face. The heat seemed to make her palms red, red as an autumn apple. The red in her palms deepened. They became red as . . . red as blood now— red as the blood of Jesus that was shed for her sins.

Abby turned her palms out and held them up in the air as if to cool them. They pointed toward Preacher Bruster now. As though pulled by an invisible rope, she stood up from the pew and stretched her hands toward Bruster, reached for him. Her palms felt just a little cooler. Pleased with the relief, she stepped out of her seat and moved to the front of the church, hands held high. They felt cooler with every step she took toward the altar. Other people joined her now, all of them with their hands in the air. Abby wondered if their palms had burned too, if the heat in their hands was bringing them to the altar.

She approached Bruster, and he held out his hands to her. Abby took his hands. Her palms immediately felt cooler, almost cold, cold as the water in Slick Rock Creek in March. Bruster fell to his knees. She followed him, and they knelt together before the altar. Bruster started praying for her. Though she tried to hold them back, the tears insisted and rolled down her face. Her palms suddenly returned to normal. As the tears fell Abby knew she had finally met Jesus. She had put her hands in His, and He had cleansed her of the foulness in the center of her soul. So, even though she might have to spend the rest of her days on Blue Springs Mountain, might have to deal with the Clacks all her life, might have to accept that her pa might never love her like she wanted and that none of her hopes might ever come true—at least she knew now that she would spend eternity in the bosom of the Lord. It certainly wasn't all she had hoped for, but whoever got that anyway?

CHAPTER
TWENTY

Daniel Porter finished up with his brickwork on the house down near Asheville in the first week of April in the year of 1917, and he was glad for it. The weather had stayed on cold all spring and he did not like the idea of spending too many more nights in a boardinghouse, which is what he had to do when the air chill dropped too low for him to sleep outside as he usually did. Picking up his wages from the boss at the back of the shed they'd set up to house the supplies, Daniel said his thank-yous to everybody, pocketed the wad of dollars the man had given him, and headed toward Asheville, a mile or so to the south.

Pulling his hat—a floppy black thing like the one his pa wore—down over his ears, he patted the bills in his jeans as if to assure himself they were safe. Hard as he worked for that money, he didn't want anything to happen to it.

It took less than thirty minutes to reach Asheville. The road under his feet turned from loose dirt to a single lane covered with bricks—a brand new road fit for the best automobile a man's money could buy. Daniel had seen lots of automobiles in Asheville, and he had no doubt the contraptions would become more and more bothersome as they multiplied on the roads. Thankfully, he didn't see many of them showing up in Blue Springs any time soon.

Truth be known, Daniel sort of liked the fact that a motor-powered buggy could take a man from one place to another so fast it might make his head spin. A man who could move that quick could find work and move to it in a hurry, could drive to the job and earn his living and still get home before dark. Always a hard laborer and a man eager to make a dollar, Daniel thought he might buy himself a car someday, just as soon as he took care of another matter or two he had in mind for his money.

Reaching the end of a row of simple wood houses, Daniel stepped up onto a wood sidewalk and through the door of a stone building with "Buncombe County Bank" carved over the front. Inside he headed straight toward a line of folks standing in front of a young woman to his left. The woman, probably twenty or so, wore a long navy skirt and a white blouse with a high collar. Her hair, pinned up in a tight bun, was the color of dry hay, and she had blue eyes. Daniel knew because he had visited the bank a lot over the last year or so. The woman was Deidre Shaller, and she worked at the bank with her father, the owner of the establishment, one Woodrow B. Shaller, who lived in a house so big, a man could just about plant a field of corn on the front porch if he had a mind to do such a thing. Daniel knew about the big house because he had helped lay the brick on it over a year ago when it was built. The house had ten rooms, an indoor privy, water that ran through pipes, and curtains over every window. And all of the windows were made of glass.

It was Woodrow B. Shaller who had given him the idea to save his money in a bank.

"You are a hardworking young man," Shaller had said to him late one Saturday afternoon back in March a year ago as Daniel labored with the bricking, his face wet with sweat. "Last one working and hardly take a stop all day."

Daniel nodded but didn't say anything. Though he had seen Mr. Shaller almost every day when he stopped by to talk to the crew boss about the progress on his new house, Daniel didn't rightly know the man and wasn't given to making conversation with strangers. Add to that the fact that he was just a common laborer and Mr. Shaller was a high and mighty banker, so he saw no reason to talk to him. He laid a brick in place, scraped off the mortar. But Shaller seemed not to notice his hesitation about conversation.

"Everybody else has already stopped," Shaller said. "Gone off to spend their pay I reckon. But not you, you still busy at it."

Daniel nodded again and kept on working.

Shaller persisted. "You thinking you will finish your bricking by the end of the month?"

Daniel wondered why Shaller would not leave him alone. Didn't the man have something he needed to do? But he knew he had to say something. "I might finish by then if I stay true with the toiling," he said. "If I don't suffer too many stops and starts . . . you know, weather and such."

Mr. Shaller missed the hint. "You are not from around here, are you?"

Daniel picked up a brick, knocked some dirt off the edge. "I live up in Blue Springs when I ain't working."

Shaller nodded. Daniel hoped he would go back to his house, a smaller one on the same property as the big one he was now laying brick for, and leave him be. But Shaller disappointed him again.

"Good workers are hard to find these days," he said, handing Daniel another brick as he laid the one he had in place. "Young man like you is probably doing all right for himself."

"I do all right," Daniel said. "Nobody getting rich these days though." *Except for bankers*, he thought. They were doing just fine by what he could see of what Shaller owned. He smoothed out some mortar, patted the brick down in it, then shaved it clean.

"What do you do with the money you're making?" asked Shaller while picking up another brick and giving it to Daniel.

Daniel tensed some at his shoulders, studied the brick he held. A man ought to know not to ask such a question. What a man did with his money was no business of any other man, especially one he had never met until that very day. He stacked the brick and worked at the mortar. Daniel said, "How long you live on this place?"

Shaller cleared his throat, letting go the fact that Daniel hadn't answered his question. "My wife's family owned it before me," he said. "Her folks settled in here a hundred years ago, built the old house." He turned and pointed to the other house on the property, a white building sitting in the middle of a stand of oaks and maples about a hundred yards from the road. "They have been here ever since. I married her twenty-three years ago. Raised a family, one son and three daughters. They are all gone now except the youngest, Deidre. Maybe you have seen her coming and going some."

Daniel nodded. He had seen Deidre a couple of times as she stepped in and out of the old house, her fine clothes something right out of the fanciest shops in all of Asheville. "Sounds like you done good," he said, stopping for a second to wipe his brow. "Married into a prime spot of land, sired a worthy family."

"I didn't marry for the land," Shaller said, his face reddening.

Daniel knew he'd said something bothersome to Mr. Shaller, though he wasn't sure what it was. "Didn't mean no offense," he said.

Shaller shrugged. "My wife is a beautiful woman. I met her in Raleigh where she attended boarding school, fell in love with her long before I knew her family owned any land."

"You don't have to explain nothin' to me," said Daniel, understanding now what he had suggested. "No business of mine."

Shaller sighed. Daniel wondered if maybe some folks thought that Shaller had come to his property by less than honorable means. Maybe that caused him some testiness on the subject. He decided it was prudent to move to another matter.

"How many acres you say you had?"

"About three hundred. Runs from here all the way up the ridge."

Daniel studied the ridge out behind the old house. Trees covered it all the way up. A stream bubbled about fifty yards behind the house. He knew because he and the rest of the workmen washed their faces in it after they finished up their labors every day. A grove of apple trees, most of them still healthy from what he could see, edged up close to the creek. Yes sir, a prime spot of land. Not as large as the spot his pa had once owned but still a piece of property to make a man's eyes sparkle. He wiped his brow again, thought of the land his brother had lost to the Clacks. Land that he had vowed to get back someday. A crazy vow, he decided, one that he had no idea how he would live out. But that didn't mean he had given up on it. No sir, he planned on keeping that vow no matter what. He glanced up at the sky, noted that the sun had about given up for the day. With Mr. Shaller's yacking, he might as well do the same.

"I expect it's time for me to clean up and head on," Daniel said. "Not much more light out there." He gestured toward the ridgeline.

Shaller stepped back as Daniel wiped his trowel off in the grass and picked up the bucket that held the mortar.

Shaller reached in his pocket, pulled out a stack of dollar bills, and handed them to Daniel. "The boss is already gone," he said. "I told him I'd give you your wages."

Hardly looking at the money, Daniel stuffed it into his pocket.

"You're not going to count that money?" asked Shaller.

Daniel took a rag from the back pocket of his overalls and wiped off his hands as he studied Mr. Shaller. He was a short bald man with a ruddy face, who wore eyeglasses with big black rims. His hands too small to hold more than one apple at a time. But he wore store-bought clothes, from his black shoes and wool pants to his white shirt and fancy coat. What difference did it make to Shaller if he counted his money or not?

"I got no reason not to trust you," Daniel finally said. "Ought to be nine dollars there, one and a half dollars per day, six days I worked this week."

Shaller cleared his throat.

Daniel could see he wanted to say something else but didn't know quite how to take up with it. He stooped to pick up his jacket, slipped it over his back, started to work the buttons.

Shaller cleared his throat again. "You ought to keep your money in a bank," he said, his words rushing out as if to say them before he could stop himself. "Not spend it all soon as you get it."

Daniel finished his buttons, then looked up at Shaller. This time it was his face that turned red at the edges. Rich banker or not, Mr. Shaller had said too much for his liking, had treaded on things no man had a right to tread on with another man.

"I am thanking you for your interest in what I do with my money," said Daniel, trying to stay calm and not jeopardize his job, "but I reckon it is none of your business whether I spend it all or not."

Shaller dropped his eyes, toed at the ground.

Daniel couldn't figure out why Mr. Shaller had so much interest. "I ain't meanin' to sound smart-mouthed. But some things is private with a man, least ways they are where I come from."

Shaller looked back at him. "Sorry," he said. "You are right, I have no business. But"—he faced his old house—"I'm a banker, you see. I make my living when folks put their money in my bank."

Daniel chuckled. At least Shaller was honest. So he was a customer to Shaller, a man whose money he could hold, make money with it for himself.

Shaller continued. "Now don't get me wrong," he said, "I don't just want your money for the bank. I believe in what I do, think it's good for me and for those who leave their money with me." His eyes lit up as he talked.

Daniel could see the salesman in him now, figured this was how he had talked a woman as stylish as Mrs. Shaller into marrying him. Shaller kept talking. "People who bank with me know their money is safe and it earns interest too, just by leaving it there it becomes more money. That way everybody does good, me and the customer."

Daniel stuffed his shirt into his pants and pondered what Mr. Shaller had said. "What is that interest thing?" he asked, curious about the idea.

Shaller smiled and picked up his bucket. "Come on up to the house," he said. "Get yourself a drink of water. I will tell you all about it."

Daniel had followed Mr. Shaller to the house that day, had sat down on the back steps while Shaller went inside to fetch some water. Shaller had asked him to come on inside, but Daniel said no, that he could wait just as well on the steps. A couple of minutes later, Shaller brought him the water, eased down on the steps beside him, and told him all about interest, how it worked to make dollars grow. Interest takes what you set aside and swells it, said the banker, swells it year by year until it comes out more than you put in.

At first the whole notion seemed like magic to Daniel, and he didn't put much stock in things like that. But then he looked out and saw the apple trees behind Mr. Shaller's house. He thought about how a seed became a bud and a bud became a flower and the flower became a piece of fruit, small at first but then larger and larger as time passed. Which sounded a lot like what Shaller was saying about his dollars. They grew as time passed, and though it was magic, it was a good magic if it worked, and he saw no reason why he should not take advantage of it. Before he left the steps that night, Daniel had decided he would take the seventy-four dollars he had saved in a glass jar by his mattress and bring it in to Mr. Shaller's bank so it could ripen like a fruit and become more than it was.

And so here he was back at the bank, his hat in his hand, his face washed to the point of shining, with his hair slicked wet against his head and his best shirt all pressed—a blue one with two pockets in the front. He was about to make his fourth deposit since Mr. Shaller told him about interest, a deposit that would bring his total to one hundred and one dollars, which was more money than most any man he knew had, his pa included. The line moved, one person, then the next. Soon Daniel found himself next in line. Waiting, he studied Deidre Shaller. Though she was about her pa's height, she had none of his stumpy body, none of his extra girth. Instead, she was willowy, almost thin. Like his ma, thought Daniel, his real ma, not Elsa. Deidre had brownish hair and a nose that sat up real cute in the middle of her face.

He dropped his eyes and looked at his shoes. Although twenty-five years old now, he hadn't spent much time with womenfolk. Not that he didn't like them. The good Lord and everybody else knew he did. He liked the way they smelled, the way they talked so high and sweet, the way they swayed some when they walked. He couldn't think of anything about a woman he didn't like. But he'd found out early that women cost a man too much—too much time when he could be working, and too many dollars from what he earned.

Deidre walked away from the counter, and Daniel's heart sank. He liked Deidre more than any woman he had ever met. She had so much style about her. So different from Ruby, that scarecrow of a woman that Laban had married, a mountain girl who hardly ever wore shoes and didn't know a thing about perfumes and such, who needed about a hundred years or so in charm school. Ruby had a tongue sharper than a skinning knife and the temperament to match.

Daniel shuddered as he thought of Laban and the downward track his brother's life had taken. Worse than a Clack. For the Clacks didn't know any better, having never had the upbringing that Laban had received. Which made it all the worse that Laban had ended up in jail more than once and had turned so full to drink that trouble followed him around like a dog after a new bone.

Picking up a stack of papers from a desk, Deidre turned back to the counter and finished up with the woman standing in front of Daniel. He moved to Deidre, his hands shaking some from coming so near to such a handsome woman.

"Hey, Mr. Porter," Deidre said, flashing him a bright smile. "You doing okay today?"

He nodded, looked in her eyes for a second but then down to his hat that lay on the counter now. Truth was, Deidre Shaller scared him to death. The only woman working in the bank, she did so in spite of what anybody said about how a woman's place was in the home. She got away with it because she was the boss's daughter and no one dared challenge her. She had more spunk than any woman he had ever known—well, except for his little sister, Abby. Abby had more spunk than most men.

"You need a slip to make your deposit?" asked Deidre, sliding a piece of paper across the counter.

Daniel nodded, his eyes fixed on her fingers. They were much longer than her pa's thick fingers. He took the paper, looked up. Deidre handed him a pencil and smiled at him again. He bore down on the pencil, marking the paper to make his deposit. Without looking up he sensed Deidre staring at him. His face blushed, and he found it hard to concentrate on his writing.

"My pa says you do good bricking," Deidre said.

Daniel wrote down his deposit amount—eight dollars. Signed his name, then handed the slip back to Deidre. Looked at her. She made him feel dizzy. "I like building things," he said, glad he'd managed to speak. "Bridges, houses, such as that."

Deidre took the paper. "You making some money from it, I guess."

"I do okay," said Daniel, amused that she was like her pa when it came to talking about money. "Since the flood last July, there is a lot of building to do."

Deidre nodded sadly. "The French Broad washed through here pretty bad."

"You taking well to your new house?" he asked, changing the subject.

"It is a fine place," she said as she wrote on a receipt slip. "You did good work."

"A lot of men put in some time on that place," he said. "Biggest house on this side of Asheville."

Deidre laughed and slid his receipt across the counter. "You keep saving your money and you can build yourself one just like it someday."

"A highlander don't need a house like that," Daniel said. "All glassed in and all."

Deidre frowned, and he knew he had hurt her feelings. His throat drew up on him and he almost choked.

"I don't mean nothing," he said, grabbing the receipt and stuffing it in his pocket. "Just . . . just that I never slept in a house with tight windows, a house where the wind can't come through all free and all. You got a fine house, one far too good for the likes of me."

Deidre held up a hand. "I take no offense," she said. "Don't give it another thought."

Daniel placed his hat on his head and started to leave. But Deidre spoke before he could. Her words surprised him, and the look she gave him did even more so.

"You ought not sell yourself short, Daniel Porter," she said. "I know how hard you work and how much money you have saved. A man like you will do well with his life. I got no question of that."

Unable to think of any proper response, Daniel just dropped his eyes. As he was about to leave, the doors to the bank suddenly burst open and Sheriff Rucker broke through, his eyes frantic, his face red.

"We done gone and declared war!" shouted the sheriff. "Just got word down at the post office. We're faced off against the Germans."

Everybody started talking at once. As if on instinct, Daniel glanced back to Deidre Shaller, but she had twisted away from him and was stepping fast toward the back of the bank where her pa kept his office. Not knowing what else to do, Daniel set his jaw and hurried out of the building. Though he had no way to know it at the time, he wouldn't talk to Deidre Shaller again for nearly three years, and he would face a lot of hard grief before that next meeting came.

CHAPTER
TWENTY-ONE

As part of the first wave of Army volunteers, Daniel set sail four months later, his brother Laban in the bunk below his on a troopship that left from Charleston, South Carolina, filled with Army men on a day all blustery with wind and rough seas. Most of the men were country boys just like Daniel and Laban—a collection of stout backs and simple ignorance from all over the country, more men jammed into one spot than Daniel had ever seen, a lot of them with peculiar ways and strange manners of talking.

Sitting back on his bunk, Daniel looked at his hands and thought about the blur of events that had passed since first hearing the pronouncement that war had come.

Like most of the fellows in Blue Springs his age, he hadn't quite known what to do when he heard about the troubles in Europe. Listening to the men who gathered at the post office almost every morning following Sheriff Rucker's announcement, Daniel heard all kinds of ideas. Some said they should wait to see if the president called up a draft—go only when the government forces them to head out. Others argued they should wait till the National Guard got formed up and go as part of the Old

Hickory Division with the boys from over in Tennessee. A goodly number said a highlander ought not go at all. Let them European boys fight if they want, but this was no business of theirs. No reason for a highlander man to go over to some country whose name he couldn't even say proper and mix himself up in another man's ruckus.

But others saw it differently, Solomon among them. "A man owes some allegiance to his country," Daniel heard him say every time the subject came up. "Not that I want my boys going over there and gettin' shot or nothing. But we got a good thing a going here in these United States and I don't want them German folks comin' over here and causing us trouble. We might as well stop them over on their home ground as to have to shoot them as they get off their boats over here."

Daniel's mouth had dropped open as he listened. Solomon hardly ever spoke so many words together in one string. Past fifty now, gray streaks ran through Solomon's hair, and his back had stooped some from all the garden work he had done over the years. He had taken to walking with a cane that he had carved, a cane at least six feet tall and four or five inches around. His pa had cut all kinds of images into his cane—carvings of a tablet like the one Moses carried down from the mountain, the Temple of Jerusalem taken from a picture he saw in the back of Preacher Bruster's Bible, a cross almost a foot high, a serpent like the one that tempted Adam and Eve, and a crown that resembled what he figured sweet Jesus would wear when he returned with a shout. He added new carvings to the cane from time to time, such as the face of Blue Springs Mountain, his cabin, or his favorite old dog Sandy, now dead. Folks had started to call Solomon "Cane Stick Man," and the kids at church would often run up to him on Sunday mornings to see the pictures he carried around on his walking stick.

People in Blue Springs respected Solomon Porter because of his steady toiling, his sober head, and his loyalty to Jesus. When Pa spoke, people listened. And Daniel was no different. Less than a month after Sheriff Rucker ran into the bank with his news, Daniel had joined up with the Army. Luke tried to go too, but he had come up with a real bad cough just a couple of weeks before he visited the recruiters, and they told him to come back in a month or so when his cough went away so they could check him out again. Daniel tried to talk some sense into the government men so they would let Luke go in with him, but they told him to shut up, that he belonged to the Army now and he didn't look like a doctor and he had nothing to say about it.

The day after joining up, Daniel spent the night at home. Solomon had told Luke not to worry, for maybe the Lord wanted him in Blue Springs a while longer yet. That settled Luke down some, and they all sat down to dinner. Daniel didn't eat much. In three days he would head out from Blue Springs to an Army camp down near Columbia, South Carolina.

"You will see the world," said Elsa, serving him supper.

"I guess this war will take me out past Asheville some," Daniel agreed.

"You're fighting for something good," said Solomon, his eyes bright with pride.

Daniel ate a biscuit and gazed from person to person at the table. His pa, a quiet man with a face that had begun to drop some, not given to big shows of any kind, joy or sadness, love or hatred. Daniel thought of an owl—never blinking, never letting on what went on behind the plain face. That was his pa, as unreadable as an owl.

Elsa sat beside him as pretty as ever. Still young looking in spite of the hard days she had spent working at the side of Solomon, the hardest toiling man around. Contrary to what many had said at the start, Elsa had turned out all right. Had given Pa two more boys, then suffered three miscarriages after that. Daniel knew because he'd heard her crying one day the year before he moved out on his own. Frozen to the spot by the unusual sound, he had listened to Elsa tell his pa that she had done fine with Junior and Walter, but her body didn't seem strong enough to see no more babies through to birthing. Solomon said that was okay and if the Lord did not want her to have no more children he was just fine with the ones they already had.

Daniel glanced at Walter and Junior. For a while there, Junior had been pretty sickly. But once he moved to the clear air of the highlands, that had ended. Though he still wasn't as big as his younger brother, Junior had filled out real nice now at the age of thirteen. Had dark hair like Pa's but more of Elsa's skin coloring, lighter in tone and not as coarse. Junior burned real easy in the sun.

Walter was just the opposite. Dark as the shell of a pecan and lean as a strip of beef jerky. Seemed born to the outdoors. While only eleven, he could shoot and throw a knife almost as well as any man.

Daniel chewed on another biscuit. Some folks said Walter had a lot of

Laban in him. Not a bad thing if they meant Laban's toughness, his ways with weapons and hunting. But a troublesome thing if they meant his weakness for drink, his rebelliousness toward the law, matters such as that.

Not wanting to think of anything grievous, Daniel looked across the table at Abby. At seventeen, Abby was the only girl who could give Elsa a run for the title of prettiest woman in Blue Springs. Seemed like since she'd come back home from down in Blue Springs a couple of years back that every unmarried man within twenty miles had traipsed up the path with his hat in hand to make Pa an offer for her hand in marriage. But Abby had said no to every one of them.

At first Daniel thought she had too high a notion of herself. Why shouldn't she take up with somebody and settle down and birth some children? What made her so special that no highlander man could win her heart? But then the more he watched and listened to her, the more he began to understand. Abby had a sense of separateness about her. Not like somebody who thought they were better than everybody else. No, Abby didn't carry herself that way. She talked to folks all the time, had more friends than anybody. When somebody got sick, she would travel to see them, a pot of soup hanging from her elbow. When Preacher Bruster needed help with the children at the church, Abby would take them to the back room and read them stories from one of the books she always seemed to have handy. Since the day she stood up and testified to the coming of the Spirit through the heat in the palms of her hands, Abby had carried herself like a woman of Jesus, and everybody started depending on her as if she'd seen far more years than her age said.

Those who knew her said Abby had a trait of royalty, like a queen bee or something. Wherever she went, the world naturally paid attention to her, buzzed around her without any question as to whether it should or not. Best thing was, the attention had not spoiled her any, so far as he could see.

Daniel took a swig of buttermilk. Although the attention hadn't spoiled Abby, it hadn't made her truly happy either. Truth was, he suspected that nothing on Blue Springs Mountain could do that trick. Abby had wanted to educate herself. Coming back to live with Pa had shut down her chances to do that, and she still grieved over it. She'd told him so the first year after she moved back in with Pa and Elsa. Mr. Holston had filled her head with all kinds of ideas about leaving the mountain and doing something wonderful with her life. She had taken his words to heart, had decided that she wanted to go down to a college somewhere, wanted it more than anything else.

"What can this mountain offer me?" she asked Daniel one day when her sorrow seemed unbearable. "Other than a husband who cannot read, a few babies who will grow up poor and ignorant, and a quick trip to a grave under some oak tree somewhere?"

Daniel started to remind her that her ma had found that kind of life just fine and only an uppity woman would see it as beneath her station. But then he realized that Abby knew this already, for the early death that had swallowed up her ma happened to prove her point exactly. So he stayed quiet and let Abby have her say.

As for him, he had mixed thoughts about it all. It was true that mountain life had killed his ma long before her natural time. But at the same time he loved the isolation the highlands brought, the stillness in the morning when he woke up just before sunrise, the sound of a creek bubbling over rocks, the feel of snow falling on his face in January. Sure, it was hard and merciless, but it was plain too, simple and straightforward. Toil hard, do good, don't poke into another man's business, and a body would do okay in the Blue Ridge. Not a bad way to live. Maybe someday Abby would see this and find a sense of peace about it.

Daniel heard a knock on the door and looked up in surprise. Walter jumped up from the table, ran to the door, and opened it. Daniel's jaw dropped open as he saw Laban step inside, his hat in hand, his eyes on the floor. Rushing to beat the others, he pushed back his chair and ran to Laban with his arms open wide to the brother he hadn't seen in almost a year. Laban gripped his hand, then wrapped his arms around Daniel's back. Daniel felt his brother's strength and knew that, although Laban had lived hard for a long time, he had not grown weak from it.

Laban broke the embrace, and they both stepped back. Daniel looked to the table, saw that everyone but Pa had stood and now waited by their chairs, waited to see what Laban wanted. Pa stayed put, both his hands on the table, his gaze locked on his eldest boy.

Daniel wondered how much time had passed since Pa and Laban last saw each other. For all he knew they had not talked since the day Hal Clack rode up to claim the land Laban had gambled away, since the day Pa smacked him full in the face. How long had that been? Eight, nine years ago?

"Sorry to upset supper," Laban said shyly.

"We about done," said Solomon, his tone as even as if talking to Elsa about shucking corn. "Shut the door and come on have a bite."

Daniel pushed the door closed and then nudged Laban, who had not yet moved, in the back. Laban jerked but then moved to the table, pulled out a chair, and sat down while laying his hat on the table. Elsa handed him a cup of buttermilk. Everybody took their seats again, including Daniel. All eyes were glued on Laban as if staring at a ghost. Daniel's shoulders leaned forward, and his hands clenched as he waited to see what all this meant. He hoped nothing bad had happened to Laban again, like when he lost Pa's land in a knife-throwing contest.

Laban sipped from his milk. Solomon stayed quiet, and Daniel wondered how he could sit so still with his eldest boy so long wayward, now sitting across from him. Did Solomon not love Laban anymore? Is that how he managed to stay so quiet while Laban ate? Did troubles do that to a pa and a son? Make it such that the two could never move past the hurts they had visited on one another?

Laban set down his cup, then wiped his hands on the thighs of his overalls. Walter squirmed, and Daniel felt the nervousness go up in the room. He wanted to shout, to tell Pa to say something, to stand up and throw his arms around Laban's neck and welcome him home. But he knew Solomon would not do such a thing. Not fitting for a highlander man to act in such a manner, even for the homecoming of his eldest boy.

"I am going to war," said Laban as though announcing he had just finished gathering eggs from the hen house. "I wanted you all to know."

Pa nodded, pulled his pipe from his shirt pocket. "Daniel is going too," he said. "Luke maybe later."

"I know," Laban said. "I talked to some boys down at the post office."

"Ain't you a bit old for it?" asked Solomon.

Laban grinned. "They ain't that particular down at the post office. If a man is under forty and real healthy they let him pass."

Solomon chewed his pipe a second, then said, "Your woman happy about you going?"

Laban shrugged. "Ain't told her yet. But I am a-going whether she takes to the idea or not."

Solomon touched his pockets for a match but came up empty. "You come on this decision without talking to your woman?"

Laban struck a match and handed it to Solomon. Solomon lit his pipe, puffed on it for a second. Laban said, "I had no chance to tell her about it. Come to my choice all of a sudden like. Didn't want little brother to go off and become a hero"—he pointed his hat at Daniel—"without me having my chance to match him."

Daniel rocked back as he figured out what had surely happened. Laban had gone down to Blue Springs for provisions or something and had stopped in at the post office to catch up with the news. Somebody there must have told him that his youngest brother had joined up with the Army. Laban had signed up on the spot.

Laban reached over and patted him on the shoulder. "You think I am gone let you have all the fun?" he said, grinning.

Daniel grinned too, but then another idea made him less pleased. Unless he missed his guess, Laban had not joined up because he worried about him becoming a hero. Laban wanted to go to look out for him, to make sure he made it through the fighting all right. *Always the big brother*, thought Daniel. Though he had not spent time with Laban in over eight years, Laban still couldn't stop protecting him.

Pa pulled pipe smoke into his lungs, stared at Laban, then over to Daniel. "Two of my boys headed to war," he said, shaking his head. "Gone be some rough fighting, I got no doubt."

"We will do okay," said Daniel.

"I trust that will be true," said Solomon.

Laban leaned forward and laid a hand on his pa's forearm. Daniel edged closer too, anxious to see what would happen between the two men.

"I will see to him," Laban whispered. "After all I done, I owe it to you."

Daniel's throat felt like somebody had dropped a walnut in the back of it. Solomon nodded as he placed a hand over Laban's. His eyes glistened, and Daniel thought for a moment he spotted some wetness in them. But the wetness disappeared fast, and Solomon cleared his throat and said, "Glad you come home, son. Glad you come home."

The night had passed with all of them sitting around the table until late, talking like a family that might never get such a chance again. For the most part, Daniel sat and listened, listened and wondered at the miracle that it had taken a war to bring peace back to a father and his son.

Now, with his stomach turning queasy as the ship plowed through the choppy waves, Daniel glanced down at Laban in the bunk below and hoped that what Laban had promised would come true. If something happened to him, if Laban failed to keep him safe, he feared that Pa would never forgive Laban. So Daniel hoped he survived the war not so much for his sake as for Laban's and his pa's. If the two of them were to come out of this scrape at peace with each other, then he had to see to it that he remained alive.

CHAPTER
TWENTY-TWO

When the ship finally landed in France after being at sea more days than Daniel had cared to count, he rushed off it like all the other men did, his legs eager to feel solid ground again, his stomach ready to feel something other than tossed and turned all the time. His group, part of the First Army Division, set up camp in some quickly built wood barracks not far from a small French village. For the first four weeks they did the same thing they had done back during their training in South Carolina. Up at dawn, march and drill, march and drill, march and drill. Over and over again the staff sergeant set them to running over an open field and then fall when they heard his whistle, fall and crawl, their guns pointed out ahead of them. Crawl through the crater holes the bombs had made, crawl through the strawy grass, crawl through the ditches and gullies. Then they came to the razor wire. Cut it with metal cutters, throw wood planks down on top of it, stand and run over the planks. Then run again—run, run, run. Then the whistle, hit the ground and crawl again—crawl, crawl, crawl.

The weather turned cold and rainy, and the men took to grumbling about it as soldiers in such situations often do. But the bad weather didn't stop them from their steady routine: march and drill, slog in the mud, run in the rain, crawl through the crater holes, the ditches, and gullies.

When not marching and if the weather allowed it, the men fired their rifles at targets, practiced jamming their bayonets into scarecrows stuffed with straw, learned how to use hand grenades and cover their faces with masks in case the Germans fired gas at them. At night they cleaned their weapons and wiped the mud off their boots and helmets. Several in Daniel's squad took a fungus between their toes and so had to lie in their bunks and sprinkle a powder that the medics gave them on their feet. Daniel and Laban stayed healthy, however, and kept right on with their marching, running, and crawling. But still their company remained in the same place. When they hadn't moved anywhere after eight weeks, some of the men took to griping.

"I did not come all the way across the wide blue Atlantic just to listen to a crazy man's whistle all day," said a man named Tom Bottles one night as they lay in their bunks after supper. "If they don't let us shoot at some Germans soon, I'm just a good mind to head on back home."

Daniel studied Bottles for a second. He had a square jaw, a bump over his left eye, and a bottom not much smaller than a donkey's backside.

"Those Germans gone shoot back," said Laban with a chuckle. "Not like hunting squirrels back home."

"Let them come," Bottles replied. "Ain't a German been born who can outshoot a good South Carolina boy."

Daniel listened but kept his quiet. Let Bottles boast, he figured. No harm to it, even if it weren't his way. When the real shooting started everybody would see who could hold his own and who could not.

The days passed with deadly monotony. But Daniel and Laban stayed busy. When not marching or doing some other soldierly chore, Laban took to gambling some, poker mostly. And he managed to find a bottle of liquor every now and again too. His face flushed when he drank.

Seeing his brother mixed up in such pursuits bothered Daniel a lot, but he knew Laban was a grown man and could do whatever he chose. Daniel himself wanted nothing to do with such shenanigans, no sir.

Trying to stay busy, Daniel took to writing letters. He got the idea when he saw Tom Bottles writing to his sweetheart one evening just before lights-out. So Daniel asked him about it, and Bottles said he wrote home about two or three times a week, to his mama and daddy too, and the letters they sent him in return sure helped make the time pass with a little more pleasure in it.

For a couple of days Daniel studied on the matter. Pa and everybody back home would surely worry about them if they didn't hear anything about their doings. And since Laban certainly wouldn't write, it fell to him. In addition, the Army furnished the paper for free so it would not cost Daniel a thing.

Liking how sensible it sounded, Daniel decided to give it a go. After the first attempt or two, he found that he liked the shaping of the letters, the chance to say out front some things he was feeling inside. Since Pa couldn't read and Daniel wasn't that close to Elsa, he addressed the letters to Abby.

Dear sister, he wrote to her about a month after they arrived in France.

> *Me and Laban made the first weeks here just fine. The food is not good—corned beef, cornmeal mush, hard biscuits and bully beef from the French, black coffee. Not like I am used to from home. But it keeps us alive, I reckon. We have not yet done no fighting. Though I can't say where we are exactly, I can say that the locals here seem glad that we came. Me and Laban venture into town every now and again when we get some leave and we met some of the French people. A couple of them speak a bit of English but not too much. So, we don't know too well what they say. But they is friendly enough.*

> *To hear the men in my squad tell it, we ought to do these German boys in within a few weeks or so and head right on back home. I don't know about that. Seems to me that a war brings out the worst in people and they won't give up none too easy once something this big has started.*

> *Laban says hey. He hopes the boys up front don't beat the Germans before he takes his shot at them. Tell everybody hey for me and keep us in your praying.*

> *Your brother,*
> *Daniel*

Folding the letter, he stuck it in an envelope, licked the flap, and carried it to the barracks that housed the postal center.

Another two weeks went by and he sent another letter of similar nature. Then, on a night that Laban stayed out late, playing cards and drinking, Daniel found himself feeling lonely so he did something quite out of character. He decided to write a letter to a woman. One Deidre Shaller to say it plain, the banker's daughter from down in Asheville.

Without knowing exactly why, he wanted to let her know he was alive, that he had joined up with the Army and was now overseas fighting for his country.

Again, Bottles gave him the notion. Holding up a picture of his girl one night, Bottles bragged about how pretty she was: "You North Carolina boys ain't got no women as fancy as this," he crowed to Daniel and Laban. "And even if you did, they sure wouldn't write you and send you a picture."

Not saying a word to Bottles, Daniel decided to see what he could do to prove him wrong. After chewing the end of the pencil for several minutes, he finally thought of something to say and so put lead to paper.

Dear Miss Shaller,

Maybe you will not expect such a letter as this. Do you remember me? Daniel Porter. I come from up in Blue Springs, keep my money at your pa's bank. I came in the day the war started. Do you remember?

Anyway, if you do, I am in France now. I joined the Army not long after I made my last deposit with you. Me and my brother come over here together, the Army lets you do that.

I am okay, no foot rot or nothing. They feed us plenty but ain't always the most tasty stuff you ever put in your mouth. Are you doing well? Do you have any family in the war? I hope not. I have seen some men coming back from the front lines. Many of them are all shot up. Others are not hurt in the body but their heads seem all troubled and their eyes look but don't seem to see nothing.

How is your pa? Well, I hope. He told me about interest on my dollars. Convinced me on bringing my money to the bank. Take good care of my money now, okay? Don't steal it and spend it. Ha, ha!

Well, I might ought to go. If you don't remember me, just tear up this letter and throw it away. But if you do and you think about it, I would appreciate a prayer said for me and Laban. If you pray . . . well, most folks pray. You do, don't you? Is that too close a question to ask?

Hey, this is the longest letter I ever wrote. Hope you remember me. Write back if you want.

Bye,
Daniel Porter

Daniel folded the letter and wrote the only address he knew for her on the envelope. Miss Deidre Shaller, daughter of Mr. Woodrow B. Shaller, Buncombe County Bank, Asheville, North Carolina. Satisfied, he sealed the envelope and walked through the rain to mail it.

The next day his company received its orders. They would head to the front in about two weeks to relieve a bunch of French boys who needed a break from the trenches. When he heard the news, Daniel turned to Laban and nodded his head.

"This is why we come over here," said Laban. "Time to prove our mettle."

Daniel stepped to his brother and hugged his neck. "We will take care of each other," he said. "If one of us makes it, both of us do."

"No question about us making it," said Laban. "Nobody tougher than a couple of Blue Springs boys."

———

Deidre Shaller received the letter from Daniel Porter on a Friday afternoon after she had finished with her duties at the bank. Remembering immediately who he was, she ran up the stairs to her room and threw herself down on the bed. Her heart racing, she tore open the letter and read it fast. Rolling over and fluffing up her pillow, she lay down and read it a second time, slower now.

To her thinking, Daniel Porter was a handsome young man. And she'd never seen a harder worker. She had noticed him doing his bricking on her family's new house long before he ever showed up at the bank to make his first money deposit. He hardly ever took a break from his labors, and when he started building a wall, it seemed to rise up almost all at once, one brick on top of another until he had finished the wall. And then he moved on to the next wall. He had a fine head of dark hair and muscles in his arms much stouter than any of her regular boyfriends. Her face blushed as she remembered him working some sunny days without his shirt on, his chest glistening with sweat.

Deidre fingered the coarse paper of the letter and sighed heavily. Daniel Porter—a mysterious mountain man accustomed to the outdoors, a man who toiled with his back and hands, a man who could hunt and fish, who was used to taking care of himself by his own wits—had written her a letter.

Laying the letter on her chest, she wondered what kind of man he really was. Was he as gentle as he seemed when he talked to her at the bank? As his letter sounded? She didn't know for sure yet saw no reason not to believe it. Just because he grew up on Blue Springs Mountain didn't mean he was spiteful or crude.

True, Daniel didn't have a lot of education. Unlike every other fellow she had courted, he had no diploma to hang on his wall, no fine history of preparatory schools. But that didn't mean he wasn't smart. Her pa had told her he took real quickly to the notion of letting his dollars earn money for him. And his letter showed he had some deep thoughts. Why shouldn't she write to him? A letter didn't mean anything. It wasn't like she was sweet on him or anything.

Standing, Deidre moved to her dresser and took out a stack of writing paper and a black-point pen from the drawer. Back to her bed again, she sat down and touched pen to paper. A brave man like Daniel Porter ought not think she didn't remember him. To leave him with that kind of idea wasn't a patriotic thing to do, not patriotic at all.

Dear Daniel,
Of course I remember you. You came into our bank. . . .

CHAPTER
TWENTY-THREE

Three days before Christmas of 1917 Abby picked up some flour and beans from the general store, tied the goods on her mule, and headed down to the post office. The weather had broke off warmer than usual for this time of year. A steady sun burned overhead, and the wind had died down to nothing. Dressed in a black wool skirt, a brown shirt and shawl, and black boots, Abby took off the shawl and laid it over her arm. Since Daniel had started writing letters, she visited the post office at least once every two weeks to pick up any mail he'd sent and to send off a letter to him from the family. Everybody looked forward to hearing from him, to knowing how he and Laban were faring over there in France. So far he had told them a lot about getting ready to fight but nothing yet about any actual shooting at the enemy. Abby hoped it would stay that way, though she knew that holding such a thought wouldn't make it so.

At the post office Mr. Boader told her that she did have a letter, and when he handed it to her, she saw immediately that the envelope had a foreign postmark on it along with Daniel's scratchy writing. She held the letter up and looked it over. It seemed bulkier than usual, and she wondered if Daniel had written some extra words. Although anxious to open the envelope right then and there, she knew she had to wait and share it with Pa and everybody else at the same time. So, fighting the urge to read it, she stuck the letter in her shirt pocket, hopped up on her mule, and pointed the animal back up the mountain.

The weather stayed warm as the afternoon passed. Several times Abby touched the letter in her pocket. She wondered what news it brought—good or bad. At least Daniel and Laban were still alive. If anything bad had happened, some government man would've come up from Blue Springs to tell them about it. But what if something had happened since Daniel wrote the letter? What if something had happened since she left the cabin that morning? That was possible, she knew it was. One person could go down to a general store and pick up some flour and beans, while another person somewhere else could take a rifle shot in the heart and keel over deader than a shovel handle. Daniel or Laban might've been shot while she was removing her shawl on the way to the post office or while she was climbing back onto her mule to ride home. Strange how that could be, but it was.

Fighting off her sad thoughts, Abby wondered about Thaddeus, a wondering that jumped into her head more than she liked these days. He had joined the National Guard as soon as he turned eighteen, about four months after Daniel and Laban shipped out.

All dressed up in his uniform, Thaddeus had come to see her a couple of days before he left. Told her pa he wanted to take a private walk with her, and would that suit him okay? Pa had said yes, and Thaddeus tipped his hat and opened the door for her, and the two of them walked out on a windy March day and headed up the hill out behind the cabin. A brown rock the size of a barn stood on top of the hill. They reached the rock and stared out over the ridgeline. A few dogwoods had started to bloom, and their white bracts made the ridge look like somebody had dropped popcorn on it.

For a long time Thaddeus didn't say anything, just kept his eyes on the dogwoods, his hat in his hands. The wind blew through Abby's hair. Her skin tingled with the light chill.

Thaddeus cleared his throat, looked up at the sky. "I am going off to war," he said as if telling her a secret.

"I know," Abby said. She leaned against the rock. "The uniform is a sure sign."

He laughed, and it sounded nice—familiar and easy. "No fooling you, is there?" he said.

Abby laughed too, then said, "Maybe you will see Daniel and Laban over there."

"Hope so, they are good soldiers I am sure."

Abby stared at Thaddeus's face. A good solid face, cut all smooth and even, like one of Pa's carvings. Blond hair and grayish eyes. She had known the face for many a year now. But when did it grow up so? Had she changed as much as he had since first meeting him back when they were children, back when Mr. Holston brought him and Lindy to Blue Springs and started his teaching?

She hung her head as she thought of Mr. Holston. Thaddeus and Lindy had kept on with their schooling after she had to quit. Thaddeus had done well with it, had learned as much as his pa had to teach him. Lindy told her that they might go to college and that they were trying to figure out a way to pay their fees. Abby tried not to feel jealous, but sometimes couldn't seem to help herself. Then the guilt started. What kind of person resented the success of her friends? Not a good Christian person, she knew that for sure.

"I wanted to see you before I left," Thaddeus said, interrupting her thinking.

"It was nice of you," said Abby. "I will pray for you on your journeys."

Thaddeus rolled his hat in his fingers. Abby knew he wanted to say something else but the words were sticking in his throat. She wondered why highlander men were so backward when it came to speaking plain what they wanted to say? Why did they keep so much inside, wrapped up like a wound they wanted to keep from bleeding?

"I know about Ben Clack and what he tried with you," said Thaddeus. "Back when we were younger. I heard you yell out. I got there just as you ran off, saw him heading down the hill, figured out two plus two."

Abby covered her mouth with a hand. Why would Thaddeus bring up such a thing now? She was about to tell him to stop, to shut up and go on off to war. She'd put the whole thing with Clack out of her head a long time ago, had sworn she would never talk to anybody about it. But Thaddeus spoke again before she could stop him.

"I wanted to kill him," he said, his eyes straight at her now. "But I had no weapon. So I just turned tail and ran off, told myself I would take care of him later."

Abby stared at the ground. "He scared me . . . but nothing happened. I have forgotten it, you should too."

Thaddeus gritted his teeth. "I won't ever forget that day," he said. "That was the day I knew for sure I loved you. I have just been too bashful to say it, knew I wasn't good enough for you."

Abby almost choked.

Thaddeus continued, his words a river of speaking now that he'd started. "But now that I am off to war, I cannot go without you knowing how I feel. I want to marry you, Abigail Porter, have wanted it for many a year. If I live through this war, I plan to ask your pa in a proper way when I come back. I am telling you this now so you can start to think on it, so you can have all the time you need until I return and make my proposal an official request of your pa and you."

He stopped and rolled his hat on his fingers again, his eyes on the ridge. Abby swallowed, unsure of what to say. She had always liked Thaddeus, knew he had feelings for her. But contrary to his notions, she was the one who wasn't good enough for him, not educated enough for a man planning to go off to college someday.

"I know this takes you some off guard," he said, looking at her again. "And I don't expect an answer today. Just study on it, will you? While I'm gone to war?" He stopped and waited on her answer.

Abby leaned back on the rock. A lazy white cloud fluttered past overhead. She had no clue how to respond. She cared for Thaddeus—she knew that. But did she love him? Yes, in a certain way. But did she love him in the way a woman ought to love a man to marry him?

She walked away from the rock, stared out over the ridge. Row after row of Blue Ridge mountaintops stretched out on the horizon, their slopes covered with trees, some green, some white, some still bare of their leaves in the early spring. She thought of the fellows who had called on her over the last few years. Some of them were good men—churchgoers and hard toilers, not given to much drink or running about. Others had carousing yet to do before they settled down. They were sharp-eyed and lean in their muscles and ready to go behind the nearest tree to kiss her. But Abby had given none of them any encouragement. Why was that? Why had she stayed so shy about such matters? Most Blue Springs Mountain girls married off by the time they turned sixteen or seventeen years, some even earlier. But she wanted no part of it. Was this because of what Ben Clack had tried with her? Had that scared her so much that she no longer trusted men? Made her fearful of their intentions? Had Ben's crude advances made her unfit for love, unable to respond to any man's courting, even that of a good man like Thaddeus Holston?

A gust of wind blew her hair into her eyes. She brushed it away. What was love anyway? A rush of fire in the stomach? A thrill running through the body like a bolt of lightning? Or was it a quiet trust, a sureness that a man would treat her well, stay loyal so long as they both lived, talk to her on the porch as she rocked on hot summer nights, kiss her softly and hold her strong when hard times came and tears ran down her cheeks?

Sighing, Abby faced Thaddeus again. Within days he would be shipping out to fight for his country. Even if she did not know exactly how she felt about him, how could she refuse his request that she at least think about his proposal?

"I am honored that you say you love me," she said. "You are a man most any woman would want as a husband. And you know that I have always cared deeply about you. You and Lindy have been my best friends."

Thaddeus dropped his head.

She knew she had embarrassed him, but that didn't stop her. "I will consider what you have told me," Abby said. "I will keep you in my prayers and will write to you. And I promise you that when you come back, and you will come back, I will give you an answer." She moved to him and laid a hand on his forearm. "Is that okay for now?" she asked, gazing into his eyes.

He put his hand on hers. They stood that way for a few seconds, their eyes locked. Then, before she could stop him, Thaddeus leaned close and touched his lips to hers. She started to pull away, but then, remembering he was going to war, she figured what harm was there in a kiss for a soldier headed off to fight for his country? She relaxed and allowed herself to feel the softness of his lips. She felt the color rise in her face.

Thaddeus swung an arm around her waist and pulled her closer. She didn't resist. Her lips parted slightly. His lips were moist. She took a quick breath yet didn't break off the kiss. He touched her cheek as he kissed her, and his fingers felt soft. Abby's stomach fluttered, and she felt her body responding in a surprising way, a way she had never experienced, never imagined before. She wrapped her arms around his waist, felt the muscles in his back.

Without warning, Thaddeus broke off the kiss. His hands cupped her face, and he ran his fingers over her lips. Abby's breath came in quick gasps now. She had never felt like this. Was this love? Had Thaddeus made her feel this way? Her old friend, a boy she'd known forever, though never considered in any romantic way? Or was this feeling caused by the fact that he was going off to war and Daniel and Laban were already there, and in times like this, everybody's emotions always rose higher, became more intense?

Confused by her questions, Abby pivoted away from Thaddeus. That had to be it, she decided, just wartime emotions and nothing else. And it wasn't fair to Thaddeus to let him think the kissing was anything but that.

She faced him again. "You come back safe," she said. "We will talk then."

Thaddeus left her then, left her and walked down the ridge and back toward Blue Springs. She had seen him only once since, on the Sunday before he left for Europe, a Sunday when all the folks down at Jesus Holiness prayed for him and the other boys who were going or had already gone to serve their country and protect the cause of freedom.

———

Abby reached home just before dark, her body weary from the travel but her mind eager to read Daniel's letter. Calling everyone into the front room, she set the letter on the eating table, and they all took their places as they always did when Daniel sent a letter—Pa at the head, Junior to his right, Walter to his left, Elsa on the other end, Abby by Junior.

Solomon pulled out his pipe, tapped it on the table, then lit it. A curl of smoke rose up in the air and hung over the table as he took out his knife. He picked up the letter and carefully sliced it open. Abby glanced around the table. Junior, at fourteen now, was moving closer and closer to war age. He had a touch of black fuzz on his chin, and his shoulders had filled out a lot since those days when he was such a sickly boy. Walter wasn't far behind him in size. Within a few years they would both move away from this cabin and take up places of their own somewhere higher up in the holler from Uncle Pierce's place. It was the mountain way. The younger moved up higher till the old ones died. Then they took up their places down nearer the valley again.

Solomon pulled the writing paper from the envelope, held it up to the lamp, and studied it. "Three pages," he said. "Longer than the others."

Abby noticed Solomon's hands as he spoke, how they had aged in the sun. His fingers shook when he handed her the letter, and she wondered if the shaking came from his age or from something else, some nervousness at what his son might have to tell him, or fear that something bad lay in the extra two pages of his son's poor penmanship. Her own hands a bit unsteady at the notion, she took the letter from him, held it over the table, looked around at everybody, and began to read.

" 'How are you all?' " Daniel started out. " 'I hope this letter reaches you before Christmas. Mail is not always real regular. Anyway, I am a veteran now, me and Laban both just come back from some days at the front. I wish I had never seen such a place. Holes tore into the ground big enough to drive a wagon in a circle. Razor wire stretched out as far as the eye can see. Trees cut into splinters by the bombs, smoke everywhere half the time.' "

Abby paused as she read the next sentence. Daniel had never told of such things as this.

"Go on," said Solomon, his hands flat on the table, his jaw set. "Tell us what it says."

Her breath coming faster, Abby started reading again.

" 'None of that was the worst of it though. Truth is, I find it impossible to tell you what the worst of it looked like, how it sounded and smelled. How does a body describe the sound of grown men whining as the bombs whistle in the air? The smell of shell smoke as it drifts on the wind? The sight of a dead man in the same trench as you, sometimes as peaceful looking as a baby asleep in a crib and at other times as crooked in the face and body as a woman giving labor? It is awful, that is what it is, the awfulest world that you can imagine, something that makes anybody that believes in Jesus wonder where God went.' "

Laying down the first page, Abby glanced at her pa. He had his eyes down, his pipe in one hand while his other was still flat on the table. The air seemed to have left the room. Abby tried to breathe but found it difficult. But Solomon pointed his pipe at her, so she focused again on the letter.

" 'Me and Laban and all the other boys from the Fighting First comported ourselves well in our time at the front. Did not back down from no fight, I can tell you that. But that don't mean we weren't scared, me anyway, I never really asked Laban. But I got to tell you he don't seem scared to me. They already promoted him a couple of ranks up to sergeant for his bravery and everybody agrees he is the one man they most want in the trench with them when the whistles go off. The whistle is the sign for us all to stand up and charge through the wire. It moves us out of the trenches and across the dead zone. We all dread the whistle but know that it has to come if we are to win this war. Can't win a war sitting on your backside in a muddy hole, you know?

" 'Anyway, Laban shows nobody any fear. Says he will personally shoot every German between here and Berlin if that is what it takes to make it safe for all the boys and girls back home in the highlands. People laugh at his accent, mine too if I tell the whole truth, but not to his face. They know he will bust them in the teeth if they poke one bit of fun at a mountain boy, he don't care who it is.

" 'We took a hundred and fifty boys to the front ten days ago. One hundred and eleven made it back. A good old boy from South Carolina named Tom Bottles took a fragment in the neck and chest. That did him in. I held him in my arms as he lay a dying, told him when I touched good South Carolina soil again I would kiss the ground that he once called home and go by to see his girl friend and tell her he died a brave man's death. He ain't the first one I done seen pass on to glory and I expect he won't be the last.' "

Abby laid down the page, took the third one in her hands. A tear ran to each eye, but she quickly wiped it away. Why should she cry over a man named Tom Bottles who she never even met? She went on to read the third page of the letter.

" 'I don't rightly know if I should tell you all this kind of thing but I don't hardly know who else to tell and I'm afraid if I don't talk it out somehow that it will get a grip on my insides and never let me go. Laban ain't much for talking. He don't stay still long enough to make much conversation, so I got nobody to listen to all this but you folks back home. I hope it is okay that I write all this and send it to you.

" 'So anyway, let me tell you this, and this is the worst of it. I did have to do what a man has to do in a war. When it is shoot or be shot, a body that can hold his nerves enough to do it has no choice but to shoot. And when the bullets run out and the shooting ends, a body has to do all else he can do to keep on living too. And that's where everything became as bad as a mind can imagine. One man against another man, both of them thinking of nothing but staying alive, staying alive so he can go back home to people he loves, to porches he wants to sit on again, to fields he wants to plow. The Germans come at us one night, when nobody expected. It had been so quiet here for a long time. I did what I had to do, God help me but that is what I did. And though I done washed my hands over and over again almost every hour since we come back from the front lines I still think I can see blood on them, blood that I can't seem to cleanse off. It comes to me that maybe nothing will wash the blood off these hands, no amount of soap and water, not even if I make it back to Blue Springs Mountain and wash them off in Slick Rock Creek.

" 'I reckon that is enough about all that. Maybe someday when I can sit down at the table and take up a cup of coffee I can find a way to say it all plainer. But I don't know that anybody needs to hear a whole lot about such things. Probably true too that nobody much will want to talk about it after all this has passed.

" 'Just know for now that me and Laban are safe, no wounds of the body at all. What will happen now, nobody really knows. We will put it all in the hands of the Almighty. What God brings to pass, we will no doubt learn to accept.

" 'Love to all and Laban says hey. Daniel.' "

Abby gently placed the page on the table. Solomon laid the palm of his hand over the letter, as if by touching it he could feel Daniel's broad back. The letter seemed sacred to Abby, like a piece of some holy garment sent to them by God.

"My boys are brave men," Solomon said. "God has been good to give such boys to me." He picked up the letter as he did every letter Daniel sent and stuck it in his pocket.

Abby thought she could see water in his eyes, and she wanted to stand up and pat him on the back and tell him it was okay to cry and say out loud that he missed his sons and worried for their safety. But since her pa had such a dislike for tears, she could not know for sure if they were really there, and if she said they were and he didn't like that, he might get mad. So she said nothing. A man like her pa wouldn't take well to anybody pointing out his grieving.

Pushing back his chair, Solomon stood and left the room. Abby glanced at Elsa, who then stood and followed Solomon.

"Time for bed, boys," she said to Junior and Walter. "Say a special Christmas prayer for Laban and Daniel. They will need all the prayers we can offer."

CHAPTER
TWENTY-FOUR

Nobody in Daniel's squad slept much on the night of July 17, 1918, due to a cloudburst that had soaked everybody in the trenches. Also, they knew something big was afoot the following morning. For two days already the German boys had pounded on the Third Division just southeast of them in an effort to take the road leading from Chateau-Thierry to Paris, not more than eighty miles away. But the boys in the Third had taken the worst of the German's whomping and handed it right back to them. Though the Third had been pushed back to the southern bank of the Marne River, they had dug in there, withstood heavy casualties and pushed back the attack. The word in the trenches said the Allies would move out on a counterthrust and cut into the Germans from southwest of the French town of Soissons. The goal was to prop up a bulge in the line and force the enemy north of the Marne.

Daniel knew only bits and pieces of the overall scheme, but he and everybody else in the First Division knew enough to write letters to their next of kin and settle any scores they had with the Lord if they were of a mind to believe in Him—just in case.

"You got all your gear in order?" Laban quietly asked Daniel as they squeezed down in a hole together about four o'clock that morning, their backs resting on the upside of the gully.

Daniel nodded. Though he had his ammo belt unfastened and his backpack lying next to his feet in the mud, he had cleaned his rifle, scraped a touch of rust off its bayonet, and tightened the chin strap on his helmet. A veteran of over a year off and on at the front, he knew now when to make ready and when to stand down.

"Gone be quite a tussle tomorrow, I expect," he whispered, staring up at the sky. "Never seen such a massing of the boys in one place."

Laban took off his helmet, hooked it on his knee. "I hope the boys ain't too wore out from marching in here."

Again Daniel nodded. They had marched into place in the trenches no less than forty-eight hours ago. But the men of the First could take it.

Laban said, "I hear there's almost two hundred and fifty thousand of us all told, Frenchies and all."

Daniel studied his brother. He had black oil smeared on his cheeks, forehead, and neck. His feet sported a new pair of boots he'd won in a poker game. Just like on his own uniform, Laban's had a sergeant's stripes stitched on both shirtsleeves. A man with a whole mess of problems in civilian life, Laban had taken fast to the military. His natural physical gifts and almost foolhardy bravery had seen him through a lot of scrapes and made him a hero with his buddies. His superiors had recommended him for officer training, but Laban had turned them down. "An officer can't gamble the shoes off the enlisted boys," he had said when the offer for promotion came.

Daniel knew the real reason Laban refused the promotion. Laban didn't want to leave his brother alone at the front.

"I hear they ain't gone do no early artillery this time," said Laban, his voice soft. "Want to take the German boys by surprise, I expect."

Daniel picked up his rifle, laid it across his lap. Jumping-off time was four-thirty or so. Before the German boys got woke up real good. According to the plan, the First Division was going to plow straight through the no-man's land that separated the two armies, cut up the razor wire, then take on the enemy machine guns. Not an easy chore, no sir.

"There is a lot of good farmland around here," Daniel said, thinking of the wheat he'd seen growing where bombs had not landed. "Fine stone houses in the villages too. No doubt real fair to the eye when they ain't no war to tear it up so."

"The Germans will use those fine stone houses as hideouts to shoot at us from," said Laban. "Would suit me if every house in France was made of paper."

Daniel smiled and checked up and down the trench. Men from the First Division rested in a number of ways as they prepared themselves for what they all knew might be their last day of living. He thought of his family back home—of Blue Springs Mountain and all its beauty, its rugged splendor that nobody who hadn't seen it could ever understand. He touched Laban on the shoulder. "We been watched over by the Lord to make it this far," he said. "But a man don't know when his time will come."

Laban placed his hand over Daniel's. "Don't you worry none about your time coming," he said. "I plan on taking care of both of us, Lord or no."

Chuckling, Daniel took a deep breath. He wanted to say something to Laban but didn't know how. He heard a rustling in the lines, saw his lieutenant headed their way, head down in the trench, hand on his helmet to hold it on. Men snapped on their ammo belts and shoved on their helmets as the lieutenant moved by. The lieutenant, a bony-faced, bowlegged man named Bruce Gorn from down in Georgia, reached Daniel and Laban.

"Saddle up," whispered Gorn. "Go time's at four thirty-five." Then he was gone, his boots splashing the mud as he hurried past. Activity in the trench notched up as everybody made ready.

Daniel stared at Laban. As usual before a fight, his tongue thickened on him and his mouth went dry. But for some reason he felt like he needed to say something this time, something he might not get another chance to speak. "You are my brother," he finally managed to say quietly. "And I pray for you every time before we go over the top."

Rolling to his stomach with his head easing to the top of the trench, Laban licked his lips and set his face toward the enemy. "I appreciate you prayin' for me," he said, "but I learned a long time ago that a man might believe in the good Lord all he wants, but when the bullets start whizzing by he better depend on his own good sense and sharpshooting."

"You ain't a believer?" asked Daniel, daring to ask the question he had long dreaded to face.

Laban shrugged. "That ain't what I said. Just that the evidence ain't all in, that's all."

"Never will be," Daniel said. "Not on this side of the river."

"Then I will just wait till I get to it," said Laban. "See what happens then."

Daniel briefly closed his eyes, thought of the picture of Jesus hanging in Jesus Holiness back in Blue Springs. His breath came quicker. Every man in the trench had now turned to face the upside of the trench. Beyond it lay almost six hundred yards of open space, one jagged crater after another between them and the Germans, row after row of sharp wire, splintered trees, and scattered weapons that had fallen from dead men's hands.

"I promised Pa I would find a way to re-claim our land," Daniel said quickly. "If I don't make it back, I want—"

"You will make it back!" interrupted Laban, his voice louder than it should've been in such a moment. "I made me a promise too, a promise that I expect to keep no matter what."

A machine gun started firing to their left. The men in the trench tensed. A few prayed so loud that others could hear them. One or two sobbed under their arms. Others tested their rifle bolts, their hands trembling visibly.

"I promised Pa I would keep you safe," Laban said. "If I can keep that promise maybe I will take another look at the Lord. That's all I ask from the Lord, to just let me get you home without a pine box around you."

Another machine gun started to sound off. *Rat-tat-tat, rat-tat-tat!*

"Stand to!" came the command from the right, its echo cutting through the line. "Stand to! Stand to!" The order sounded up and down the trench now as each man took up the yell.

Daniel felt tears in his eyes. He wiped them off, grabbed Laban by the elbow. "You are my brother," he whispered fiercely. "And I got nothing against you, you hear that! Nothing against you at all, no matter what happened back at home with the land. You are my brother and we gone both make it home, you and me together, back to Blue Springs!"

Laban turned and grinned, and Daniel wiped his eyes again. The whistle then sounded and somebody shouted, "Over the top!" and the time for talking ended. Thousands of men just as scared as he and Laban scrambled up the side of the trench and out to the field. A shell screamed overhead, and artillery started to rumble. Daniel wanted to turn again to Laban and tell him straight out that he loved him, but then the German machine guns kicked up the mud at his feet and artillery shells thumped to the ground, spraying his face with dirt. A man to his right fell with his chest torn open, and Daniel had no time to say anything else, so he just lowered his head and started to run.

Bullets cracked and hissed. Men fell forward and backward and sideways. One man rolled over in a somersault when a piece of shrapnel hit him between the eyes. Screaming, Daniel rushed on, his rifle firing in the direction of the machine guns ahead. To his left he spotted Lieutenant Gorn behind an Army tank. His bowed legs were crossing the field behind the giant machine, like a rabbit running from a fox. Smoke covered the ground, and Daniel wiped his eyes to see. He glanced quickly to his left to search for Laban but didn't see him anywhere.

Dropping himself into a crater, Daniel reloaded his rifle, rubbed the mud off his face, and rushed back up onto level ground. A shell whistled overhead, landed no more than thirty feet away. His feet felt the ground rumble, and his ears rang from the roar of the artillery. He jumped over a body in his path. He saw that it was Gorn and he wanted to stop to see about him, but it wasn't the time for that. The German machine guns seemed to fire even faster now. Mud kicked up at Daniel's feet. He smelled the fumes from all the shooting and bombing, an acrid smell that made his nose moisten. A stream of machine-gun fire tore his way, a sideways rain of death ripping the air toward his body.

He heard a man moaning, and he thought he recognized Laban's voice so he rushed to his right, skidding to the ground. Flipping over the body of the man lying there, he saw it wasn't Laban at all but some stranger with red hair and a flat nose. The man's right arm was missing below the elbow. Daniel took the shoelace that he kept in his pocket for just this kind of thing and tied off the man's stump with it. The man's face had already turned an empty white, and Daniel figured he had seen his last day. Unable to do anything more to help, Daniel started to ease away. Nothing more dangerous on a battlefield than to stay in one place for too long. But the man grabbed his pant leg.

"P-please take this," he said, moaning. He held up his remaining hand. "My wedding ring. Take it back to my . . . my wife back home . . . in Raleigh."

Daniel ducked down lower. Bullets whizzed all around them. The noise was deafening. He couldn't just leave the man alone as he was dying. So Daniel pulled the ring from the man's finger and stuck it in his shirt. He then wiped the man's face with water from his canteen. The morning shook with rumble and rifle fire.

"I will take your ring," Daniel said.

"Her name is Lydia Gant," said the man. "She is a good wife. My name is Oscar, Oscar Gant. Tell her . . . tell her I love her."

"She will hear those words from my lips," said Daniel.

"I thank you," he said.

Daniel touched the canteen to Oscar's lips. Oscar's head tilted and then moved no more. Daniel closed the man's eyes, put up his canteen. He breathed a quick, silent prayer for Oscar's family. Then, gritting his teeth, he pushed off the ground and ran again toward the German machine guns. All around him, the Allies' line advanced, soldier after soldier pushing ahead in the face of a punishing defense by the enemy. Rushing past a shattered tree and up a steep incline, Daniel saw a German helmet straight ahead, then another. The helmets bobbed up and down, this way and that, and Daniel knew he'd spotted a machine-gun nest. The Germans fired at him from the hole where they had dug in. The bullets cut a furrow in the ground at his feet but missed his flesh.

Pulling a grenade from his belt, Daniel primed it and heaved it at the Germans. A second later a burning cut into his right hip, and he stumbled and fell down. Crawling to a nearby crater, he dove headfirst into it. A shell whistled overhead, then landed. Shrapnel splintered the air. A piece ripped through Daniel's left shoulder. The bomb's roar filled his ears. Another piece of shrapnel caught him in the middle of the back. He grabbed the wet ground and tried to pull it over him, tried to cover his body with earth and so protect himself from the death falling from the sky. But he couldn't hold enough of the dirt in his hands to make it a full enough blanket. The shrapnel kept falling, and after another few seconds, Daniel closed his eyes and everything faded to black.

The First Division pushed the Germans back all day, and Laban fought steady with the rest of his unit, step by step, crater by crater, machine-gun nest by machine-gun nest. The sun rose fast after the battle got started, then beat down hard and hot as it reached its worst moments. The Fighting First made their first objective by noon but didn't stop there. By early afternoon the Germans were giving up more and more ground. The wind picked up a notch as the hours went by. The First fought their way through a wide ravine and up the other side. Bodies littered the ground, looking like cut logs after lumberjacks have taken their axes to a forest. Airplanes buzzed overhead, some of them fighting in aerial combat, while others blasted away at the soldiers running on the ground below.

A wound on Laban's right cheek had caked over with mud and blood and throbbed from his neck to his eye, yet wasn't bad enough to slow him down. Laban's eyes had glazed over hours ago. His face wore the look of a man who had seen so many bad things that another one didn't matter anymore. Though his finger kept pulling the trigger on his rifle, and his legs kept pushing forward, his mind had taken him somewhere else—a place that let his body keep functioning but not his feelings.

Grabbing at his ammo belt, Laban saw that he'd emptied it. He halted in the middle of a tattered field and stared down at his empty hands as though seeing them for the first time. From off in the distance he heard someone yelling. He looked around to see who it was but saw no one. Searching the field, it suddenly dawned on him that he needed to find some ammo, and what was more, he needed to get on the ground to stay alive while he looked.

Laban quickly dropped and started crawling, his hands and elbows pulling him along. Overhead he heard a plane approaching and he wondered if it was a friend or enemy. He looked up at the sky, saw white clouds moving and the plane dropping through the clouds. The plane was German and had set its sights on him.

Laban's senses snapped back into place. He rolled to his right and landed in a shell hole. Three other men lay beside him. He recognized a lieutenant from the First but didn't know the other two. The plane raked their position yet hit nothing but the ground. After one more pass, it buzzed away. Then the field turned suddenly quieter. While a few guns continued to fire, the artillery had largely stopped for the moment.

"We got 'em running," panted the lieutenant. "We'll dig in here for the night."

His canteen in hand, Laban saw no cause to argue. The boys of the First had already done more in one day than anybody expected they could. He took a drink of water, then offered the canteen to the others in the trench. The lieutenant took a swallow. Laban lay back and took a deep breath.

"You cut up your face there," the lieutenant said, pointing to Laban's cheek. "A bayonet get you?"

"It weren't no woman's fingernails, I can tell you that much," s.
Laban.

The lieutenant grinned. Laban screwed the cap back on his canteen, then rolled over and stuck his head over the top of the crater. Bodies lay in every direction. But American soldiers were now crawling in and out among them, checking on the wounded, taking prisoners, and grabbing up ammo and provisions off the dead. Smoke drifted low over the field, close to the ground like morning fog back in the hollers in Blue Springs. The shooting had almost completely stopped now. Laban figured the men on both sides of the line were too weary for any more meanness for the day. The day had just about disappeared.

Immediately, Laban began searching for Daniel. He felt the same queasy feeling that always came when he didn't see his brother after a battle. Nothing worse than the sickness such times brought, when he wondered if he'd failed again, if he'd messed up like he always did by letting something happen to his little brother. He knew of course he couldn't stay with Daniel all the time. War just didn't allow such a thing. When the shells started falling and the officers shouted "Over the top!" a soldier had to stand up and run, with his rifle shooting and bayonet stabbing at anything that got in the way. Not possible for a man to keep up with another man in such a circumstance as that, no matter how much he loved him or what kind of promise one had made to the other.

Laban faced the lieutenant. "You seen my brother?" he asked. The lieutenant shook his head. Laban spoke to the other two men. "He is about my height, Daniel Porter is his name, got black hair, a scar on his chin from where a dog bit him back home."

The men said no and then looked away. Laban knew they figured Daniel was dead. Men in war always figured that about those missing. That way they never came up disappointed. But Laban knew better. He and Daniel did this at the end of every battle. Started looking for each other. Moving from trench to trench, crater to crater, calling out each other's names, asking the other soldiers. So far it had worked out good. Sometimes they found they were close by during the entire battle. Maybe that was how it was today, with Daniel only a short ways off. He knew Daniel was okay. All he had to do was find him.

He grunted, took another swig from his canteen, and reset his helmet. "Got any spare ammo?" Laban asked the lieutenant, pointing to his own empty belt.

The lieutenant handed Laban a belt full of ammo and also a couple of grenades. Laban nodded his appreciation, then climbed out of the hole and headed to the one beside it. But he found no one there. He moved to a third hole, then a fourth. Still no Daniel. He knew a couple of guys in the fifth hole, and they said they'd seen Daniel earlier in the day but not for several hours. Laban left them and kept looking. Within an hour or so he had checked out the line in both directions for about a half mile—the distance he figured the battle might have separated him and Daniel. But Laban hadn't found him.

Although he didn't want to consider the possibility, he finally asked a medic where they were taking the wounded and made his way over there. He saw a hospital sign over a large stone house located near what had once been a grove of thick trees. He checked in with the guards. They pointed him to a big canvas tent, and he walked over there and ducked inside the makeshift hospital. A quick glance over the beds showed him a scene he didn't want to see but looked at anyway because of wanting to find his brother. But Daniel wasn't there. Not on the blood-soaked beds or the grungy floor, either. For a moment Laban just stood and stared at the wounded men. From somewhere deep within a feeling he had long thought destroyed rolled up inside of him. A rush of bile came to his throat, but he pushed it back down and ran outside, his lungs sucking in air as desperately as a beached trout. Clenching his fists, he thought of one other place to look yet refused to do it. Daniel was not in the stack of bodies the death detail collected after battle and laid out behind the hospital for burial. Even though he knew he might be fooling himself, Laban sensed in his bones that Daniel was still alive. That he had taken a hit, maybe he could believe that. But dead? No! No bullet had done that to him, no piece of shrapnel. To believe that Daniel was dead meant he had done a worse thing than he had ever done, a thing for which he could never be forgiven, that would show him once again he was unworthy of the Porter name.

A hard sweat broke out under Laban's armpits, and his throat felt like somebody had shoved a whole orange down it. It had never taken this long for him and Daniel to find each other. Truly scared now, Laban squatted down by a tree that a bomb had split down the middle. Sap ran from the broken trunk like blood from an open wound. Laban touched the sap, tasted it. He closed his eyes. The sap felt like blood on his fingers. He wiped it off on his pants, then opened his eyes and glanced toward

the sky. Full dark had fallen. Laban heaved a sigh and knew he had to face the possibility that something had happened to Daniel, something no brother ought to have to consider about another. He squeezed the barrel of his rifle, and his knuckles turned white. Then he stood and looked back over the ground the First Division had taken that day. If Daniel wasn't in the trenches at the front and if he wasn't in the makeshift hospital, then he had to have fallen somewhere between where they started and where they finished. That being the case, Laban had no choice but to go back and look.

He took a sip of water, holstered his canteen, and headed off to find his lieutenant. It took about thirty minutes. Laban quickly told him what he planned to do.

"You a crazy man," said the lieutenant. "It's pitch black. No way to find one man in all that." He waved his hand over the carnage behind the trenches where he sat. "Wait until morning, see if he don't turn up by then."

Laban considered the matter. If Daniel was still alive but shot up so bad he couldn't call out for help, then he probably had no more than a night before his chances ran out. A wound would bleed him to death or the gangrene would set in.

"I got to go find my brother," he said, his decision firm.

"Might still be Germans out there," the lieutenant warned.

Laban nodded. A battlefield at night, even a conquered one, held all kinds of danger. Enemy wounded lay all over the field, and they often became loose in the head because of their pain and shot at the first thing that moved. And other German soldiers out on the field may not be wounded at all. They were healthy men who had played dead as the First overran their positions, who buried their faces in the mud or pulled dead bodies over them when the Americans charged past. Later they would try to make their way back to their lines under the cover of darkness and would shoot a man faster than a crazy drunk on a Saturday night in Blue Springs. But Laban didn't care about any of this.

"I got to find my brother," he repeated.

"I ought to order you to stay."

Laban smiled grimly. "Ain't no order gone stop me."

The lieutenant nodded. "Go on then. But mind yourself."

Laban touched his helmet in a half salute and walked away. Overhead a black sky looked down on him. The smell of smoke had largely disappeared, and the air smelled almost normal now, like a summer night ought to smell. A dog barked from off near the hospital, and Laban thought of home.

He looked up at the sky. "This here is your chance to hand over some evidence," he said to the darkness. "A mighty good chance."

The dog barked again. Laban hunched low, his rifle at the ready as he moved back across the ground he had helped take just a few hours earlier in the day.

When Daniel first woke up he couldn't tell what time it was. His eyes felt crusty, as if someone had poured molasses mixed with dirt in them. He rubbed them out and they gradually opened better. Rolling over from stomach to back, he winced as his hip hitched up in pain. He tried to touch the hurting spot, but his right arm wouldn't move. He lay still for a moment, trying to get his bearings. Then he sensed another presence in the dark. He squinted to his right, saw a body about ten feet away. The dead man wore a German uniform. Daniel closed his eyes and remembered what he could of the day's events. Most of it blurred up on him; he didn't know exactly how he'd come to where he was.

He looked up at the moon. Must be a good bit past midnight, he figured, maybe near three or four. With his good arm he checked his condition, noted the wounds in his hip, back, and right arm. Blood seeped from the wounds, and Daniel wondered how much he had already lost. Maybe too much?

He took a heavy breath and stared at the moon again. It looked the same here as back in Blue Springs, he decided, exactly the same. No matter where a man went, the moon looked the same. How strange that such a notion would come to him here. The whole wide earth and all the people on it, all under the same moon, even the German soldier lying dead beside him in the trench. For a second, Daniel wondered about the soldier. Did he have a wife back home? Children maybe? Did he hunt and fish in the woods by his cabin? Or did he live in a city and drive a fancy car?

Daniel heard feet moving. He drew up in the hole, tried to make his body as small as possible. The feet moved closer. Daniel looked around his crater, hoping to see a rifle. One lay next to the dead German. Gritting his teeth against the pain, Daniel pulled himself to the weapon. A voice drifted over the battlefield as a ghostly whisper, but he couldn't tell whether it spoke American or German. He grabbed the rifle and quickly checked it.

Holding the rifle in his left hand, he forced his body to the crater's edge. He held the rifle to his left shoulder, his finger on the trigger. The voice called out again. Daniel could make out the word now—it was English.

"Daniel!" The word rang out as a steady whisper. "Daniel!" It was Laban! Squinting in the dark, Daniel saw his brother moving toward him, his body low to the ground as it searched from hole to hole.

Daniel grunted as he threw his good leg out of the crater and jerked out to level ground. "Over here," he called quietly. "I'm over here."

Laban stopped and stared Daniel's way. Daniel raised high his left hand, and Laban saw it and ran toward him. Ten seconds later Laban reached him and threw himself to the ground beside his brother.

"Glory be!" whispered Laban, rubbing his head like a mother blessing a child. "You are alive!"

"Not easy to kill a Blue Springs boy," Daniel said, happier now than he could ever remember. "You said so yourself."

They scrambled back down into the hole where Daniel had spent the night. Laban handed him a canteen. Daniel drank deeply from it, gave it back to Laban, who also took a long drink.

"I been looking all night," said Laban. "But now I done found you."

Daniel heard a catch in his brother's throat. "You done good," he said, laying his left hand over Laban's. "I'm proud you are my brother."

For a moment they stayed quiet, letting the emotions settle, leaving time for the unsaid to be thought. Laban took another drink of water, offered it again to Daniel, but he refused.

After capping the canteen, Laban suddenly became a soldier again. He glanced around the hole and nodded toward the dead German. "Not real safe out here," he said. "Best we get on back to our lines."

"That suits me fine," Daniel agreed. "But I got to tell you, crawling is gone be mighty slow for me." He pointed to his hip.

"I reckon I got to carry you then."

"Isn't that what big brothers are for?"

Grinning, Laban took Daniel by his good hand and threw it over his shoulder, then hoisted him onto his back.

"How far you reckon it is to the lines?" asked Daniel.

"Don't rightly know. I been out here lookin' for you for hours, so probably at least a couple of miles back to the front."

"The First did okay today then?"

"We tore up them German boys like a mountain cat on a rabbit."

Pleased but tired, Daniel rested his head on Laban's shoulder. Laban raised up and climbed out of the crater and started to pick his way over the battlefield. His head bouncing in all directions, Daniel saw shapes and shadows in all directions. The ground was uneven, chock-full of bumps and bulges. Bodies lay scattered as far as the eye could see—German boys mostly but every now and again an American or two that the medics or body detail hadn't found.

Seeing the Americans, Daniel wanted to stop and check them, carry them back with him and Laban. But he knew Laban couldn't do any more than what he was already doing.

Stepping carefully, Laban moved with a steady pace, his strong body staying close to trees and burned-out buildings whenever he could find them. Overhead, the moon disappeared behind some clouds. Listening to his brother's breathing, Daniel said a quiet word of thanks that he had a brother as brave as Laban. No doubt he would have died had Laban not come searching for him.

It seemed to Daniel that at least an hour had passed since they began their journey back to the front. He felt sweat on Laban's back. But Laban never paused, not even for a swallow from his canteen. Daniel wished he could walk and thought about telling Laban to let him try. But then he remembered he couldn't feel his left hip much less stand on it. So he kept quiet as Laban moved ahead.

Daniel wondered if he would lose his leg, maybe his right arm too. He pushed away the notion. If it happened, nothing he could do about it. But he would fight any doctor who came to amputate any of his limbs, unless he became convinced he would die otherwise.

Laban kept on walking. From time to time Daniel thought he saw movement, a jerk of something here or there, a German soldier maybe, coming to consciousness and about to shoot at them. But Laban paid it no attention. Daniel glanced up at the sky and thought he could see the first signs of the sun rising. He wondered how much time had gone by since Laban found him. His mind drifted in and out, and his eyes opened and closed with fatigue and shock.

From what seemed like a long ways off, he heard Laban whisper to him. "We are not far now," he said. "I recognize that house over there.

We tore into some German boys late in the day there. Our lines are no more than a hundred yards or so."

Daniel squinted hard, saw the outline of a large stone house to his left maybe forty yards away. "Don't let no sawbones take off none of my body parts," he said weakly.

"We ain't there yet," said Laban. "Don't count no chickens." He pushed past a burned-out tree and then headed up an incline.

Daniel tensed. They were coming at their lines from the rear. Their boys might think they were Germans trying to sneak through and shoot them before they could identify themselves. Or a wounded German trying to reach his own lines might do them the same trick.

Daniel heard something move off to his right. He twisted that way and saw a shadow rising off the ground. He opened his mouth to warn Laban, but the shadow fired a rifle before he could say anything. Daniel saw the flash of the bullet and somehow knew before Laban ever felt a thing that his big brother would not make it all the way back to Blue Springs.

As if watching something that had been decided before the beginning of time, Daniel saw Laban's head snap back and felt his brother's arms relaxing their hold on his legs where they had carried him piggyback through the night. Dropping to the ground, Daniel saw Laban spin in the direction of his enemy and point his rifle at the shadow. A shot fired. The shadow jerked backward and fell down face first, the limp form once more on the earth from which it had arisen.

Daniel crawled quickly to Laban, who was lying now on his back, his eyes on the sky, a small puddle on the ground by his right ear. Tears poured down Daniel's chin and onto his throat.

Laban reached up and touched Daniel's cheeks, brushed away the tears. "Pa says cryin' never did anybody any good," he said.

Daniel gripped Laban's hand but did nothing to stop the tears. "You just hold on," he said, "I will—"

Laban touched a finger to Daniel's mouth to quiet him. "It is okay," he said. "I done kept my promise. It is okay."

Daniel kissed his brother's hand, his tears too strong to let him say anything else. Good soldiers knew when to let the truth stand as it was. No reason to pretend that anybody could do anything to make Laban better.

"You will tell Pa, won't you?" asked Laban, his voice pleading.

Daniel lifted Laban's head, laying it gently into his lap. He rocked him back and forth. "You know I will," he wept. "I will tell Pa you kept your promise."

"I am sorry about losing the land," Laban said. "I didn't mean to hurt nobody."

"I know," said Daniel. "We all know."

Laban breathed heavily.

Daniel kissed him on the forehead. "I will get the land back for you," he said, repeating the promise he'd made to his pa the day they moved away. "You kept your word to Pa. I want you to know I will keep mine to you. I will get the land back . . . for you and for Pa."

Laban nodded. "Thank you . . . brother. I . . . I would be much obliged to you for that." Daniel's tears fell faster and dripped onto Laban's face. Laban took Daniel by the collar and pulled him low. Then, his face peaceful, he whispered, "I got me some evidence now."

"What?"

"Evidence," Laban whispered again. "I got me some . . ." Laban's eyes closed and his head dropped. And Daniel held his brother's head in his lap under the light of a French sun coming up, and he cried in spite of what his pa said about it, and he wondered why it was that God let some men live while other men died.

CHAPTER
TWENTY-FIVE

S till walking with a limp, Daniel arrived back in North Carolina early in September. Abby and the others met him in the morning at the train station in Asheville where he had come after a stopover in Raleigh for a few days to clear up some business from the war that he didn't want to talk about. They put him in a wagon for the trip back to Blue Springs. Though he had already told them in a letter how Laban had died saving his life, Daniel repeated the story as they ate a late supper that night in the cabin. Solomon smoked his pipe and kept saying how proud he was of his boys and how he hoped Laban knew that. Watching her pa, Abby wondered why he had not said such things to Laban before it was too late, but then she realized he was the same way with her so maybe she shouldn't ever expect anything different. Solomon Porter had kept his feelings wrapped up inside his chest all his life, and neither she nor anybody else had any reason to expect him to change.

The supper ended and everybody headed off to bed. The next morning came and then the next and a week followed that and then a month. Daniel didn't talk much about the war, and nobody pressed him because they knew that some things a body had to say when they wanted or not at all. Sometimes, late in the night, they heard him scream out from the mattress where he slept by the fire, and they figured he had some night-mares rolling around in his head. But they knew of nothing they could do to make the bad dreams go away. Elsa fed him well, and Abby joined him for slow walks through the woods. Other than that, their hands were tied.

His hip a little better, Daniel pitched in with the chores where he could, and the work seemed to cheer him up some. About six weeks after coming back to the mountain, he told everybody he thought his hip had mended enough for him to move out on his own. Nobody argued. A man of his years made his own decisions, and who were they to question him?

By the middle of October he had rented a three-room house down near Asheville and paid for it with some of the wages he had saved from the war. By the end of the month he had sent them a letter saying his arm had healed to the point that he thought he could lay brick again and planned to work whenever the weather allowed.

Since Laban had not spent much time at home in years, Abby's days didn't change any as a result of his death. This fact seemed real strange to her as she pondered on it but then she realized maybe it shouldn't. People died every day and it didn't change anything in her life, so why should the fact that this time it was her brother make things any different. Laban was dead and buried somewhere way over in France, and Daniel had a limp and dark circles under his eyes, caused by him waking up at night with his bad dreams. But nothing in her life had altered one bit. She still woke up every morning a resident of Blue Springs Mountain, a back-ward highlander woman with no hopes for anything but a life of poverty, ignorance, and sunup-to-sundown labor.

In a way she envied Daniel for what he had done and seen. At least he had traveled somewhere. He had visited some of the world, painful as some of that visit had been. In the meantime, her life had brought nothing but more and more days of hard work on a mountain that grew suffering and loneliness as its best crops. Yes, she had come to love Junior and Walter, and she and Elsa had long since come to peace with each other. Still, living on Blue Springs Mountain had left a hole inside Abby, a sense that something more awaited her, something she ought yet to do. Though she had given up any notion of getting more education, she still had not managed to push off the idea that the Lord had more in store for her than just to live out her days as a backwoods mountain woman.

As the leaves on the trees fell off and November approached, Abby fell more and more into a dark mood, a bout of melancholia the likes of which she hadn't felt since Hal Clack threw her out of his house in Blue Springs. While she had managed for years to hide her resentment of her situation, she now took to fussing and fuming every time something happened that she didn't like. Elsa usually gave back to her whatever she dished out, but Junior and Walter started shying away when the worst of her moods hit. As winter approached she felt more and more alone.

Occasionally, Abby tried to figure out what was eating at her. Was it just that she thought too highly of herself? Better than others around her? Did she have a big head because she wanted to move off the mountain and take up some career? She did not think so, but she knew that some folks, especially some of the men who had tried to court her, explained their failure to win her hand by saying she didn't think any man was up to her standards.

Examining the matter closely, Abby dismissed the idea. It wasn't that she thought herself better, just different. And with that she could not argue. She was different—different because the isolation of her highland home did not satisfy her like it seemed to satisfy the others who lived there. She didn't know why this was the case.

Was it the fact that the highlands did not give her the chance to test her potential? To go on to school like Mr. Holston had said she ought? Would she be happier if she could leave the mountain, become a teacher or . . . or whatever women down in Asheville became? She knew her mind had a lot of space in it that nothing had ever filled. She had read every book in Blue Springs, but that was few, and she had a thirst for knowledge worse than any man's desire for the doublings. At times her brain seemed as empty as a cabin where everybody had moved out, leaving behind only cobwebs, rats, and dust.

But Abby knew that her failure to achieve more education wasn't all of it. Though it pained her to admit it, she also felt bothered that she was a full-grown woman without a husband. Elsa and Lindy kept telling her she ought to find a man and marry up with him, but most of the men under thirty-five had joined the Army and only those wounded bad had come home so far. So her choices were as thin as the hair on a turkey's neck. Besides, she would not marry for anything less than love, no matter how desperate her circumstances.

She thought often of Thaddeus. He had written her a lot of letters during his time at war, each one pledging his love to her. Fighting in another division, he had spent as much time at the front as Laban and Daniel and managed to come through it with nary a scratch. And, if the news from the paper down in Blue Springs told it true, the war would be ending just about any day now. Then Thaddeus would come home and ask for her hand in marriage, and that would place a decision in her lap that she didn't know if she wanted.

True, when she thought of Thaddeus, a warm rush rolled into her stomach and her face flushed. Once he had finally managed to say that he loved her, he said it afterward with steady frequency. Abby liked it when his letters arrived, liked sitting down and reading his flowery words. One thing about Thaddeus Holston—his pa had taught him how to write, and he used the knowledge at full force when it came to what he wrote from the front. Abby studied over every letter he sent, trying to determine if the feelings they created in her rose up because it was Thaddeus doing the writing or because she just wanted a letter from somebody, a man of any kind is better than none kind of notion. If Thaddeus returned and she married him, would it be because she loved him or because he was the only man available? Was she settling if she married him, settling for less than what she wanted or what she deserved?

She knew if she married Thaddeus, she would never leave Blue Springs Mountain. He had made it clear enough more than once that he loved the place. So where did that leave her? Settling for the mountains and a hard life? Giving up her sense of destiny? All to marry him. Though she fought against the emotion, this idea left her empty.

When she got right down to it, Abby wondered if marrying Thaddeus would make her happy, if it would fill up the loneliness she had carried around all her life, the sense that she wasn't connected to anybody. Would marrying him change the fact that her ma's dying on the day of her birth had cut her off from the rest of the world as surely as a knife had cut the umbilical cord between her and her ma's body? She wondered if she was so cut off that nothing could ever connect again. Maybe even a husband could not bridge the gaps she felt, the separateness that existed between her and others.

Abby knew she ought to feel complete because she had Jesus in her life, and that her connection to God should give her all the relationship she needed. Yet, she had to admit, even the Lord did not completely soothe the ache in her chest, the longing that made her shoulders droop and her head hang low. She wondered why. Didn't a person who had

Jesus have everything? Well, the Good Book said so. But maybe Jesus made his presence known through the people who loved you, the people who gave you the hugs you craved and the words of encouragement that anybody, even the most saintly of Christians, ought to hear from time to time. Deep in her soul Abby felt that no one did any of that for her. She couldn't remember the last time somebody had held her tight. And only Thaddeus and Lindy had ever told her they loved her, and they weren't even family, at least not yet.

As the cold weather hit, Abby's spirits dropped even lower. Then Walter, Junior, and Elsa took sick with the flu, and everything she had ever known flipped upside down. Suddenly she had no choice but to stop worrying about herself, because Death now hung out at the door, and she and her pa were the only well people in the house. Abby realized that a family needs everybody fighting as hard as they can when the Grim Reaper knocks, and so she rolled up her sleeves and took to fighting it with all she had.

Abby had heard of course about all the people the flu was killing all over the country. Some said the Germans had started it by dropping germs in the harbor in Boston. Others said the outbreak started in Kansas with a bunch of soldiers burning manure from their mules. But no matter where it all started, the influenza had become a killing machine, an enemy as deadly as anything the Germans could come up with in a hundred years. The newspaper said it had spread all over the world and that thousands were dying. The epidemic had not come to Blue Springs until the middle of October. By the time it reached her family, the flu had already killed ten people on the mountain, including Preacher Bruster down at Jesus Holiness.

The sickness struck Walter first, on a Saturday, the first weekend of November. At noon he started complaining about an aching in his head and arms. By the time the shadows outside had stretched over the whole yard, he had a fever hotter than a washtub sitting out in the August sun. Grumbling because he owned no automobile to make the trip faster, Pa left for Blue Springs on his horse to fetch the doctor. At nightfall Junior started with the same hurts that Walter had. Pa came back a couple of hours later but only to say that Doc Booth had at least four other people in town with the same ailments and would come as soon as he could. He had given Pa a bottle of aspirin to help with the fever. Other than that, the doctor's only advice was to sponge off Walter and Junior with cold rags, to help keep the fever down, and to take to their knees for praying.

All night long the two boys lay on their beds moaning and coughing. The coughs pushed up a nasty sputum, some blood mixed in it from time to time. Abby and Solomon and Elsa did all they could, soaked their faces with cold rags, piled blankets high on their chests, shoved aspirin down their throats every couple of hours. They prayed too, harder and louder than Abby had ever prayed. But nothing seemed to matter. The boys cried out in pain, and nobody knew anything else to do.

At daybreak Elsa started complaining too. Within an hour she had joined Junior and Walter on the sickbed, her fine face marked by a bleached-out look. Solomon sat beside her, his hands on her forehead, his mouth muttering his prayers. Elsa got sicker. About midday Solomon left Elsa's bedside, went out to the barn, and brought back a sack of onions and started boiling them in a pot.

"I heard down at the post office that some woman up in Pennsylvania swore she kept her family alive with onions," he said. "She made a poultice, put it on their chests, made them breathe onion steam and eat hot onion soup."

Knowing nothing better, Abby didn't argue. Pa made the poultice, wrapped it in a clean rag, then laid it on Junior and Walter and Elsa. Finished with that, he carried the pot of boiled onions to each of the beds and made the three of them breathe from the fumes.

Abby prepared a soup of squashed onions, salt, and water. When she fed it to the sick ones they gagged and spit, but she just cleaned off their chins and gave them some more. By the second night, Walter had drawn down in his bed, his legs pulled up to his stomach, his face a bluish color now. He coughed up more and more blood from his throat, and Abby figured he wouldn't make it.

Doc Booth called out from the yard a few hours after dark. They brought him in, and his heavy body was breathing hard. With no road the last mile up to the cabin, he had no choice but to walk the distance, and his heft made it a rough climb. After he caught his breath, he checked on the ill, shook his head over Walter, and motioned Abby and Solomon over to the fireplace.

"This flu is the worst I ever saw," he said. "Thousands already passed on, all over the world. Not much anybody can do, not even the experts in the big cities."

"Some say it's the Lord's vengeance for all the killing over in Europe," said Solomon.

Doc Booth sighed. "Hard for me to see how the Lord can blame the folks here in Blue Springs for all of that."

Solomon took out his pipe and lit it, let the doc's words go unchallenged. "Thank you for coming," he said, patting Booth on the back. "I know this is hard on you too."

"I am getting long in the tooth," Booth said. "Seen too many good people take up lodging in early graves."

Solomon just puffed his pipe and shook his head.

Booth picked up his bag from the kitchen table. "Praying is all you got left," he said. The doctor left the cabin then, his bulky body covered in a big black coat.

Abby moved back to Walter, took a chair by his head, and held his hand. Solomon moved from one bed to the other—Walter, then Elsa, then Junior, then back to Walter. Knowing that Walter was the worst sick, Abby stayed with him. He never woke up. A couple of hours before sunrise, he took a full breath, shuddered for a second, and then stopped moving.

Pushing back her tears, Abby called for her pa, who was at Elsa's bed at the time. His pipe in hand, he rushed into the room. Seeing Walter, he knelt down by his son and kissed his forehead. Abby watched him for several minutes. His mouth moved in prayer.

Finished, he faced her. "I want a moment with him by myself," he said.

Abby bit her lip. She didn't want to leave him in a time like this, to let her pa suffer alone. She wanted to put her arms around Solomon and tell him she hurt with him. She wanted to say that the two of them had more in common than anyone else, that they had not only lost Walter but Rose Porter too, and that gave them a bond nobody else could match. But she'd never touched her pa in that way and didn't know how he would take to it if she did. In addition, he had asked her to leave the room, and who was she to argue with him? If he wanted to suffer by himself, then so be it.

Standing, she kissed Walter on the cheek and left the room.

They buried Walter four days later in a space up the hill out behind the cabin. Even though grieved beyond speaking, Abby felt grateful that he had trusted Jesus as his Savior the previous summer and been baptized in Blue Springs Creek. Since the flu had taken Preacher Bruster, and they had no replacement for him to say words over Walter, a few of Walter's friends told what a good buddy he had been, Solomon read some Scripture, and Lindy and Abby sang a song together. That was the end of it. Blowing on their hands to keep them warm, everybody moved slowly back down to the cabin to check on Elsa and Junior, who had survived the flu yet were still too weak to come to the graveside. A table full of food that the neighbors had brought waited for them in the cabin. After looking in on Elsa and Junior, Abby joined Lindy by the fire. They talked for a while about how much suffering the flu and the war had brought.

"Thank the Lord the war is over," said Lindy. "Everybody coming home soon."

"You mean Thaddeus," Abby said, staring into the fire.

Lindy smiled. "He loves you, you know."

"That is what he tells me," Abby said, too shy to admit she liked hearing it.

"You plan on marrying him?"

"You gone marry Jubal?" Abby asked.

"As soon as he comes back and we can find a preacher."

Abby chuckled. Lindy and Jubal had started courting when they were young and had stayed at it all along. He was stationed in Charleston, South Carolina, because he was too short for real fighting. But Lindy didn't care about his stature.

"So what you thinking about Thaddeus?" Lindy asked, her tone insistent.

Abby studied the fire. Why not marry Thaddeus? He loved her. She loved him too, at least in a certain way. Whether it was the kind of love she ought to feel to marry, she still did not know. She'd never had a chance to compare it to anything. Should she wait for what some people claimed you ought to have—fireworks blasting and sweaty palms? But she might wait forever and not find that kind of thing. Maybe she should accept his proposal. But that meant she would never leave the mountain, never fill up her head with knowledge. Was Thaddeus worth that? Even

HIGHLAND HOPES

if she didn't marry him, nothing said she would ever receive the learning she wanted. Then she would not only be ignorant but alone too.

Abby faced Lindy. Thaddeus was a good man. Maybe her hopes were too grand for a simple highland girl; maybe she had no true reason to hold out for anything else. "I expect I just might marry him," she said.

"You mean it?" asked Lindy as if unable to believe her ears.

"I reckon I do."

Lindy jumped up and hugged her neck. "You are the best friend anybody could ever have! The best friend ever!"

Abby felt tears testing her eyes and she wondered if they came from joy or grief. Then she heard someone hailing them from the yard. Lindy walked to the door and opened it.

"It's Sheriff Rucker," she said to Abby.

Abby stood as Lindy beckoned Rucker inside. Sheriff Rucker stepped over to the fireplace, a thick coat on his back and his hat in his hand.

"Sorry to bother you at a time like this," he said, warming his hands.

"You always welcome here," Abby said. She pointed him to a chair.

A few seconds later, Solomon came in with Elsa holding to his elbow, her face real pale. Solomon led Elsa to a chair by the fire, eased her down, then went over and shook the sheriff's hand. Abby and Lindy took their seats.

"Sorry about your sorrow," said Rucker, looking from Pa to Elsa to Abby. "Seems there is a lot of it going around these days."

Solomon thanked him and sat down in his rocker by Elsa's. "What brings you out so far on such a cold day?" he asked, not bothering to make idle chatter.

Rucker hung his hat on his knee, pulled an envelope from his back pocket. "Two things," he said. "I wanted to pay my respects to Walter."

Solomon nodded his gratitude.

"And I brought this for your missus," he said, handing Elsa the envelope.

Her eyebrows touching with confusion, Elsa took the envelope and held it up to the light. She looked at Solomon, then to Abby and Lindy. "It is from my ma," she said.

Rucker cleared his throat. Abby remembered the last time Rucker had come to their place, the time he helped Hal Clack evict them from their land. Was this more bad news?

273

"Mrs. Clack died a week ago," Rucker said without ceremony. "Flu got her like it did your Walter."

Elsa gasped and her face, already pale, seemed to lose all the rest of its color. Solomon reached over and took her hands in his.

Abby's heart sank. Though she hadn't really talked to Mrs. Clack in a long time, she still cared for her. How sad that she had died too. How sad that anybody had died.

"Mrs. Clack left the letter with a lawyer," Rucker said. "But since he has fallen sick, he asked me to bring it to you. I am supposed to stay until you open it." He indicated the letter.

Abby watched as Elsa fingered the envelope. Tears ran down Elsa's cheeks. Abby wondered what all this meant. Why had Mrs. Clack sent it through a lawyer?

Her fingers slow, Elsa wiped her eyes, opened the envelope, and stared down at the page. After a couple of minutes, she looked back up, first to Solomon, then over to Abby. Her hands trembled as she held the letter up to the light again. Abby couldn't tell if she was still weak from sickness and grief or scared by what the letter might say.

"I will read it aloud," Elsa said.

Nobody moved.

" 'Dear Elsa,

I will make this short and simple. I am giving you in my will the sum total of eight hundred and nineteen dollars to use as you see fit. I know this will make your pa madder than a preacher with a empty offering plate because he don't know I been stealing money from him all these years while he was passed out drunk. But he can't hit me no more now so let him be as mad as he wants.

" 'God bless you, child. You are a good person, and Solomon ended up making you a good husband. Take this money as my way of making up some for the bad things your pa did to you, and think of me from time to time while you are spending this on fancy clothes.

Love,

Your ma, Amelia Clack

" 'P.S. I am also leaving a hundred dollars for Abby for her to buy some books. It won't purchase her all the education she wants but it will help some. She aided me around the house when she lived with me and never made me feel bad about what my husband had done to her family. I took a true liking to her, like she was my daughter since you left me to marry. So I wanted to do what I could for her. Wish it could be more but even this much will make my old man plumb crazy.' "

Elsa stopped reading and laid the letter on her lap. Her face appeared blank, her lips shocked into silence. The fireplace crackled.

"Glory be," Solomon finally whispered. "Eight hundred dollars. We maybe can buy back our land with that."

As if waking from a deep sleep, Elsa turned to him slowly, her eyes gradually focusing. "That won't happen," she said. "No way my pa will let you buy back your land with money my ma gave me."

Abby recognized the truth of what she said. Solomon hung his head. Abby thought about how many books she could buy with a hundred dollars.

The letter in her hand, Elsa stood and eased to the fireplace, propped her back against the mantel. Her shoulders squared up some, and Abby could see she had something she wanted to say in spite of her weakened condition. A feeling of admiration rose up in Abby then, an appreciation for Elsa that she had never experienced. In spite of her grief over the death of her son and her mama and her weakness from the flu, Elsa had courage.

"We could use this money to buy my ma's old place down in Blue Springs," said Elsa. "Pa don't care about that property."

Solomon pulled out his pipe. "I know this might sound mean right now, but you know I don't take to no town," he said.

Abby felt a tension spring up in the room, and she forgot about the books for a second. Mrs. Clack had left them a pot of gold, but it was already creating an argument between Elsa and her pa. And just after Walter's death too. Money might be a curse.

Elsa faced the fire, gazed into it. Quiet settled on the room. Pa lit and puffed his pipe. Sheriff Rucker shifted his feet.

Elsa licked her lips, stared down at the letter, then slowly turned back and faced everybody again. "I need to say something," she said.

Abby tensed as she looked at her. At thirty-eight years, Elsa had matured into a beautiful woman. With only a touch of gray in her hair, she looked much younger than most women her age. Except for when she was grieving like now, she had a glow in her skin, and birthing two boys hadn't broadened her figure all that much.

"When I moved here with Solomon I expected to stay for a couple of years," Elsa said, "then convince him to move down to Blue Springs. But as you know"—she smiled weakly and glanced over at Solomon—"my husband is a stubborn man. So, we are still here." Elsa paused, holding herself up with a hand on the wall.

"When Laban . . . well, when we lost the land, I thought I had another chance to convince Solomon. But again, no luck." She pushed her hair from her face. "Then Solomon returned for us. I wanted to fight him about coming back up the mountain . . . but I did not want to hurt my marriage. So I brought my boys and followed him here."

She took a breath. Abby saw moisture on her forehead. She looked feverish again, but that didn't stop her.

"My boy Junior, who had been so sickly in Blue Springs, turned off for the better. That pretty much ended my plans to go back to Blue Springs. A mama will do about anything for her child."

Elsa moved back to the rocker by Solomon and took his hand. "It has not been easy," she said. "But we have made it. And, well, when Preacher Bruster married us, I said I would honor my husband. So I stopped fighting him on the matter. You know that has not been easy on me—I am a fighter by nature."

Solomon chuckled lightly.

"I gave up my desire for fine things," she continued. "Going to Jesus Holiness all these years taught me that, taught me to care less about worldly goods and more about what matters." Letting go of Solomon's hand, she fingered the envelope and glanced around the cabin.

"Now this comes along, more money than any of us ever thought we would see. If you had talked to me fifteen, eighteen years ago, I would have shouted for joy at having this. But now . . . now if I can't use it to buy back my husband's land, which I know I cannot, and if he won't let me use it to buy my mama's old house, which he will not, then I got no more use for it than a man in a desert needs a boat." She paused for a second, and her eyes filled with tears. "My boy is buried up the hill on this land," she said. "I don't plan to leave him, I reckon."

Abby couldn't believe her ears. Though Elsa had changed a lot in recent years, she had always liked nice things. These dollars could go a long way toward making her life a lot easier.

"Here is what I want to do," Elsa said. "I will give fifty dollars to Jesus Holiness in the name of Preacher Bruster."

Everybody nodded in agreement.

"I will keep two hundred dollars to buy some things for the cabin, a couple of tools to make Solomon's load a little lighter." She smiled through her tears at him. "He is not getting any younger, you know."

"Hey, watch it now, woman!" said Solomon, responding to her teasing.

Elsa faced Abby. "Here is what I will do with the rest of the money," Elsa said. "I will give it to Abby so she can leave Blue Springs and go to school."

Nobody moved. Abby's face burned, and her mouth turned dry as ashes. The room started to spin. Then Elsa stood and walked to her, put her hand on her shoulder.

"You nursed me and my boys," said Elsa. "I am grateful for that."

Abby started to protest, but Elsa shook her head. "This money will just cause us trouble," she said. "But it will give you what you have always wanted."

Abby finally found her voice. "But I can't take it," she said. "Your mama gave it to you."

Elsa leaned over, whispered so only Abby could hear. "Mama told me once that you became like a daughter to her. The letter says it too. She would like this, I know it. And I don't need it anymore; I am content with what me and Solomon have here."

Abby was about to argue some more, but then Solomon stood and eased to Elsa's side and put his arm around her.

"You are a gifted young woman," said Elsa, standing again. "And this money is just temptation to me, a temptation to make me start coveting again, to make my heart unsettled on this mountain. I don't want that. It won't be good for me or your pa." She faced Solomon, then Abby again.

Abby considered what it meant if she took the money. A whole new life, she realized, a new start that might fulfill all her hopes. But it also meant she couldn't marry Thaddeus, at least not yet. It meant she would leave Blue Springs to go study at a college somewhere. Who knew if she would ever come back? She turned to Lindy. Her friend's eyes brimmed with tears, and Abby knew what she was thinking. Yet how could she turn down this chance, her only opportunity to live out her dreams? It seemed like a miracle to Abby, a miracle that God had put the money into Amelia Clack's hands, that Amelia had given it to Elsa, and that Elsa had changed so much that she could give it away to her. Had God planned things this way all along? Did that mean God did not want her to marry Thaddeus?

Her head throbbing with questions, Abby rubbed her forehead and knew what she had to do. Whether God had put this money in her lap or not, she did not know. But she did know that if she didn't take it and use it for her education, she would regret it the rest of her life.

Raising her eyes, she stood and hugged Elsa. Behind her, she heard Lindy weeping. In that moment, though, Abby didn't weep because her heart soared with the hopes that now sprang up in it.

SECTION III

1922–1929

CHAPTER
TWENTY-SIX

Her head tilted into a stiff September wind, Abby adjusted her umbrella to protect herself against the blowing rain, turned a corner, and headed down Boone's main street. She was dressed in an ankle-length gray skirt, tan blouse, and a waist jacket that matched the skirt. And she had her hair pinned up and under a wide-brimmed hat—the picture of a young woman of good breeding. Having gained some weight since she left Blue Springs, her figure filled out the jacket and skirt to a most attractive degree but with no hint of any excess. The men of Boone usually paused as she passed them on the street or in the hall at school, their eyes following her with silent approval.

Preoccupied with other matters—like her studies or her toil at the boardinghouse where she stayed—Abby paid little attention to the men. On this particular day, she not only had to do the shopping for Mrs. Duper, the owner of the boardinghouse, but also needed to study for a math test and prepare for the Bible class she taught at the Gospel Spirit Church every Sunday morning.

A gust of wind pulled at her umbrella so she held it with both hands.

Her feet moved quickly, rushing through the rain. She stepped over a mud puddle.

Life was busier now than she'd ever dreamed it could become, and the three years she had spent in Boone since leaving Blue Springs in August of 1919 had gone by in a blur. After spending a year preparing for the tests that would determine whether or not she was ready to enter the Appalachian Training School, she had passed and then entered classes the fall of 1920. Her first year as a regular student had gone hard. Many of the students were far superior to her, especially in the languages and math that the program required. But she studied longer than anyone else, and so by the beginning of 1921, she had caught up to most of the three hundred or so men and women who made up the student body.

The years in Boone had suited her. She had met plenty of new and interesting people. And the school had music and debate and theater and art, and her mind had spread out like an oak tree widening its branches above the ground. Though the town wasn't nearly as large as Asheville, it had a train running through it and modern inventions like electricity and telephones in most of the public buildings and more than a few automobiles running up and down the streets.

Now she'd started her next to last year, and the only bad part about leaving Blue Springs was that she saw Pa and everybody only at Christmastime each year. Which had made it difficult to keep up with all the changes in the family. Daniel had married a banker's daughter in June. Abby had taken her first trip to Asheville with Pa and everybody to take in the big event. Although he had not wanted to leave Blue Springs, Daniel took up residence in a house his wife's pa owned outside of Asheville because nobody in Blue Springs needed any brickwork done, and since he had chosen that for his livelihood, Asheville it was. He labored harder than any man around, Solomon said, and hardly ever spent any money, so he ought to become rich someday. Abby had smiled when Pa said that. Daniel had always toiled that way—like sweat was liquid gold and he wanted to make as much of it as possible.

Abby reached the corner and eased off the wood sidewalk to cross the street.

Luke was doing what he always did—picking and singing and traveling all over the state and into some others too. She saw him even less than Daniel because he didn't even make it home to Christmas sometimes.

A car drove toward Abby from the left. She took a step back. The car rushed her way; the driver hit the horn and honked at her. She stepped back another pace. The car honked again and seemed to speed up. She started to back up some more, but the car reached her before she made it. The car's tires hit the water puddle at the corner, and a thick spray of muddy foam splashed off the wheels. The spray covered her skirt before she could move, a gush of wet that flooded her shoes and soaked her calves and ankles. The car turned right and disappeared around the corner.

A gust of wind grabbed her umbrella and again tore it away from her face. Rain washed over her eyes. Jerking the umbrella back into place, Abby stepped in the direction the car had sped away, her teeth clenched, a fist in the air toward the car. Rude people, she fumed, rude people in infernal machines. She hated this part of living in a town, even one as small as Boone, hated the noise and commotion caused by such vehicles. Maybe a place like Blue Springs didn't have electrical lights and inside privies and hard-surfaced roads yet, but a person could still hear herself think when she took a walk and she could do so without getting run over or splashed with dirty water.

Sighing, she turned away, lifted her skirt off her ankles and shook as much water as possible from it. Maybe she could borrow an old rag in the general store, she figured, and dry off some with it. She moved across the street and up the block. A couple of minutes later, she heard another car headed her way, this one from the direction the last one had disappeared. She decided to just ignore it. Head down, she quickly crossed a second street. The general store was only a block away.

She heard the car drawing closer. She faced straight ahead. The car pulled up beside her. Confused, she glanced over, recognized the car as the same one that had splashed her. She started to shake her fist at the driver but thought better of it and instead looked away and kept walking. The car rolled along at the curb. Then she heard a man's voice calling to her.

"Hey, ma'am," he said.

Abby turned and saw that the driver had rolled the window down halfway. She shook her head and looked down at the street again, her feet moving faster now.

"Just hold on there, ma'am," the man called through the rain. "I suppose I owe you an apology."

Abby stopped and faced the car, her face flushed. "You suppose?"

The car stopped as she did. A man in a pinstriped black suit, a round-collared white shirt, and a gold tie stared out the window. "Let me offer you a ride," said the man.

Abby shook her head. "It is not fitting for a woman to ride with a man she does not know," she said. "And I am only going another block." She pointed up the street.

"I can see you are a lady," he said. "And I can appreciate your decorum. But please know that I am sorry that I splashed you so thoroughly."

"I accept your apology," said Abby. "But now, if you will excuse me, it is raining out here and I am soaked. So I will go now."

The window closed and the car moved away. Abby lowered her head, pulled the umbrella closer, and headed to the store. Three minutes later she reached it and ducked under the awning while lowering her umbrella. At the door, her mouth dropped open. The man from the car stood there holding the door open for her. He bowed at the waist as she approached.

"Allow me to introduce myself," he said. "My name is Stephen Jones Waterbury. And since you would not let me give you a ride, I am here to do a service for you to make up for my previous rudeness."

Abby studied the man for a second. He looked close to twenty-five or so, maybe nearer thirty. His hair was light but was slicked back with some kind of oil and so seemed darker. He was close to six feet and fairly thick in the shoulders. His eyes were grayish and his face was round. All in all a handsome face—not that she cared about such things these days, but handsome nonetheless in a soft sort of way. But he looked too full of himself for her liking, like a prince or something talking to one of the servants of the manor.

"What do you mean 'a service'?" she asked, her eyes narrow with suspicion.

"Oh, some deed, you know, something that will help you in some way."

Abby shook her umbrella. "I don't need any help."

"You're not from Boone, are you?"

"I live here now," she said, unwilling to reveal anything. "And I got things to do." She closed the umbrella and pushed by him into the store. To her surprise, he followed her. She faced him again.

"Look," she said. "I don't know your intentions but I have shopping to do so I have no time for any nonsense."

He smiled as if indulging a child. "I have no intentions but to make amends for my behavior."

"A rich man like you does not pay this much attention to a strange woman without having some kind of intentions."

Stephen stepped back a pace. The smile left his face. For the first time he seemed a touch unsure. He cleared his throat. "You are right," he said, appearing to try another approach. "I do have intentions. When I splashed you on the street, I just kept on going. But then I caught a glimpse of your face as I drove by, saw that you are a woman of unusual beauty. So I turned around and drove right back." He took a breath.

"You want to know my intentions. Well, they are these." His confidence returned, and his tone took on a note of the high and mighty again. "I intend to find out your name and where you live. Then I intend to ask you to accompany me to dinner at the finest restaurant in this fair town. Then I intend to get to know you and let you come to know me. And after that? Well, only the Fates can know anything beyond that." He stopped and stared boldly into her face.

Abby swallowed hard. No man had ever talked so honestly to her, and it made her feel strange—flattered in a way but scared too, scared that such a man as this had far too much sense of himself for somebody like her. A worldly man like this could swallow up a simple mountain girl, like a frog pulling in his supper.

"I have no desire to have dinner with you, Stephen Jones Waterbury," she said.

He smiled but didn't back away. "I will not take *no* for an answer," he said. "Unless you are married, of course."

"No, I'm not married," said Abby, perhaps a bit too quickly.

"Excellent," said Stephen. "So what is your name?"

Abby considered for a moment. What harm could come from telling the man her name? He had come back to apologize after all. So he did have some manners. "My name is Abigail Porter," she said. "I am from Blue Springs and I attend the Appalachian Training School, want to become a teacher."

"A noble desire," he said. "I am a lawyer myself. Like my father in Raleigh."

"You keep it in the family."

Stephen chuckled. "That is the idea. So what about that dinner?"

Abby thought of Thaddeus. But she hadn't seen him in over a year.

He never wrote either, even though she had sent him a couple of letters. And Lindy didn't talk much to her these days. She recalled the few dates she had accepted during her time in Boone. The men seemed so immature, so unfocused. None of them had attracted her enough for more than a few engagements. Why not go out with somebody like Stephen Jones Waterbury? Just like that, she made her decision.

"I will go to dinner with you," she said. "I live . . ." She gave him her address, and they agreed that he would pick her up the following Saturday at six o'clock. Then he bowed at the waist and left. She watched him walk away in his fancy suit and climb into his fancy car, and she wondered what in the world she had done accepting a dinner engagement with such a man.

Just over seven months later Abby took Stephen Jones Waterbury home to meet her family. Though she felt a little strange about asking him, she didn't want to keep on courting a man who had not seen the place of her origins. Stephen hesitated when she first suggested the visit, but she refused to accept his hesitation.

"We have been seeing each other long enough," she said. "One day to meet my folks is not too much to ask."

"This is important to you?" Stephen asked.

She said it was, and since he had no real reason to say no—except that he didn't take much to visiting a place where he couldn't drive his car to the front door—he finally gave up and agreed to the trip. So, on a Saturday just two weeks after her twenty-third birthday, he picked her up in his car and drove them from Boone to Blue Springs. The sky overhead started out blue but by the time they made it to Blue Springs it had turned cloudy. In Blue Springs, they stopped to pour some water in the car's radiator and to take a bite to eat. Abby had made chicken-salad sandwiches and hard-boiled eggs. Hoping it would not rain, she spread out the food on a blanket under a tree near the general store.

"I don't suppose this place has a diner," said Stephen as he eased down on the blanket's edge, his tone indicating a certain disdain for any town without a proper restaurant.

Abby smiled. Stephen sometimes seemed snotty, but that was just his way. Though Boone had a college for teachers, it wasn't exactly a huge city with a hundred fancy eating places. "No diner within miles," she answered. "Folks around here grow their own food. Why pay somebody to cook it for you?"

His mouth busy with his sandwich, Stephen didn't say anything. Abby stayed quiet too. In the months since they first met, she'd learned a lot about Stephen. An only child from an aristocratic family, he liked only the very best. He was one of three lawyers in Boone, and everybody seemed to know him. He spent hours and hours in his office, working mostly on land contracts and timber deals. Always ready to shake a hand or pat a back, folks said he had natural political instincts, might become the mayor of Boone someday.

Abby bit from her sandwich. She liked the way people looked at her when Stephen escorted her into a room. She felt like somebody important, somebody that others would see as valuable. She wiped her mouth. Yes, it bothered her some when Stephen had told her that she needed to buy new clothes, that hers were not appropriate for this or that affair they were to attend. Yes, it bothered her some when he snapped his fingers at somebody and snipped at them when they didn't move quickly enough to meet some need of his. And yes, it bothered her some that he seldom attended church, even though he claimed he and his family were staunch Methodists. But she forgave him these faults because he was a young man enjoying the fruits of his success—a success that made him too busy to attend church, caused him sometimes to act bigger than his britches. That would settle down as he matured, she figured, as he took on more dignity to go with his dollars and fame.

She watched him eat, his mouth working fast. At times she wondered why he continued to court her. Couldn't he have any woman in Boone? Or in Raleigh back where his folks lived? He spoke plain enough when she asked him that very question about two months after he started calling on her: "I have courted enough city women," he had said. "On the whole, they are quite uninspiring."

Abby started to ask him what that meant, but he kept talking. "You, on the other hand, are so . . ." And here he had hesitated, gently fingered her cheek, then said, "You are so basic, so honest, so . . . so incredibly beautiful . . . well, it leaves me speechless is what it does, quite speechless."

Both embarrassed and flattered by his outburst, Abby didn't question him on the issue anymore. To do so seemed too much like fishing for compliments. If he wanted to court her, she would let him. What harm could come from it? He had always remained a gentleman and treated her with respect. And she had to admit, she liked the benefits of courting a wealthy man: riding in a car, attending motion pictures, eating meals cooked by somebody other than herself. What was wrong with that?

Finishing their meal, she and Stephen quickly packed, climbed back into the car, and headed out of town. Less than ten minutes later they reached the spot where the road stopped at the base of Blue Springs Mountain.

"We walk from here," said Abby. "A mile or so."

"I'm sure it will be quite the treat," said Stephen, his tone too complicated for Abby to figure out.

"You ought to be grateful," she said. "Up till five years ago when they cut in this road, you had to walk more like three miles to reach our place."

"For you, I will go as far as I need to go," he said. "Journey back to the land of the primitives."

Abby couldn't tell if he was teasing her or being serious. She decided to let it go. Taking a deep breath, she took his hand and led him up the mountain. It felt so strange coming home this way, with a man in tow, a man whose intentions she wasn't entirely sure of. Up to now Abby had reached no conclusions with regard to Stephen. Would he someday make this same trip to ask Pa for her hand in marriage? Was that why he continued to date her, why he had finally accepted her invitation to come to Blue Springs? But what would she do if he asked? Did she love him? She did not know.

A quarter mile up the trail, the wind picked up and it started to rain. Stephen looked at the sky and cursed, and she chastised him about it. He hung his head like a boy, just as he always did when she spoke to him about his occasional use of foul language. Once or twice she had smelled liquor on his breath too, and that bothered her even more than the swearing. He had told her that such habits were hard to break but he was trying, and how could she refuse such a sincere apology? Practically every man in Blue Springs except her pa took of the spirits from time to time. And this was in spite of it being Prohibition. Fact was, moonshining had mushroomed into a bigger business than ever since Prohibition started. So if Stephen took a sip of liquor every now and again, that just made him like most every other man. No reason to get too riled up over such a thing.

The spring rain fell in a slow drizzle—not enough to soak Abby and

Stephen but plenty enough to make a walk up a steep incline a less than enjoyable stroll. By the time they stepped onto the rutted path that marked the beginning of her uncle Pierce's property, they were both spattered with mud where they had slipped a couple of times.

"Not far now," said Abby.

Stephen wiped his hands on his corduroy pants. "Middle of nowhere," he muttered. "Hard to believe civilized people still live in such a place."

Abby's face flushed and she started to defend her home, to tell Stephen about the beauty of a mountain slope in October, about the soothing cascade of a stream washing over rocks, about the touch of a corn silk on your face as you walk by it. She started to testify to the strength of highlander people who bowed their necks and wore out their backs and callused up their hands as they made this hard land yield to their living on it. But then she noted the irony that she, a woman who had wanted to leave Blue Springs for as long as she could remember, now thought she should defend the place. Confused, she said nothing. Stephen just didn't know any better, she decided. After he met some people from Blue Springs, he would understand.

Hurrying through the rain, they reached her pa's cabin a few minutes later. Two dogs ran at them when they entered the clearing, their ears pinned back and their teeth bared as they barked. Abby didn't recognize the dogs. Before she could stop him, Stephen grabbed a rock in each hand and faced the dogs, his face looking pale. The dogs halted about fifteen feet away, growling and slobbering.

"Filthy beasts!" Stephen shouted. "Another step and I—"

Abby heard a door open, saw her pa walk out. He held a shotgun.

"Pa!" she shouted, waving her arms.

"That you, Abigail?"

"It's not the Queen of England," she hollered back. "Call off these dogs." The growling animals had not moved.

Solomon laughed but didn't move. Abby wanted to run and throw her arms around him, but had long since learned that such public displays didn't happen in the Porter household. Her heart dropped as it always did when she remembered how it had forever been between her and her pa.

"Them is good dogs," Solomon said. "Couple of pups I traded for down in Blue Springs."

For the first time in her life, Abby noticed her pa's poor grammar. It sounded strange to her, backward and . . . well, just plain ignorant. A touch of shame ran through her as she wondered what Stephen thought about her pa. Did he wish he had not come here? That he had not courted a woman who came from such an uneducated family? Another idea entered her head. A good daughter wouldn't feel embarrassed by her own kin, no matter how poor and ignorant they were. A touch of guilt mixed in with her shame.

"You plan on calling these dogs off any time soon?" she asked her pa, pushing away her thoughts. "We're getting mighty wet."

"Who you got with you?" asked Solomon, acting like her answer might determine what he did about the dogs.

"Stephen Jones Waterbury," she said. "I wrote you about him a couple of times. Said I was bringing him home."

"Didn't get no letter saying any such thing," Solomon said, his tone indicating he was leaning toward not believing her. "And I been to the post office most every week."

Abby laughed out loud. "Well, he is not a robber either way," she said. "Nor a revenuer either. So call off these dogs, lower that shotgun, and act like you are glad to see your only daughter."

As if suddenly making a decision, Solomon nodded, lowered the gun, and whistled. The dogs ran back to him, stopped at his feet, then lay down on the porch. Abby took the rocks from Stephen and threw them down, and then the two of them moved to the porch and she introduced Stephen to Solomon.

"He is the gentleman I have been seeing," said Abby.

Stephen and Solomon shook hands, and everyone except the dogs stepped into the cabin. After Abby and Stephen dried off, they all sat down at the table. Elsa offered some corn bread and honey and hot coffee. Solomon lit his pipe and puffed on it but didn't say much. Junior kept his eyes fastened on Stephen as though watching a freak show at the circus. Elsa patted Abby on the back several times, obviously glad to see her but unsure how to express it.

"How's Daniel?" asked Abby. "He still in Asheville?"

"Yep, layin' brick," Solomon replied. "I think his wife is expecting."

Abby glanced at Elsa. "He writes me some," she said. "But he hasn't told me about any baby."

"Too busy working, I guess," said Solomon. "That boy is doing well, I can tell you that."

"What about Luke?"

"He comes in and out," Junior said. "Always pickin' and singin'. Nothing has changed with him, I can tell you that. He is all over the western part of the state, has a regular band now."

Abby nodded at Junior. He had become a man now and almost a dead cross between Solomon and Elsa. Eighteen years old, he wouldn't be staying with Solomon and Elsa much longer. When a highlander boy reached his age, he almost always moved out, took a wife, and built his own cabin. Of course more and more highlander boys left the mountains now to find work, like Daniel had done. She thought of Walter, wondered what he would have become if he had lived.

"Luke played on the radio," said Solomon. "We heard him down in Blue Springs. They got a radio in the general store."

Abby glanced around the cabin. Electricity had not reached this holler yet. Might not for years. And Pa had no means to get any kind of radio even if it had, not even with what Elsa had kept from her mama's money.

"Glad Luke is doing good," Abby said. "He got a girl?"

"More girls than he can ask for," said Junior with a smirk. "But not a one has talked him into walking down the aisle."

"He moves around too much to marry," said Elsa. "Playing all over the place, town to town."

Abby munched her corn bread. The room fell quiet, and everybody stared at their coffee. Abby cleared her throat. She would ask more about her brothers later, but the time had now come to say something about Stephen. She laid a hand on his arm. "Stephen and I have been courting," she announced. "He is a lawyer down in Boone."

Solomon eyed him over the end of his pipe. "A lawyer, huh?"

"Like my father," said Stephen. "Up in Raleigh."

Solomon grunted and bit his pipe. Abby wondered why he was acting so distrustful. Suddenly the whole idea of bringing Stephen up here seemed foolish, the notion of an idealistic young girl. What made her think Stephen would like this place? She wasn't sure she even liked it.

"Why did you come all the way up here?" asked Solomon.

"Solomon! Mind your manners!" The words came from Elsa standing at the stove.

"I am just asking," said Solomon. "Any other pa would do the same."

He faced Stephen again. "You stayin' honorable with my daughter?"

Abby had never seen this side of her pa. He seemed almost belligerent, like a man protecting his property or something. She couldn't decide if she liked him this way or not.

Stephen looked at her, then back to Solomon. "I can assure you that I am a decent man," he said. "Your daughter is a lady and I have treated her as such."

Solomon puffed his pipe and leaned back just a touch. But he had not put down his guard.

Abby decided to change the subject. "Is Daniel's hip doing okay?" she asked.

"Seems so," said Elsa, apparently eager to assist her in guiding the conversation. "Not keeping him from working, I can tell you that."

"Abby tells me he got wounded in the war," said Stephen. "Too bad. The whole thing was a waste far as I could see."

Abby touched Stephen's arm again, her grip telling him to go easy here.

"You don't think the war was a noble thing?" Solomon asked, his tone neutral. Abby prayed that Stephen would see the danger of the question.

Stephen shrugged. "The war didn't concern us," he said. "Let the Europeans fight if they want, just don't involve us."

"I take it you did not join up with the Army?"

"No sir, I did not. I stayed right here. My father, a man of much influence, kept me right here in the good old U.S.A."

"Lot of good men died in that war," said Solomon, his lips working harder on his pipe.

"A sad thing," said Stephen. "And a damn waste. Every one of them that died, a useless sacrifice that didn't solve a thing. A lot of smart men say we will have to fight the whole thing again someday, maybe sooner than later."

Abby gulped at the swearword. Solomon Porter didn't take to such in his house. Not to mention the fact that he'd suggested that Laban's death had been a waste.

Solomon placed his elbows on the table, cupped his pipe in both hands, and cleared his throat. "You are welcome in my house," he said, glaring at Stephen. "And I am pleased to hear that you are a gentleman with my daughter. But"—he leaned toward Stephen and spoke in a rough voice—"I will not allow no profane talk at my table. And I would have you know that my eldest boy died in that war. And . . ." Abby heard a catch in his voice. "And his sacrifice was *not* useless, no matter if we do have to go back. His death was not useless, nobody can . . . nobody can convince me of that."

Then, as if too weary to continue, Solomon rose from the table and left the room. Horrified by the scene, Abby squeezed Stephen's arm and wished she had never asked him to come to Blue Springs. The whole thing had turned out to be a disaster. A man from outside could never understand her people. Trouble was, she no longer knew if she did either. She felt like a woman cut off on all sides, certainly not a woman of the city but no longer a woman of the isolated hollers either. At that moment, she didn't know where she belonged, and the sense of loneliness she had felt since she was a little girl settled like an anvil on her heart once more.

CHAPTER
TWENTY-SEVEN

When Abby returned to Boone after the awful visit with her pa, she threw herself into her studies and work. Up before daylight, she helped Mrs. Duper prepare breakfast for the boardinghouse and clean up after everyone had finished. Then she attended classes at the training school. As usual, she liked English best, the books it put in her hands to read, the language it taught her to use, the stories the words allowed her to make up in her head. In her stories, nobody's ma ever died when they were born, and everybody always felt like they belonged somewhere special. For the most part, her rushed days kept her mind so occupied that she had little time to worry about her future.

Stephen didn't call on her for almost two weeks after their visit to Blue Springs, and Abby thought maybe the experience with Solomon had soured him on seeing her anymore. No wonder. He and Pa had started out as wrong as any two people could. Muddy weather, mean dogs, and differences in politics could cause all kinds of splits among folks. Truth was, a city boy like Stephen had no business courting a woman from such a coarse background. Butchered grammar and outdoor privies did not match well with a man of his refined taste.

The idea that she wouldn't court Stephen anymore caused her chest to tighten and an ache to flood through her throat, but it didn't knock her into as big a tizzy as she might have thought. Did that mean she didn't love him? That she liked him more for the social status he brought than anything else? She didn't know. She thought of Thaddeus from time to time but Lindy still barely spoke to her when she visited Blue Springs and so she had no idea where he was or how he was doing. Apparently, though, he had decided to move on with his life without her. That grieved her some, but she had no way to do anything about it.

In the first week of May, Stephen showed back up on the front porch of the boardinghouse and said he wanted to take her to dinner. Glad to see him and not thinking of any reason to say no, Abby took his hand and they went to dine, and the pattern of the past few months returned with no real discussion of what it meant. Abby wanted to talk about the future but believed the man ought to initiate such conversation, and since Stephen didn't seem eager to do so, she held her piece. It wasn't like she had lots of options in terms of men in Boone. Since everybody at school and in town knew she was courting the most eligible bachelor around, nobody else dared approach her.

Summer rolled in hot and dry. The days scorched down and dried up the flowers almost as soon as they bloomed, and everybody moved a little slower in the vain effort to keep from sweating so much. With classes at the school taking a break for a few weeks, Abby spent a good part of every afternoon sitting on a swing on the boardinghouse porch, a book in one hand and a cardboard fan in the other. On the first day of August she put herself in just such a spot, a glass of lemonade replacing the book this time. A bird chirped a couple of times in one of the maple trees that fronted the house. A fly buzzed by her head and then disappeared into the yard. Abby sipped her lemonade. She heard a horse clomping, then saw a buggy turn the corner about a block away. Abby pushed her hair away from her eyes and wondered how much longer buggies would be around. From what she saw, it seemed automobiles would replace them someday soon and scare the horses right off the streets. She didn't like the idea but knew that her like or dislike made no difference in the matter.

The buggy moved her way, stopped a couple of minutes later directly in front of the boardinghouse. To her surprise, she saw Elsa holding the reins.

Abby stood and placed her lemonade glass on the porch railing. Elsa climbed out of the buggy. Fearing something bad, Abby ran down the steps toward her.

"Don't worry," Elsa said quickly, apparently reading her thoughts. "Nobody's hurt nor dying."

"Thank goodness," said Abby, hugging her tightly. "You gave me a start showing up here without some warning."

Elsa smiled. Abby led her to the porch, pointed her to a rocker by the swing. "I'll get you some lemonade," she said.

"Much obliged."

When she returned with the lemonade, she handed it to Elsa, took hers off the railing, and perched herself in the swing. Elsa sipped the lemonade. Abby smoothed her skirt, told herself to relax. Elsa had said nobody was hurt or dying, so it wasn't bad news. But why had she come? Nobody from Blue Springs had ever visited her in Boone. Elsa held her lemonade glass with both hands as if to cool herself.

"You look well," she said to Abby.

Abby nodded. "Passable. I like my schooling here. Will be a teacher someday soon I reckon."

"We're all so proud of you."

Abby stared into her glass. Elsa had made her education possible, and she could never repay her. But the two had never been that close. Not anybody's fault, just the circumstances of their lives. Abby had Aunt Francis as a ma when Elsa first joined the family. By the time her aunt died, Elsa had children of her own to look after, so not much time for Abby. Then Abby stayed on in Blue Springs with Amelia when Elsa moved back in with her pa. One thing led to another after that and so the years passed. Now here she sat with a woman she'd known most of her life but who felt almost as much a stranger as somebody she had just met on the street. Odd how that was—how living in the same house with somebody didn't always mean that you knew them.

"Pa doing okay?" she asked.

Elsa smiled and said, "Solomon is steady as the sun, you know that. Never changes."

Abby sipped her lemonade. Though always a challenge, Elsa had made a good wife for Pa, had given him children, companionship, and another set of hands to help with the toiling. All of it wrapped up in a package as pretty as anything on the mountain.

"I guess you are wondering why I'm here," said Elsa, her tone indicating the time had come to end the small talk.

Abby nodded. "I am curious," she said. "First time anybody from home has come all this way to see me."

"I feel sad about that," Elsa said, her eyes down. "But you know how it is, busy on the farm, still some awful roads between here and home. Seems that time just rushes on by and before you know it two years have passed and you haven't done some things you ought."

"I'm not blaming," said Abby. "You have done far more than anybody expected you to do. I'm just saying."

Elsa started rocking. "Your pa is worried," she said. "Worried that you might do something not best for you."

Abby pushed off the floor, setting the swing in motion. Her heart rate notched up. "He's worried about Stephen?"

"You still seeing him? Your letters don't indicate."

Abby pursed her lips. "After my last trip home I figured nobody would want to know about him. But yes, he and I are courting."

Elsa rocked some more. "Your pa has some concerns," she said.

A sense of resentment pushed into Abby. What right did Pa have to stick his nose in this? She had made her own way for a long time. Not right for him to interfere now. "Why didn't Pa come to tell me about his concerns?" she asked.

Elsa looked out to the yard. A squirrel scampered up a maple tree, chattering as it climbed. "You know how your pa is," she said. "He don't take well to a lot of talk."

"He had plenty enough to say when I brought Stephen home," said Abby.

"That he did," Elsa agreed, staring at Abby again. "And I will not try to defend his manners. But you got to remember he lost a boy in France not long ago."

"Laban was my brother," said Abby. "I don't think it is something I will forget."

Elsa bit her lip.

Abby felt ashamed that she had spoken so harshly. Her swinging became more vigorous. She squeezed her lemonade glass and told herself to calm down. A pa has a right to speak his mind about his daughter's suitors. No matter what the situation between them. That didn't mean she had to listen, but he did have his right to a say. "So you came to tell me that Pa thinks I ought to stop seeing Stephen," she said.

"Yes," said Elsa. "He believes Stephen is wrong for you. You are a highlander, nothing you can do about it. Easier to breed the ears off a rabbit than to take the Blue Ridge out of a mountain-born baby."

"Pa say that?"

"He can be right eloquent at times, that's for sure."

Abby stared out into the yard. Was Pa right? Could she ever truly escape her origins? Did her beginnings hang on her like the mist that hung over the mountains in the morning? Was she destined always to be connected to the backwardness of her birthplace? Tied forever to the ignorance and poverty, the abuse of liquor, the harsh way that men usually treated their women?

She studied the squirrel as it sat on a branch. Blue Springs was more than backwardness, she had to give it that. It was also the breathtaking view of tree-covered ridges and the smell of wet leaves in autumn. It was a family toiling together in the fields and then eating the fruit of that toil at the table that night. It was a group of neighbors who would walk miles in rain or snow to bring a pot of soup when somebody came up sick. It was a church filled with people shouting out their faith to Jesus and a general store that sold peppermint sticks two for a penny. It was a pack of cur dogs that would take on a bear to protect their master. Abby loved the Blue Ridge Mountains. And she hated them too.

"Your pa wants the best for you," said Elsa.

Abby stayed quiet.

"He loves you," she added.

Tears pushed their way into Abby's eyes. Surprised, she quickly brushed them away. "I reckon I would like to hear him say that," she said.

Elsa leaned forward and set her lemonade on the porch rail. She took Abby's hand, patted it. "Your pa wastes few words," she said. "But you know he loves you."

Abby pulled her hand away, folded her arms around her waist. "I have told myself that all my life," she said. "But the older I get the less able I am to just accept it." She stood and leaned over the porch rail. The squirrel left the maple tree, chattered at her from the ground. Abby turned and faced Elsa. Though it was warm, she shivered as she considered what she wanted to say, whether she should go ahead and finally speak out what she had held inside so long. But Elsa had given her the money to leave Blue Springs. And Elsa had to live with the same shadow that cast its arms over her. Now seemed the right time to let her feelings free in the open air.

"I have felt this ever since I can remember," she started, her voice almost a whisper. "A feeling that Pa did not like me for some reason, that he resented the fact that I was there, that I reminded him of my ma so much that he wished I would just disappear."

She looked down at her feet for a second, then continued. "I know it might not make much sense, but since I have had a lot of time to think about things in the last couple of years . . . it just seems to me that Pa is mad at me for some reason—"

"But that's not true," Elsa interrupted. "Your pa—"

Abby threw up a hand to stop her. "Let me finish," she said. "I'm not saying he's mad on purpose. In fact, I don't even believe he knows he's mad. But I just think he is, that's all I can say. It's a feeling I get, an intuition. Yes, he loves me, but he's scared of me too, and whatever it is about me that scares him keeps him so distant I don't even feel like I know him. He is a rock to me, strong and stable, yes, but unbreakable too, so hard you can never hold it, never feel close to it."

She moved back to the swing and sat down. "He has never told me he loves me," she said. "And I can't remember the last time he hugged me. So . . . you have to excuse me when I say I resent the fact that he sends you down here to say something he ought to have said for himself a long time ago. If he loves me, let him come tell me. If he wants me to stop seeing Stephen, let him come say it in person. Otherwise, I will do what I think regardless of what Pa says or doesn't say." Abby pushed her feet and the swing moved.

Elsa drank from her lemonade, licked her lips, started to speak but then stopped. Abby waited. Elsa sighed as she stared down into her glass. She opened her mouth again but then paused once more.

"You say what you want," said Abby. "I have been honest. So can you."

Elsa shook her head. "It's too hurtful," she said.

"No more so than a pa that won't say he loves you."

Elsa brushed a tear away. "I believe your pa wishes you had died. I believe he thinks that if you had died, your ma might have lived."

Abby stopped swinging and looked back at the squirrel. Finally, somebody had said what she had long thought. She closed her eyes, covered her mouth with her hands.

"I didn't . . . didn't want to say it," sobbed Elsa. "Because . . . because I know what it says . . . about me too. He wishes your ma . . . your ma had lived. He would never . . . never have married me."

For several minutes the two women sat, both caught up in their own emotions, neither of them brave enough to break the silence. Abby's shoulders shook, but as always she held back her tears. Why let something she had always known bother her now? What difference did it make that Elsa had finally voiced what Abby's heart had always instinctively felt? It didn't change a thing. Somehow, though, Abby knew she was trying to fool herself. The words spoken had changed things, had changed everything. Words had a way of doing that, she knew from her study of them. Words had the power to become living beings, arrows fired into the sky that never came back, that always found a target, penetrating to the core of what they hit.

"He loved my ma," Abby forced herself to say. "But he loves you too. A man can love two women."

Elsa nodded. "I know. I just fear that what he feels for me will never match what he felt for her."

Abby wiped at her eyes. "I don't expect it should," she said. "Match it, I mean. It is different for sure, but that does not mean it's not just as deep."

Elsa took a drink of lemonade. "Thank you for saying that, Abby," she said, her emotions in check again. "I expect your words are true, just hard to remember sometimes."

Abby started the swing moving once more. "Did you ever know my ma?" she asked.

Elsa nodded. "I met her a couple of times. But I was pretty young. She was a beautiful woman, a good Christian too, everybody said so. Strange that both your pa and mine loved her so."

"She must have been a real jewel," said Abby. "I envy anybody who knew her. Even now, as old as I am, I still wish I could see her just once, have one talk with her, a long one mind you, but one chance to hear her voice, listen to her advice. Just one chance, that's all I want."

"If you got that one, you would surely become greedy for another," Elsa said.

Abby smiled. "I expect you are right. But right now I would settle for just the one."

Elsa stared into the yard again.

Abby felt close to her for the first time. In a strange way, her pa's love for her ma had given her and Elsa something in common.

"You still got that letter she left you?" asked Elsa.

Abby shrugged, not sure what she meant. "What letter?"

Elsa sipped her lemonade. "You know, she wrote you a letter. The night she died."

Abby stopped moving. "I . . . I never saw any letter," she said. "Never even heard of such a thing."

Elsa furrowed her brow. "Your ma wrote you a letter. I had it at one time. But then I left it with all your aunt's things at my mama's place when I moved back in with Solomon. Just figured you got it somewhere along the line. You saying you never saw it?"

Abby stood and paced the porch. "That is exactly what I am saying. I never saw any letter." She stopped and faced Elsa. "You are telling me that my ma wrote me a letter the very night she died? You sure of that?"

"I saw the letter with my own eyes," said Elsa. "Solomon told me that Rose wrote it as she lay dying, wanted you to have it when you got older."

Abby put a cheek in the palm of her hand. She wanted to ask Elsa if she had ever read the letter, but that notion about scared her to death. If Elsa had read the letter, Abby would want to ask her what it said. Yet, if she had read it, that would have been years ago. No way would she be able to remember the words exactly like her ma had said them. And to hear the words spoke out in a general way after so much time had passed would take away the power of hearing them from her ma.

"You say you left the letter at your mama's house," Abby said, making sure she had heard right. "You reckon it's still there?"

"Don't know," said Elsa. "Pa and the boys cleared out a bunch of stuff after my ma died. Threw out some things, stored some other things away."

"Your pa still own the house?"

"Yeah, he stays there some when his leg bothers him. But he has let it run down pretty bad."

"You think he would let me in to see if the letter is still there?"

"Hard to say. I haven't seen him in a while. You want me to ask him?"

Abby rubbed her forehead. Knowing what she did of Hal Clack, she figured he wouldn't go out of his way to do anything polite for her, not even if his daughter requested it. Even worse, if the letter was there and Hal Clack found out she wanted it, he might just take it and tear it up just to spite her. No reason to think he had changed his mean ways over the years. She remembered the carving her pa had made for her, recalled that she'd left it at the house when she moved out. Was the carving there too? Or had it and the letter been destroyed?

"You reckon you can get into the house without him knowing?"

"Maybe," Elsa said. "If I can catch it when he is not there. But I got no key. And Sheriff Rucker keeps a close eye on the place."

"How about you ask your pa if you can look for something in the house?"

"Sure, but he will want to know what."

"Then you better not ask him," said Abby. "I will have to think of another way."

"I expect you are right," said Elsa. "My pa is not a nice man."

Abby smiled ruefully. "Yours is not nice and mine is not talkative. We each got our own kinds of problems, don't we?"

Elsa nodded, and the two women sat on the porch and sipped lemonade as the sun disappeared. Elsa spent the night at the boardinghouse. The next morning, when she was getting ready to leave for home, Abby thanked her again for coming and asked her to think about how they might get into the old house and search for the letter. Elsa agreed she would.

After Elsa left, Abby got busy with her chores but her mind never left the fact that her ma had written to her in her dying moments. All these years she had wanted one talk with her ma, and the letter offered her a chance to have it. If she didn't do anything else in the next year, she would find out if that letter still existed. Then, if it did, Abby would take possession of it and read it. And that, she had no doubt, would help the loneliness of her life finally to go away.

CHAPTER
TWENTY-EIGHT

On September 10, Daniel kissed Deidre on the cheek, told her that if everything went well he would see her again in a couple of days, and stepped off the porch. Whistling, he brushed his hair out of his eyes and patted his coat pocket before climbing into the car—a four-year-old Model T, Tin Lizzie Ford that Mr. Shaller had loaned him. Five minutes later he turned right and headed north toward Blue Springs. The sun warmed the car, and Daniel leaned back and patted his coat pocket again. Inside the pocket a paper sack held a wad of money totaling over seven hundred dollars—all the money Daniel had managed to save since the day he took his first job laying brick about six years ago.

While driving to Blue Springs, Daniel did some thinking. He was thirty-one years old and still had a limp from the war. Heavier now by about twelve pounds than when he had gone off to France, yet still not a portly man. Married to a finer girl than he had ever hoped to snag and the pa of two strong kids—Marla Suzanne, three years old, and Laban Edsel, barely one.

Since marrying and settling down in Asheville, he had moved up from laying brick to become foreman of a building crew, and at the present

time things in construction were busting out all over. The city seemed
bound and determined to fill up every space of ground available in its
part of the mountains, and Daniel toiled as hard as anyone else to make
that happen. Every now and again he missed the quiet of Blue Springs,
the simple pace of his boyhood days. But who had time for such quiet
when all about him he saw men working and a town growing and his
opportunities to better himself spreading out?

"You will make a mark in this town," Mr. Shaller had told him and
more than once. "You got the smarts for it, and no man ever labored
harder than you."

Daniel liked the praise and the way Mr. Shaller smiled when he said
it, his pride in his son-in-law visible for everybody to see. But, truth be
told, he hadn't worked as hard as he had in order to make a mark in
Asheville. He patted the money in his pocket again. He had other ideas
for these dollars, ideas he had not even told to Deidre.

It took him just over half a day to make the trip to Blue Springs. Driving in on the only road—a gravel, single-lane path that cut through the
mountain like a long white snake—he stopped at the general store, said
hey to the three men playing checkers by the wood stove, and purchased
a can of beans and an apple.

"How long you in town?" asked Tatum Butler, the new owner of the
store.

"A day or so, not much more," Daniel replied, laying out the money
for the food.

"You looking prosperous," Butler said. He scooped up the money and
put it in a cigar box.

Daniel dropped his eyes. "Doing all right for an ignorant mountain
boy."

"Your pa says you married above yourself." Butler shoved the box
under the counter.

Daniel chuckled. "He's got no room to talk. He did it twice."

"That be true," said Butler. "Solomon Porter is one lucky man when
it comes to womenfolk."

Daniel agreed and then asked, "You see Elsa's pa in these parts much
these days?"

Butler rubbed his stomach, an ample mound that hung way past his
belt. "Time and again," he said. "Comes in here with his boys. You know
the war got one of them, don't you? The flu another."

Butler leaned forward and whispered so only Daniel could hear, "You ask me, we could do with a couple more of them gone. Like maybe Topper and Ben, they the meanest of the bunch."

Daniel cleared his throat. "Clack ever at his place here in town?"

Butler nodded. "More so than a few years ago," he said. "He's slowed a mite since that bear trap got him. Stays in the house a lot when the weather turns cold."

Daniel gathered up his apple and beans. "You reckon he's there now?"

Butler eyed him close. "Don't know. He came in a couple of days ago, though. Bought up a bunch of provisions. Maybe he is still there." He leaned closer again, his belly resting on the counter. "You got business with Clack?"

Daniel shrugged. "Thanks for the goods," he said. "Maybe I see you again before I go back to Asheville."

Again Butler rubbed his stomach and then nodded his good-bye. Daniel walked out onto the porch. The sun warmed his face, and a slight breeze blew on his hair. A one-eared dog walked over and lay down at his feet. Other than the dog, the porch was empty.

Daniel stepped to the porch rail, sat down on it. A flood of memories ran into his head as he opened his beans and fingered them out. He thought of Laban. The beans went down hard. He missed his brothers, both Laban and Luke. He hadn't seen Luke since last Christmas and only for a short spell.

He bit into his apple. *Is a shame that life takes people away*, he thought. One brother here, another there, a third dead in a field in France. With a sister in Boone and Pa and his family still here in Blue Springs. Like a bunch of leaves, he decided, folks grow up on the same tree all green and fresh, but when they take on some age and crinkle up a bit, the winds of time blow them all away in their own separate directions. Kind of sad when a man considers about it.

Finishing the apple, Daniel threw the core into the yard, then ate the beans and tossed the empty can in a trash bucket by the porch rail. He patted his coat pocket as he walked off the porch toward his car. He drove about a mile up the hill and parked it in front of the house where Abby had lived with Mrs. Clack. For several seconds he just sat there and studied the house. It looked bad. The paint was all peeling, a couple of windows had been busted out, shingles were missing off the roof, and the yard was overgrown with bushes and vines. A bunch of no-gooders, he recalled of the Clacks, sorry men who made their living selling whiskey, much of it to folks who barely had enough money to keep food on the table much less pay for liquor. True, the Prohibition had made whiskey running even more profitable, making it a trade where mountain men sold their product to big-time people in faraway cities and so made more dollars than from anything else a body could do in the mountains. But that didn't make liquor running right. Men like the Clacks charged high dollar to everybody and kept the law enforcement in their hip pockets and roughed up anybody who crossed them.

Daniel gritted his teeth and wished he didn't have to deal with such sorry men. But promises had been made. First to his pa a long time ago and then to Laban as he lay dying. Promises he planned to keep, no matter what. For a second he felt guilty that he had not told Deidre how he would spend the money he had saved. Husbands ought to stay straight with their wives, he figured. But somehow he hadn't seen fit to tell her this. It was *his* money after all, at least half of it put away before he had even married her. So why should she have a say in how he spent it? And what if she had wanted to do something else with it, something that wouldn't allow him to keep his promises?

His jaw set, Daniel climbed out and stalked to the house and knocked hard on the door. To his surprise, he heard a voice almost immediately.

"Who is there?" The words sounded slurred.

"Daniel Porter," he called. He heard movement, like somebody dragging something. A few seconds later, a haggard face appeared in the window by the door. Daniel took a step back. The door opened and a smell like sour milk poured out. Hal Clack stood in the doorway, his eyes black and sunk back in his head, his body thin as a starved dog, with his overalls hanging loose on his shoulders. For a man with so much money, Clack looked like a beggar.

"What you want?" Clack asked.

Daniel stuck his hands in his pockets. Suddenly his tongue felt as though it were sticking to his teeth. He wanted to say this in the proper way. Heaven only knew he had thought about it enough, talked the words in his head over and over again, making sure they sounded just right. But now that the time had come, he found the words hard to get out.

"I ain't got all day," said Clack, hitching up his overalls. "Speak up or get off my porch!"

Daniel cleared his throat. "I come to . . . to make you an offer," he said, his voice gaining speed now that he'd finally started talking. "An offer to buy back the land you took . . . uh, I mean, the land my brother lost to you back some years ago."

Clack's eyes widened and he straightened up some. Daniel thought he saw a touch of a grin play on his mouth, but then it quickly disappeared. "That fool brother of yours got hisself shot up in the war, didn't he?" asked Clack.

Daniel's fists clenched. For Clack to even mention Laban felt disrespectful. But Daniel fought off his urge to hit Clack. Such business as that would do him no good in his efforts to get back the land. "Laban died in France," he said. "Heard you lost a boy too."

Clack grunted and stepped back. "You wanting to come in?" he asked. Though not trusting the man, Daniel shrugged and followed him into the front room. Clothes lay all over the floor, and he could tell by the smell that the place hadn't had a cleaning in a long time. Cobwebs hung in the corners.

"Have a seat," said Clack, pointing to a chair by the fireplace. Daniel sat down, and Clack took an identical chair a few feet away.

"I guess my Elsa is still with your pa," Clack said.

"That she is," said Daniel. "She and Pa have done good together."

Clack grabbed a jug from off the floor, drank from it, offered it to Daniel. He refused.

"How's that oldest boy of theirs? He still a whiner?"

Daniel wondered if maybe Clack had a warm spot for his grandson. "Junior is all growed up. A handsome boy, a lot like his mama."

"The other boy die?"

"Flu took him."

"Flu took a lot of young'uns," said Clack, sucking from his whiskey jug again.

"Bad business," Daniel said, glad for some point of agreement with Clack. Maybe this would go better than he had figured. Maybe age had taken some of the bark off Clack, made him a touch softer.

"You say you come with an offer for the land," Clack said. "What kind of offer?"

Daniel studied his feet for a second. Laban had wagered the land against two hundred and forty dollars. But a long time had passed since then. Timber people had come into their part of the world, had started buying up some of the acreage, pushing up the prices. But he had over seven hundred dollars on him. Surely that would make a good offer, a three times profit for Clack from what Bluey would have given up if he'd lost the wager.

"I got four hundred fifty dollars," said Daniel. "That is a fair price."

"That is a right smart of money," said Clack with a crooked grin. " 'Course I hear you married up with a woman of means."

"I took no money off my wife," Daniel said, his face reddening at Clack's suggestion. "I saved this money myself."

"Don't get your bowels in no uproar. Don't matter to me how you come by your money. "

"I got it right here." Daniel patted his coat pocket. "Just hand me over the deed and I will give it all to you right now."

Clack shook his head. "Ain't enough," he said. "And I'm betting that you got more than four hundred fifty dollars in that pocket. A smart man like you knows to keep some back, make a higher offer if the first one ain't taken."

Daniel eyed Clack harder. The man wasn't a fool. A drunk and a snake, yes. But a sneaky snake, the kind a man really had to watch. "I can go up some," he said. "Make it five twenty-five, that's all I can do."

Clack shook his head, swigged off his jug, and said, "Not enough."

Daniel clenched a fist. He wanted to hit Clack, wanted to go over and smack him right in the mouth. He wanted to make Clack sorry he'd ever taken the land from Solomon Porter, that he'd made Laban feel so bad about himself that he went to war thinking he had to protect his brother to make up for his own mistakes. Out of guilt, Laban had gone out looking for his brother in that field in France, gone out and never came back. So now he still lay in that field under a grove of trees in a land that spoke a different language than he did. Now he would stay in that field forever and never come home.

Clack wiped his mouth with the back of his hand. Daniel unclenched his fist, knowing he couldn't punch Clack, at least not until he held the deed to his pa's land in his hand.

"Seven hundred and fourteen dollars is my best offer," Daniel said. "All the money I got in the world." He pulled out the paper sack, dumped the money into his hand, then held it up for Clack to see.

Clack put his jug on the floor and took the money from Daniel. Licking his lips, he fingered the bills. His eyes, red from whiskey, gleamed as he counted it. "Seven hundred and fourteen exactly," said Clack. "You done well for a Porter man, sorry as all of you are."

Once again Daniel had to push back his anger. "It's yours," he said. "All of it. Just hand me the deed to the land and I can take my leave. Then we can be done with each other. That will please us both, I expect." He said it lightly, trying to make a joke of their mutual dislike for each other.

Clack stood and wadded up the money in his hand. Daniel held his breath. Within seconds, he would have the deed, would pay off the promise he'd made to his pa and to Laban. Then Laban could rest in peace.

But then, to his shock, Clack stepped over to him and threw the money on the floor. "Ain't enough," he said. "You ain't got enough to buy back that land from me."

Daniel jumped from the chair, stood toe to toe with Clack. "You're a thief!" he shouted. "A no-good slacker of a man not fittin' to breathe the same air as my pa! That money is a high offer for that land and you know it!"

Clack chuckled, and Daniel could smell his foul breath. Clack reached out and put a hand on Daniel's shoulder, patted him as if consoling a small child. Confused, Daniel pulled Clack's hand away and stepped back. Clack's chuckle turned into a laugh, a full-throated crazed cackle.

"You idiot!" bellowed Clack. "I ain't got your land no more. Why would I keep it? I sold it right about two years ago." He slapped his knee and grabbed for his jug again.

Daniel seized his arm. "What you mean you sold it?" he shouted.

"Clean out your ears, boy. I sold it, plain as I can say it." He pulled his arm away and tipped his jug to his lips.

"Who owns it?" shouted Daniel, finding it hard to believe what Clack was saying.

"A timber company. From Asheville, your neck of the woods. A man paid me almost eleven hundred for it."

The veins in his neck bulging, Daniel grabbed Clack by the front of his overalls and jerked the man close to him. They stood face to face, and Daniel had never hated anyone more than he hated Hal Clack at that moment, not even the German soldier who had shot Laban.

"I ought to break your sorry neck," Daniel growled. "Snap it like a twig."

Clack laughed some more.

Daniel drew back a fist. "What company?" he shouted. "Who owns the land?"

"I ain't gone tell you," said Clack. "Why should I do your work for you?"

Daniel threw him against the wall and held him up by the front of his overalls. Clack's feet dangled in the air. "You will pay for this, Hal Clack!" he yelled. "I promise you that!"

Clack just grinned back at him. "The timber company is buying up acreage all over Blue Springs Mountain," he said. "I expect they'll cut down every tree they can find off that precious land of yours." His face said the idea greatly pleased him.

"You better hope not," said Daniel, dropping him to the floor. " 'Cause if they do, I will personally come back here and stick a knife in your liver, you can count on that."

"But I thought you was a Christian man!" cackled Clack, picking up his jug. "A Jesus man like your pa. What happened to the Jesus man?"

Grinding his teeth, Daniel picked up his money, stomped out of the house, and sped out of Blue Springs in the loaned Model T, his thoughts a jumble as he tried to figure how he might find out who had bought his family's land and how he might go about buying it back from them.

CHAPTER
TWENTY-NINE

Abby had hoped to visit Blue Springs before winter set in, but the opportunity never presented itself. Between her work at the boardinghouse and her studies she barely had time to breathe much less take a trip back home. Besides, she had no car, and even though she and Stephen had taken up their courting again, she dared not ask him to take her after the last painful episode at her pa's house. As November moved in and then off the calendar, she pondered over and over how she might find out if the letter from her ma still existed but she came up with no good plan. If she went to Clack and asked him about it, he would certainly deny her any request to search his house. But she couldn't just break into the place. Or could she? She considered the idea. But what if one of the Clacks showed up and caught her? Ben maybe? She shivered at the thought and gave it up.

December rolled in wet and cold, and she finished up with school until February and started to make plans to go home for Christmas. The deliveryman who brought groceries to the boardinghouse traveled real close to Blue Springs on one of his trucking runs, so Abby talked to him about a ride. He said he would take her the week before Christmas Day.

On the Friday before she was to leave, Abby went out with Stephen for dinner. She'd spent a couple of dollars from what she made at the boardinghouse and bought him a navy sweater for his Christmas present. They ate at the best of Boone's three eating places, a room in the Boone Inn that served dinner four nights a week. Stephen ate a steak, rare with white potatoes, and she chose fried chicken with mashed potatoes and gravy. Stephen seemed quieter than usual, and she wondered if he felt okay. He'd planned to go to Raleigh for Christmas. Abby worried about his driving that far. The roads were narrow and slick for most of the way out of the mountains, and if he had any sickness with it raining and all, he might wreck and hurt himself.

Finished with her meal, she put down her fork, leaned over, and touched his cheek. "You got any fever?" she asked. "You seem all quiet."

Stephen took her hand, kissed her palm. "You are a wonderful woman," he said. "Far too good for the likes of me."

Abby blushed. Not accustomed to such open compliments from where she came from, his words embarrassed her.

"I don't want you to go to Blue Springs," he said. "I want you to come to Raleigh with me."

Abby blushed even more. "A proper woman does not travel such distances alone with a man," she told him. "Not if she wants to keep her reputation."

Stephen smiled and laid her hand on the table, covered it with his. For a brief time he said nothing. Abby also kept silent. Stephen looked so handsome tonight, all dressed out in a gray pinstriped suit with a blue shirt and white collar, his hair well oiled and combed back from his forehead. He ran his fingers over the top of her hand. She closed her eyes, allowed herself to enjoy his touch. Over the last few months she and Stephen had been seeing each other three or four times a week. They had moved past the hand-holding stage soon after he called on her again following the unpleasantness of their visit together to Blue Springs. He had kissed her the first time they were together again, and she hadn't resisted. They had kissed often since then, and she'd decided that she liked it, liked the feel of his arms around her shoulders, the smell of his cologne, the scratch of his face on her neck, the touch of his lips. From time to time she tried to compare his kisses to the one she and Thaddeus had shared. But she had trouble remembering the kiss Thaddeus gave her. Did it measure up to these from Stephen? Did Stephen take her breath away as

Thaddeus had? She didn't know, so after a while she stopped trying to compare them.

Stephen removed his hand from hers, breaking her thoughts. "I want you to come to Raleigh to meet my parents," he said as simply as if ordering a cup of coffee.

"I would like to do that someday," said Abby.

Stephen reached into his suit pocket and pulled out a handkerchief. His hands trembled. "I don't mean *someday*," he said. "I mean this Christmas." His voice took on an edge.

Abby smiled. Sometimes he could become as persistent as a spoiled child. "I only see my family a couple of times a year," she said. "Christmas is—"

"Hold it right there," Stephen said. "I want you to see this before you say anything else." He handed her the handkerchief. She saw it was new and made of silk. She ran her fingers over the smooth cloth.

"Unfold it," he said.

Although confused, she obeyed him and slowly opened the handkerchief. Her eyes rounded wide. A ring lay inside the handkerchief. A small diamond flashed from the center of the ring.

"I am asking you to marry me," he said. "An engaged woman can ride in a car with her fiancé to go meet his parents, can't she?"

Abby's breath caught. She stared at the ring as if hypnotized.

Stephen took the ring out of the handkerchief, held it close to the light of the table candle. "It is a beautiful stone, don't you think?"

Abby nodded but still couldn't talk. While she knew that Stephen cared for her, it had never dawned on her that he would see her as high-bred enough to marry. How could he? A man of his background, his education and style? How could a man from the upper crust of North Carolina society stoop so low as to marry a common girl of highlander origins? It didn't make sense. And what would her family say? Pa especially? A chill ran through her as she considered Solomon's reaction.

"I wish you would say something," said Stephen. "And it will please me most if what you say is a simple *yes*."

Abby finally found her voice. "But you didn't ask my pa," she said.

Stephen's eyes narrowed at the edges. "You are right about that," he said. "But after our last visit, I assumed he might say no. So I decided to ask you without his permission." He handed the ring back to her.

She held it reverently. The candle flickered. Abby knew that if she slid on the ring, her whole life would change once more. Blue Springs Mountain would recede even further into the background. Her pa and family would become less and less important. Lindy and Jubal and Thaddeus would . . .

Abby's stomach knotted up as a wave of mixed emotions churned inside. Stephen loved her, he had said it more than once. He loved her and he had style and education, and he promised her a life filled with the same. How could she refuse such an offer as that? At the same time, though, a life with him meant a sure end to any connection to her roots, the place and people whose lives had intertwined so much with her own. To marry Stephen would mean to say good-bye to the backwardness of the isolated highlands, which she both loved and hated.

Abby took a deep breath. If she married Stephen without at least telling her pa face to face, he would never forgive her. That would cut her off from him even more, and though she no longer held to any childish dreams that they would ever feel close to each other, she also had no desire to make it any worse.

She squeezed the ring and wished she had a way out of this dilemma but knew she didn't.

Stephen touched her lips with a finger. "I am waiting for an answer," he said.

She nodded. Stephen leaned forward and kissed her, his lips touching where his finger had touched. "Is that a yes?" he asked.

Pulling away, Abby studied the ring again. "I . . . I still have to ask my pa," she said.

"He will not agree to it," said Stephen. "You saw how he responded to me."

"I know," she said, taking his hand and wishing she could explain her complicated relationship with her pa. "And I will not abide by his decision if he denies us. But . . . well, in the highlands a well-raised girl does not marry without at least making the attempt to gain her pa's approval."

Stephen leaned back. "So you're insisting that you go see him," he said, not at all pleased.

Abby nodded. "I will go this week and tell him what I plan to do. Ask him to bless it."

"And if he doesn't?"

"Then he and I both will know that at least I tried."

"And you will still agree to marry me?"

Abby glanced at the candle. She thought suddenly of Thaddeus but pushed away the memory. "Let me wait until I see my pa before I make it official," she said, handing Stephen back the ring. "Keep the ring for me until then."

His teeth set, Stephen took the ring, wrapped it in his handkerchief, and tucked it into his pocket. Watching him, Abby told herself that no one from Blue Springs had ever had it so lucky. No matter what her pa said, she had no reason not to marry Stephen Jones Waterbury. Yet, before she could, she had to go to Blue Springs one more time and not just to see her pa either. While she was in Blue Springs, she had to see if she could find the letter from her ma and then have one more talk with Thaddeus Holston.

Abby stepped down from the truck in Blue Springs late in the afternoon exactly eight days later. Thanking her truck-driver friend, she pulled her black coat tighter to keep out the icy wind and shoved her neck deeper into the collar. The air had a wet feel to it and, though she hoped it would wait a few days, she had a sense that snow would come soon. For a couple of seconds she just stood and looked around the place. It seemed smaller to her since she last visited, like somebody had taken the buildings and shrunk them somehow. Otherwise, not much had changed. The town still had just the one main street, paved now with a crushed white powder but only six blocks long. Unlike Boone, no cars sat on the edges of the road. Except for the wind blowing, Abby heard nothing—not even a bird or a dog.

She tipped her head and began moving against the cold, up the street toward Lindy and Jubal's house. She'd made a phone call from the boardinghouse to the post office in Blue Springs and told Jubal to let Lindy know she was coming home and hoped to see her. To her relief Lindy had called her back that night and invited her to spend the night with her before traveling on up the mountain. Hesitant at first to put Lindy to any trouble, Abby had finally agreed to the arrangement. After what she'd done to Thaddeus, if Lindy wanted her for an evening, how could she refuse? Besides, this was the first sign of any thawing in Lindy's feelings toward her. Best not turn her down if she wanted to rekindle the friendship.

At the gate to Lindy's small house, she stopped and stared at the wood-frame dwelling. Similar to almost every other house in Blue Springs, it had a front porch. A chimney rose up from the left side, smoke curling out of it. A cluster of trees, all bare now, towered high from the back and off to the right. A light seeped out from the two square front windows. Abby knew they weren't electrical lights. That modern convenience had made it only to the buildings along the main street. Thankfully, indoor bathrooms had reached most of the private homes now.

Shivering, Abby hurried to the door and knocked. A few seconds later Lindy opened the door. For a second, the two just stared at each other. But then, hoping to put any lingering hard feelings behind them, Abby stepped to Lindy and opened her arms. The two hugged each other, then moved inside to the fireplace. Jubal stood when he saw Abby and hugged her too, and she felt grateful that they'd forgiven her for hurting Thaddeus.

"Sit down here by the fire," said Lindy. "You must be all frozen."

"I am a mite chilled," Abby said, keeping on her coat.

Jubal handed her a blanket as Lindy brought her a mug of hot coffee. Abby drank the coffee, letting its warmth run down into her stomach. Then Jubal and Lindy pulled up in chairs beside her. For a minute or so, they sat quietly and gave her time to warm up. Abby looked around the room. Plain white walls but clean. A picture of Lindy's pa hung over the mantel on the fireplace. A low table sat in a corner with a large black Bible lying on its top. A two-seat sofa made of brown cloth. Yellow curtains framed the windows. A Christmas tree about five feet high stood in a bucket in another corner, several strings of red ribbon hung around it. A cloth angel rested on top. The room contained little else except for the chairs where they sat. But it was warm and clean and smelled like coffee and burning wood.

"You got a cozy place here," Abby said.

Lindy beamed. "Me and Jubal work hard," she said. "I help some down at the general store. Jubal is postmaster, of course you already knew that." She laughed, and Abby liked the sound and wished she could hear it more often.

"You hoping for kids soon?" Abby asked.

"We doing our part," said Lindy, blushing slightly.

Abby drank from her coffee. Lindy had become a pretty woman— thick dark hair and a better figure than most mountain women. True, she had some crooked teeth and a back with a bit of a curve in the spine, but such things as that happened often in her part of the world.

"Thanks for letting me come," said Abby. "And for inviting me to spend the night."

"We have been wanting to see you," said Jubal. "You are not around these parts enough these days."

Abby studied Jubal. He had grown a good bit, now stood almost as tall as Lindy. But his hands and feet were small for a man, gave him an appearance almost girlish. But Lindy loved him and that was all that mattered.

"You said you had some big news," Lindy said, obviously anxious to know what brought her friend back home.

Abby slid her chair closer to the fire. For some reason she felt hesitant to tell out loud that Stephen had asked her to marry him. It seemed like a betrayal in some way, a turning of her back on her people. But that made no sense. She had every right to marry Stephen. Why shouldn't she?

"I am here to ask my pa to approve my marriage to Stephen Jones Waterbury," she said, forcing herself to keep her tone flat. "He asked me a few days ago to become his bride."

Lindy held her coffee cup in her lap and looked over to Jubal. He was staring at the floor, unable to meet his wife's gaze. Abby started to take issue with Lindy's stony response but realized she had no right. Even after she left Blue Springs to go to college, Lindy still believed Abby would someday end up with Thaddeus.

"I know this is hard on you," Abby said, her head down, "but I would hope you would feel happy for me. Stephen is a wonderful man."

Lindy stood and walked to her. "I'm sorry," she said. "I . . . I just didn't think . . . well, I always figured . . . even when I heard you brought a man home with you . . . I always wanted you and Thaddeus . . ." Her voice trailed away. Then she leaned forward and put her arms around Abby's neck and said, "I do want you to be happy. And if Stephen makes you happy, then I am glad."

Abby hugged her tighter. "I know he is not a true highlander," she said, hoping to comfort her friend. "But he is good to me and he has such wonderful taste and education. I don't know why he wants to marry me, but—"

"Because you're the prettiest girl in Boone, no doubt," said Lindy.

"And the smartest too," added Jubal. "Smartest girl anybody around here ever knew."

They all remained quiet for a while, each dealing with what the news meant for them. Then Lindy let go of Abby's shoulders, took her spot back in her chair. "I hear your pa did not take too well to your fellow," she said.

Abby laughed lightly. As always, news traveled fast in the highlands. Nothing that happened there stayed a secret for long. "He thinks Stephen is a snobbish city boy," she said. "What do you expect?"

Lindy smiled and said, "Your pa just wants the best for you. But what he sees as the best may not agree with your viewpoint. He know you're coming to see him?"

"I sent a letter," Abby said.

"He picked it up," said Jubal, looking at Lindy. "He knows."

They all drank from their coffee again. The fire crackled. Abby wondered whether to mention a second reason she had come to Blue Springs before giving her answer to Stephen. To do so seemed unfair in a way, like rubbing their noses in it or something, and she had no intention of doing a cruel thing like that. But she also knew that if she didn't ask, she would never forgive herself, would always wonder what might have happened. She gripped her coffee cup.

"Does Thaddeus have his own place?" she asked, trying to keep her voice light and easy. "I would like to see him while I am here."

Lindy glanced at Jubal again. Jubal hung his head like somebody had shot his best dog. Abby's heart pumped faster. Something had happened to Thaddeus!

"Thaddeus lit out some time ago," said Lindy.

"Right after you brought your gentleman friend home," Jubal said. "Told me he had no more reason to stay around here."

"But Stephen had said nothing about marriage at that time," objected Abby. "Why should Stephen's visit bother him?"

"You figure it out," said Jubal, just a little testy.

Abby considered the matter for a second. Her heart sank. Without intending to, she had hurt Thaddeus's feelings. "But he swore he loved this place!" she said. "Swore he would never leave."

Lindy sighed. "People change their minds," she said. "Thaddeus changed his."

Abby felt faint. The notion that she would not see Thaddeus again before she accepted Stephen's proposal made her dizzy. But what had she expected? That Thaddeus would just wait around forever to see what she would do? That he would never marry if he didn't marry her? Did she really think that a man as smart and good-looking as Thaddeus Holston would go to his grave a bachelor just because she chose not to marry him? What arrogance on her part!

"I am sorry I will not see him," Abby said. "He has always been a friend."

"He will wish he had seen you too," said Jubal. "But maybe it is for the best. He would not take well to this news you have brought."

The room fell quiet. Even the fireplace stopped popping. Only the wind rattling against the windows made the room seem anything more than a still-life picture. It suddenly dawned on Abby that her desire to see Thaddeus was much more than just wanting to see an old friend. Before she married Stephen she needed to see him, needed to test what she felt for Stephen with what she remembered feeling for Thaddeus. Were the two the same, or was one better? One worse? Now she would never know, and that scared her more than most anything she had ever experienced.

Lindy stood and took Abby's cup. "It is about time for supper," she said. "And I am sure you are tired from your trip. Why don't you go rest for a while and I will make ready the meal."

Though her upbringing told her the mannerly thing was to help Lindy, Abby felt too stunned by the news about Thaddeus to argue. A couple of minutes later she lay down on Lindy's bed and turned her face to the pillow and buried her head. A clog rose up in her throat, but she swallowed it down and told herself that she and Stephen were meant for each other. But the clog insisted its way back, and she lay on the pillow and grieved because her pa didn't like the man she would marry, and because she hadn't been able to see Thaddeus one more time to make sure she was marrying the right man.

––––––

When Abby awoke the next day, she looked out the window and saw nothing but white. White on the ground and in the sky, miles and miles of white as the snow fell like it had a plan to make movement impossible for a month. Watching the snow, she thought back to the previous night. After supper she and Lindy and Jubal had talked by the fire, one story leading to another, revisiting the old days in Blue Springs. When they had finished, they hugged one another and headed off to bed. All in all it had been a sweet visit, everything she'd hoped except for the fact that Thaddeus had not been there.

Climbing out of bed, Abby dressed quickly and moved to the fireplace in the front room. She found Lindy and Jubal already there.

"Don't reckon you will go to your pa's place today," said Jubal, pointing out the window. "Maybe not for a few days."

Abby nodded. Snows like this shut the mountain down. She thought of the letter she'd sent Elsa telling of her plans to visit Lindy for a day. If she had not stopped, she would have made it home late yesterday. Would Pa be mad that she had stayed over at Lindy's?

The day passed slowly. The snow continued to fall. Abby knew she couldn't travel up the mountain until it stopped and maybe not until a couple of days after. It all depended on how fast it melted. If it turned off real cold, she might not get to her pa's place at all. What would she do then? Would she have to give Stephen an answer without first talking to her pa? Or would she tell Stephen to wait, then come back to Blue Springs Mountain when the weather broke later in the spring? Too confused to answer, she turned her thoughts to other matters. Like what to do about Hal Clack, about the letter and the carving she hoped to find in his house. Should she just go find him and ask him straight out if she could look for the items? But no, she knew that was silly and wouldn't work.

Her nerves on edge, Abby told Jubal and Lindy she wanted to walk some, even in the bad weather. She tied a wool scarf on her head and left the house just after noon and trudged up the hill to the Clack house. Smoke curled from the chimney. The Clacks were home. But which ones? Old man Clack, or Topper and Ben? Maybe all of them plus a couple more. Not sure what to do next, she turned and made her way back to Lindy's.

As the afternoon went by, Abby wondered if she had made a mistake coming home. At just after dark someone knocked at the door. Lindy glanced at Jubal, then to Abby.

"Crazy time for visitation," said Jubal, going to the door and opening it.

To everyone's surprise, they saw Solomon Porter standing on the porch. Jubal quickly let him in.

"You must be plumb icy," Lindy said. She then pointed Solomon to a chair by the fire.

"It is a touch frigid outside," said Solomon, taking the seat and sticking his feet close to the flames. "Must be at least five inches of snow done fell."

Abby walked awkwardly to her pa. *Normal people would hug each other here*, she thought. But she and Solomon had never had that kind of relationship. So far as she knew, Solomon didn't hug much of anybody, except Elsa maybe. And even with her, not in public, not that Abby had ever witnessed. Solomon nodded, and she leaned down and kissed him on the cheek. It felt strange and he looked somewhat stricken as she stepped back, but she decided it didn't matter. Even if he didn't know how to respond to her, she wanted to show him at least some measure of affection. Living apart from the family had taught her that much, given her at least that much freedom.

"You looking healthy," Solomon said as she found her seat again.

"I am well," she said.

"I'll fix you a cup of coffee," Lindy said to Solomon. "Jubal, you come help me." The two quickly left the room.

Abby cleared her throat and wondered why her pa had come.

"I knew the weather would keep you from getting to us," he said as if hearing her thoughts. "So I come down to you."

"I appreciate it," said Abby. "I wanted to see the family for Christmas."

"Maybe it will clear up some before then," he said. "Got a couple of days yet."

Abby nodded. Silence came for a while.

"You want to talk to me about your fella," said Solomon, his hands held toward the fire.

Pleased that he'd taken the initiative, Abby nodded.

"He ain't my first choice. You know that."

Abby nodded again.

"But I won't stop you," he said. "You are old enough to know your own head."

Abby held her hands in her lap. "I thank you for that. He does love me, I know that for a fact."

Solomon sighed. "You deserve some loving."

Abby's heart welled. Her pa had his own ways, ways that left her feeling cut off from him, but he was not a mean man. "Everybody does," she said.

Solomon stood and threw a log on the fire. Abby wanted to cry in appreciation for his acceptance of her marriage to Stephen, but she knew her pa would not like it if she did. No reason to test his generous spirit any more than needed.

Solomon faced Abby, his hands in the pockets of his coat, an old black thing that he'd probably owned for close to ten years. He studied his shoes and shifted from foot to foot. Abby suddenly sensed something else going on in him, something apart from what he had come to say about Stephen.

"I hear Elsa told you about your ma's letter," he said without introduction. "Must have come as a shock to you."

Abby squeezed her hands together. "I was glad to hear it," she said. "But to be honest, it seems long gone now. No way to know whether it still exists anymore and no way to put my hands on it if it does."

"I meant to tell you of it a long time ago," he said. "But life got all mixed up, time passed, I let it slip my head."

Abby sighed. "It's okay, Pa. Nobody is blaming anybody."

Solomon looked down at his shoes again. "I never had nobody read it to me," he said. "Didn't want to hear what your ma said private to you. You think I did the right thing?"

Abby shrugged. "Don't know. Everybody has to do what they feel is best at the time."

"Elsa read it," he said. "But I never asked her what was in it."

Abby stared into the fire. Would it make any difference if she read or didn't read the letter? But how could it? The words had been written years ago, long before anything of her personality had even developed. Words were important, she believed that with all her heart, but did they have enough power to truly change anything in her life, in the lives of those around her? Surely not.

"You reckon it's still at the Clacks?" Solomon asked.

Abby sagged back in the chair. "No way to tell without going through the house."

Abby shook her head. It was all crazy. A letter—and a carving too for that matter—had so much meaning to her. But that was her only hope. That the letter and carving still existed and Clack didn't know it. If that were the case, then maybe somewhere down the road she could find a way to search his house. But not now. No way could she go to Clack now. An unexpected visit to his place would surely send him on a search to find and destroy anything and everything with any taint of connection to her.

"I'm sorry I can't go fetch the letter for you," Solomon said.

"It's all right, Pa," said Abby. "Nothing to be done about it now."

Solomon rubbed his beard, and the room fell quiet. Abby said a silent word of thanks to God that her pa had said okay to her marriage to Stephen. She let her thoughts about the letter recede to the back of her head.

CHAPTER
THIRTY

Abby married Stephen Jones Waterbury at the Grace Methodist Church in Boone on the last Saturday afternoon of May 1924, just three weeks after taking her last class of the year at the Appalachian Training School. Only a couple of classes short of earning her degree, she figured she would go back in the fall to finish up. The weather broke off perfect for her wedding day. She wore the white dress and lacy veil she had bought with some of the money Elsa gave her, with a strong sense of joy that she wasn't lying by wearing the white. A minister in a black tail-coat led them in their vows, while Stephen's mother and father looked on from one side and her pa and Elsa, Junior, Luke, and Daniel and Deidre and their two children watched from the other.

Abby could see that Stephen's fancy friends and folks made her pa uncomfortable. Even though he wore the black coat, white shirt, and string tie Daniel had bought for him, he kept tugging at the tie like he wanted to tear it from his throat. He arrived in Boone only one night before the wedding, then lit out for home within a couple of hours after it ended. The two families, while polite enough to each other, didn't mix much, and Abby had the distinct sense that both sides believed the marriage to be a bit of a mismatch, though for different reasons of course.

For her part, Abby had already decided to ignore everything but Stephen. She loved him and he loved her, and no matter what the kinfolk thought, their love would see them through any family feuding that might occur. Besides, her folks and his lived pretty far apart and they would never see each other, so what did it matter that they had so little in common?

Lindy and Jubal had also attended the wedding. Abby wanted to ask them about Thaddeus, but that made no sense given the circumstances so she let it pass. Thaddeus had been a childhood friend; that was all, no more and no less. And girls always remember with fondness the first boy who ever kissed them, don't they? No harm in that.

Following the wedding, she and Stephen took a trip by car and train down to the beach in southeastern North Carolina, and Abby saw the ocean for the first time and realized anew how much the mountains had confined her. Standing on the beach as the wind blew her hair back, she relaxed in Stephen's arms and studied the horizon and wondered what kind of people lived beyond the point where the water and sky met in the distance. She thought of her ma and pa, who had never journeyed to the ocean like this and felt sad for them. But then Stephen kissed her neck and walked her back to the hotel where they were staying. Soon afterward, she closed her eyes and forgot everything else.

About the only negative moment on the honeymoon occurred on the fourth day when an old friend from Stephen's college days in Raleigh took him out for an evening meal without her, and Stephen staggered back to the hotel room near midnight, smelling of whiskey and cigars. At first she started to fuss at him, to tell him she'd never spent time with a man who drank, especially with it being Prohibition and all, and what if he had gotten caught and put into jail? Then where would she be? But Stephen threw his arms around her and gave her a wet kiss, and she figured that men did such things from time to time so why cause a fight on their honeymoon when he had treated her so well since the day she met him? Deciding to leave well enough alone, she led him over to the bed and pulled off his boots. Then she covered him up and lay down beside him while he slept it off.

By mid-June they had returned to Boone and set up housekeeping in a six-room white house about a quarter mile out of town on the main road. The house had a porch on the front, a living room area, three bedrooms, and a kitchen all to itself. Electric lights burned in all of the rooms, and the bathroom had a tub with claw feet and running water. Stephen's mother and father had picked out the house and furnished it just two weeks before the wedding. Though Abby felt a twinge of guilt every now and again when she walked through it—kind of like she had done nothing to deserve such fine surroundings—that didn't keep her from quickly growing to love the place. All through that summer she rose early to make breakfast for Stephen—eggs, biscuits, grits, ham, jelly, with all the fixings. Stephen left for his office soon after. Abby stayed at home a lot, making sure everything stayed spotless, prim and proper. Stephen liked a clean house and an orderly life, and she saw no reason not to give him one.

Neighbors and friends of all kinds dropped over to make her feel welcome—women from her church and the Methodist church, wives of Stephen's friends from work, members of the Ladies of Boone Improvement Society. After reading scores of books on etiquette and social graces, Abby entertained them as best she could and kept a stash of tasty treats on hand for whoever happened to come by.

When fall arrived Abby talked to Stephen about maybe going to the local grammar school and doing some teaching while she finished her classes at the college, but he argued against the notion and they had their first real fight.

"I don't want you to do any teaching," he had said. "I thought for sure you understood that. I will provide for you."

"But I have always wanted to do this," Abby told him. "And it has nothing to do with your provision for us; I know you do well in that."

"No wife of mine will work," he said, obviously concerned that the people of Boone would think less of him if Abby took a job. "You will have enough to do around the house, especially when children come."

"But I want to help a lot of children," continued Abby, her face red. "Some who don't have such privileges as ours."

Stephen stepped to her, gathered her hands in his. His eyes took on a softer look. His voice soothed her. "I am sure you would make a wonderful teacher," he said. "You have real gifts, I know that. But let's give it a year. Not put so much pressure on you this first year of marriage. Stay and make our home a perfect place. Teaching can wait. Your final classes can wait too. See how things are after this year. If you still want to do these things later, we will have another talk."

Although unconvinced, Abby relented. A woman ought to follow her husband's wishes where she could, shouldn't she? After all, he did earn enough to take care of them both. The nice house and surroundings, the good food she ate, the stylish clothes she wore—all of it resulted from his hard labors. He had a right to say what she did or did not do in regard to her future.

When college opened again the middle of September, it made her sad that she wasn't returning to finish her degree but she didn't fuss any to Stephen. He had so much on his mind from the office she didn't want to burden him with her minor complaints.

Not knowing why, Abby took up her sewing at this time. A blanket emerged first from her busy fingers, a brown piece that matched the colors on the chair in the living room. After that she started on a sweater. She wasn't sure whether she would give it to Stephen or her pa, yet knew even as she drew her first stitch that she wanted it ready by Christmas.

By Christmas she had not only finished the sweater but two others as well. She gave the first one to Stephen, the next to her pa, and the third to Junior. When she saw everybody in Blue Springs on Christmas Day, Daniel and Luke complained that they hadn't gotten a sweater, so she promised she would do better next time. Everybody laughed in response when someone said, "Don't work yourself too hard, you got someone else to sew for now." Abby laughed with them and patted her stomach. She had found out in November that she had a child on the way, and though it scared her some because her ma had died giving birth, she also felt her body had come alive in a fashion she'd never experienced since she heard of the baby coming. She could put up with some fear for something like that.

Her water broke in the middle of the night on the 10th of June 1925, and at about the same time that the sun rose, Abby gave birth to a boy with hair like Stephen's and a birthmark the shape of a small knife blade on his left heel. She agreed with Stephen that they ought to name him Beaufort James after Stephen's father, and so the boy took that name and they called him Jimmy. She read to him every night by the fire and dressed him up in fine clothes and took him to church every Sunday. Stephen only attended church with her every now and again and only then when she pressed him on it and agreed to go Methodist for the day. He said he had too much work to do at the office. But Abby knew for a fact that sometimes he didn't go to the office when he stayed out of church, knew it because she had stopped by his building a couple of times after services and didn't find him there. She wondered if he dropped by the hotel instead, maybe to play some cards with his friends and have a drink or two.

Fearful, she thought about asking him about his whereabouts on those days she dropped by his office and didn't find him, but since she didn't know how to pose her questions, she let them pass. The months peeled off the calendar, and it seemed Stephen stayed out late on Saturday nights drinking with his buddies with more and more regularity. Abby found the problem growing bigger and bigger. But how does a wife tell her husband she dislikes something he's doing? Every now and again she hugged him and told him she missed him and worried about him when he didn't come home by the time she crawled into bed. But he usually just shrugged and told her not to let it bother her, that he could take care of himself, and all the successful men in Boone liked to carouse just a little.

Sometimes when Stephen came home drunk she wondered about Thaddeus and if he ever did anything like this. Not to a wife of course, because Lindy had told her he hadn't yet taken a wife. But did he have a wild streak too? Did every man do these kinds of things from time to time? Every man but her pa? Her thoughts of Thaddeus made her feel guilty. She knew such questions about another man were out of place and not fitting for a good Christian woman who loved her husband, and so she shut them out of her head.

Abby never told anybody about Stephen's bouts with liquor. Not Lindy and not any of her family. Not in person or in the letters she sent home every few weeks. What could they do about it? Remind her they had spoken against the marriage in the first place, that they saw this kind of behavior in Stephen from the beginning? No good in that. So she kept her chin up and her mouth closed. Time moved on, and Abby poured her love into her boy, Jimmy, and the Gospel Spirit Church and made life as pleasant as possible for Stephen. If she stayed pretty and tended the house well and brought up some children worthy of his pride, then he would have no reason to gallivant too much now, would he? That hope, though, didn't always pan out.

One time in November, about a year and a half after Jimmy was born, Stephen staggered in way past midnight, and since she was feeling kind of sick from some unknown ailment, Abby forgot her pledge not to fuss at him. Her face red and her fists clenched, she told him what she thought of his ways.

"You are drinking too much!" she had said through gritted teeth, remembering how such shenanigans had led Laban down a bad path. "Not even counting the fact that the sheriff could arrest you and throw you in jail. Then what would happen to me and Jimmy? Not to mention your practice and reputation?"

Stephen smiled crookedly at her. "The sheriff sat right beside me down at the hotel," he said. "So I don't think he will do any arresting . . . any . . . any time soon."

Seeing that he wasn't repenting any, Abby decided to change her approach. She stepped close to him, tried to put her arms around his waist. "I worry about you," she said, her voice soothing now.

Stephen pushed off her hand. "I'm a grown man. I don't need a woman worrying about me."

"My brother lost everything with this kind of behavior," said Abby, her words running ahead of her good judgment.

"I am not an ignorant mountain boy," Stephen said, almost snarling. "So stop your complaining. You have it pretty good around here from what I can see."

Stunned by his anger, Abby started to fight, but then not sure what else to say, she bit her tongue and fled from the room. The next morning Stephen acted like nothing had happened. At first she didn't know what to do. How could he act so unconcerned about their fight? Then she realized that maybe he had forgotten the whole scene. Just like that. He had been so drunk he had no recall of the previous night's ugliness. She decided to leave it alone. If he had no recollection of the episode, then why should it matter to her?

Stephen had so many good qualities. His strong drive to work hard, the way he could charm a crowd, his education, his ability to talk about just anything. So what if he drank some every third or fourth weekend? It wasn't like he came home and beat her or anything. And when he wasn't drinking he was as sweet as any man could be. So she had no reason to feel sorry for herself. What woman would in her situation? Deciding once more to make the best of things, Abby remembered that life had taught her one thing if nothing else: God never gives anybody a road that always slopes downhill. So she better just bow her back and walk up the steep places when they came and leave behind all the complaining and the self-pity.

Around Christmas of that year, Abby found out she had another child on the way and she felt glad. A second baby would make it plain to Stephen that he had to slow down some, both with his work and his activities afterward. Surely another child in the house would remind him of his responsibilities, keep him home more, cut down on his drinking.

Abby delivered another boy on the 27th of May 1927 and named him Stephen Jones Junior, Stevie for short. For a few months it seemed that Stephen had indeed calmed some. He spent more time at home than he had since their first year of marriage, and Abby thanked the good Lord for it and prayed the change would last. But it didn't. Within a year after Stevie's birth, his father had fallen back into his old ways, and Abby knew of nothing she could do about it but pray some more and not stew over it too much.

She didn't see her family too often in those years, usually only at Christmas or every now and again in the summer when she could talk Stephen into giving up a weekend to drive her back to Blue Springs. He usually fought her over it but then relented at least once a year and let her go. When she did go home, she always thought of her ma's letter and the carving her pa had made and whether or not they might still be in the Clack house. But having no way to find out, she always pushed away her hopes of ever seeing either object and told herself life was okay without them.

The visits home were never easy. Stephen stayed on the porch a lot, his eyes searching the mountains' ridges as though he might see gold in them at any second. Never given to much small talk, Solomon left him alone, and Abby knew better than to interfere. If her pa and her husband did not like each other, so be it.

For her part, she talked with Elsa a lot, caught up with the news of the rest of the family, and showed off her two children to the neighbors who dropped by when they heard she'd come home.

The visit she took in August of 1928 followed a pattern similar to all the rest, at least at the beginning. Stephen shook hands with Solomon, talked for a few minutes about the weather, the lack of rain and such, and then headed to the porch. Solomon pulled out his knife and a piece of wood and joined him, neither saying anything. Elsa and Abby made their way to the kitchen that Solomon had built on the back of the house. Abby noticed how much Elsa and Solomon had done to the cabin since the day they first moved in so many years ago. The place had five full rooms now, glass windows in each one. Elsa had hung chintz curtains on all the windows. And Solomon had smoothed down the floors to a point where even bare feet wouldn't pick up any splinters. Not only did they have a fireplace in the front room, they also had an iron cooking stove in the kitchen. Although the cabin still lacked indoor plumbing and a privy, it was far better than what they had when they first started. As usual, Solomon had worked hard all these years to make the best of the land his brother had allowed him to farm. That plus the money he earned from making his chairs enabled them to make the cabin more than passable.

The two women took their seats at the kitchen table. Jimmy and Stevie were napping in Elsa's bedroom. Elsa gave Abby a basket of corn to shuck and she started in on it. Elsa began shelling peas and catching her up on all the local news.

Solomon Jr., a strapping young man of twenty-three now, was working with the county as a law officer. Married to a girl from over in Edgar's Cove and living halfway between there and Blue Springs. He drove home a couple of times a month on a Sunday to see Solomon and the family. A good-looking boy, he was making his way well in the world.

Listening to Elsa, Abby wondered what it would feel like to live so close to family—to have them dropping by, to see their wives and husbands, their children on a regular basis. She saw Stephen's family less than she did her own, usually only once a year and always in Boone. In her over four years of marriage, she had never traveled to Raleigh. Stephen had never asked, and his parents had never invited. Beaufort James and Gertrude Katherine Waterbury remained little more than strangers to her and nothing—not even the fact that she had birthed their two grandchildren—seemed to incline them to change anything.

Sometimes Abby wondered if they were ashamed of her, if the reason they didn't invite her to Raleigh was because they didn't want to introduce her to their high-society friends. But, like so many things, she had never questioned Stephen about it. If he wanted her to go see his home, he would say so. Until then, she would leave it alone.

"What about Daniel and Deidre?" she asked, forcing her thoughts back to Elsa and the present moment. "Anything new from them?"

"Nothing he probably hasn't already written you," Elsa replied. "He toils like a slave hand. Saves his money. He and Deidre seem happy. They came up back in June, stayed a few days. Daniel's kids are growing fast, fighting with each other all the time."

"You see his car?"

Elsa laughed, pulled up another bowl, started throwing peas into it. "A noisy thing. He parked it down at the fork. Complained we ought to put a road in here so he wouldn't have to walk so far on his bad hip."

Abby laid an ear of corn on the table, picked up another. "He is doing well. I wish I could see him more often. Luke too."

"That Luke has a radio show," said Elsa. "We hear it every now and again down at the post office. Jubal lets us listen."

Abby shook her head. How strange where events had taken her family, how the twists and turns of life had split them up, one here and one there. She hardly knew Luke anymore. She had seen his picture in Boone last year on a poster in the store where she shopped. The poster said Luke was going to sing at a nearby church and all were welcome. When the day arrived, she went to hear him, sat in the back during the service. Though still slow of speech, Luke had grown into a capable man. In fact, his stuttering had seemed to draw the crowd as he spoke at the church, had seemed to tell them that the good Lord could use anybody, even a man with a hesitant tongue, a man who didn't have a lot of learning in his head. Luke had said something almost like that: "A man with J-J-Jesus in his heart don't need a lot of learning," he'd stated, his stuttering almost absent. "Just find the Lord's w-w-will for your life and do it, and the Lord will bless you."

At the end of the singing time, Abby had made her way through the crowd to see her brother. He had shuffled his feet and apologized for not telling her he was coming to town.

"But I s-s-stay so busy," he said. "And I ain't one for writing m-m-much."

Abby hugged him and told him he didn't need to apologize, she was his sister and she was so glad to see him and he looked real good.

They talked a few minutes and he told her he had a woman friend who lived in Hickory, but they had not decided yet if they would marry. "I ain't s-s-sure she likes the notion of traveling around and all. And I don't kn-kn-know no other w-w-way to make a living but to travel and sing."

"Sounds like you got some deciding to do," Abby had told him.

Luke agreed and laughed, and they talked for a while longer. Then a man came and took Luke by the arm and said they had to head out to the next town. Abby had watched him drive away.

"I miss my family sometimes," she said to Elsa, focused on the corn again.

"Only natural," said Elsa. "You are all by yourself down there in Boone."

Abby peeled away the corn shucks. "I stay busy though," she said, not wanting Elsa to hear anything too deep in her words. "Something going on all the time."

"Busy is good," said Elsa. "Idle hands are the devil's workshop."

"I'd like to see the devil try to keep up with me," Abby laughed. "You know how it is keeping up with kids."

Elsa snapped some more peas. Then she asked, "You stop in Blue Springs on your way up?"

"Nope, Stephen saw no need." She dropped an ear of corn onto the table.

Elsa worked on the peas another minute, then said, "My pa has put our old house up for sale. Building a new place a couple of miles further out."

Abby's fingers tugged at the silks on the corn, but her mind wasn't on it. She thought of the Clack house, the last place anyone had seen the letter from her ma, the last place she had seen the carving. Since her marriage, she had pretty much put aside her plans to find either of the things. Just like finishing up her schooling. Leave all that in the past, she figured. But now the house was for sale?

Her tongue thickened. If somebody new bought the place, they would clean it out, throw away any junk, including any papers they found. Or Clack would do it before the new folks moved in. She tried to stay calm.

"How long since he put the house up?"

"Only a month or so. I started to write you, then thought better of it. No reason to tell you something you can't do anything about."

As Abby set down a piece of corn, an idea came to her. "You know if your pa has any offers on the house yet?" she asked.

"Don't know. But probably not many folks around here that can come up with enough cash money."

Abby worked on a new ear of corn. Elsa snapped her peas.

The afternoon passed, then the night. Abby drove home with Stephen and her boys near the end of the next day. But her mind stayed in Blue Springs this time, in the old house where she had spent much of her childhood, in the house she planned to buy from Hal Clack before he sold it off to somebody else.

CHAPTER
THIRTY-ONE

Sitting by the window in his bedroom, Daniel Porter studied the ledger book he had resting in his lap. The building season had been one of his busiest ever, and he had earned a right smart stack of dollars. Now, as September ended, things had finally slowed enough for him to add up the profits, take a look at where he stood. A grim smile crossed his face. Since returning from the war, he had labored as hard as any time in his life, spending long hours in the sun, laying brick for a while and then taking the job of overseeing a group of builders. His home life had suffered some in that time and he knew it. His children, a girl and two boys, the youngest boy barely six months old, saw him only when the sun went down or when the weather turned too bad to do any building.

Daniel made a notation in the ledger and added up the figures. Deidre hadn't bothered him too much about his long hours working, and he loved her for her patience. Maybe soon he could repay her for her understanding. He stared out the window and thought of his wife. She had stopped work at the bank after Marla Suzanne arrived, took quickly to her chores as a mama. Kept the house in apple-pie order. Cooked good food too, enough to feed a small army. She guided the children with a firm but loving hand and stayed as pretty as any woman in any town anywhere. God had done him a good service by bringing her into his life.

His spirits high, Daniel jotted down another list of numbers and closed the ledger. His shoulders relaxed as he gazed out the window again at the yard. He'd lived here for over eight years now, far longer than he had wanted. At times he felt guilty about staying in his in-laws' old house, felt that he'd failed somehow, taken advantage of another man's good heart and not made his own way with his family. That pricked at his pride some—made him feel less than a man. He didn't like it when that kind of notion ran into his head, yet he couldn't always keep it out.

When this notion came to him, he would remind himself that living on Mr. Woodrow Shaller's property had given him a chance to save his dollars to buy back his pa's land. That and that alone gave him the reason he needed to swallow his pride and live on in a house another man had paid for. About the only good thing was that Mr. Shaller had never thrown it up to him, and Daniel was glad for that. Deidre's pa was a good man. He had no complaints with him, none at all. The house in Asheville had been a good deal all around, a place to start his family, to settle in and do his best to forget the war.

He had not managed to do that of course, certainly not completely. In fact, the harder he worked and the more money he saved, the more vivid the memories—the recollections of his last minutes with Laban and the promise he'd made to his brother. If he didn't know better, he would have sworn that the dollars piling up in the bank made him more fractious, not less so, more on edge as he drew nearer to trying again to purchase back the land Clack had stolen from his family.

Telling himself to stay relaxed, Daniel stood and put the ledger in a dresser drawer by the bed. He checked his appearance in the mirror. White shirt, black string tie, the best pants he owned, and a black coat only a year old. His best clothes by far.

Pleased, Daniel turned and left the room and the house. A minute later he climbed into his car and pointed it toward town. Just over twenty minutes later he reached his destination—a six-room office building only ten blocks from the bank where Deidre had once worked.

Daniel sat in the car for a while and stared at the words painted in black on the front window of the building. *Tillman Timber and Logging, Inc., Robert Tillman, President.* Climbing out of the car, he squared his shoulders and smoothed down his coat. Then he walked over and pushed through the door of Tillman Timber.

Five minutes later a secretary led him into a corner office in the back and pointed him to a seat. "Mr. Tillman will join you in a minute," the secretary said.

Daniel nodded his thanks and the secretary left. He looked over the room—a spare, plain space with only one window and no pictures. Stacks of paper were piled on the desk, and the room smelled like old cigarettes. The office told him almost nothing about the man who occupied it. But Daniel didn't care about the room decorations, and he didn't need it to tell him about Robert Tillman, president of Tillman Timber and Logging. He already knew plenty. While saving his money over the last five years, he had dug up as much information as he could. Had discovered that Robert Tillman was the man who had taken ownership of his family's land after Hal Clack sold it to him. Had found out that Tillman had bought up land all over western North Carolina, that he had bought up the land not because he wanted to log it himself but because he wanted to sell it to somebody else and let them log it. Tillman was really a salesman more than a logger, a middleman who gathered up as much land as possible for as cheap a price as possible, then turned around and sold it to the highest bidder. That bidder, usually an actual logging firm, would then send out crews to cut down the trees and haul them away from the mountain soil that had given them life.

Thankfully, Daniel knew that Tillman hadn't sold his pa's land yet, because nobody had started cutting on it. Daniel had a number of friends keeping an eye on the property back home, and they had sworn to let him know fast if they saw a logging crew on his old place.

He heard footsteps and a second later, Robert Tillman bounced into the room. The man had a handlebar mustache and gray hair slicked back on his head. He wore a gray suit and a blue shirt and yellow tie. His eyes landed on Daniel for an instant but didn't stay there. Without shaking Daniel's hand, he took a seat behind the paper-covered desk. Daniel cleared his throat and decided to move right to the point. A man like Tillman probably spent little time with small talk.

"I am Daniel Porter," he said. "I come to talk to you about some land you own."

"And what land would that be?" asked Tillman, picking a piece of paper off his desk and examining it.

"Up on Blue Springs Mountain," said Daniel. "You bought it five or so years ago from a man named Hal Clack."

Tillman put down the paper. His fingers found his mustache and twirled it. "I recall that land. Fine logging property, I believe."

Daniel nodded. "I come to buy it from you," he said, his voice sterner than he had planned.

Tillman searched his face. "You seem mighty intent. That land got special meaning for you?"

Daniel wiped his hands on his pants, tried to figure what to say. Would Tillman jack up the price if he knew his family once owned the property? Or did he already know from the old deed and just wanted to test him, see how honest he was? Not knowing how to respond, Daniel decided to stick with the truth.

"It belonged to my family," he said. "I want to buy it back."

Tillman fingered his mustache. "A noble act," he said. "Wish I could help you."

"What do you mean?"

"I mean I don't own it anymore. Or I won't own it soon. I'm talking to some folks up in Raleigh about it."

Daniel felt his face turning hot. "I done had to go through this one time already. I went to Clack right after he sold it to you."

"Not my problem," said Tillman, picking up a piece of paper again, his interest obviously disappearing.

"Who you selling to?"

"I can't divulge that," he said without looking at Daniel. "Business is business."

"How much you gettin' for it?"

Tillman laid the paper down and licked his lips. His eyes looked bright, like a man staring at easy new money. "More than you got," he said.

"How much?" insisted Daniel.

Tillman fingered his mustache. "Nineteen hundred dollars. Don't reckon it hurts for you to know that."

Daniel pressed his palms into his thighs, and the blood ran out of his face. Tillman had doubled his money from what he gave Clack for it. Did land always do that? Double every few years, go up so high that no normal man could buy it?

"You got that much?" asked Tillman. "My deal ain't finished yet. You pay a bit more, maybe I will sell it to you."

His shoulders slumped, Daniel shook his head. Counting the seven hundred he had taken to Clack's house five years ago, he now had about thirteen hundred dollars, enough for Tillman to make a profit but not enough to match the offer from Raleigh.

Tillman leaned forward, his face as friendly as a dog about to receive his dinner. "Tell you what," he said. "It will take another few months for this deal to make its way to the finish. You go on out there and see what you can come up with. If you can match the offer from Raleigh, I will sell it to you, straight out as that. What you think? Is that a good deal or what?"

Daniel stared at the man, unsure if he was playing with him or not. But he seemed sincere; maybe he . . . but then he knew how crazy that was. No way could he save up another six hundred dollars in a few months. He thought of Mr. Shaller, the money in his bank. He could go to him and ask for a loan, that's one of the things banks did. They loaned money all the time to people for just this kind of thing. Mr. Shaller would loan him the six hundred, wouldn't he?

His heart racing, Daniel started to tell Tillman he could get the money, bring it back and buy the land outright. But then he thought about his pa and knew that if Solomon found out he had borrowed money to purchase back the land, he would never accept it. Highlanders didn't do business that way, didn't borrow off another man. Highlanders saw such borrowing as a kind of charity, and their pride would not allow such a thing.

Daniel's head bent low. He realized he couldn't take out a loan from Mr. Shaller. Which probably meant he could never buy back his family's land. He faced Tillman again.

"I thank you for your time," he said.

"Glad to talk to you," said Tillman. "You bring me back the nineteen hundred and I'll keep the offer open."

"Don't wait on me," Daniel said. "I don't expect I will be seeing you again."

Tillman shrugged. "Too bad. I expect they will start cutting a couple of months after the deal is finished."

Daniel trudged from the office, his shoulders slumped. With all his obligations, he saw no way to save enough money soon enough to stop Tillman from selling his family's land to another company, this time one that would surely start logging on it real fast. But that didn't mean he would give up. A Porter man didn't know the meaning of the word. He would go back to work and would save every dollar he could scratch aside. He would not give up on the promise he made to his pa and brother. No matter what happened to him, he would take that promise to his grave if he couldn't fulfill it before then.

CHAPTER
THIRTY-TWO

It took Abby almost two months to gather up her courage to the point where she could go to Stephen and tell him what she wanted. In the meantime she talked to Elsa from the boardinghouse phone a couple of times and asked her to check about the price of Clack's old house. Elsa reported back that her pa wanted nine hundred dollars for the place and that he had a standing offer of seven eighty-five from a preacher's family that had moved in over the summer to pastor a new church the Baptists were starting.

Afraid that Clack might take the offer if he didn't soon receive a better one, Abby decided she had to do something fast. She approached Stephen on a Tuesday night the first week in October, a night he arrived home from work early and appeared in a good mood. Having fixed him his favorite meal—a steak seared in an iron skillet with onions, mashed potatoes and gravy, hot biscuits, and sweet potato pie—she waited until an hour after supper. She found him in the living room, his feet up on a stool, a cigar in his mouth, the fire going hot at his feet. He held a newspaper. Though she had planned her words down to the last one, Abby's tongue turned thick as she started to talk.

"You are tired, I reckon," she began.

"Always tired after a day downtown," Stephen said, not looking up. "I am not lying around in a hammock at the office, I can tell you that."

Abby folded her hands in her lap. Stephen talked a lot these days about how hard he worked, almost as if to justify what he did. "You are a good provider," she said, keeping things positive. "I thank the good Lord every day for what you do for me and the children."

Stephen didn't answer. She cleared her throat, decided she might as well go ahead with what she had to say. She asked for so little, spent frugally on the house and almost nothing on herself. But Stephen drove a nice car, dressed in the best suits, bought cigars and liquor like they weren't going to make any more of them and he had to buy up enough to last a lifetime. Surely Stephen had nine hundred dollars he would give her. She deserved it for all she did.

"I know what I want for Christmas," she said, her voice even.

"Good. Another dress like last year?"

"Not quite. Something that might surprise you, I think."

He lowered the paper, stared at her over the edge. But he didn't say anything. Abby swallowed, brushed back her hair. "You know the house where I grew up with Mrs. Amelia Clack?" she said.

"Yeah, you point it out to me every time we go through Blue Springs. The place is falling apart now, isn't it?"

Abby nodded. "Yes, but . . . well, it has come up for sale."

"So, what's that got to do with you and Christmas?"

She saw that he hadn't figured it out yet. The idea was so out of the ordinary, so beyond the scope of what she would normally ask. For a second she wondered if she ought to continue or if she should just shut her mouth and forget it forever. But then Stephen spoke and what he said made her so mad she just had to press ahead.

"Somebody ought to burn the place down. Burn it down and start all over."

Her face red, Abby recalled the day somebody burned down her first house, the day she and her family got thrown off their land. If that had not happened, the letter from her ma would never have gotten lost. She would have read the letter by now, would have heard her ma's dying words. Losing that house had meant the loss of so much more than the house, and she was determined never to let that happen again, not if she had any chance of stopping it.

"I want to buy that house," she told him sternly, knowing it sounded crazy even as she said it.

Stephen laughed so hard, his cigar almost fell out of his mouth. "You want to what?"

"You heard me. I want to buy the Clack house."

He stopped laughing for a second and studied her. She pressed on. "Clack is asking nine hundred dollars," she said. "He might take eight hundred fifty."

"You already checked on the price?"

She nodded, proud of her prior investigation.

Stephen puffed his cigar, obviously thinking about her outlandish idea. "You mind telling me what you want to do with it if you buy it?" he asked.

Abby squeezed her hands together. Here was the question she didn't know how to answer. Stephen knew she didn't want to live back in Blue Springs. So why did she need a run-down house? If she told him about the letter, would he laugh in her face again? Would he tell her to grow up, to realize that the letter probably had long since disappeared? Would he say that he wouldn't spend nine hundred dollars on the off chance the letter still existed somewhere on the property? Probably so. She decided to keep her reasons to herself.

"I can't say why exactly," she said. "But I need to buy that house."

Stephen grunted and lifted the newspaper again. "I am a practical man," he said. "Not going to put that kind of money into a piece of property I don't ever plan to use."

"See it as an investment," said Abby, a touch of desperation riding her words. "New people are moving into Blue Springs all the time. It's got close to fifty acres of land out behind it. I can fix up the place and in a couple of years sell it for a whole lot more than what we paid for it." She stopped and waited. What she said made sense. Even if the letter and carving weren't there, the money would be well spent. A businessman like Stephen would see that.

Stephen lowered the paper once more. His eyes narrowed. "What do you know about investments?"

Abby shrugged. She wanted to remind him of her education. Instead, she kept it simple when she answered, "I read. Keep up with things. I know some about finances."

Stephen tilted his head. Then he laughed again and said, "Well, it makes no difference what you know about finances, I will not spend money on a beat-up old house in a two-bit town I would prefer to never even see again. So you better just choose something else for Christmas."

"But that's all I want," Abby said, about to lose her nerve but fighting against it. "It is all I have ever asked from you. In our four and a half years of marriage, name one other thing I have asked, just one, for myself I mean, one thing I have really come to you and said I wanted."

Stephen put his feet on the floor and leaned toward her. His face became serious, and she believed for a second that she had touched him, given him something to consider.

He placed a hand on her knee. "Look," he said, "I know I haven't said this to you . . . and I don't want to upset you with this, but . . . well, I don't really have that kind of money right now. You know we moved, built a new office this past year, hired a couple of people. And . . . well . . . we have lost some business too, a couple of clients, not many but enough to make a difference. So you see . . . even if I agreed with you about the Clack place . . . well, I just don't have the dollars to make it happen."

Abby couldn't believe her ears. Stephen had never given any clue about any money problems. Like he said, he had moved to a new office, hired new workers. A lawyer doing those kinds of things had no cause to claim poverty. She stared at him and questioned whether she could trust what he said. Something about the way he'd said it made her wonder. But if she didn't trust him about this, what else should she call into question? A wife who does not believe her husband is a woman on a bad path, and that scared her. But that's the way she felt, and what could she do about it?

She took his hands in hers. When she spoke, her voice came out more serious than she could remember. "So you are telling me you will not, that you cannot, help me with this one thing I want more than anything else," she said.

He dropped his eyes. She waited. "That is what I am saying," he said, still looking down. "At this time, I have neither the means nor the will to do it."

For several seconds they stayed that way. The logs in the fireplace burned lower. Abby let go his hands, sighed heavily. He glanced up at her, then back down. Still not sure whether to believe him or not, Abby stood and stalked out. Once again, her hopes of finding the letter from her mama were dashed. Maybe the Lord simply didn't want that hope fulfilled. If so, maybe she ought not to blame her husband for that.

CHAPTER
THIRTY-THREE

His shirt lying on a chair beside him, Solomon Porter shivered for a second as Doc Booth pressed the end of his stethoscope up against his chest.

"Breathe again," said Booth.

Solomon took a heavy breath. Booth moved the stethoscope to the other side of Solomon's chest. "Once more." Solomon breathed again. Booth moved the stethoscope to his back, made him repeat the breathing four more times. Booth hung the stethoscope around his neck.

"You say you been coughing a lot?" he asked.

"It come on me about two months or so ago," said Solomon. "Hacking all the time. And I can't seem to get my breath neither."

Booth shook his head, and Solomon knew he disapproved. "And these coughs bring up some blood?"

"Yeah, in the morning mostly. Seems that part of it eases a mite as the day passes."

"Lie down here a second," said Booth, pointing Solomon to a table by the chair where he sat. "Let me check another thing or two."

When he was flat, Booth took to pressing on Solomon's stomach and chest. Booth's hands were chilly.

"You ought to warm up them fingers some," said Solomon. "Before you go a-pokin' on a man in the middle of November."

Booth grinned but didn't stop working. "You lucky I am seeing you at all," he said. "You know I retired last year."

"But I ain't going to no other doctor. Put off coming to you long as I could as it is."

Booth shook his head again and kept probing. He came to a spot just under Solomon's right rib, near the top of the stomach. He pressed hard on it. Solomon winced but tried to hide it.

"That hurt?" asked Booth.

Solomon shrugged. "A touch maybe, but you pushing like a man digging for worms. Not a surprise that it bothers me some."

Booth pushed again, dug his fingers in. Solomon gritted his teeth against the pain. Sweat broke out on his forehead in spite of the chill in the room. Booth let off the pressure and stepped back.

"Put on your shirt, old man," he said.

Glad to have the visit finished, Solomon obeyed quickly. After he had buttoned his shirt, Booth pointed him back to the chair, took one across from him, then leaned forward and put his hand on Solomon's knee.

"Solomon," he started, "how long have I known you?"

Solomon counted a second. "Oh, I don't know. You come here in eighteen and ninety, if I recollect. That would make it thirty-eight years, I reckon. Long time, that's for sure."

"And you trust me, right?"

"As much as a man can trust any doctor, yeah, I reckon I do."

Booth nodded and straightened up. "Then listen to what I'm telling you," he said. "I don't like what I've found here today. But I'm not sure of anything just yet. You need to go to Asheville for some tests."

Solomon immediately shook his head. "I ain't going to no Asheville doctors. A bunch of city folk just dying to start a-cutting on a body."

"But I don't have the equipment here to give you a complete check," insisted Booth. "The medicine either. They're doing all kinds of new things in the hospital down in Asheville."

"What you thinkin' I got?" asked Solomon, changing the subject.

Booth stared at the floor.

"Spit it out, Doc. I ain't a child you got to protect from the truth."

Booth looked him in the eyes. "It's the cancer," he said. "If I'm guessing right, it's in the right lung. I can feel something, a tumor maybe, under the rib. Don't know how far it's spread or if it's the bad kind or not. And I can't tell much of anything yet about the left lung."

Solomon rubbed his hands together. "You reckon it's the same thing that got Francis?"

"Who knows? Hers was in the stomach, mostly. But remember, I'm still guessing here. That's why you need to go to Asheville." Booth's voice took on a pleading quality, and Solomon knew he ought to do what the doc said. But the thought of spending time in a hospital in Asheville scared him a whole lot worse than dealing with the cancer in his own cabin on Blue Springs Mountain. In addition, few people he knew who got the cancer ever got better from going down to Asheville. Cancer won soon enough either way. So he saw no reason to spend his last days in some strange city with doctors who didn't know his name, stuck inside a dull brick building when he could spend them sitting on his own porch, scratching his own dogs and listening to the bobwhites as the sun went down.

"I appreciate your checking me out," said Solomon, standing and grabbing his cane. "What do I owe you?"

"You owe me a trip to Asheville," Booth said.

"Too high a price. How about a rocker come Christmas? These chairs here"—he pointed to the one where he had sat—"will tear up a man's back in a hurry."

"A rocker will do just fine."

Solomon turned to leave, then twisted back to Booth. "How long you reckon I got left?" he asked.

Booth shook his head. "No way to guess without some more tests."

"Take a stab at it," said Solomon. "From what you found just now."

Booth stared at his friend for a moment. "You making this mighty hard on me," he said.

"I know and I am sorry for that. But I need to know how much time you figure."

"Maybe a year," said Booth. "More or less depending on a whole lot of things."

Solomon studied his shoes for a second. He looked back at Booth, stuck out his hand. Booth took it.

"You a good friend," Solomon said. "And I will bring you that rocker by Christmas. Should have brought you one a long time ago."

"You sure you won't go to Asheville?"

"You want that rocker or not?"

Booth grinned. "I will do some studying on your sickness," he said. "See what medicine I can give you."

"I will appreciate any medicine you can come on," said Solomon. "And thanks again."

Solomon left the office and made his way back to the street. Then he stopped and let his eyes take in the little town where he had lived all his days. In one way, a lot had changed in the last fifty years or so. A few more people now, mostly loggers, and some who had come to build roads, a new doctor, and a man from the government who wanted to do something about protecting the forest. Other than that, Blue Springs hadn't taken in too many outlanders. The town had electrical lights and telephones in the general store, post office, sheriff's office, and a couple of the rich folk's houses, though not much in any others. Most of the people had run some pipes into their places to run water and provide for indoor-relief matters. About fifteen people he knew had cars.

Progress, he thought, staring at the town. That's what Daniel called it. No way to stop it. Changes had come and were still a-coming.

Other things—some good and some bad—hadn't changed at all. A ghostly mist still covered the valley most every morning, the ridgeline still looked down on the town like a thick forehead covered with trees, the apples still snapped in your teeth when you bit into them in the fall, and the water from Blue Springs still tasted fresh and cold in a dipper. People still took care of one another in hard times, and you could still go down to Jesus Holiness on a Sunday morning and hear the preacher shout out a Jesus-praising sermon. On the other hand, Hal Clack and his kin still ruled the town with their liquor money and bullying ways, a sick person still had no real medical treatment close by, few roads connected them to the outside world, and except for logging, jobs were scarce as hens' teeth. Adding it all up, he figured he was as happy to have lived his days here as anywhere else on God's green earth.

Pulling his coat tight, Solomon gripped his cane hard and headed out into the November wind. The trip home gave him some time to do some thinking. Finding out that you only have a short time to live will set a body to doing that, he figured—cause you to see the final chores you need to finish, some fences you ought to mend, some words you should say.

By the time he walked into his yard, he had come to a pretty good idea of what he wanted to do with the months he had left.

After warming up by the fire, he took the coffee Elsa had made him and sat down at the table in the cooking area. Busy as always, Elsa stood at the stove, cutting some apples into a pan. Solomon reached out and tugged at the bottom of her apron.

"Come sit for a minute," he said. "You always working."

"You want some apple pie for tomorrow or not?" she said.

"Sure I do, but I want you to sit with me for a spell first."

Shaking her head, Elsa quickly finished the apples, set the pan to the side, and turned to Solomon. He pulled her over and, still sitting, hugged her close. She kissed him on the head. He looked up at her.

"You a good woman," he said. "I did a right smart thing when I married you."

Elsa smiled. "You doing a lot of flattering for a quiet man," she said. "What you got on your mind?"

Solomon grinned. "Maybe not what you got on yours, least not right now. Sit down here for a mite." He patted his lap and she accepted the invitation. He hugged her tight for several moments, letting himself enjoy the smell of her body, the softness of her skin. God had blessed him twice, he thought, first with Rose, then with Elsa. In spite of all the hard knocks he had suffered—little Solomon Jr. lost at birth, Rose dying, losing the land to Hal Clack, Walter succumbing to the flu, Laban being killed in the war, three babies gone before they were born—God had given him more than he deserved. And if he kicked off and went to glory tomorrow, he could still say he had lived a good life. He lifted his head from Elsa, took her face in his hands, kissed her on the cheek. She stared at him curiously.

"What you up to?" she asked.

He took her hands, held them to his chest. Then he told her, just as plain as that, what Doc Booth had said. How he had the cancer, maybe a year to live. How he had told the doc he would not go down to Asheville for more tests. How he would take whatever treatment Booth could give him but nothing more.

Elsa listened with her teeth set, her hands squeezing Solomon's. Halfway through his talking she started to cry. But he hushed her and told her not to worry, that he would fight the sickness and outlive anything old Doc Booth had to say. Brushing back tears, Elsa told him she wanted him to go to the Asheville hospital. He reminded her that some things nobody but the Lord could help. Besides, if he went to Asheville that meant he would have less time to be with her, and he didn't want that separation. She told him she could stay at Daniel's house, but then he said it didn't matter, that he wouldn't spend his last days away from Blue Springs Mountain. Elsa stopped arguing at that point and just kept on crying for a long time. Finally, when her tears had subsided a bit, at least for the moment, Solomon wiped her eyes with the end of her apron and hugged her again as tight as he could.

"I want you to write some letters for me," he said after a while. "One for each of my kids. Tell them you want them to come home for Christmas. Make it plain they need to come but don't tell them exactly why."

She leaned back and stared at him. "You want to tell them face to face about your sickness," she said.

"That's the idea," he said. "I want them here in the cabin, all together one more time, maybe the last time. I want to let them see I am not afraid of this. The Lord took good care of me all my life. I don't want them thinking anything but that. They need to hear me say I am still a Jesus man, ready to meet the Lord if that is the will the Lord has for me."

Elsa patted him on the chest. "You are a brave man," she said.

He shook his head. "Just trying to stay faithful. If I believe what the Good Book says, this ain't no time to go running scared."

She laid her head on his shoulder and they sat that way for a long time. The sun outside disappeared and night fell. The fire burned low but they didn't seem to notice. They had only a few months left, and they wanted to hold each other like this for as long as they could.

CHAPTER
THIRTY-FOUR

Christmas arrived on Blue Springs Mountain with a howling wind and a dusty snow that whirled in the air like dancing bits of salt. Daniel brought Deidre and his kids back to his pa's house. Abby came alone, explaining to everyone that Stephen had insisted he and the children ought to stay in Boone and see his folks this year since they had traveled to Blue Springs only a year before. Solomon could tell that Abby found that hard to take. The letter Elsa had sent her had her suspicions up, and she wanted her husband beside her when she discovered what it meant.

Luke didn't make it at all, but it was not his fault. Playing in a church over in Knoxville, Tennessee, he got stuck in a heavier snow than the one that hit Blue Springs and therefore couldn't make it. With the shortest distance to come than anyone, Solomon Jr. and his wife met everyone down at Jesus Holiness for the afternoon services on Christmas Eve, then joined them all on the trek back up the mountain. They made it home just after dark.

On the trip up, Solomon thought long and hard about keeping his sickness quiet until he could gather Luke with everybody else under one roof, and he told Elsa his notion when they got home. But she reminded him that he might never have another chance to do that so he might as well go on and tell those who had managed to come home. After a few minutes he agreed with her and asked her to gather everybody in the front room.

When she had done that, Solomon eased his way into a chair by the fireplace and looked around. One of Daniel's kids sat on his knees, Deidre beside him, his youngest baby asleep in the loft. By them sat Solomon Jr. and his wife, she a thin-faced woman with big eyes and bony shoulders. Abby rocked beside Solomon Jr.

Solomon feared for Abby sometimes, what kind of man she had married that he wouldn't come home for Christmas with her. But that was out of his authority now, nothing he could do.

Everybody still wore their coats to help the fireplace out. A small evergreen tree, decorated with popcorn and red ribbons, stood in the corner. The smell of fresh coffee hung in the air. The fireplace crackled as the dry wood burned. Elsa sat beside Solomon, her apron on and her hair pinned back.

A sense of peace and comfort rushed through Solomon. Whatever happened, he could deal with it, he and the Lord and his family together. He breathed a silent prayer for Luke, stuck in the snow, and Stephen, even though he didn't like him much, and his two grandchildren over in Boone. Even if he did not cotton to his son-in-law, the man had still sired his grandchildren and provided for his only daughter. Nothing all bad in a man that Abby would pick, he knew that for a certain.

Solomon cleared his throat and the room fell quiet. When he started speaking, his voice came out stronger than he had expected. "I am recalling Romans eight," he said, "the twenty-eighth verse. 'And we know that all things work together for good to them that love God, to them who are the called according to his purpose.'"

Heads nodded after he'd finished. They knew the verse too.

"Now I am not a-saying that the good Lord causes the bad things that happen to us in life," Solomon continued. "I'm just a-saying that in everything that comes to us, hard or easy, the good Lord can work out something helpful to us, something to make us better people."

Everybody but Elsa looked at him, puzzled as to where he might be heading with this. They had all suffered some and knew that. Life had knocked them about a bit and they had the scars to show for it.

"I found out a few weeks ago that I am a sick man," he said, seeing no reason to postpone the saying of the thing. "That is why I had Elsa send you a letter asking you to come home for sure this Christmas. Doc Booth tells me I got maybe a year, he can't say for sure, but that is his guess."

He paused to let the words sink in. Abby started to speak, but he held up a hand. "Let me finish," he said. "Then I will answer any question that I can."

Abby dropped her eyes, and Solomon spoke again. "Doc Booth told me to go to Asheville to the hospital down there. But I told him no. So, I don't want any of you trying to talk me into any of that nonsense. I come into this world in a log house, I plan to go out of it in one." He paused again but nobody spoke.

"Doc Booth will give me some medicine," he said. "And I will take what he gives me. But he says maybe it won't do much but ease my pain some when it comes. I don't hurt much now, let me say that plain so you won't worry. I am okay, for now. What will happen at the end, well . . . only the good Lord knows, and I will trust Him to see me through that when it comes."

He stopped and glanced around the room. Abby had her head down. Daniel stared at him with a look of confusion.

Solomon pointed to him. "You got something you want to say, Daniel?"

Daniel pushed his hands through his hair. "You ought to come to Asheville," he said. "Any man knows that. They might could help you there, give you longer."

Solomon shook his head. "I done said not to try to talk me into nothing. You will just waste your breath. One thing you know about me by now, when I make up my mind, there ain't no changing it."

Everybody nodded. They knew that about Solomon.

"Elsa will go on living here when I am gone," he said, hoping to put their minds at ease about a few things. "Solomon Jr. and his wife, Jewel, will come see her at least once a week. Later, if she needs them, they can move here or she there. She will decide that when the time comes. But she is a lot younger than me so that will not come for a long time." Solomon grinned and took Elsa's hand and squeezed it.

Abby lifted her head. A surge of anger ran through her, and she spoke before she could figure out why. "So what is the good that the Lord is doing in this, Pa?" she whispered. "Can you tell us that?"

Solomon heard the fear in her voice. He sagged in his seat. Of all his kids, he felt like he knew Abby least of all. It had been that way since the day of her birth, a distance between them like a canyon between two mountain peaks. He figured he carried most of the blame for that. A good pa would have fast put away his resentments about her living while her mama had passed on. A good pa would have found a way to warm up to her, to tell her plain out how much he loved her, how she made him proud with her studying and all, her ability to take care of herself all these years. But he had never found the words for such a thing and now the years had passed and he could see Death gaining on him from the back and time had about run out.

"I ain't sure just yet what the Lord is a-doing in all this," he told her honestly. "But I am trusting what the Book says. Somehow, before I move on to glory, I am expecting something worthy of praise to come forth, something that we will point to, or at least those of you left behind, will point to and say, 'There it is, that is what Jesus was doing.' I am trusting that will happen."

Abby shook her head, and Solomon could see he hadn't convinced her. But he had done his best to make her look for what God might do. Now she had to deal with it in her own heart as sweet Jesus wooed her spirit.

The fire crackled. Daniel asked a few more questions about how long Doc Booth thought he had left, and Solomon answered as best he could. Then the talk just frittered out, and everybody stood up and hugged one another and made their way toward their sleeping places.

Solomon lay down by Elsa and stared up at the ceiling, thinking about the night, realizing with sadness that Abby had not hugged him nor cried any. Of course, he hadn't gone to her either. And his eyes had stayed dry too. With a sudden insight that folks facing their last days sometimes get, he realized he couldn't remember a time when he really had hugged her, not a single instance when he had just wrapped her up in a big warm squeeze. Not when she left him to live with Mrs. Clack, not when she left Blue Springs to go to school, not when she married Stephen Waterbury. Try as he might, he could not recall a time when he had really held her close, and that made him sadder even than when Doc Booth had given him the news about his cancer.

Solomon found sleep hard to come by. He knew he needed to do something about the way he'd treated Abby all her life, but he had no idea what that was, and that scared him. He didn't want to die and have his baby girl wonder forever if he truly loved her. But after all these years, how could he go to her now? How could he convince her that he loved her? How could he change his ways at such a late hour?

His hands clasped on his stomach, Solomon fixed his eyes on the ceiling and tried to find an answer to his questions. Then it dawned on him, the way to show Abby how he felt. Since he didn't do well with words, he would have to go another way. And he now had a clear view of what that way was.

CHAPTER
THIRTY - FIVE

T he snow that had started falling just before Christmas took a break the next day—stopping just long enough to let all the Porter kin leave Solomon's house. But then it began dropping again, larger flakes this time, and so wet they stuck to your hat like they had molasses mixed in with them. The snow continued off and on for another three weeks, the white covering the mountains so thick it hurt the eyes just to look at it. Boxed up inside the cabin, Solomon studied long and hard over his intentions toward Abby. He examined the notion from every side, testing it to see any flaws, anything that could go wrong, what he could do if this happened, what he could do in case of that. From all he could tell, his idea seemed smart, maybe downright brilliant.

As January turned into February, the snow finally relented. But the cold set in next and locked the snow in place, a freeze so solid that Solomon slipped and slid a lot bringing wood in from the porch. He and Elsa spent the whole month holed up in the cabin, leaving only to feed the animals and bring in wood. Solomon saw no change in his health during this time. He still coughed a lot in the morning, but the amount of blood in his spittle stayed about the same and the lump in his side grew no larger from what he could tell. He thanked sweet Jesus for the fact that nothing became worse. To do what he wanted for Abby would take some time, though he didn't know exactly how much. So he prayed with all his breath that he would stay well long enough to do it before he died.

He nearly shouted on the first Tuesday of March when he woke up, made his way to the porch for wood, and heard the sound of dripping water. Afraid to believe his ears, he glanced over to the edge of the porch and saw the icicles melting. Moving to the steps, he looked up at the sun, noticed how warm it felt through his coat. From out of nowhere a robin landed in the yard and skipped toward him, its red breast plump. Taking a deep breath, Solomon grabbed up an armful of wood and stepped back inside.

"Looks like winter has broke!" he shouted to Elsa. "Snow is melting everywhere."

Elsa walked out from the cooking area, wiping her hands on her apron. "You mighty anxious for spring this year," she said.

Solomon nodded. He hadn't told her about his plans for Abby. "I got something to do," he said. "Gone take me away from home soon."

She went over to him and hooked her hands through the suspenders on his overalls. "What are you up to, old man?"

He laid his hands on her shoulders, looked into her eyes. "I am not long for this world, and I want my only daughter to think as well of me as you do. So I got something I got to do for her."

Elsa snuggled her head to his chest and said, "You mighty mysterious today."

Solomon smiled.

Daniel spent all winter and early spring in a state of low spirits. The frigid weather kept him from working much and that caused him some of his heartache. And the fact that his pa had the cancer added to it. But that was not the worst part. No, the truth was that loved ones took sick and passed on to their eternal reward all the time. Everybody knew that. It came with the territory. No extra cause to feel blue over that. What caused Daniel the most trouble was the understanding that his pa would die before he had a chance to regain his land for him. Which would mean that he had failed both Laban and Solomon, that his promises were no good, just empty words spoken when hard times visited but nothing more.

As April arrived and the weather warmed up enough for him to go back to his toiling, he thought long and hard again about going to Mr. Shaller and asking for a loan to buy back the land. After all, only a truly selfish man would let his pride keep him from doing something so good for somebody else. But then he remembered that he already lived in a house owned by Mr. Shaller, that Mr. Shaller had given him and Deidre a car and taken care of doctor bills more than once when his babies turned up sick. The truth of it was that Mr. Shaller had already given him a loan over and over again, and if he had had to pay for all the things Mr. Shaller provided for nothing, he wouldn't have as much money as he already did. To go to Mr. Shaller again wasn't just a matter of pride, it was a matter of what was right.

While convinced he'd reached a right conclusion, Daniel still wanted to make sure. So, on the second weekend of April, he took a trip to Blue Springs and met with Solomon down at the general store. The two took seats by the wood stove near the back. Solomon propped his cane on the wall by his head. A barrel with a checkerboard on top sat between them. The room smelled like sawdust and onions all mixed in together. Mr. Butler said hello to him and Pa, then left them and took up his broom to sweep in the back room. Solomon pulled off his hat and set it on the checkerboard.

"You looking healthy," Daniel said. "You didn't just make up that cancer talk so you can slack off your laboring, did you?"

Solomon chuckled. "Wish I was that smart," he said. "I would have done it a long time ago." He pulled out his pipe, knocked it on the bottom of his boot, and stuck it in his mouth but didn't light it.

Watching him, Daniel wondered if he would stay so calm when his time came, when the doctor said the words that told him how much time he had left on earth. Only a man of faith could meet Death with such a steady way.

"I made you a promise a long time ago," Daniel said, deciding to say right off what he had come to say. "You remember what that was?"

Solomon smiled. "Sure I remember. But sometimes things make promises hard to keep."

Daniel picked up a checker, rolled it in his hand. "I promised Laban the same thing," he said. "Right before he passed on."

Solomon pointed his pipe at Daniel. "You wanted to comfort your brother, no sin in that."

"But I meant what I said," insisted Daniel, his teeth together. "I meant it when I said it to you and when I said it to him."

Solomon laid his pipe on the checkerboard, placed his elbows on his knees, leaned forward. "You are a fine son," he said, "and a loving brother too. Nobody ever questioned you on that. But I got to say to you that what a man promises can't always be kept. Try as he might, a man comes up against things sometimes, things that he nor nobody else can stop, things he can't figure out, things that just knock him for a loop before he even sees it coming."

Listening to his pa, Daniel knew the truth of what he said. But he hated the notion of accepting it.

"You think I wanted to lose our land in the first place?" asked Solomon. "Of course not. And I have wondered ever day since then what I could have done to stop Hal Clack. Then I wondered what I could do to go re-claim my property. But you know what? I couldn't do nothing, not that day nor any day since. Sometimes a man just has to accept that. Just accept that he ain't got all the power under the sun, that his strength is limited and so is his ability to bend life to his will. It's a hard lesson, but it seems that the sooner a man learns it, the better off he will be." Solomon paused and leaned back.

Daniel thought about Solomon's words. His pa had just said more in one minute than he usually said in a month. But Daniel didn't like what his pa had said. "That sounds like giving up," said Daniel. "Just bending to the will of whatever comes to you. But Porter men don't give up."

Solomon chewed on his pipe, then said, "That is one way of looking at the thing. But I see it more like coming to peace with things. Striving as hard as you can strive, but then, when all is said and done, coming to peace with what is there, not always feeling like you failed just because something stays past your reach. Kind of like the apostle Paul saying he had become content in whatever way he found hisself."

For several minutes Daniel stayed still in his seat. Mr. Butler walked back in and started sweeping behind the counter.

"Pa, I have saved a lot of money," he said finally, "but I still don't have enough to buy back the land. So I want to take out a loan at Mr. Shaller's bank to pay for the rest."

Solomon stuck his thumb in the pipe, dug at the bowl. "I ain't one for taking no loans," he said. "The Good Book says 'Neither a borrower nor a lender be.' If a man can't pay for something up front or trade for it, then he don't need whatever it is he is buying."

"But I can pay it back," said Daniel. "In a few years, I can—"

Solomon held up a hand, stopping him in midsentence. "I forbid you to borrow money to keep a promise you made to me a long time ago. If you buy that land with borrowed money, then I won't take it, simple as that. I expect Laban would feel the same way if he could talk to you today."

Daniel lowered his head. What he'd figured would happen, happened. His pa didn't approve of him going to Mr. Shaller.

"It pleases me that you want to do this," Solomon said, his tone soothing. "But I hereby free you from the promise you made to me and Laban. Now all you got to do is free yourself. I expect that will go much harder."

Daniel wrapped his fist around the checker and squeezed hard. Solomon surely had it right. No matter if his pa freed him, he hadn't yet freed himself. So, as long as Solomon kept breathing, he would keep trying, even without a loan from Shaller. For Laban, for Pa, and for his own peace of mind, he wouldn't rest easy till he had the deed to the family land in Solomon Porter's hands once more.

CHAPTER
THIRTY-SIX

The rains fell hard and often the spring of 1929 and kept the creeks and streams in and out of Blue Springs running fast and foamy through almost all of May. Watching the rains, Solomon had to bide his time. But that did not mean he wasn't making some preparation for what he had to do.

Rising early, he walked down to Slick Rock Creek every morning, bent down and took a handful of water into his palm. He lifted the water to his nose and sniffed it, then poured the water into his mouth, worked his tongue over it for practice, rolling it out and back through his teeth and tasting it. If his plan had any chance of success, he had to know the water—the aroma, the touch and taste of it on his tongue.

As May ended, the rains stopped and Slick Rock started dropping lower, the water settling into its normal path, a soft splashing over the rocks—a trickle here, a bit of foam there. Kneeling by the creek at dawn during the second week of June, Solomon swallowed a handful of water and knew the time had come. The blood in his spittle was thicker by the day now, and the lump under his rib had started to hurt when he touched it or turned on it in the middle of the night. If he waited much longer . . . well, he would not consider that.

Standing, he moved back to the cabin and called Elsa to her chair by the fireplace.

"I got to go out now," he said. "Like I told you a few weeks ago. Don't rightly know how long my duties will take."

Elsa rubbed her hands on her apron. "Mind telling me what you going to do?"

Solomon coughed. He knew Elsa might fear for him if she knew his plans. But maybe, given his condition, her fears did not matter anymore. "I am going to make Hal Clack sell me that house of his," he said. "That way, Abby can see if Rose's letter might still be there."

Elsa laughed. "That's a silly notion," she said. "Wasting money like that."

Solomon shrugged. "Not a waste even if the letter ain't there. After I pass you might want to fix the place up and live there."

Elsa raised an eyebrow. "That's possible," she said. "As I get older, I might need to live in town again. So how do you plan to get Pa to sell you the place?"

"Your pa is piling up a whole lot of money from his whiskey-making. Everybody knows that the Prohibition has made it such that a man like him has more customers than ever."

Elsa nodded. Nothing new in any of this.

Solomon continued. "He must have four or five stills working all at once, maybe twenty to thirty men toiling for him."

Elsa scowled and said, "I still can't figure what this has to do with you."

"Easy," said Solomon. "I am going to find those stills. Then I am going to go to Clack and tell him that if he don't sell me that house, I will go to the revenuers with what I know."

Elsa caught her breath. "But a highlander who turns in another mountain man commits the worst kind of sin," she said. "To choose an outsider over a highlander, no matter how bad the highlander's deeds, is just not done."

"It's Clack or my girl," he said. "Which would you choose?"

Elsa nodded again, then asked, "How do you plan on finding the stills when revenuers all over the mountains can't manage it?"

Solomon grinned and rubbed his hands together. "That is the best part," he said. "I know an old trick. . . ." Then he told her what he planned to do. Her face lit up as he talked.

"I never heard of such a thing," she said. "But it makes some sense. A man with enough knowledge of the creeks could maybe do it."

"If the weather stays dry and the creeks stay low, I might just have a chance."

"You are a smart man, Solomon Porter."

"I been trying to tell you that for many a year," he said, grinning. "About time you took notice of it."

Solomon stayed out most of the next two months, coming home only when he needed provisions or to rest up for a couple of days. His beard grew out and became a scraggly mess, and his body lost at least ten pounds from all the walking he did up and down the mountain paths that surrounded Blue Springs. Spending the night wherever he found himself when the sun dipped, he ate cold food most of the time and didn't sleep well. All alone at night, he stared up at the sky when sleep didn't come and counted the stars and wondered why life took some of the twists it did. But the stars gave him no answers, and he figured maybe he should just trust the Lord in such matters and accept things as they were.

All day long for day after day he held to his cane and trudged up and down the creeks and streams that flowed into Blue Springs River, kneeling by the banks, dipping his hands into the water, tasting it, rolling it over his tongue. He carried a sack of provisions and a rifle, which were slung over his back. His side pain cut into him now when he moved a certain way, a stabbing pain that made his face hot and his right arm numb at the worst of it, and his breath seemed harder and harder to push in and out of his chest. He coughed a lot too, a hacking in his throat that shook his whole body and brought up stuff from his insides that he spit on the ground and covered over with his boot. He leaned on his cane as he pushed his body up and down the slopes, his hands turning white from the grip. The figure of Moses and the cane reminded him that others had struggled in the wilderness before him, that others had seen their hopes dashed at one point but raised again in another. God had seen Moses through his wilderness, so God would see him through his.

Holding to that belief, Solomon refused to let his sickness beat him. He would not give up and go home. The hope of pleasing Abby drove him forward, the goal of showing his girl that he did love her, of proving what he had so much trouble saying.

Moving upstream, he tried the water over and over, testing this small branch and that one, following the taste of the water where it took him and guessing some when he couldn't get the right flavor. Gradually, the tasting took him where he wanted, to one still after another hidden in the coves and hollers above Blue Springs. Over the summer months he found eleven different stills, each of them hidden beneath green thickets of laurel and rhododendron. Hiding in the woods to watch, he studied the size of the working area and the faces of the men who plied the illegal trade. Of the eleven stills he uncovered, he immediately left eight of them alone and moved on. The other three, though, he carefully marked on a piece of paper he carried in his shirt pocket. These three—one on a ridge just past Edgar's Knob, another in a cove about four miles past his old cabin, and a third to the northwest of Blue Springs in some wild territory he had never crossed—belonged to Hal Clack. Solomon knew this to be true because he hid in the woods and watched the stills long enough to see one of the Clack boys at each of them.

Armed with what he'd found, Solomon made his way back home near the end of August and told Elsa everything.

"I want to look for another week or so," he said, holding back a cough. "I expect there is at least one more big outfit out there. Probably over to the west just a little farther; I haven't checked over there too well just yet."

Elsa took his hands in hers, her eyes worried. "You are looking real tired. You sure you are not ready to go to my pa?"

Solomon shook his head. "I want to find every still I can. As long as Clack has one out there I don't know about, he will try and stonewall me. He knows that even if I shut down the three I've marked, that he can keep on making money, wait me out."

Elsa nodded. "You know my pa pretty well," she said. "He won't take easy to what you plan to do to him."

"I will take care," said Solomon. " 'Course there isn't a whole lot he can do to me. A pistol shot might be a favor."

"Don't even say such a thing!" Elsa said.

After a day and a night at home, Solomon left again, a sack of food over his shoulder, his side hurting bad. That night he camped as far west of Blue Springs as he had been in over ten years. But that didn't matter. He had one more still to find. When he had that one marked on his paper, he would leave the paper with Elsa and go have a talk with Hal Clack.

It took Solomon another two weeks to find Hal Clack's fourth still. Now his side felt like somebody had lit a fire in it, a fire that was burning him from the inside out. And he had come to the point where he coughed almost all the time, a cough that rattled around worse than marbles in a barrel. But again he refused to let his sickness stop him. Holding his cane as if clinging to life itself, he pushed on.

Near the end of the day of the second week, he tasted the water one more time, spit out the tainted liquid, and eased his way from the edge of Turkey Foot Creek, being careful to keep quiet. The sun overhead sloped away from him and everything fell into shadow. About thirty feet up from the creek he saw a narrow trail leading higher up the hill. Crouching, he picked his way up the trail. The underbrush thickened. The shadows shut out most of the day's light. A chill descended on the mountain, and Solomon knew he needed to pick up a heavier coat the next time he traveled home. Even in summer the higher elevations took on a nip when the sun went down. He stepped around a big rock, heard men talking. Pausing to listen, he tried to make out the voices. Hal Clack maybe? Or Topper or Ben? He couldn't tell.

Moving slowly, he lifted the sack of provisions from his back and set it on the ground. His cane followed. Then he took his rifle and gripped it steady, his eyes searching through the thick underbrush. The talking sounded closer. Sounded like at least four or five men, maybe more. A lot of men for a still, and they were not too careful about staying quiet.

Solomon's heart pumped harder. That many men meant it was a big still, and the fact that they took so little care about their talking meant they knew their boss had paid off the government men. The still had to be one of Clack's.

On his belly now, Solomon inched around a corner and found himself among a bunch of large boulders. The boulders provided an outlook over a small glade. The glade backed up to Turkey Foot Creek. The still was set up by the creek. Solomon saw five men sitting around it, Hal Clack among them. Pleased, Solomon closed his eyes for a second. He could go home now. See Elsa for a day, take a hot bath and shave, eat some good food, and gather up his strength. Then he would go see Hal Clack.

Something crunched behind him. Solomon froze in place, his finger on his rifle trigger.

"Hold it there, old man. I got the drop on you."

Solomon dropped his head to the ground. Ben Clack. He would recognize the voice anywhere.

"Throw that rifle over here," said Ben. "Real easy like."

Seeing as he had no choice, Solomon obeyed. Ben picked it up, told him to stand, then shoved his rifle into his ribs. Solomon ground his teeth against the pain in his side. A couple of minutes later, Ben Clack called out to his buddies as he pushed Solomon into the glade and threw him down at the fire beside the still. All the men except Hal Clack stood in a circle around Solomon. Hal Clack laughed out loud, his voice cackling over the mountains like a madman.

It took Clack a few minutes to stop laughing. When he did, he poked Solomon in the shoulder with a muddy boot. "What you doin' way up here, Solomon?" he said. "Ain't my daughter woman enough to keep you close to your own fire?"

Solomon's eyes blazed at the coarse man. What kind of pa would make such remarks about his own daughter?

"You lookin' mighty mean for a man in your position," said Ben. "I believe if I was you, I would try some sweetness."

Solomon's glare didn't change any.

Hal Clack toed him again and said, "I asked you what you was doing up here. A man don't get this far from home without some purpose."

"I was looking for you," Solomon said. "Except I didn't plan on you knowing about it."

"What you want with my pa?" asked Ben, raising his rifle to shoulder height.

Solomon coughed and spit out what the cough brought up. Hal Clack kicked him in the shoulder once more, and Solomon grabbed his boot and twisted it in his hand as hard as he could. Ben smacked him in the neck with his rifle butt. Solomon grunted against the pain but didn't let go of Clack's foot, so Ben grabbed him by the legs and pulled him away from his pa.

"Tie him up," Hal Clack ordered.

Ben obeyed quickly. Now Solomon lay on the ground with his hands tied behind his back, his feet also bound. The Clacks and the others all took their seats again.

Clack lifted a jug to his lips, then pointed the jug at Solomon. "You still ain't answered my question," he said. "What you want with me?"

"And how did you find us?" asked Ben.

"Yeah," said Clack. "How did you come to us here?"

Rolling over to face them, Solomon figured he had no reason not to answer. "An old trick," he said. "When you make as much whiskey as you do, you throw away a whole lot of meal and mash, still-slop, you know what it is. The stuff smells loudly. You throw it in the creeks where you get the water for your makings. If enough still-slop is thrown in, it fouls the stream. When the water is low and moving slow, a body can taste it if he is careful for it. Then all you do is follow the water upstream, go in the direction of the taste. I been trackin' your stills for a couple of months now. Done found four of them, expect that's close to all you got."

Hal Clack grunted, glanced at Ben and his other men. "You are a smart man," he said to Solomon. "You go to all that trouble to find me. But why not just go to Blue Springs? You know I stay there a lot these days."

"You can figure that out," said Solomon. "It ain't just you I wanted to find."

Clack squinted at Solomon. "You tryin' to locate my stills?"

"That's right."

"Dangerous thing you're doin'," said Ben. "A man better have a good rifle and a lot of help to do something like that."

"I got only one out of the two," Solomon said.

"Then you ain't as smart as you might think," said Hal Clack.

Solomon stayed quiet. The fire flickered in his eyes.

"We're waiting," Ben said. "Assuming you got some explanation."

Solomon knew he had no choice but to tell why he had come. Not the way he planned it, but maybe it didn't matter. "I've found all of your stills," he said. "I have them marked on two pieces of paper, one kept with Elsa and one down at the general store in Blue Springs. If I don't come home by the end of the week, Elsa will go to the sheriff down in Asheville with the papers, show them where to find your makings."

Hal Clack stood and leaned over him. Ben and Topper edged closer, their rifles in their hands.

"You got a good reason for such fool hardly actions, I figure," said Clack.

"I do," said Solomon. "You got your house in Blue Springs up for sale. I want to buy it."

They all laughed now, the sound of it rolling through the mountain air. Solomon let them play out their amusement.

"That's a crazy thing," said Ben. "What you want with that old house?"

Solomon hesitated, not wanting Clack to know his intentions but not wanting to lie either. If Clack knew he wanted the house so Abby could search it for her mama's letter, he might burn it down for spite. "Elsa wants it," he finally said, not untruthfully.

"She wanting to move back to town?"

"Who knows what a woman wants? I can offer you a hundred and fifty cash dollars for it."

Clack turned serious. "I got an offer of seven eighty-five. Why should I sell it to you so cheap?"

"Because if I tell the sheriff about your stills and he shuts even one of them down, much less all, that will cost you close to a thousand a week the way I figure it, given today's prices. That's why you will sell the house to me so cheap."

Ben raised his rifle, pointed it at Solomon's head. "Let me shoot him, Pa," he said. "Put him out of his misery."

Hal Clack raised his hand, stopping his son. "Why shouldn't I let him kill you?" he asked. "Then go get them papers from Elsa and the general store."

Solomon stared into Clack's eyes, tried to connect to whatever decency the man had left inside. "Don't matter none if you shoot me. I got the cancer. Doc Booth says I got less than a year. But Elsa, what you gone do to her? Shoot her too? Have you sunk that low, Hal? So low you would hurt your own flesh to get what you want? I know you ain't got much manliness left in you, but even somebody as mean as you won't sink that low, will he?"

Hal Clack looked at him a long time. Ben never lowered his weapon.

"You a crazy old coot," said Clack. "I ought to just shoot you like Ben says."

"Be doing me a favor," said Solomon.

"I can just move my stills," said Clack.

"A lot of trouble to do that. Cost you a whole lot of money. And they is mighty hid where they are. Sell me that house and leave your stills alone. Otherwise, the minute you get them back up and running, I will just start lookin' for them again. Will keep on doing it so long as I got breath."

Clack laughed once more, but Solomon thought the edge had gone out of it. "We been fightin' this battle a long time," Clack said. "Sworn enemies since we were no more than boys."

"That is the mountain way," said Solomon. "Feuding is as regular as frost in January."

"We both have paid a price for it. You lost your land, me my daughter."

"A high price," Solomon agreed.

"We both lost boys in the war too," said Clack, his tone gentler than Solomon had ever heard before. "Maybe it is time to let some old things die down some."

"I don't believe what I am hearing," said Solomon. "You going soft on me?"

Clack let out a cackle and kicked him in the ribs as if to quell any such notion. "You the Jesus man," he laughed. "Can't an old man change his ways?"

Solomon bit his lip against the pain. "Reckon so," he grunted.

"I got enough money for any ten men," said Clack, settling down some. "So what does it matter to me if you take that old house? I'm building a new one anyway." He turned to Ben and Topper. "It's too much trouble to move the stills," he said. "Let him go."

Ben started to argue, but Hal Clack stopped him with a shake of his head and said, "I ain't gone shoot him. Sheriff Rucker might not take kindly to that. And I'm too old to spend even a night in jail. So just keep your mouth shut and do what I say. Cut him loose."

Pulling out a knife, Ben sliced through the ropes on Solomon's wrists and ankles. "You ain't heard the last of this," Ben whispered as Solomon threw the ropes down.

Solomon nodded to Hal Clack. "I will see you in town next Monday," he said.

"You crazier than I am, Solomon Porter."

"Just bring me that house deed," said Solomon.

"Only because I don't want to move my stills," said Clack. "Not 'cause I'm going soft."

Solomon grinned under his beard, hurried back to the rocks, and picked up his cane and provisions. Then he left the glade, his ears on the ready just in case he heard anybody lifting a rifle behind him.

CHAPTER
THIRTY-SEVEN

D aniel slipped into the back of the church house and took a seat in the row farthest from the front. Wiping sweat off his face, he looked around the plain rectangular building, glad for a moment to catch his breath. The place was packed with men in overalls and women in simple cotton dresses. A row of men's hats hung on pegs on both sides of the building. Flies buzzed in and out of several open windows but no breeze came with them. A string of children darted up and down the aisles, their faces red with heat and excitement.

A door opened from the front right side, and five men walked in, two with guitars in their hands, one with a banjo, another with a mandolin, the last one with a black Bible. Daniel kept his eyes on the man in the front of the group, a shorter version of himself, but softer at the edges and thicker from less physical work and no doubt better food. The man was his brother Luke, the brother he hadn't seen in nearly a year. Luke wore a white shirt and a black string tie, a pair of gray pants, and black shoes with silver buckles on top. Oil slicked back his hair, and his lips curled up in a bright smile. He looked happy.

The man with the Bible stepped up to the wood pulpit that stood front and center and said, "It is good for all you fine folks to join up with us for tonight's singin'. The Good Book says we ought always to stand ready to make a joyful noise unto the Lord." He grinned and turned to the musicians. "These old boys don't just make a noise," he said. "They make some sweet music."

"Amen!" somebody shouted. The preacher faced the congregation again. "You know these boys," he said. "They have blessed our hearts more than once. But in case you are just coming to our church for the first time, these boys are the Jubilees for Jesus Band and they gone bless our hearts tonight with some music that will make you swear you done died and gone to heaven."

"Praise the Lord!" somebody hollered from the back. Holding up his Bible, the preacher said, "Now, let me tell you right before we start that when we are finished with this, I am gone ask you to give what you can for an offering for these boys. The Good Book says a laborer is worthy of his hire, and these boys got to make a livin' like everybody else. So when the time comes, I am asking you to drop in what you can. Don't make your kids go hungry and don't give to the point that they gone throw you out of your house next week, but remember that the Good Book says that God loves a cheerful giver. So dig in your pockets with a smile on your face and give these boys what you can. All right?"

The congregation nodded. A child ran from the front pew to the back, disappeared out the door.

"All right then," said the preacher. "We gone pray and then we gone just lean back and let these boys sing us right into the presence of the Master." He bowed his head and everybody followed suit.

His eyes closed, Daniel put his face in his hands and considered his troubles. The busy season for his work had just about ended for the year, and he had saved only a little more money. Elsa had sent him a letter saying that Solomon had become so sick he had to cut back on his laboring, that he now spent at least half of every day just sitting on the porch or lying flat in his bed. He coughed nonstop now, and his belly had swelled up so much that the skin felt tight when she touched it. She didn't know how much longer he might make it, and maybe Daniel ought to come see him real soon.

The prayer ended, and Daniel opened his eyes. Luke edged a couple of steps toward the congregation and began strumming his guitar and singing. While listening to his brother, Daniel kept his head down. He hadn't told Luke he was coming to hear him. Fact was, he hadn't known himself till about three quarters of the way through the day. He had seen a poster a couple of weeks ago in the hardware store where he bought a lot of his bricking supplies. It said that Luke Porter and the Jubilees for Jesus Band were coming to the Valley Branch Revelation Church on the last Saturday night in September to sing for the Lord. But the church was a good ten miles west of Asheville, and trying to do as much work as possible before winter set in, he didn't know if he could find the time to get there or not. About halfway through the day though, he just got the feeling he ought to go.

The feeling fell on him right after he ate a piece of fried chicken about two in the afternoon. A sense that he wanted to see his brother, to talk with him. Maybe it was because he knew his pa was looking at his last days. Or maybe it was because he felt like such a failure in regard to his promise about the land. Daniel didn't know for sure. Whatever the reason, he started to feel lonely after he'd finished eating and knew that, no matter what else, he wanted to see Luke that night. At a time like this, brothers needed to do some talking with each other.

Leaving his crew to finish up, he drove fast to his house, told Deidre his plans, washed off and changed his clothes, then headed out to Valley Branch. It took longer than he figured to reach the place. The last couple of miles he drove over a road so narrow the wheels of his car just about covered it on both sides.

Luke finished his song, and the crowd shouted "Amen" and "Praise Jesus," and before they had all quieted down, he had started in on another one. Watching him, it amazed Daniel that he did so well in front of all these people. When Luke sang, his stuttering all but disappeared so that nobody could tell that his brainpower didn't measure up to everybody else's. His musical gifts covered up a whole lot of his other shortcomings.

Daniel wondered about his own gifts. Sure, he was smarter than Luke, but not so much so that it gave him any real advantage over the rest of the world. And yes, he got along well with people, but not enough to take up politicking or something like that. To be real honest, he didn't see anything that made him stand out from the crowd, except maybe that he could work most men into the ground, a tolerance for labor that maybe only a strong-backed mule could match.

The singing up front kept right on moving. And Daniel, though he kept one ear tuned in, kept right on doing his thinking. Right near the end of the hour and a half of singing and picking, it dawned on Daniel that maybe this was at least a partial reason he had come to see Luke—he needed some time to just sit down and mull over a few things. Things like Pa dying. And a brother he no longer knew too well. Plus, his own failings, the worst one being that he didn't keep promises too good.

Daniel hung his head, his heart heavy. The Jubilees for Jesus finished up with a rambunctious version of "When the Roll Is Called Up Yonder," and the people in the church called out "Amen" and "Hallelujah" so loud that Daniel thought the roof might come off the place. But it didn't, and the preacher got back up and prayed again. Then four men in overalls stood as one and passed two wicker baskets down the pews to take up the collection.

Easing out of his pew, Daniel walked out the door, slipped on his hat, and made his way around the side of the church to the door Luke had used when he entered the building. The sun was almost gone, and the air chilled him some. He stuck his hands in his pockets. Since he didn't often take this much time off from work, he knew his coming would surprise Luke. He kicked a boot at the ground, wished he had spent more time with his brother. Time sure moved along fast, he decided. Here he was thirty-seven years old already and he still lived in another man's house and felt like a stranger to his own family. What kind of life was that? True, he had a good woman and three upstanding children and a reputation as an honest man and a fine bricklayer. Yet, somehow right now, that didn't seem like enough. His pa's sickness had made that plain to him, had told him that time moved along quicker than a river after a heavy rain, and if he wanted any changes in his life, he better do something about it pretty quick.

The door to the church opened. Daniel stood up straight. Luke led the group out, his guitar slung over his back, his face smiling. Strange, thought Daniel, how in spite of the fact that Luke was older, he had always seen himself as the big brother. Reckon this was because Luke was slow. Right now, though, he wanted Luke to act like the older brother that he was, wanted Luke to somehow comfort him, offer him a strong shoulder to lean on.

He balled his fists in his pockets and told himself to stop wishing such useless things. About halfway down the steps, Luke spotted him.

"Hey, brother," said Daniel, opening his arms. "You singing mighty good there."

Luke laughed, and the two hugged. Luke turned back to the rest of the Jubilees. "You b-b-boys recall my little b-b-b-brother Daniel, don't you?"

Each of the Jubilees shook Daniel's hand.

"Y'all are mighty good," Daniel said. "Best I've heard in these parts."

The Jubilees thanked him. Luke handed his guitar to one of them, and then he and Daniel stepped away by themselves.

"You just sh-sh-sh-showed up from nowhere," said Luke.

"I just decided today," explained Daniel. "Wish I could hear you more often."

"Mighty g-g-glad to see you."

They came to a car. Daniel noted that it looked pretty new. Luke placed a foot on the front bumper and asked about Daniel's family. Daniel leaned against the hood, said everybody was fine. He then asked Luke about his woman friend. Luke grinned and said he had broken it off with her.

"I s-s-s-saw Pa a couple of weeks ago," Luke said, obviously wanting to change the subject. "He d-d-don't look too good."

Daniel nodded. "I reckon that's a big reason I come to see you," he said. "Seems we both ought to go home and sit with him every chance we get now."

Luke hung his head. "I d-d-don't get home as much as I sh-sh-should."

Daniel patted his back and said, "None of us do. Life gets pretty busy."

Luke gently kicked the bumper of the car. "I am g-g-g-grieved that he is so sick. He d-d-d-deserves to live a whole lot longer."

"I wish it worked that way," said Daniel. "But I reckon we don't always get what we deserve. Good for us, though, huh?"

Luke grinned. "You and me might be long g-g-gone by now if a body got what he d-d-deserved."

Daniel laughed but then turned grim as he remembered all his failings again. The two brothers stayed quiet for a moment. The crowd from the church started leaving, with a rush of children coming out first.

"I w-w-wish I could do something for him," said Luke. "To m-make his last days easier."

Daniel shook his head. "You and me both. I been wanting to do that for a long time." He brushed his eyes to keep from tearing up.

Luke put a hand on Daniel's shoulder, then said, "You have done all you c-c-could. All anybody could do."

Daniel pulled away from his brother, faced in the opposite direction. People passed by them on the way out of the church, but other than throwing up a hand to say good-bye, nobody interrupted them. Daniel wondered if it was just their mountain shyness, or did the people sense something between him and his brother. He squared his shoulders and faced Luke again.

"I let Pa down," he said, his head low. "Let him down bad."

"What you mean?" asked Luke. "You worked harder to please Pa than any of us. G-g-go see him a lot more than me."

"A promise I made him," said Daniel, his heart aching to let out what he had kept bottled up so long, to confess to somebody else how bad he'd messed up. "A long time ago."

"What kind of p-p-promise?"

Daniel moved back to the car, leaned on the hood again. Luke kept his eyes straight on Daniel. Taking a deep breath, Daniel told him then, poured out to his big brother how he had told Pa and Laban that he would re-claim the land. How he had worked all these years trying to save money to buy back the property. How he had gone to Clack, then to Tillman, thinking he had enough money but then finding out he did not.

Luke listened without comment, his eyes never leaving Daniel's face, his body not moving. When he'd finished, Daniel put his head in his hands and stared at the ground. There, he had said it out, all his failures as a son and a brother.

He thought he heard Luke chuckling softly. Not believing his ears, he glanced up at his brother. Sure enough, Luke had a grin on his face. For a second Daniel couldn't respond. How could he? He admits what a bad man he is and his brother starts to laugh? What had come over Luke?

Anger rushed to Daniel's stomach. "I see no cause for mirth," he said. "A man should not poke fun at another man's failings."

Luke's whole body began rolling with laughter. Daniel jumped off the car and grabbed him by the arms, squeezed his hands into Luke's flesh. But Luke just kept on laughing, louder and louder.

Confused, Daniel let go Luke's arms and started to draw back a fist. A man couldn't take such embarrassment as this, not even from his brother!

Luke held up his hands, palms out. "D-d-don't go to pounding on me," he said, gaining enough control to talk. "I know how s-s-s-strong you are."

"Then stop laughing!" said Daniel as he dropped his hand. "And tell me what is so funny."

Luke put his hand over his mouth and pushed back a final laugh. "I ain't a-laughing at you. Just how crazy life c-c-can be sometimes." He took another second and then his face became more serious. "All this t-t-time. You needing money. And me with enough to pay for that land three t-t-times over but never thought of d-d-doing it."

Daniel sagged back against the car. Words failed to come for several seconds as he thought about what Luke had just told him. "I don't figure it," he finally said. "How in the world—"

"I been l-l-living alone for all these years," said Luke. "Makin' good money from all over and with nothing really to spend it on. I got a whole s-s-stack of dollars at my place over in Hickory. How much you need?"

While he knew that highlander men did not do such things, Daniel didn't fight the tears that rolled from his eyes. Instead, he hugged his brother as hard as he could and breathed a prayer of thanks to the Lord that such miracles as this still happened in the backwoods part of the world where he lived.

CHAPTER
THIRTY-EIGHT

Abby stood in front of the Hal Clack house in Blue Springs on the third week of October, her shawl pulled tight around her shoulders, her hair pinned back in a bun. A light wind played on her cheekbones, and a scattering of leaves blew over her black boots. The house looked awful. Paint peeled off the walls, and one side of the front porch sagged where the wood had rotted out. Two of the four front windows were broken, and weeds ran wild up and down the yard.

Clutching the deed to the house in her hands, Abby wondered again how it had come about that she now had ownership of the property. Elsa had brought her the deed less than three weeks ago, handing it to her on the front porch of her house without any explanation how she got it. After she had recovered some from her initial shock, Abby had pressed her on the matter, asking again and again how she had obtained the house. But Elsa just shook her head and dropped her eyes.

"Did you go to your pa?" Abby pushed. "Ask him for this?"

Elsa said nothing. Abby thought it over some more yet saw no other possibility. Elsa must have decided to press her pa to give up the old house. Maybe she wanted to live in it after Solomon passed. Then, for reasons she couldn't imagine, Hal Clack had given in to his daughter's urging. Seeing that Elsa refused to say anything else, Abby finally gave up, hugged her, and accepted the house deed.

It had taken her almost a month to put things in order enough at home to make the trip to Blue Springs. Not that she didn't want to come earlier. Truth was, she had thought of little else since Elsa first brought the news about the house. And that in spite of her having learned for certain that another baby was now growing in her body. The first of the month had made it so plain she couldn't deny it any longer. But for today the new baby could wait.

Stephen could wait too. Abby bit her lip as she remembered how Stephen had responded when she told him that Elsa had given her the house, and she wanted to go to Blue Springs to see it.

"Why do you want to do that?" he demanded to know when she'd told him after supper a few days before. "It is just an old house."

Not knowing what else to say, Abby told him about the letter from her ma, how she needed to see if it still existed.

Stephen chuckled and shook his head. "Why don't you grow up?" he said roughly. "No reason to go poking around in the past like that. Leave it alone. You have too much here at home to do to go running around up in that godforsaken place."

"I am going to do this," said Abby, the words rushing out before she could think to stop them.

"What if I say you cannot?"

Abby squared her shoulders. Her face flushed. It wasn't like her to conflict with her husband in such a way, but she had waited her whole life to hear a word from her ma, and she wouldn't let anything stop her from it now, not even her husband. The trip would only take a couple of days, and then she could return home and never clash with Stephen like this again.

"I will do this," she insisted. "No matter what you say or do."

Stephen stood from the table and walked out of the house. When he came home about three hours later, he smelled like whiskey and refused to speak as he dropped off into bed. The days since then had brought more silence. But this had not stopped Abby from carrying out her plans.

Her breath coming quickly, Abby pushed through the weeds and stepped onto the porch. Again she stopped. A flurry of feelings swirled in her stomach. Despite the problems her family caused, Mrs. Clack had made her time here reasonably happy. She had left here every morning to go to school and come back every night to do her studying. Without this house she would never have left the mountain, would never have gotten an education and bettered herself.

But the house had brought her pain too. Like the scare she had when Ben Clack tried to pin her down and take advantage of her; like the day a drunken Hal Clack attacked her; like the day the Clack men ran her out and sent her back to Blue Springs Mountain.

Abby wondered what, if anything, she would find inside the house. Had Mrs. Clack kept the carving she left behind? Perhaps so. And what about the letter? The wind picked up at her back. Only one way to know for sure. Go into the house and search it.

Abby took the key that Elsa had given her and stuck it in the door lock. Twisting it, she opened the door and stepped inside. The room smelled of sour whiskey and old sweat. Brown leaves lay in one corner where they had blown in through the broken windows. Bits and pieces of worn-out clothes were strewn on the floor in every direction.

Moving slowly, Abby stepped from room to room, not looking for anything in particular but taking in the sights and sounds. All the rooms had the same feeling that the entry area had—a sense of haphazard use and poor housekeeping. The house had only two closets: one in the bedroom where Mrs. Clack had slept and one in the bedroom where Abby had been allowed to stay. Both closets were empty.

Though she'd told herself not to expect anything, Abby's shoulders still slumped as she moved to the kitchen and searched the pantry next to the sink. Other than a dusty jar of pickles and a few potatoes that had molded on top, she found nothing. She stood in the center of the kitchen floor and wondered what to do next. Then she remembered the old shed in the backyard. Maybe the Clacks had left some things out there. Passing the kitchen sink on her way to the back door, she recalled the day Clack had knocked her down, how Mrs. Clack ran to her rescue as she lay on the floor by the trapdoor to the cellar. She smiled. Mrs. Clack had turned out just fine. Gratitude rushed through Abby.

She walked over to the trapdoor that covered the ladder going down to the cellar. For several seconds she stood over the cellar and thought of Amelia Clack. How strange. The woman she had figured would dislike her the most had come to care for her almost like a daughter. What at the time seemed so bad—living with her after Laban lost the land—had

380

turned out for the good. It occurred to Abby that such a thing happened pretty often in her life, maybe in others' lives too. Grief leading to joy, hardship to achievement. Was that the way it was for everybody?

She pondered on the notion and decided not. At least not all the time. Some people never seemed to find the good after the bad, the joy from the sorrow. Some people just kept right on suffering, one misfortune acting like quicksand that pulled them down lower and lower until they suffocated under the pull of it all.

Abby wondered why. Was it that the people who never found a way out of the bog didn't do the right things to escape it? Was it a flaw in their character that kept them all sucked down in their living? Or did the good Lord have it all stacked out against them that way from the beginning? A load of bricks hanging over them that was going to drop on their shoulders no matter how much they dodged this way or that? But this seemed unfair to her. Why would God give her a way out of life's ditches but not somebody else?

Rubbing her forehead as if to push away the mystery of it all, Abby started to leave the house. At the back door, though, it suddenly dawned on her that she needed to check the cellar. The Clacks could have stored a few odds and ends down there over the years.

She turned and walked back, dropped to her knees, and unhooked the latch on the trapdoor, then lifted it up. A musty smell rose up from the dark hole. Unable to see to the cellar floor, she stood and wondered where she could find a match. She saw a drawer by the sink and went and opened it to find some tangled fishing line, three black socks, and a bent spoon. Beneath the socks she found half a candle. By the candle was a box with four matches inside.

After lighting the candle, Abby held it down into the cellar, planted her feet on the ladder, and eased down. At the bottom she swept the candle in all directions. A rat scurried away, and she involuntarily took a step back. But then, gritting her teeth, she bent low to avoid bumping her head and moved to the center of the square space. Turning from side to side, she peered into each corner. Spider webs draped down from the ceiling in a ghostly blanket of gray. A couple of empty wood boxes sat to her left. A man's hat, the top crumpled inward, rested by the boxes.

By the hat Abby spotted a pair of yellow eyes staring at her. The rat! The eyes reminded her of Ben Clack's eyes when he had caught her among the cedar trees, his foul breath breathing on her neck.

Feeling sick to her stomach, Abby almost stumbled as she backed up. She wanted to run from the place, to get away from anything and everything connected to the Clacks. Surely she would find nothing here. She started to move toward the ladder, but something stopped her. A fluttering in her chest that said if she left the cellar without searching it completely, she would never forgive herself. She'd come this far, so she might as well see it through, rat or no rat.

Abby steeled her spine and turned one more time to see into the last corner. She almost dropped the candle when she spied a round basket in the corner's shadows. The basket was at least two feet high and about half as wide. Could it be Aunt Francis's basket? After all these years?

Forgetting the rat, Abby clenched the candle with both hands and told herself to calm down. It might not be Francis's basket at all. And even if it was, it might be empty, might not contain anything but a bit of string and a few sewing needles.

Not allowing herself to hope yet, Abby stepped to the basket, leaned over and picked it up. A second later, with her hands shaking, she took a seat on one of the boxes, placed the candle on the floor, then flipped open the basket. A black Bible lay on top of a stack of gray wool cloth. Thinking the letter might be in the Bible, she quickly flipped through its pages but found nothing. She lifted the cloth and unfolded it and shook it out. Nothing there. She looked back into the basket. A tan dress was lying under the cloth. Abby pulled out the dress. Beneath it she saw the carving of her mama her pa had made so many years ago.

For a moment she sat perfectly still and stared at the carving as if it were a snake that might bite her at any second. But then she reached for it, her hand moving slowly toward the finely cut wood. The carving rested on another piece of gray wool. Abby pulled the carving out and held it up to inspect. The face on the figure looked almost alive as the candle flickered on it, the shadows making the lips and eyes seem to move. Abby sucked in her breath. The face mirrored her own, the curve of the cheekbones, the sweep of the eyebrows, the purse of the lips. Anybody seeing the carving and her at the same time would swear that the carver had used her as a model. No wonder her pa looked at her strangely sometimes, like he had just seen a spirit come to life. And no wonder he found it hard to take to her. Spending time with her no doubt brought up too many painful memories to do it very often.

A sense of understanding suddenly rolled through Abby, a sense unlike anything she had ever known. Her pa's hesitance around her came from the fact that he had loved her ma so deeply. Why should she hold that against him?

But then she shuddered. Why should he take out his hurt on her? She deserved better than that. It wasn't her fault that she took after her mama. Why couldn't Solomon just see her as a gift, a living reminder of all the good times he shared with Rose instead of as a reminder of the hurt that came over him when she died?

Abby held up the carving once more, then started to put it back in the basket. She saw the gray cloth, pulled it out to wrap around the carving. A folded piece of paper lay inside the cloth. Abby's heart nearly stopped. The paper was brown at the edges, and a small piece had torn off. Not sure whether to believe it or not, she gently touched the paper with her index finger, poked it as if to see if it were real. When it didn't disappear at her touch, she lifted the paper from the basket and placed it in her lap. She left it there for several seconds, her mind reeling. Was this the note from her mama?

In one way, she hoped not. Who knew what such a note would change in her, how it would make her different. Would that change make her life better or worse? Sometimes when a body wishes so hard for something, it turns out bad when they actually get it. Abby picked up the paper. Another, much bigger part of her hoped desperately that this was indeed her mama's final words to her.

Her fingers trembling, she unfolded the paper, pressed it out flat, and held it up to the light. The candle's flame made shadows across the page. Abby studied it closer. The handwriting was small and scratchy. Her throat closed, like somebody had it in a vise. The candle seemed to stop flickering. Time felt still as Abby read the letter.

My dearest Abigail, I will not be with you when you read this. Not much time. I love you. Your life springs from mine. I am about gone. Sorry I will not be there for you. Your pa is of few words. Will take my passing hard. Might not know how to love you right. Listen. If anything comes between you and him, it will be your need to go to him. He won't know how to come to you. Won't have the necessary words. He will love you. I know it. But it won't go easy for him. Whatever happens, you say what needs saying. That is my hope. I am tired. Going to Jesus. You are a highlander woman. Be proud of that. I love you always.

Rose, Mama

Abby put the letter back in her lap. The candle flickered again. She took a deep breath. For the first time since the death of her aunt Francis, she ignored her pa's words about crying and let the tears stream down her cheeks.

It took Daniel almost two weeks to track down Tillman at his place of business. When he finally did find him, he received the news that the land deal Tillman had told him about last September had already gone through, only some final paperwork left to finish to make it official. Though worried about the news, Daniel refused to accept it.

"Is the deal final?" he pressed Tillman.

"Not exactly," said Tillman, twisting his mustache. "But everything is in place. You came about a month too late."

"I'll give you two hundred dollars more than the Raleigh folks are paying you," insisted Daniel. "Make it worth your while to sell it to me."

Tillman eyed him from under an arched eyebrow. Daniel tried to look confident. "How do I know for sure you even got that kind of money?" asked Tillman. "That if I stop my deal in Raleigh, that you can come through with what you've promised?"

Daniel glanced around the office. "You got a phone?"

"Yeah," Tillman said, pushing out his chest with pride.

"Call up the Buncombe County Bank then," said Daniel. "The money is right there, all of it and then some." Daniel realized he had sounded high and mighty, but still, he did have it, thanks to Luke, who had handed him over two thousand dollars.

"Every d-d-dollar I got," Luke had said as he took the wadded money out of a wood crate he kept under his bed. "You can have it all for P-P-Pa and Laban."

Tillman rose from behind his cluttered desk and walked around to Daniel. "You are a mighty determined man," he said, fingering his mustache. "My friends in Raleigh won't like this sudden change."

"I am determined," Daniel said. "Make it four hundred more than they are paying you."

Tillman paused and twirled his mustache. Daniel could see he had him thinking. A man like Tillman sold to the highest bidder. Daniel felt sure he was trying to decide if he could get more from the Raleigh people, match or go past his four-hundred-dollar increase.

Tillman cleared his throat, then stuck out his hand. "It will take a few days to contact the folks in Raleigh," he said. "Deal with the paperwork for a switch like this. But for four hundred dollars I would just as soon sell the land to you as to a bunch of strangers from downstate. You bring me some proof you got the money, I will see what I can do. You deliver me the cash, maybe the land is yours."

Trying to keep his emotions in check, Daniel stood, took Tillman's hand and pumped it hard. A smile beamed across his cheeks. In just a few days he would go to Solomon and give back to him the one thing he wanted most in the whole world, and Daniel's promise would find its finish.

"I want it settled as soon as possible," he said. "I got a sick pa. Would like to get this done before he passes."

"Just get me the money, I'll do the paperwork."

CHAPTER
THIRTY-NINE

Abby made her way to Blue Springs Mountain on Monday, the last week of October, a day of clear blue skies and warm temperatures. She came without talking to Daniel or Luke and took along Jimmy and Stevie, leaving Stephen in Boone. "Too busy" he had said when she pleaded with him to come with her. "And your pa could care less." Her mind occupied with other matters, Abby decided not to argue.

She arrived in Blue Springs about midway through the afternoon, left the children with Lindy and Jubal, and climbed alone up the holler to her pa's place. Though she'd thought about little else since discovering her ma's letter, she still didn't know how to respond to it. She knew she needed to do something, but she didn't know what. Her mama had said she should go to Solomon. But why was it her responsibility? He had never come to her, had never shown her anything but a separateness—a space of silence she had no clue how to cross. Truth was, her mama's words had made her angry, upset that they put so much pressure on her to make things right with her pa.

When she approached the cabin, Abby found Daniel and Luke already there, the two of them sitting on the porch, three sleepy dogs at their feet.

As usual, Luke had his guitar in his lap. Abby realized for the first time that his guitar playing might have started because he didn't have to talk much while strumming. But then it had become a way to live, a gift and a job all at the same time. She envied him, his nimbleness on the strings.

They stood to greet her, all of them expressing surprise to see one another.

"You by your lonesome?" Daniel asked, giving her a hug.

"My husband is a busy man," she said as explanation. "People depend on him." Abby felt bothered that Stephen had refused to come yet she didn't let it show.

Daniel opened his mouth as if to speak but then apparently thought better of it and said nothing. She studied him a second. He seemed pleased about something, his eyes all lit up. She and Luke hugged.

"Where's Deidre and your kids?" she asked Daniel.

"They staying up with Uncle Pierce and Aunt Erline. Not enough room here."

"Uncle Pierce and Erline doing okay?"

"Yeah," said Daniel. "But they don't get out much, not even down to church."

Abby nodded. Though her pa's brother and sister-in-law lived only a short distance away, few people ever saw them except when they went to their place.

"When did you two come?" Abby asked.

"J-j-just a l-little while ago," said Luke.

"Been here no more than a couple of hours," said Daniel. "Ain't even talked to Pa yet. He's asleep."

Elsa stepped onto the porch, wiping her hands on her apron. Abby hugged her, genuinely grateful for all Elsa had done for her over the last few years. Elsa led everybody into the house.

"Daniel said Pa is resting," Abby said.

Elsa nodded. "He mostly sleeps a lot these days. Doc Booth gave him something that knocks him clean out."

"Probably half whiskey," said Daniel, grinning.

"Just don't tell Solomon that," Elsa said. "He will refuse to drink it if you do."

Abby looked around the cabin. Over the years, Solomon and Elsa had taken a rough-cut bunch of logs and made something right presentable out of them. Curtains hung over the glassed windows, and a couple of pictures adorned the walls. A hat tree had replaced the nails in the walls.

Solomon had made a fancy mantel with wheat-shaped carvings and put it over the fireplace. He had also put in some new floors, all shiny and smooth with store-bought varnish. For highlander folks, they had done real well—a testament to her pa and Elsa both.

"I'd like to look in on Pa," Abby said.

"Come on then," said Elsa. "Just stay quiet so as not to wake him."

Abby nodded. Daniel and Luke stayed by the fireplace. Elsa led her down the narrow hallway. At the door to their room, Elsa stopped and looked at Abby, her eyes searching her straight through.

"He has asked about you a lot," she whispered. "Wants to talk to you."

Abby knew that Elsa had told Solomon about giving her the Clack house. Maybe he wondered if she had gone there yet, if she looked for her mama's letter, if she found it and what it said if she had. It suddenly dawned on her that Elsa may also be wondering if she had the letter, wondering if Rose Porter's words would change Abby's life any, or her connection to Solomon. Although she hadn't yet figured out what she wanted to do with her mama's last words, Abby now knew she had to speak to Solomon about them, could not let him pass on without telling him she'd found the letter.

"As soon as he's awake, I will speak with him," said Abby, keeping everything else to herself.

Elsa nodded in acceptance, and then, pushing on the door, she led Abby into the bedroom. Abby stepped past her and saw Solomon on the bed. An oil lamp burned on a table beside him and cast shadows over his body. His hair had grown out and turned grayer. It was spread out behind his head, all long and wavy. His eyes were closed and sunk deep into his skull. Always a strong man, he looked skinny now, his bones sticking to the edge of his skin. He snored softly.

Abby wrinkled her nose. The room smelled stale. Abby remembered the smell of the room where Aunt Francis had passed on. The smell in Solomon's room matched that one. Her heart felt as heavy as a big rock.

She turned to Elsa and left the room. Back with Daniel and Luke, she held back her tears and prayed with all her heart that her pa would wake up one more time so she could talk with him before he crossed the river to glory.

Daniel spent the next twenty-four hours trying to keep from walking into Solomon's room and grabbing him by the shoulders and shaking him until he woke up. Here he had the best news he could remember inside his head and he couldn't tell it to his pa. Wanting Solomon to be the first to hear, he hadn't told it to anybody else either, not even to Deidre. Truth was, she did not even know about the new money in the bank because he had sworn to secrecy the teller who took the cash deposit.

Unable to sleep, Daniel passed the night in a dither, his head aching. What if Pa never woke up? What if he never had the chance to tell him he had the money to buy back the land, that it was as good as theirs? All they had to do was wait on some papers to come back from Raleigh and then everything Laban had lost so long ago would return to them.

The notion that his pa might die without hearing what he had done made Daniel's chest hurt. Could it happen like that? If so, then what did it all mean, his efforts all these years, his hard toiling and steady saving? Could all that come to naught? His life's hopes shot to pieces, like a jar busted up by a rifle bullet? Daniel felt quivery in the stomach at the thought.

Doc Booth stopped by about midday on Tuesday and checked on Pa. He came out shaking his head, not wanting to look anybody in the eye. But Elsa cornered him, held him by the arm, and told him to give it to her straight.

"He's in a coma," said Booth. "Not much longer for this old world."

Daniel's neck tensed. He saw Abby grab her throat. For a long minute, silence hung in the room. Then Luke stuttered out what Daniel wanted to ask but couldn't dare. "Y-y-you reckon he's g-g-gone come to anymore?"

The air sucked out of the room.

Booth inspected his boots. "It is up to the Lord," he said. "Maybe, maybe not."

Daniel's throat closed on him. Booth hugged Elsa and Abby, shook Luke's and Daniel's hands, and left. Another night passed. Nobody talked much. Quiet fell on the cabin, kind of like the silence in a church right before the service starts, a quiet when everybody waits on the next thing to happen. They all knew of course what that next thing was.

Wednesday broke off a whole lot colder, the sky turning gray. A frigid wind whipped through the holler, and when Daniel ventured out to bring in some firewood and feed the animals, he felt the cold and thought how it matched his insides, a place so chilled now he wondered if it would ever warm up again.

A few folks dropped in during the day, stepped into Solomon's room, watched him for a couple of minutes, bowed their heads to say a prayer, then left. Knowing how hard it was for people to travel this far back in the holler, Daniel thanked them for coming. Even now, no decent roads led to Solomon Porter's cabin.

By nightfall a light rain had started to fall, and Daniel figured it might snow before morning. The quiet that had begun the day before stayed in place throughout the evening and night. But this time nobody even tried to go to sleep. The vigil was in place and in earnest now. Somebody sat by Solomon's bed at all times.

Daniel took his turn every few hours, holding Solomon's hand, wiping his brow, praying over him as the night grew darker. He knew what would happen by the end of the week—his pa would take his last breath. They would wash him up good, put him in his best clothes, lay him out in the front room in the wood coffin Solomon had already built to hold his earthly remains. Somebody would go down to Blue Springs to let out the word. Then the crowd would gather.

In the highlands, a man like Solomon Porter still carried a lot of weight. His passing would bring folks from all over the mountain for the Sitting Up Time, the time from when the body died to when it was put in the ground. Neighbors took turns sitting by the deceased, praying to Jesus, singing songs under their breaths. They brought food when they came too, and they told stories of all that the deceased had done. How he had helped them with this, how he had taught them that, how his living among them had shifted the life they lived, made it all for the better.

Daniel propped his head in his hands, his elbows on his knees as he studied his pa's face. Solomon Porter had made life better for a whole lot of folks. Life had never come easy for him, but he had toughed it out, and his faith in sweet Jesus had held him together when everything else threatened to tear him apart. His hand trembling, Daniel reached over and touched his pa's forehead, brushed his hair off his face.

He wondered what would hold him together. Now that his pa was about gone. Now that he had done all he could but still not managed to give back to Solomon what he most wanted. Now that he had failed in his promise. Hanging his head, Daniel closed his eyes to stifle the tears. He had failed.

Solomon groaned and stirred in his sleep.

"You okay, Pa," Daniel said. "Rest easy now."

Solomon groaned again. His head rolled toward Daniel, then back the other way. Daniel took a rag from the table, dipped it in the water pan on the floor, dabbed his pa's face with it.

"I'm gone miss you," Daniel whispered. "You been a good pa."

Solomon's eyes opened, and Daniel froze. Solomon blinked twice.

"Pa?"

Solomon licked his lips.

"Pa? You awake?"

Solomon's head turned a touch. Daniel wanted to shout. Instead, he quickly grabbed a glass of water and touched it to Solomon's lips. Solomon stirred some more. His eyes steadied. He looked at Daniel, and Daniel saw that he recognized him.

"Elsa," whispered Solomon.

"She's right outside," said Daniel, standing. "I'll get her."

Solomon took hold of Daniel's sleeve. "In a minute," he said. "I saw Laban."

"What?" Daniel said, sagging back down to the chair.

"I saw . . . Laban," repeated Solomon. "He come . . . come to me. Said I needed to wake up, to talk to . . ." his voice trailed away as his eyes closed. Daniel thought for a second that he'd lost him, but then Solomon's eyes popped open again and focused on Daniel.

"I am here," Solomon said. "Laban said you had . . . had something to tell me. . . ."

"What about Elsa?" asked Daniel, feeling he ought to let her know that his pa was now awake.

"Soon," he said. "But not yet. You got . . . something to say first?"

"I do, Pa," said Daniel. "I do."

Solomon nodded, licked his lips. Daniel told him the story then. As fast as his voice could tell out the words, he told his pa how he had saved his money, how he had gone to Tillman, how he had saved some more but it wasn't enough. His eyes burning with joy, he told how he had gone to hear Luke and how Luke had started laughing when he told him how much money he needed.

"Luke had the money all along, Pa," Daniel said, straining not to yell it so everybody in Blue Springs could hear. "He gave it to me, and I put it in the bank down in Asheville. The papers from Raleigh will come in any day, maybe they are already there. I don't know since I been up here. But I done it, Pa. I got back your land and will keep it for the family. I can go up to Mama's grave again, back to where I made you my promise. I will talk to her for you, tell her we're all doin' okay now, that you are on the way to her. I won't ever let your land go again." Daniel paused to catch his breath.

Solomon smiled at him as he took his hand and squeezed it. "You done a good thing, son," whispered Solomon. "It . . . it brings me joy to hear it."

Daniel smiled back, and his heart raced. He laid his head on his pa's chest and listened to the weak thump of his heart. Solomon placed a hand over his head and patted him lightly.

"The Lord . . . gave the land back," Solomon said. "Let you keep your promise to me and Laban. Don't never . . . never forget that."

Daniel raised up, looked into his pa's face.

"Your effort, true," Solomon continued, "but the Lord's grace . . . don't ever . . ." He lost his voice again, and Daniel knew that he better tell Elsa so she could see him before he passed off again, maybe this time for good.

He kissed his pa on the forehead. "I tend to forget the Lord's part in all this. Your reminder does me good."

Solomon pointed to the corner by his bed. "My cane," he said.

Daniel stepped to the cane, handed it to his pa, then sat back down.

Solomon pointed to the carving of Blue Springs Mountain. "My pa used to say he could see God's face on our mountain," he said.

Daniel nodded. He had heard Solomon say this before. "If you look for it," Daniel said.

Solomon handed Daniel the cane. "This is yours. Keep it as a reminder. No matter where you are, what you go through, God is still here, on this mountain. You can see His face . . . if you look . . . for it." He closed his eyes and licked his lips.

Daniel started to protest, to say Luke should get the cane, not him. But how could he argue with his pa at such a time?

"Now bring Elsa," said Solomon.

His throat choked, Daniel left the room, the cane tight in his grip. A minute later he roused Elsa from her chair and brought her to the bedroom. Leaving her with Solomon, he walked to the porch and sat down on the steps and looked up into the sky. Snow fell lightly on his face. Wind clicked through the trees. Light from the fireplace seeped out from the cabin's front windows. One of the dogs walked to him and lay down by his feet. Staring at the carving of Blue Springs Mountain on the cane, Daniel felt at peace. Though his pa would no doubt die real soon, Daniel's heart rested for the first time in many a year. God was still on the mountain and now that mountain belonged to his family again.

Abby woke with a start. Her neck ached. She saw Elsa standing over the rocker where she sat, her eyes bright. "He is asking for you," she said. Abby wiped her mouth and pulled the afghan off her knees. She thought immediately of Daniel. But why would Elsa come tell her that Daniel wanted to talk to her? Her eyebrows furrowed in confusion.

"Your pa," said Elsa. "He woke up a while ago."

"Pa's awake?" The words sounded strange. She couldn't believe them.

"That's what I'm saying," insisted Elsa. "Daniel was with him when he woke. Solomon talked to him, then me. He is asking for you now."

The words finally sinking in, Abby jumped up and rubbed her eyes. The notion that maybe God had worked a miracle and made Solomon well entered her head, but then Elsa quickly dashed the idea. "He is real weak," she said. "I fear he won't stay with us much longer."

"Then I better go to him."

Elsa nodded, and Abby left her and rushed to her pa's bedroom. At the door she paused for just a second to gather her bearings. She had found the letter. Her mama had told her to go to her pa, to say what needed to be said to make things right with him. But could she do that after all these years? Could anybody say anything to change the time they had lost, the moments they could have shared, the way they could have known each other so much better?

Still unsure what to do or say, Abby prayed a silent prayer and pushed through the door. A pillow propped Solomon up on the bed. He opened his eyes as she stepped to him. A hint of a smile creased his face.

He patted the bedside and whispered, "Come sit."

Abby quickly obeyed, taking his hand as she sat down. "Glad to see you awake," she said. "You gone beat this thing yet."

Solomon grunted. "Don't go telling no fibs. My time is short."

Abby remembered her mama had said the same thing in her letter. "Everybody's time is short," Abby said.

Solomon nodded. Abby rubbed her pa's hand. She wanted to cry, but trained by years of holding in such feelings, she pushed back the tears. Solomon stayed quiet, his eyes staring at the ceiling. She glanced out the window, saw that light had started to creep into the yard. The rooster would start crowing soon.

"I hear you got Clack's old place," Solomon said.

Abby looked at him. His eyes seemed to twinkle. A notion she had not imagined came to her. "What do you know about that?" she asked.

Solomon shrugged. "I know a thing or two."

Abby rubbed his hand. He squeezed her fingers. "You have something to do with that?" she asked.

"A little."

"Tell me."

Solomon shook his head. "It don't matter," he said. "What matters is you got it back."

She thought of pressing him but knew he wouldn't respond. When Solomon Porter said no, it stayed that way. Silence came again. Solomon closed his eyes. For a second she wondered if he had slipped away again. She tensed against the fear that he had.

"Pa?"

"I'm still here," he whispered.

Abby stared at his face. Saw the lines that life had carved into it. It dawned on her that life carved lines on everybody, just like Pa carved lines on his wood figures, lines that showed who a body was, what they had done, where they had been. She had lines too, lines like her mama's. She studied Solomon's face some more. The lines around his mouth curved downward, and she suddenly realized she had the start of similar markings on her chin and neck, markings like her pa's.

She looked back out the window, not wanting to admit what she knew. Maybe she looked most like her mama, but she'd turned out a lot like Pa—quiet and to herself, not given to emotion. A stiff woman afraid to give over to the feelings that rumbled so deep inside. Even though she had loved words all her life, she loved them best when she read them on the page of a book or heard them from the lips of another person. And while she had studied hard to understand words, she hadn't become a good sayer of them. Her mama had feared that her pa wouldn't have the necessary words to say what needed to be said between them. But sadly, neither did she.

Abby's shoulders slumped. Solomon breathed quietly. The rooster crowed. Abby stared again at the lines around Solomon's mouth, the lines like those on her face. She recalled her mama's last words, the encouragement for her to do the saying, for her to go to Solomon and take the step he had no ability to take, to say what was needed. That was her mama's last hope. That she, Abigail Faith Porter, would say what somebody had to say. The words of Jesus rose up in her head. *"For if ye forgive men their trespasses, your heavenly Father will also forgive you."*

As if reaching for a diamond, Abby reached into the pocket on the front of her dress and pulled out an envelope. The letter from Rose waited inside. She hadn't let it out of her sight since the day she found it. Gently she took out the letter and laid it on her pa's chest.

Pa," she said quietly. "I need to show you something."

Solomon opened his eyes. She held up the letter.

"It's from Mama," she said.

Solomon picked up the letter and held it to his face. "She wrote this the day she died," he said. "The day you come into this world."

"I know," said Abby. "You want me to read it to you?"

Solomon smiled. "I been wanting that for a long time."

"The words aren't easy to hear," she said.

"Not easy to write either."

Abby nodded. Solomon handed her the letter. She took a breath and started to read.

" 'My dearest Abigail, I will not be with you when you read this. Not much time. I love you. . . .' "

Solomon held her hand as she read on, his grip tightening when she said the words about his not knowing how to love her right, how he would not know how to come to her.

Feeling his grip, Abby stopped. "You all right?" she asked.

"It is hard," he said, "to hear her voice again."

Her emotions strangely calm, Abby nodded.

"She told it true, though. I am not much count as a pa."

"Don't say that," pleaded Abby. "That's not what she said. You did the best you could, you worked so hard—"

"Read the rest," he interrupted. "I got to hear it."

Abby stared again at the letter. Was she doing the right thing, reading this to him, making him hear such hard things?

"Read it," he said, giving her no choice. "Time is a-wasting."

She squeezed his hand and started again.

" 'If anything comes between you and him, it will be your need to go to him. He won't know how to come to you. Won't have the necessary words. He will love you. I know it. But it won't go easy for him. Whatever happens, you say what needs saying. That is my hope.' "

Abby finished the letter, then placed it again on his chest. Solomon gently folded it and held it in the palm of his hand. Seconds passed in silence. Abby heard the wind blowing outside. Solomon stared up at the ceiling.

"I am not good," he said, "with the telling of what is inside me."

"I know you love me, Pa," Abby said, hoping to relieve some of his guilt.

Solomon swallowed. "I do," he said. "But I got to tell you I wanted your mama to live no matter what."

He paused, and Abby saw a pair of tears in the corners of his eyes. She waited to see if he would wipe them away, but this time he didn't.

"No matter what," he repeated. "I wanted her to live no matter what."

Abby understood what he was saying. If God had given him a choice, he would have chosen to let her die instead of her mama. She hung her head. The calm she had felt now threatened to disappear. Her pa had just said the one thing she feared most.

More silence fell. Another pair of tears replaced the first ones that had fallen from Solomon's eyes. Something strange suddenly happened to Abby. The words she had expected to hurt more than anything she could ever imagine had now been spoken. But instead of cutting her heart out, the admission from her pa had created a sense of relief in her, a realization that now that she'd heard the worst, nothing more unsettling could ever be said to her. The hurting words seemed to hold healing in them, a salve given over with the thorn.

"I am sorry I did not do better by you," said Solomon, his voice growing weaker. "But I don't know . . . somehow I feared you . . . getting close to you . . . feared that maybe if I got too close, something bad would happen to you too . . . like happened to your ma. So I did the only thing I knew to do, stayed my distance."

Abby felt like someone had lifted a wagon off her back. All these years her pa had been as scared as she. She squeezed Solomon's hand again. "You did okay, Pa," she said. "It all turned out okay."

"I am glad you found your ma's letter," he said. "No matter how hard it is to hear what she said."

The cabin creaked in the wind. Abby thought again of how the Clack house had fallen to her, the way Elsa would not tell how she had come by the deed.

"How did Elsa get the Clack house, Pa?" she asked. "And don't tell me to ask Elsa."

Solomon brushed his tears away now, raised an eyebrow. "Don't go giving me no orders," he said, "no matter how sick you think I am."

Abby waited. Solomon lifted up some on the pillow and shrugged, then said, "Let's just say that Hal Clack and his boys are still making their doublings. Leave it at that."

Abby's brow wrinkled. "You threaten him or something?"

"I done said all I plan on saying," said Solomon. "Anything else, ask Elsa."

Abby patted his hand and let it go. Solomon closed his eyes. Feeling lighter than she had in years, Abby knew she still needed to say one more thing, maybe the toughest thing of all. "I am sorry, Pa, for all the years we let pass between us."

A ray of sun broke through the clouds, ran through the window onto Solomon's face. Abby saw tears form again in his eyes.

"I am the one who is sorry," he said. "I should have put your ma's death behind me a long time ago. Seen you for what you are—a fine highlander woman. Your ma would have been real proud."

Tears rushed to Abby's eyes now, and not fighting them anymore, she had trouble seeing her pa.

"Will you forgive me my foolishness?" asked Solomon. "Let me die knowing I am in good stead with my only girl?"

Abby threw her head onto her pa's chest and let her tears run down her face. "You don't even have to ask," she cried.

Solomon put his arms around Abby and patted her on the back.

"I found the carving too," she sobbed. "It looks just like me."

"Like you and your mama."

"I love you, Pa," whispered Abby.

"I love you too, child," he said. "Always have."

Abby hugged him as close as she could, and the rooster crowed again.

"Sweet Jesus has done a good thing in all this," Solomon whispered. "A mighty good thing."

Her tears soaking her cheeks, Abby listened to her pa's heartbeat and knew his words were true. And even though the words were the last ones he ever spoke to her alone, it was okay because she had heard what she needed to hear, and her deepest hopes had come to pass.

EPILOGUE

W e buried Pa six days later," said Granny Abby, "on a day so cold it made your nose hurt to stand out in it. Took Daniel and Luke almost a whole day to dig out Solomon's spot in the frozen ground. A nephew of Preacher Bruster's, a man named Bobby, did the words over him."

"But he died at peace," I said, glad for the way that Abby and her pa had made things right in the final hours of his life.

"Yes, thanks to the Lord. He died the night after our talk. We were all there—me and Daniel, Luke, Elsa and Solomon Jr., sitting around the bed talking to him. Even Pierce and Aunt Erline showed up to see him on to glory. He stayed alert until about halfway through the night, then fell asleep. Right before dawn, he just turned a mite in the bed, opened his eyes and took Elsa's hand. The next thing we knew his eyes closed and he took another couple of breaths and then stopped. Just like that. With us one second, gone to Jesus the next."

Sighing, I laid down my notebook and relaxed my fingers. The sun outside had just about disappeared. Granny Abby and I had spent the last three days together, sleeping and eating only enough to keep up our energy. I had run through a stack of videotapes and the two notebooks I had bought earlier, plus two more I had purchased a day or so into our talk. Abby had told me almost thirty years of her life, a tale that made me see that maybe I didn't have it too bad, that my problems—a discontent with my career, my love life, and my faith—though giants to me, didn't measure up to what she had faced so long ago.

I stared into the fireplace. Was my self-pity out of place? Had I gotten so soft that I let things swell up so much they threatened to overwhelm me? Did I have any right to feel angry at the tough breaks that had come my way?

Not knowing how to answer my own questions, I focused on Granny Abby again.

"I'm glad Daniel finally got the land back," I said, thinking of how Daniel and Luke had re-claimed Solomon Porter's property. "I know that must have made Solomon's death a little easier."

Granny Abby grunted and pushed back a wisp of hair. "Well, that didn't turn out quite like we all thought it would," she said.

"What do you mean?"

She shook her head. "We'll talk about that next time," she said. "Leave it be until tomorrow."

A hundred questions ran through my head. Why wouldn't she tell me what happened to Daniel? And what about her and Stephen? Did their marriage improve? Did she ever get to teach? And Thaddeus? Did Abby ever talk to him again? What became of Elsa after Solomon died?

I gazed into the fire. I knew so little about her life it astounded me. How had I grown up without paying more attention to my family history? The clock ticked by the hallway.

"So did Daniel make out okay?" I finally asked, hoping she would say more.

Granny Abby waved me off. "I am tired," she said. "Maybe this is a good time to cease our talking for the day."

I didn't want to stop, but I knew if she said she was tired, I needed to accept it. "You think seven tomorrow morning is too early to begin again?" I asked, eager to know the next chapter of the tale.

Granny Abby smiled. "You know I get up by five every day," she said. "But if you want to waste half the morning before we start, that is okay by me."

I laughed, then stood and stretched my back. "Let's make it six," I said.

Standing from her rocker, Granny Abby grinned and eased her way from the room. After she left, I walked to the fireplace and took a deep breath. My family's story had brought two endings. Abby had heard from her mama, and she and her pa had come to peace with each other. The letter had changed her life for the good and brought forgiveness and healing to their relationship. And Daniel had regained the family land. But I still needed to know so much more.

I was not quite one third of the way through my family story. If the first thirty years had brought this kind of adventure, heaven only knew what the next thirty would bring. Throwing a fresh log onto the fire, I brushed off my hands and sat back down. In the morning Granny Abby would continue the story. Though not exactly sure how all this was affecting me, I was sure I couldn't wait until tomorrow.